THE
WARRIOR
HEIR

CINDA WILLIAMS CHIMA

HYPERION PAPERBACKS
NEW YORK

Acknowledgments:

Heartfelt thanks to my agent, Michelle Wolfson, who made all the difference; to my editors, Arianne Lewin and Donna Bray, who believed; to Hudson Writers (Deb Abood, Pam Daum, Cathy Fahey-Hunt, Anne Gallagher, Ellen Matthews, Marsha McGregor, James Robinson, and Jane Sahr), who gave the gift that every writer needs: thoughtful and loving critique; most of all, thanks to Rod, Eric, and Keith, who understood.

Text copyright © 2006 by Cinda Williams Chima

First Hyperion Paperbacks edition, 2007
15 14 13 12 11
This book is set in 12-point Bembo.
Library of Congress Cataloging-in-Publication Data on file.
ISBN-13: 978-0-7868-3917-9
ISBN-10: 0-7868-3917-1
Visit www.hyperionteens.com
ILS No . V475-2873-0-11252

For my mother, Carol Bryan Williams,
who told stories

PROLOGUE
OLD STORIES

COALTON COUNTY, OHIO
June, 1870

The scent of wood smoke and roses always took him back there, to the boy he was and would never be again.

The Roses came for them during his tenth summer. In those days, Lee was slight of build, though his father always said his big hands and feet predicted height and broad shoulders when he was grown. He was the youngest, a little spoiled, the only one of four children to display the telltale signs of a wizard's stone. His parents complained that it took him two days to do a day's worth of work. Not lazy, exactly, but largely inefficient.

They had been back only a fortnight after a month on the run. It was a mistake to come back. Lee knew that, afterward, but his father was a farmer, and a farmer can't afford to stay out of the fields too long during the growing season. Besides, the Roses' previous attacks had been hit-or-miss affairs. They would sweep through the village on the river, search the outlying farms, and then disappear, sometimes for as long as a year.

Bandits, their neighbors called them, and speculated that they'd been soldiers in the recent War of the Rebellion. Only seven years before, Confederate General John Morgan had led his raiders through these southern Ohio hills.

Lee's family knew better. Knew what these raiders were looking for, and why. The Roses had followed the lineages west from the port cities in the east. They hunted the descendants of the Silver Bear, harvesting the gifted for the Trade. His brother Jamie had been taken when Lee was just a baby, while they still lived in Pennsylvania. Jamie had been an enchanter. Lee didn't really remember him, but they always burned a beeswax candle for him on the holidays.

Lee was just happy to be home, back in those green, blunted hills tailor-made for a dreamer. On that fateful day, he had left the house early in order to avoid any chores that might be assigned. He'd spent the morning on the riverbank, and the product of it was a stringer of cat-fish that he planned to offer up for supper. He ambled back along the road that led up to the house, just two wagon ruts, really, detouring whenever something caught his interest.

As he drew closer to home, he caught a strong scent of wood smoke. It was odd, because it was summertime and the stone fireplaces and woodstoves that heated the house had not been in use since April. Perhaps his father was clearing land or burning off brush. If so, Lee should have been home to help. From the angle of the sun, he knew he was already late for the midday meal. His mother would be in a fine state about it.

It was then that he saw a dark column of smoke climbing into the sky through the tops of the trees up ahead. From the location, he knew it must be coming from the home yard. Perhaps the kitchen had caught fire. He broke into a run, the fish swinging awkwardly at his side.

As it turned out, it *was* the kitchen, and the barn, and the garden shed. They were all ablaze, wood and thatch buildings ready-made for burning, and half devoured already. The main house, though, was stone, with a slate roof, and so more resistant. His father had teased the stones for it out of the surrounding hills. A fine house for that part of the world, and perhaps that was why it had drawn attention. Lee stood in the fringes of the forest, unsure what to do. The fish slid unnoticed from his fingers.

Why was no one fighting the fire, pumping water from the well, passing buckets, and soaking down the wood that had not yet caught? He scanned the yard. No one was there, not his father, nor his brother, not anyone.

Keeping within the shelter of the woods, he circled around to the back of the house, knowing the hedges and walls that quilted the gardens would give him cover. His father had come over from the Old World, and he was proud of those gardens. They were civilized, hemmed in by stone, like those in their family's ancestral home.

Instinct told him to stay hidden. He crouched, fading into the shadow of the stone wall where it ran near the forest, following it back to the house. The skin on his face tightened from the heat of the kitchen fire as he slipped past it, through the vegetable garden, to the back door of the house. The door was standing partly ajar. He pushed it wide open.

It was a mess inside. Clearly, his family had been at the table when the attack came. Had he returned on time, he would have been among them. Food lay scattered, ground into the floor—bread and pieces of fruit and the small cinnamon tarts that Martin liked so well. The furniture had been chopped to pieces and set ablaze like kindling, tables were overturned, crockery shattered against the wall. Someone was either very angry or wanted to make a point. Lee circled around the shards of glass on the floor, aware of his bare feet.

He crept farther into the house, barely breathing, keeping flat to the wall, his ears straining for any clue that would tell him the intruders were still inside. As he moved toward the great hall, he became aware of a sound, a rhythmic banging. It grew louder as he drew closer to the front of the house. As he slid his hand along the wall, he encountered something wet. Bringing his hand close to his face, he caught the metallic scent of blood. Blood was splashed all over the floor and walls. Dark red puddles were congealing between the stones in the floor. His heart clamored in his chest; he had to fight to get his breath, but he forced himself to go on.

A body lay in the doorway to the hall, a man dressed too fine to be local, in a waistcoat and a silk shirt and cravat, not homespun, like Lee's. He looked middle-aged, but was probably much older. A man who carried no obvious weapons, and needed none. A wizard, it must be.

Lee's brother Martin lay facedown just beyond the doorway, his body nearly torn in two. Most of the blood must have been his. He was ten years older, big and broad shouldered, known as a hard worker. Practical. Not a dreamer like Lee. Anaweir: no magic in him, no match for wizards.

"Martin." Lee's lips formed the word, but he had no breath to make a sound.

Lee crept into the room, feeling the tacky blood under his toes. There were the bodies of two more wizards, and then he saw his father sprawled across the hearth, his legs in the fireplace as if he'd been thrown there.

His father, who told him stories of castles and manor houses across the ocean. Who could steal fire out of the air with his fingers and spin shields out of sunlight. Who called him wizard heir and had begun to teach him the charms that would shape magic to his use. Who had been powerful enough and smart enough to protect them from anything. Until now.

Lee fell to his knees retching, and lost what little remained of his breakfast. Then he heard the noise again, the banging sound.

His mother was huddled in her rocking chair next to the fireplace, her knitting on her lap. The sound he'd heard was the slam of the rocker against the wall. Now that he was closer, he could hear her knitting needles, clicking together in a businesslike fashion. But she had picked up no stitches. Although she had yarn in her basket, and on her lap, she was knitting nothing.

"Mama?" he whispered, drawing close to her, looking warily over his shoulder. "Was it the Roses?" She stared into the hearth where Papa lay cold and broken. Rocked, and knitted nothing, and said nothing. She didn't have to. He knew it was the Roses; of course it was the Roses, who else would it be?

"Are you hurt, Mama?" he said again, a little louder. He wormed his hand into hers, but her fingers didn't close around his, and in her eyes there was a dreadful nothing.

He fought back a sob. No crying. He was the man of the family now. "Where's Carrie?" he asked. His sister was not among the bodies on the floor, which made sense because the Roses would want Carrie alive.

His mother didn't answer. Carrie could be taken, or she could be hiding. If she were taken, they would head south toward the river, and then west to Cincinnati or east to Portsmouth, where they could catch a boat. If she had been taken, he didn't know what he would do.

If she was hiding, he knew where she would be. He left the house the way he'd come in.

They called it the root cellar, but it was really a cave that tunneled into the side of a hill some distance from the yard. In that cool damp space they stored food: potatoes and turnips and carrots and dried beans and peas in sacks.

The mouth of the cave was covered with red climbing roses, and flat white and pink wild roses. They were all in bloom, their fragrance cloying. He parted the thorny canes and stepped inside.

"Carrie?" he said softly. "It's me."

For a moment, there was nothing, and then a rush of movement in the darkness, and his sister wound her arms around him, whispering, "Lee! Why did you come here? It's too dangerous. You should have run away when you saw they'd come back."

"Carrie, they killed Papa and Martin, and there's something wrong with Mama, she won't talk to me." The words tumbled over each other, louder than he intended.

Carrie sucked in her breath and pulled him tight against her, so the rest of what he had to say was spoken into her shoulder. She murmured soothing words to him, but not for long. Her back straightened and her hands traveled down to his elbows.

"Listen to me now." She held him out at arm's length. She wore trousers and rough-woven shirt, her knife belted at her waist. Their mother hated to see Carrie dress like a man, but sometimes she did anyway. "You're going to have to be very brave," she said.

"Don't worry," he said, standing up a little straighter, trying to make his voice deeper like Martin's. "Papa taught me how to protect you against the wizards."

She swallowed hard. "Silly. You *are* a wizard. You are going to have to be brave enough to go for help." He tried to interrupt, but she went on. "I want you to head straight south to the river and follow it to town. Stay under cover and away from the roads. When you see someone you know, tell them what happened and ask them to send help for Mama."

"Aren't you coming with me?" He felt lonely already. He tried not to think about Martin or his father, because he knew the tears would come again.

"I'm going away for a while," she replied. "It's too dangerous for me to stay with you and Mama. The Roses are looking for warriors. Not wizards or Anaweir. They'll leave you alone if I'm not around." Seeing his expression, she hurried on. "I'll come back when it's safe."

Lee thought of his mother, silent and scary in the house. He knew it was wrong, but he didn't want to go back there alone. "Take me with you, Carrie. Please."

Carrie shook her head. She was practically an adult, yet tears were streaming down her cheeks. "You have to stay, Lee. Mama is Anaweir. She needs someone to look after her."

"Oh, all right," he said petulantly, not wanting her to know how frightened he was. He might as well get started, since he would be taking the long way to town. He raked the roses aside again, sticking himself in the process, and stepped out into the broken sunlight. And into the arms of the wizards who waited there.

"Carrie!" he screamed. Hands grabbed him, holding him tight, lifting him away from the mouth of the cave. He struggled and kicked, slamming his elbow into someone's face, feeling the cartilage give way followed by the rush of hot blood. He twisted his body, but he couldn't get free.

There were too many, a half dozen of them. Strangers with bearded faces, dressed for Sunday, like the dead wizard in the hall. Lee didn't know any attack charms, really, but he could find fire, so he plucked it out of the air and sent it spiraling into the men around him. There was more cursing, and then they threw him to the ground.

The wizard with the bloody nose pointed at Lee, muttering a charm. An awful cold went through him, and he went limp. The wizard slid his hands under Lee's arms, hauled him upright and held him there, his feet off the ground, dangling like a puppet.

"Call her out," the bloody-nose wizard commanded, and flamed him with his hot hands. Lee's muscles seized, and he screamed—he couldn't help it—but then he clamped his mouth shut stubbornly.

"We haven't got all day. The White Rose is right behind us." The wizard released power into him again, like hot molten metal running into his veins, but Lee was ready this time. He sucked in his breath, but didn't make a sound.

"Come out or we'll snap the boy's neck!" Bloody Nose shouted. The roses that obscured the mouth of the cave trembled, dropping petals as they were thrust aside. Carrie emerged into the sunlight in a half crouch, knife in hand. Seeing Lee in the hands of the wizards, she straightened and let the knife drop to the ground.

Bloody Nose gave Lee a triumphant shake. "You led us right to her."

Carrie dropped to her knees, bowed her head. "Please, my lords. I'll come with you. Only, let my brother go."

Lee tried to speak, to tell Carrie to get up off her knees, that they would fight the wizards together. "Carrie, don't. . . ." His protest became a scream of pain as Bloody Nose sent flames into him.

"Wylie. Enough." This from a gray-haired wizard with a seamed face, seemed to be in charge. "Bring the reader."

Wylie tossed Lee aside as though he weighed nothing, then fumbled in a pouch at his waist. He produced a silver cone and handed it to the leader. Two wizards moved to either side of Carrie, grasping her arms and lifting her to her feet. The leader yanked her shirt free of her trousers and thrust the cone up against the skin of her chest. Carrie flinched, but looked to one side and said nothing. After a moment, he nodded and withdrew his hand.

"There is a warrior stone," he said in an Old World accent. Satisfied, he returned the cone to Wylie. "God knows, we've paid a price for it. Let's get her out of here before the White Rose catches up to us."

The wizards brought their horses forward and began to mount up while their leader bound Carrie's hands in front of her with a silver chain.

Wylie slammed Lee down against the trunk of a dead tree. The wizard knelt beside him, pushed his chin back, and placed his fingertips against his throat. Lee looked into the flat gray eyes and knew he was about to die.

The leader noticed. "Let the boy be, Wylie," he said gruffly, pulling on his riding gloves.

Wylie looked up. "He's a witness. We killed a wizard, and if word of that gets back to the council . . ."

"There's three dead on our side as well," the leader pointed out. "If the boy's father had stayed with his own kind, he'd still be alive. This is a child. Let's not make matters worse."

"You're not the one who did the killing. This one may be a wizard, but he's of mixed blood." Wylie's lips tightened in disgust. "Wizards, warriors, sorcerers, even Anaweir comingling as equals. It's unnatural."

"Perhaps they're on to something." The leader gestured toward Carrie. "At least the girl's healthy. Which is more than I can say for the warriors at home."

Wylie's fingers still pressed against Lee's throat. Lee could feel the power in them, a faint vibration against his skin.

"I told you to leave him be," the leader said. "We've lingered too long already."

Wylie finally stood and moved away, looking for his mount.

Carrie had been lifted onto one of the horses. She stared straight ahead, her mouth in a tight line, spots of bright color in her cheeks. The leader took the reins of her horse and then mounted his own. He pointed at Lee, disabling the charm that had been laid on him, but Lee just lay there, afraid to move, knowing finally and for true that he was, at heart, a coward.

And then it happened. A bolt of light blazed through the trees, blue-white and deadly, trailing flaming stars— like the fireworks Lee had seen once in Cincinnati. The air crackled with electricity, and even at a distance, his hair stood on end. The blast struck its target dead-on, and for a moment, Carrie and the horse beneath her were outlined in flames, like some heavenly bodies that had passed before the sun. There was a shimmer in the air, a kind of visual vibration, and then they were gone, horse and rider vaporized, as if they had never existed.

"It's the White Rose!" one of the wizards shouted.

Turning his horse, he charged through the trees. The other wizards wheeled their horses and followed, screaming in rage, but the White Rose had done what it came to do, and was in full retreat. In a matter of minutes, the horses and riders were gone. Dust settled slowly through shafts of sunlight, and the clearing was quiet, save the sound of the wind moving the branches overhead.

By the time darkness had fallen, Lee was already miles away, sitting cross-legged on the riverbank. When the moon finally cleared the trees, it shone on the Ohio, which ran like a silver ribbon in both directions. Across the river lay Kentucky, a mysterious darkness pierced by the lights of scattered settlements.

"I won't be a bear any longer," he said to himself. He would be fiercer, more invincible. "From now on, I'm a dragon."

Before he continued on, he took his sister's knife and wrote something in the soft mud at the water's edge, wrote it in order to fix it in his mind.

The word was "Wylie."

TRINITY, OHIO
More than 100 years later

The baby awakened when Jessamine uncovered him. She thought he might cry, but he only gazed at her solemnly with bright blue eyes while she opened his shirt and examined the incision. Still a little red and puffy at the edges, but no sign of infection. Perfect. She'd half expected that the procedure would kill him, but he seemed to be thriving. Only a month post-op, her patient had gained weight, his color was good, pulse and respiration normal.

No reason he couldn't travel. None at all.

She snapped the baby's shirt closed, feeling pleased with herself. Those fools at the hospital had been difficult about everything: her methods, that she'd brought her own people to assist, that she wouldn't let them observe the procedure.

Idiots. Perhaps she should have allowed a few of them into the operating theater. It might have been worth it to see their faces before she wiped their minds clean.

Of course, it would be years before she would see how the experiment played out. Considerable time invested if it failed, but much to be gained if it succeeded. Perhaps an end to the shortage of warriors. An unlimited supply of fodder for the Game. Final victory to the White Rose.

She glanced around the nursery. It was full of baby things, more paraphernalia than she could possibly carry. She could always buy more when they reached their destination. What would a baby need to travel? Diapers and clothes. A seat to travel in. What would he eat? Formula? She shrugged. Pediatrics was not her specialty.

She found a large bag on the floor of the closet that already held diapers and a box of wipes. No bottles, though. She yanked open a dresser drawer and found layers of tiny clothes. She shoved some of the clothes into the bag, which was decorated with elephants and giraffes in primary colors. Jessamine frowned and ran her hands over her elegant suit, swept a curtain of dark hair away from her face. She did not relish the idea of walking around with a diaper bag on her shoulder and a baby on her hip. She should have hired someone to take charge of the brat from the start.

She pulled a plastic infant seat from the closet and set it on the floor next to the crib. The catch resisted when she tried to lower the side, so she stretched over awkwardly and scooped the baby from the mattress. She laid him in the seat and began fussing with the straps.

How does one go about finding a nanny? She had no idea.

"What are you doing here?"

Jessamine jumped. The enchanter Linda Downey stood in the doorway. She was just a child, really, barefoot, in jeans and a T-shirt. Linda was the baby's aunt, Jessamine recalled, not his Anaweir mother. Good. Not that it would have mattered, but she preferred to avoid a scene.

Jessamine stood, leaving the baby in the seat and the straps in a tangle. "I didn't know anyone was home," she said, instead of answering the question.

Linda tilted her head. She was a pretty thing, with long dark hair woven into a thick braid. She moved with a careless grace that Jessamine envied. But then, if Jess had to choose one gift over another, she would always choose her own.

"Of course there's someone home," the girl said, in the insolent way of teenagers. "You don't leave a baby by itself."

At least the sudden and awkward appearance of the enchanter solved one problem. "I'm glad you're here,"

Jessamine said imperiously, with a sweep of her elegant hand. "I need you to pack up some things for him, enough for a few days, anyway. Food, clothes, and so forth."

"Why? Where do you think you're taking him?"

Jessamine sighed, flexed her fingers with their long, painted nails. "If you must know, I'm taking him back with me."

"What?" It came out almost as a shriek, and the baby threw out its arms, startled. Linda took a step forward. "What do you mean?"

"I'm taking him back to England with me. Don't worry," she added. "He'll be well cared for. I just can't afford to leave him lying about."

"What are you talking about?" Linda demanded.

"Since the surgery, he has . . . appreciated in value," Jessamine said calmly.

Linda knelt by the car seat, looking the boy over as if she could discover something through close examination. She extended a finger, and the baby grabbed on to it. She looked up at Jessamine. "What did you do to him?"

"He needed a stone, and I gave him one. A miracle. Something no one has ever done before. I saved his life." She smiled, turning her palms upward. "Only, now he's Weirlind."

"A warrior?" It came out as a whisper. "No! I told you! He's a wizard. He needed a wizard's stone." Linda shook her head as she said it, as if by denying it she could change things. "It's all in his Weirbook. He's a wizard," she repeated bleakly.

Jessamine smiled. "Not anymore, if he ever was.

Be reasonable. A wizard's stone is hard to come by. Wizards live almost forever. But warriors . . . warriors die young, don't they?" The last part was intentionally cruel.

Now the enchanter stood, her hands balled into fists. "I should have known better than to trust a wizard."

Jessamine drew herself up. She was losing patience with this scrap of a girl. "You didn't have much of a choice, did you? If it weren't for me, he'd be dead by now. I'm not in the business of providing charity care. I did it because I intend to play him in the Game. And I think you'd better remember to whom you are speaking and hope I don't lose my temper."

Linda took a deep breath, let it out with a shudder. "What am I supposed to tell Becka?"

"I don't care what you tell her. Tell her it died." The Anaweir and what they thought were of no consequence.

"But why do you have to take him now? He can't play in a tournament until he's grown." The girl's voice softened, grew persuasive. Jessamine felt a gentle pressure, the touch of the enchanter's power. "He's alive, but how do you know he'll manifest? And what will you do with him in the meantime?"

Jessamine shrugged. "Perhaps I'll bring you along to watch him," she said. "In a year or two you can go to the Trade." The girl would bring a pretty price, too, if Jess was any judge. Enchanters and warriors were both hard to come by.

Linda took a step back. "You wouldn't!"

"Then don't try your enchanter's tricks with me.

I've spent quite a bit of time on him already. I intend to keep an eye on my investment while he's growing up."

"*If* he grows up. If someone else doesn't get to him first." Linda extended her hands in appeal. "Everyone knows you are Procurer of Warriors for the White Rose. How long do you think he'll last if he's with you?"

The girl had a point. The stone Jess had used on the boy had come from a seventeen-year-old warrior, her last prospect. A girl who would never play in a tournament. She'd been butchered by agents of the Red Rose when they'd been unable to steal her away. Illegal, but then rules relating to the Anawizard Weir were made to be broken. "I assume you have a suggestion?"

"Let his parents raise him. Come back and get him later."

The baby scrunched up his eyes and let out a screech, his face turning an angry blue-red. Unfathomable creatures, babies, Jessamine thought. Unfathomable and unpredictable and messy.

"He might be hard to handle later on if he's not raised to it." Jessamine said.

Linda lifted her eyebrows. "You're saying a wizard can't manage a warrior?"

Jessamine nodded, conceding the point. "What if someone else takes him to play?"

"In Trinity? No one will ever look for him here. It's perfect. You're a healer-surgeon. Suppress him, so he won't stand out." Linda sat down next to the baby, smoothing down his fringe of red-gold hair. "You can easily keep watch on him. His parents are Anaweir. They can be managed well enough. Tell them you need to see him on a regular basis. Becka will do whatever you ask. You saved her son's life."

Jessamine had to admit, the enchanter's suggestion was appealing. It would be years before this boy could be put to use, and he would be nothing but trouble in the meantime. This way, she could keep the warrior brat out of harm's way and out of her hair until he was old enough for training.

She looked into the enchanter's blue and gold eyes. "What about you? Are you *manageable*? Are you going to be able to give him up when the time comes?"

Linda looked down at the baby. "As you said, I don't have much choice, do I?"

"Jack!"

His mother's voice cut into his dreams and he reluctantly opened his eyes. It was late, he could tell. The light had lost that early-morning watercolor quality and streamed boldly through the window. He'd stayed up too late the night before, stargazing. It was the night of the new moon, and some of the key constellations hadn't slid over the horizon until after midnight.

"Coming!" he shouted. "Almost ready!" he lied as his feet hit the wood floor. His jeans lay in a heap next to the bed, where he'd stepped out of them the night before. He jerked them on, pulled a fresh T-shirt from the drawer, and threw a pair of socks over his shoulder.

Jack careened around the corner into the bathroom. No time for a shower. He washed his face, wet his fingers and ran them through his hair.

"Jack!" His mother's voice had a warning note.

Jack leaped down the back stairs and into the kitchen.

His mom had granola and orange juice waiting for him. She must have been distracted, because she had also poured him a cup of coffee. She'd left her muesli unfinished and was sorting through a stack of papers.

That was Becka. His mother was a woman of a thousand passions. Although she had a PhD in medieval literature and a law degree, she had difficulty managing the household economy: things like school schedules, lunch money, and getting the library books back on time. Jack had taken on the task of organizing both himself and his mother from an early age.

Becka looked at her watch and groaned. "I've got to get dressed! I'm supposed to be at a meeting in an hour." She shoved a large blue bottle across the table toward him. "Don't forget to take your medicine." She thrust her papers into a large portfolio. "I'll be at the library all morning and in court this afternoon."

"Don't forget I have soccer tryouts after school," Jack said. "In case you get home first." His mother was a worrier. She always said it was because he'd almost died when he was a baby. Personally, Jack thought such things were hardwired. Some people always worried, others never did. He supposed his father fell into the latter category. Maybe it was hard to worry from three states away.

"Soccer tryouts," Becka repeated solemnly, as if to fix it in her mind. Then she raced up the stairs.

Someone pounded at the side door. Jack looked up, surprised. "Hey, Will. You're early."

It was Will Childers, stooping to peer through the screen. Although Jack was tall, Will towered over him, and he was built solidly enough to play tackle on the varsity football team. His trumpet case looked like a toy next to him. "Jack! We gotta move! We've got jazz band practice this morning for the concert next week."

Jack slapped his forehead and carried his cereal bowl to the sink. Pushing his feet into his shoes without untying them, he grabbed the book bag waiting by the door. Fortunately his saxophone was at school. "School starts early enough in the day as it is," he grumbled as he followed Will down the street at a trot.

They cut across the grassy square and threaded their way between the classic sandstone buildings of the college. Trinity was a postcard Midwest college town; its streets lined with stately Victorian homes and ancient oaks and maples. Full of people who could recite every sin Jack had ever committed. He'd lived there all his life.

Thanks to Will, they were only a few minutes late for practice. It wasn't until Jack was seated in homeroom and the first bell had already rung that he realized he had forgotten to take his medicine.

What was amazing was that it had never happened before. The perfect record so far was his mother's doing. The medicine was priority one with her. She never forgot, not once, not this time either. He was the one who'd messed up.

Jack knew the history well enough. Jessamine Longbranch, the famous London heart surgeon, had swept in from overseas to steal him from the jaws of death. She still visited the States once or twice a year, and would give Jack a checkup.

Her bedside manner left a lot to be desired. He'd strip to the waist and she'd do a brief physical, run her hands over the muscles in his arms and legs and chest, listen to his heart with an unusual cone-shaped stethoscope, check his height and weight and blood pressure, and proclaim him healthy.

He always felt like a piece of meat during those meetings with Dr. Longbranch, poked and prodded for fat and bone, interrogated about his exercise habits. Their tenant, Nick, said it was a failing common to surgeons; they preferred to deal with people under anaesthesia.

Each visit ended with a reminder to take his medicine. Dr. Longbranch always delivered a new supply on her visits, and his mother ordered more from her office in London. The medicine in the blue bottle had taken on a kind of talisman quality, the elixir that kept evil away.

No one was home to bring it to him, he knew. Becka would be in the library at the university, and then in court, unreachable at both places. His mother didn't carry a cell phone because she was convinced they caused brain tumors.

Perhaps he could reach Nick, though, at the house or his apartment. Nick would answer the phone if he was doing handyman work in the house, though he never checked his voice mail. Or maybe Penworthy could be persuaded to let him walk home and get it. It was worth a try. He asked for a hall pass just as the final bell rang.

Leotis Penworthy, the Trinity High School principal,

was working cleanup in the school lobby, intercepting students who hadn't yet made it into their classrooms and taking names from the unfortunates who still trickled through the front door.

Penworthy wore ankle-length pants and a powder blue polyester sports jacket that was three sizes too small. His stomach poured over a belt hidden somewhere beneath. His face was always flushed, as if the constriction at his waist had forced the blood upward into his temples.

"MISTER Fitch!" he crowed, collaring a boy who was trying to slip past him. "Do you know what time it is?" It was a comical matchup. Fitch's clothes were a chaotic mix of Goodwill bargains and oversized military surplus chic, sleeves rolled to fit, pants belted to keep them from sliding from his slender frame. His pale hair was bleached white at the tips, and he wore three earrings in one ear.

"Sorry, Mr. Penworthy," Fitch said. He glanced up at Jack, over Penworthy's shoulder, then looked back at the floor. The corners of his mouth twitched, but his voice was solemn. "I had some updates to do online this morning, and I guess I lost track of time." Fitch was webmaster for the school's site, and unofficial systems administrator for the high school. A cheap source of high-grade technical expertise.

"Don't think you can use the Web site as an excuse, Mister. We gave you that computer so you could do the work on your own time."

Harmon Fitch had run late for a lifetime. His mother worked nights, and Fitch had four younger brothers and sisters to get on the bus.

"Mr. Penworthy," Jack broke in. "Excuse me. I, ah, forgot something at home and wondered if I could go get it." He kept his tone neutral.

The principal turned his attention to Jack.

Penworthy despised him, an opinion he communicated in a hundred different ways.

"Mr. Swift," Penworthy said, lips spreading in a predatory smile. "I find it incredible that a boy of your intelligence could be so utterly disorganized."

"You're right," said Jack politely. "And I apologize. I can be home and back before homeroom is over, if you'll let me go." Fitch was already halfway down the hallway. Penworthy didn't notice. He had a new and better target.

"I'm sorry," the principal said in a way that had no sorry in it. "Students are not allowed out of the building during school hours. It's a matter of liability."

Jack didn't feel like explaining about the medicine to Penworthy. It wasn't something he liked to talk about. But he knew an explanation was his ticket home. "I have to go home to get some medicine. It's for my heart. I forgot to take it this morning."

Penworthy scowled, rocking on his heels like one of those inflatable dolls that pops back up when you knock it down. Jack knew it would be difficult to deny this request (a matter of liability). But the principal had weapons of his own.

"Fine," Penworthy snapped. "By all means, sign yourself out in the office and go home and get it. But plan on serving a detention this afternoon to make up the time."

"But I can't," Jack protested. "I have soccer tryouts."

"Well, Mr. Swift, let this be a lesson to you." Penworthy's pale eyes gleamed with triumph. "Nothing reinforces memory like consequences."

Jack knew he was stuck. If he didn't make it to try-outs, he wouldn't make the team. And he thought he had a chance to make JV at least. "Never mind, then," he said, turning toward the pay phones next to the school office. Becka wouldn't allow Jack to get a cell phone, either. "I'll call home and see if I can get someone to bring it in to me."

"Just make sure it's an adult," Penworthy warned. "We have a zero tolerance policy regarding drugs in school."

There was no answer at the house or at Nick's apartment. Surely a few hours' delay in taking his medicine couldn't hurt. In his sixteen years, he couldn't recall so much as a single symptom. The surgery had cured him, as far as he could tell. Longbranch had never even explained exactly what the medication did. His mother, who was usually so full of questions, treated it like a magic potion.

He felt fine anyway. If any symptoms developed, he would say he was sick and they would have to let him go home. He returned the phone to its cradle and headed back to homeroom.

Jack hadn't been back in his seat for more than a minute when Ellen Stephenson touched him on the shoulder.

"What kind of measurements did you get in the res-piration lab?" she whispered. "I was working on my lab report last night and my numbers were all over the place."

Jack fished in his book bag and passed his science folder to Ellen. "Mine were, too. I was wondering if the machine had been calibrated."

She bent her head over his data sheet, squinting at his sloppy notes and raking her chin-length brown hair behind her ears. It hung, straight and shining, like a kind of helmet. She half turned in her seat, extending her long legs into the aisle. There was something different about her today, but he couldn't put his finger on it.

Lipstick. She was wearing rosy pink lipstick. Jack couldn't remember seeing her wear makeup before. He drummed his fingers lightly on the desk, contemplating Ellen's lips at close range as she read down the page. It had been a long time since he'd looked at anyone but his ex, Leesha.

"Your data are at least as variable as mine," she agreed, passing his folder back. Their hands collided, touched for a moment, and she jerked hers back quickly. The folder fell to the floor, scattering his papers.

"Oh, man, I'm sorry." Kneeling next to his desk, she frantically scraped the pages into a pile. She looked up at him, mutely extending the wad of papers toward him. Her eyes were clear gray under a smoky fringe of lashes, and her nose had a little bump at the bridge, as if it had been broken once. Jack resisted an urge to reach out and touch it. Instead, he stuffed his papers back into his folder and extended his hand to help her up.

This seemed to unsettle her again. She brushed at her skirt and fussed with her hair. "Well. Maybe we can ask Mr. Marshall about it in class."

"Ask him about . . . ? Oh. Sure, okay." Jack cleared his throat. "If you want."

The bell rang, startlingly loud. Jack began shoving books and folders into his book bag.

"Um . . . Jack?"

He looked up to see Ellen standing between him and the door, her backpack slung over her shoulder. "I wondered if you felt like studying together tonight for the social studies test. I took some good notes," she added. "We . . . ah . . . could compare them. . . ."

Jack looked at her in surprise. Ellen had never shown any interest in him before, other than as a benchmark of sorts. She was new to Trinity High School, but she already had the reputation of being a high achiever. In fact, she had a few points on Jack in some of his honors classes.

Maybe she doesn't have much else to do, Jack thought. It sucked that she had to change schools in her sophomore year. Ellen didn't hang out much. He didn't recall seeing her at dances, or at Corcoran's after a game.

She was really cute, though, and he wasn't going out with anyone. Not since Leesha dumped him for that jerk Lobeck. He'd probably be at tryouts and . . .

Tryouts.

"I'd love to. I mean, I wish I could," he said, slinging his backpack over one shoulder. "But I've got soccer tryouts tonight, and I'm not sure what time I'll be done."

"Soccer tryouts?" she repeated, looking him up and down. "Really? Do you play?"

Jack sent up a prayer to the gods of soccer. "Hopefully."

"All right," she said, dropping her gaze away from him, the color coming up into her cheeks. "Sure. Maybe another time." She shifted her book bag again and headed for the doorway, moving with a lithe, athletic grace that sucked the breath right out of him.

"Stephenson!" he called after her. She stopped in the doorway and turned around. "Another time, promise?" He grinned at her. She returned a tentative smile, and then was gone.

Dumb, he grumbled to himself. Really deft. He knew from experience that girls wouldn't ask twice. He had lots of friends who were girls, had known most of them since they'd shared apple cider and oatmeal cookies at the Trinity co-op nursery school. It wasn't easy to figure out how to move on from there. Small towns were kind of . . . incestuous.

Leesha Middleton had been different. She'd moved to Trinity the previous year. You didn't make friends with Leesha. You surrendered. She could have gone out with anyone, but she chose Jack. And now she'd chosen Lobeck.

Ellen was new blood, too. Well, he'd probably have to make the next move.

Jack tried to call home again at lunchtime. Then he tried his mom's office, but Becka hadn't checked in with Bernice. He shuddered, imagining his mother's reaction if she got the message in the late afternoon. With any luck, he'd beat her home. Anyway, he felt fine. Great, in fact.

By the time Jack and Will came out onto the field behind the high school, some of the early arrivals were helping Ted Slansky, the soccer coach, set up the goals. The sun emerged from the clouds at intervals, but it was a cold sun that seemed to draw away more heat than it provided.

The stands were peppered with a few spectators: interested parents, community coaches, friends. Jack shaded his eyes, scanning the bleachers to see if there was anyone he knew.

"Run up the colors," Fitch said behind him. "'Tis the queen and her court."

Turning, Jack saw a handful of varsity players collected in a reverent half circle at one end of the stands like wistful planets around a glittering sun. Leesha.

"What's *she* doing here?" Jack said irritably. "She *hates* soccer." Knowing the answer even as he said it.

"'Tis not for us to ask, but only to serve, admire, and desire."

Maybe Fitch had no idea how annoying this was. Maybe. "Shut up, Fitch."

Fitch's smile disappeared. "Dude. You're better off. Trust me."

Jack deliberately turned his back to the stands.

There was a large turnout. Jack tried to be optimistic. He was a good player, playing midfield and forward most of the time, but he had never been a star.

"Look who wandered into tryouts. It's Jackson Downey Swift. Or is it Swift Downey Jackson? I get so confused." The sneering voice came from behind him, but Jack knew who it was right away. Then a soccer ball hit him right between the shoulder blades. Hard.

"That's called a pass," said Garrett Lobeck. "Better pay attention if you want to play with the men."

Jack swung around. Lobeck had a crooked grin on his face, thinking he'd made a witty remark. He was one of four brothers, known for their good looks, bad habits, and a talent for violence on and off the field. At seventeen, Garrett was the youngest, and on pace to be the worst of the lot.

"Maybe you'd better paint your name on your butt, so Coach knows your mama's on the school board," Lobeck went on. "That's the only way you'll make the cut."

"I'm surprised to see you, too, Lobeck," Jack replied. "I thought they made you ineligible after that game against Garfield last year."

Lobeck had broken the goalie's leg on a nasty penalty play. There'd been a huge stink about it. But Lobeck was a talented running back, and his father owned half the town, so they'd let him play football in the fall. Becka had been the only member of the school board to vote against it.

Jack lifted the ball with his instep, juggled it a moment, then passed it off to Fitch. "So assault and battery is okay. Did they scrap the academic standards, too? Or are you in some kind of mainstreaming program for idiots?"

There was a kind of time delay while Lobeck processed this. The word "idiot" must have been the give-away, because his face flushed a deep russet color and he took a step toward Jack.

Suddenly Will was there. "What's up, Lobeck? No sixth graders to pick on?" Lobeck was big, but Will was in the same weight class at least, and he was all muscle. Lobeck didn't like the new odds.

"Ease up, Childers. Don't get your shorts in a bunch." Lobeck scowled at Jack, then trotted off down the field.

They started out doing drills, dribbling and passing, throw-ins and goal shots. Jack was standing on the sidelines, waiting his turn for the throw-in, when he heard another familiar voice behind him.

"Jackson." She said his name in two disappointed syllables. "Aren't you even going to say hi?"

He had to turn around then, or make it plain she was getting to him. "Hi, Leesha."

She wore a pale pink hoodie, and her masses of dark curls were pulled back in a clip. She put her hand on his arm. He stared at it, swallowing hard, trying to ignore the pulse pounding in his ears. "I still miss you sometimes, Jack." Guileless gray eyes looked into his.

He knew better than to fall into that trap. "Sure you do, Leesha." He thought he was managing to keep his voice light and even. He gazed off across the field, knowing without looking that she was pouting, a little frown line between her brows, her lower lip thrust out. Her hand was still on his arm.

"I'm still not sure about *Garrett*," she said. "Sometimes he's so . . . possessive." When Jack didn't respond, Leesha said, "Are you coming to my party?"

Jack blinked and looked down at her. "What?"

"Are you coming to my party? It's at the Lakeside Club."

Jack's turn on the field was coming up. He removed

Leesha's hand from his arm. But she grabbed a fistful of his sweatshirt, stood on tiptoe, and kissed him on the cheek. A virtuous kiss, for her, but Jack reared back like he'd been burned.

"I'll send you a special invitation, Jack," Leesha promised, letting him go.

Something made him look up, over her head, into the stands beyond. Where Ellen Stephenson stood, staring at him and Leesha. Then Ellen turned away, leaping nimbly from her seat to the ground. In a few long strides, she was at the gate, and then gone.

Swearing under his breath, he turned back toward the field—to see Garrett Lobeck glaring at him like a thundercloud come to earth.

"Swift!" It was Jack's turn. Finally. He blew the throw-in.

They began a series of scrimmages, switching off positions.

Jack rotated through fullback, midfielder and then forward. *Mentally*, he was a mess, but *physically*, he felt good, not tired at all, although he'd been constantly on the field. It was good to be outside again after the long winter. The late-afternoon sun slanted across the grass, almost blinding him when he faced into it. The field was still wet and, after an hour and a half of punishment, was getting slippery.

Jack had just accepted a long pass from Harmon Fitch, and turned to move it upfield, when suddenly his legs were swept from beneath him. He landed hard, flat on his back in the mud. It took him a moment to regain his breath. Propping himself up on his elbows, he saw Lobeck heading the other way with the ball. Lobeck: king of the sliding tackle.

Fitch helped him to his feet. "You okay, Jack?"

Jack shook off his hand. He stared after Lobeck. Maybe it was time to teach him a lesson.

Fitch noticed. "Come on, Jack. That way lies morbidity and mortality. You gotta pick your battles. Wait till there's a mathathon or something. Kick his butt." He grinned. "If you want, I'll hack in and change his grades, but I doubt I could do much damage there."

Jack wiped his muddy hands on his sweatshirt. Fitch was right. There was no way he'd win a fight with Lobeck. Besides, he wasn't hurt. He was soaked through, but not cold at all, despite the wind. His extremities tingled, as if his blood were returning after a long absence. He looked downfield with a sudden clarity, judging the players, mapping the obstacles in his path.

Lobeck's team had scored and kicked off. Once again, Jack's team was approaching the goal. Jack had dribbled the ball into the corner of the box when Lobeck loomed up in front of him like a wall, grinning in anticipation. Jack feinted to the left and drove for the center. He felt rather than saw Lobeck right behind him, saw his massive shape headed for him out of the corner of his eye just as he took his shot. He half turned, raising his hands, palms outward, and steeled himself for the impact.

Jack couldn't say what happened next. As his shot flew past the goalie, he extended his arms to fend off the tackle. There was a detonation at his center, and something like hot metal surged through his arms and out his fingertips. Lobeck screamed and then went flying, following the ball into the net. He hit with such force he almost bounced back out onto the field. He lay there, dazed, for a good five seconds before he slowly rolled to his stomach and got to his hands and knees. It took him another minute or two to catch his breath. Then, like an engine slowly sputtering to life, he began to swear.

"You fouled me!" he gasped, jabbing a thick finger at Jack. "You slammed me into the goal." He was literally shaking with anger and indignation.

"I didn't touch you!" Jack was sweating, practically steaming. Still tingling, yet somehow drained. He glanced over into the stands. Leesha was leaning forward, watching avidly. Leesha might be bored by soccer, but she loved a fight.

Lobeck staggered to his feet. His entire front was layered in mud, and his lip was bleeding. "You threw me into the net!" He turned to the goalie for backup. "Didn't he?" The goalie shrugged. He had been busy trying to block Jack's shot.

Jack widened his stance and raised his hands, ready to fend off an attack. To his amazement, Lobeck flinched and stepped back a pace. And Lobeck outweighed him by fifty pounds at least.

"Give it up, Garrett," Will said. "There was daylight between you and Jack. You must have tripped. Besides, the shot was clean away. It didn't look like you were going after the ball at all."

Coach Slansky had followed the ball to that end of the

field and stood, watching, just outside the box. Lobeck squinted at the coach, then glowered at Jack.

"All right, boys, we're done," Slansky said. "I think I've seen all I need to see today. Besides, it looks like it's going to snow or something."

Lobeck grabbed his gym bag and water bottle and stalked off the field. Will and Jack and several other players helped Slansky stow the equipment. The sun had slid behind the clouds, and the horizon to the west looked threatening. Will and Jack retrieved their gear from their lockers and headed for the parking lot. Leesha had disappeared.

"Funny," said Will. "I thought it was supposed to be nice today."

They cut between the buildings to the street. The swings pitched crazily in the wind as they passed the playground at the elementary school. The tops of the evergreens along the border of the parking lot tossed and shimmied. Bits of debris skittered along the ground. Jack shivered, feeling exposed under the boiling sky.

"Great shot, Jack." Will was grinning. "I wish I'd had a camera. The expression on Lobeck's face was priceless."

Jack shrugged, pulling his jacket closer around him. "I didn't really see what happened. I guess he did trip." He scanned the street ahead, an empty tunnel under the heaving trees. A gauntlet. The flesh on his arms prickled. Why was he so jumpy? Lobeck had left before they did, but it was unlikely he would try an ambush. Not with Will around.

He glanced back over his shoulder in time to see

someone emerge from between two houses and move quickly toward them, as if he were floating over the grass. Someone dressed in a long coat that flapped around his legs, too tall and spare to be Garrett Lobeck.

"Will!" Jack grabbed his friend's arm. Will turned, following his gaze. Then he grinned.

"Hey, Nick!" Will shouted. "Where'd you come from?"

And the dimensions of the stranger changed, became suddenly recognizable. There was the neatly trimmed beard, the piercing black eyes, the fringe of white hair. Why had he seemed so unfamiliar? But when Nick Snowbeard spoke, the voice was as unfamiliar as the image. "Jack!" It stung like a lash, sent him staggering backward. "Go home now and take your medicine! Hurry! Your mother is waiting for you."

"Nick?" Jack said uncertainly.

"I said go! Will, you see that he gets there. We'll talk later." Nick turned away from them, his face fierce and intent, looking back down the street at the high school. Will grabbed Jack by the arm, literally dragging him home.

They broke into a run, side by side, feet thudding on the pavement. Jack remembered the message he'd left on the answering machine. Becka must have sent Nick out looking for him. She was angry he'd gone to soccer practice instead of coming right home. He was toast.

He began to wonder if he really should be *running* home to take his heart medication, but by then they were turning on to Jefferson Street.

The neighbors were out in force, despite the weather.

Mercedes was in her front garden in a heavy cotton Japanese jacket. With her long, thin legs and pointed features, she looked like some exotic wading bird.

"Jackson!" she said, looking greatly relieved when she saw them. "You'd better get into the house. Your mother's looking for you."

Iris Bolingame leaned over her front gate to tell him the same thing. She was a tall, imposing woman, who wore her long blond hair in a single fat braid decorated with glass trinkets, like some Norse goddess. Even Blaise Highbourne was walking up the street, swinging his leonine head from side to side, searching the cross streets. It was as if the entire street were ushering him home.

But then, that's the way it was in a small town. Everybody knew your business.

Sleet slanted across the street as he and Will parted on the sidewalk. Jack went in to take his medicine. Literally and figuratively.

His mother was seated at the kitchen table, her face blotchy from crying, surrounded by a garland of tissues, like offerings at a shrine.

"Jack!" she cried, leaping to her feet. "I didn't get home until an hour ago. When I got your message, I was so worried. And when you were late . . ." Her voice broke.

"I'm sorry, Mom. I wanted to come home and get my medicine, but Mr. Penworthy wouldn't let me. Well, he would have, but then I'd have had to serve a detention. And then I would have missed soccer tryouts." He hesitated, realizing he was making matters worse.

"Remember? I told you about tryouts this afternoon?"

"Soccer tryouts! You should have come right home! I've already called the school, the hospital, and the police station. The neighbors are out looking for you." Now she was really pissed.

He nodded, his face hot with embarrassment. "I know. I ran into Nick."

"Nick?" She blinked, distracted. "I didn't even talk to him." Then she refocused. "How could you be so thoughtless? What if something happened to your heart?"

"Really, Mom, I feel great." And it was true. Despite a three-hour workout, being thrown to the ground and covered with mud, he felt positively light on his feet. It was hard to explain. The world seemed unusually sharp, more in focus. There was a keen, primitive edge to everything. The wind shrieked, and he could hear the harsh splatter of ice on the roof. The old windows rattled in their wooden frames. He felt like going back out into the wind, shaking his fist and howling back.

"Well, you look awful! You have mud in your hair!" she said, pulling him in for a hug. She reached for the bottle on the table. "Here, you'd better take your medicine right away. Dr. Longbranch said if you ever forgot a dose, to take it as soon as you remember."

She poured out a tablespoon of the nut-brown liquid and handed it to Jack. It carried the scent of damp basements and old paper, last fall's leaves stirred from the bottom of a pile. He swallowed it down.

"Now, you'd better get upstairs for a shower. And maybe lie down for a little while before supper. I have some work to do tonight. How's Thai food sound?"

"Sure. Great," he said, the flavor of the medicine lingering on the back of his tongue. It tasted somehow of old sorrows, old regrets. He brushed his fingers across his eyes, feeling an uncanny sense of loss.

Becka was unloading her briefcase. "Your Aunt Linda is coming tomorrow."

"She is?" Jack's head snapped up. It had been more than a year since his aunt had visited. What was even more surprising was that she'd called ahead to warn them. "What's up?"

"Don't know," said Becka. "She says she's coming to see you."

Ted Slansky was seated at the battered table in the equipment room, nursing a cherry soda and reviewing his notes from the afternoon's scrimmage. He rubbed his chin, informally matching players and positions, faintly conscious of the stench of old sweat and leather that permeated the place. The papers stirred with a sudden movement of air as the door opened.

He looked up, expecting to see one of the players, someone hoping for some early feedback. But two men stood in the doorway, long coats hanging loosely from their shoulders, open in front, as if they did not feel the cold. One was an older man, tall and slender, with a scholarly beard. The other was young and athletic looking, with a sharp jawline and straight dark hair. They glanced quickly about the room, and then back at Slansky.

"Was there a boy here?" the older one asked. It was an

odd question, and spoken with a faint accent, as of someone born overseas.

Slansky might have laughed, but didn't. Somehow it didn't seem like a good idea. "There were about thirty boys here, as a matter of fact, but I think they're all gone now," he replied. "Did you look out front? Some of them may still be waiting for rides."

"There are no boys out front," the older man said, as if it were Slansky's fault.

Slansky shrugged, feeling uneasy. There was something threatening about the two men. "Which one is your boy? I can tell you whether he was here or not." He laid the sign-up sheet in front of him on the table.

"We don't know which one it is," the younger man hissed. "That's why we are here." At this, the older man lifted a hand to still the other. He picked up the sheet from the table, scanned it quickly, then folded it and put it in his pocket.

"Hey!" Slansky protested. "I need that." He would have said more, but the bearded man put out a hand and rested it on his shoulder. Slansky was very conscious of the shape and weight of the man's hand, the heat of it burning through his sweatshirt. He fell silent, eyes wide, overtaken by an unreasoning fear.

The building shuddered under the assault of the wind. The younger man stood, head cocked as if listening. "This shouldn't be so difficult if the boy's untrained," he growled. "There's some disruption about, someone interfering . . ." His voice trailed off.

"Why were thirty boys here?" the older man asked

softly, speaking to Slansky. He tightened his grip, and Slansky felt his heart respond, as if the man could stop it with a touch. Sweat trickled down between his shoulder blades.

"Soccer tryouts," he replied, swallowing hard.

"Soccer tryouts," the man repeated, as if in disbelief. "There was a release of power here," the man continued. "Was there, perhaps, a fight?"

Slansky shook his head. "It gets pretty competitive sometimes, but . . ." He shook his head again. "No fights."

"Did you notice anything unusual? Did any of the players . . . stand out? Perhaps a new player who did something remarkable?"

Slansky desperately reviewed the afternoon's scrimmage. "There were some good plays, but . . . perhaps if you tell me what the . . . what you're looking for, I could help you."

The bearded man made an impatient gesture. He pulled the list of players out of his pocket and thrust it at Slansky. "Circle your five best players," he ordered. "We'll start there."

When the coach had done that, the stranger slid the list back into his pocket. The younger man shifted from one foot to the other, as if impatient to be off. The questioner moved his hand from Slansky's shoulder to his head. His scalp prickled, as if all of his hairs were standing at attention. He quivered with dread.

"*Ana memorare*," the man whispered. That was what it sounded like, some kind of Latin phrase Slansky might have remembered from Catholic school.

Slansky awoke some time later and lifted his face from the table. He realized he must have been asleep for a while, because it was getting dark and the room was cold. Somehow, he'd knocked over his can of cherry pop. He wondered why the door was open and where the sign-up sheet had gotten to.

After supper, Jack slipped out the back door and crossed the gravel driveway to the garage, carrying his social studies book and notebook under his arm. He climbed the stairs to Nick's apartment, and was lifting his hand to knock, when he heard Nick's voice from within. "Come on in, Jack."

As usual, the old caretaker's apartment was tidy, though several books lay open on his desk. Only three rooms, and the place was packed with stuff: books, model airplanes, a miniature steam engine that Nick and Jack had built the year before, jars of chemicals and plant extractions. Bunches of drying plants hung from the ceiling, like some exotic upside-down garden. There was a large wooden cabinet that had been a store display, with rows of tiny drawers full of antique hardware and scavenged items. One whole room was devoted to books, layered two deep on shelves from floor to ceiling on every wall. The apartment always smelled of paint and varnish and spices and dust: exotic, like one of the Indian markets down by the university. Nick at home somehow reminded Jack of an old bear denned up for the winter.

Nick Snowbeard looked up from his solitary dinner. "Sit down, Jack. You're just in time for dessert." Warily,

Jack dropped into the offered chair. Nick shuffled around the apartment, clad in his usual attire of flannel shirt and work pants.

Dessert was chocolate marshmallow ice cream. Jack got partway through his dish before Nick started in on him.

"So you forgot to take your medicine," Nick said abruptly. "Your mother must have been beside herself." He still seemed unusually hard-edged and intense.

"I guess." Jack looked away from Nick, toward the window. A shallow tray was laid out on the table. It had been spread with different colors of sand, raked into an intricate design, littered with small metal objects.

"Why didn't you come home and get it when you remembered?" Nick's voice broke into Jack's reverie.

"Mr. Penworthy said I'd have to serve a detention after school if I left school to go get it. And I didn't want to miss soccer tryouts."

Nick shook his head, his exaggerated brows drawing together in a frown. "You should have come home anyway, detention or not. It's a small thing for your mother to ask, your cooperation in taking care of yourself. What you did today could have important consequences. You cannot imagine what it is like to lose a child."

The old man spoke as if from personal experience. Jack sighed, a frustrated explosion of air.

"You're an adolescent. You think you're immortal." Nick collected their dishes and set them in the sink, put the teakettle on to heat. "How did tryouts go?"

Jack told Nick all about the business with Lobeck. By

the time Jack finished his story, Nick was frowning again. "Garrett Lobeck went flying through the air? And you didn't touch him?"

Jack shrugged. "I don't really know what happened. He was pissed about it. I think he was just looking for an excuse for blowing the play."

"Was he hurt?" Nick persisted.

Why this sudden interest in Lobeck? "His lip was bleeding. He'll have a fat lip tomorrow. To match his head," Jack added.

"Do you think he'll make a big deal about it? Tell people he was attacked, and so on?" Snowbeard leaned forward, placing his hands flat on the table in front of him as if he were holding it down. The old man's hands looked smooth and remarkably young for someone his age. Whatever his age was.

"Who knows? He said I fouled him. Seriously, someone should've hurt him a long time ago."

Nick smiled thinly. "Don't misunderstand me, Jack. It is not that I object to a little butt-kicking when it's deserved." He stood abruptly and walked to the window, nudging the metal tokens on their bed of sand with his forefinger.

"What's that?" Jack asked, eager to distract Nick, who seemed intent on interrogating him.

"Mmmm? This? It's nothing. A charm against evil. Old magic. The eccentricities of an old man." Typical Nick Snowbeard. He could say any outrageous thing that came into his head and get away with it.

When Nick had things arranged to his satisfaction, he returned to the table. And the topic of Lobeck.

"Did anyone else see what happened? Was anyone there to watch the tryouts?"

Jack shook his head. "The goalie was the closest, and I don't think he saw it." He tried to think of who was in the bleachers. Thought of Leesha. "There were some people in the stands." Jack regarded Nick curiously. "Why, do you think he'll sue me or something?"

The kettle shrilled. Nick rose, lifting it from the heat, and poured hot water into the teapot. He set out a china cup, cream and sugar.

The weather was getting worse. Sleet clattered against the glass of the windows, and the oaks behind the garage creaked in protest. A damp chill seemed to find its way through a hundred unseen passages, running cold fingers down Jack's spine.

Jack was still irritated about the medicine. Today, he hadn't taken it, and he'd felt . . . different. More alive. Now he felt . . . anesthetized. As if he were being smothered.

"I just don't see what the big deal is about the medicine. Dr. Longbranch says I have to keep taking it. She never runs any tests, so how would she know? I feel fine, and I felt good today without it. Maybe it's time I weaned myself off the stuff. I think we should find another doctor, someone from around here. I've never liked Dr. Longbranch that much anyway."

"Have you told your mother how you feel?"

"I've tried, but she doesn't want to hear it. It's like she thinks Longbranch is some kind of . . . of wizard."

Nick choked, sputtering, spraying tea across the table.

"Are you okay?"

"Perfectly." Nick blotted at his beard with a napkin. "I suggest you speak with your Aunt Linda before you do anything rash."

Jack stared at him. Aunt Linda? Why did he need to get a second opinion from her? Becka often joked that Nick had been a present from Aunt Linda, since she was the one who had recommended him. All of her presents were unusual, from exotic African carvings to a chemistry set his parents had vetoed when he was three, to sailing lessons and beach weekends. Some gifts were dangerous, some extravagant and impractical, but all were interesting. Never a golf shirt or a gift card.

Nick never said much about his personal history, if he had any family, or how he knew Aunt Linda. Somehow, he seemed to be able to deflect those questions effortlessly. He was from northern Britain, had attended Cambridge, though he never finished his degree. Aunt Linda had attended private school in Britain when she was Jack's age. Perhaps they'd met there.

It didn't matter. Jack was tired of being the miracle child, the survivor, tired of swallowing down the medicine that was emblematic of his special status. "Sure, Nick, whatever. I'll ask her. She's coming tomorrow, you know," he said.

Nick's black eyes glittered under bushy brows. "Is she? That's a good thing, I suppose," he said.

Impatiently, Jack grabbed his social studies book and leafed through until he found the appropriate page. "Well, back to important stuff. I have a social studies test tomorrow. Can you quiz me on the explorers?" He pushed the book toward Nick, a little rudely. History was Snowbeard's specialty. Sometimes he spoke of events long in the past as if he had participated personally.

The old man sat for a moment, tapping a forefinger against his pursed lips. He sighed and rotated the book so he could read it. He found the spot with his finger. "Vasco da Gama," he said.

◈ CHAPTER TWO ◈
THE ROAD TRIP

Jack awoke, momentarily confused by the sound of voices from downstairs. He threw back the quilt, then lay back regretfully for a moment. It had been another late night.

But there was something else, some vestige of a dream that made him shiver. Something about dead people, somebody looking for him. And Nick. He frowned. It had been a long time since he'd had a nightmare. One he remembered, at least.

The weather had improved. The wind was finally quiet after shrieking most of the night. There was the promise of a fair day in the brightening sky. The back-yard was gilded, every leaf and blade silvered with ice, and gleaming.

When he rounded the corner from the back stairs into

the kitchen, she was there, seated at the kitchen table with his mother. His aunt Linda.

Her hair was gold and platinum this time, and short and spiky all over. Her skin seemed bronzed a bit, no doubt the result of recent travel in the tropics. She wore blue jeans and a fitted T-shirt, with sturdy leather hiking boots.

They must have been talking about him, because conversation stopped when he came into the room. There was an awkward little moment until Aunt Linda rose to embrace him. Jack towered over her, but she tilted his chin down so she could look him in the face. Her eyes were blue speckled with gold, like some exotic stone.

"You've grown so tall, Jack," she said, releasing his chin but still studying his face. "I do believe you've passed up your father. It seems boys become men before you know it." She looked a little sad for some reason, but he felt inordinately pleased, as if he had personally brought the change about.

"I was just telling Linda some news. I guess I forgot all about it after that scare we had last night." Becka looked as excited as a child at Christmas. "I've been awarded a fellowship to do some research in Middle English literature at Oxford this summer."

"Oxford? You mean England? But what about your practice?"

"Mike Mixon's agreed to pick up any court work for me this summer. Things are pretty quiet right now, anyway. It's been a long time since we've had a real vacation. I won't be working all the time, and there's so much I'd like to show you" Becka said.

"You'll love England, Jack," Aunt Linda added. "Our family comes from there. So many old voices, and so much history under the ground," she said, as if that comment required no further explanation.

"Well." Jack was torn between excitement and apprehension. "Dad said maybe we could finally build that sailboat this summer."

"I'm sure we can work something out," Becka said lightly, pretending it might actually occur.

"Maybe we could visit *you* for a change," Jack suggested to Linda.

Linda didn't meet his eyes. "I'd love for you to visit, but unfortunately I've sublet my flat in London, since I've been doing so much traveling."

Aunt Linda's livelihood had always been rather mysterious. She was in real estate, she said, representing manor houses and castles throughout the UK. Jack assumed she must be good at it; she always seemed to have plenty of money and the leisure to spend it.

"Mom said you came to see me," he said bluntly.

She nodded, steepling her hands. "I was hoping you could come with me on a road trip."

"Road trip?"

"I'm going to dig up some dead relatives," she went on, "and ask them where the family money is."

"Dead relatives?" All he seemed to be able to do was parrot what she said.

Aunt Linda laughed. "I came back to the States to do

some genealogical research," she said. "I'm going to drive down to Coalton County and look through some old records."

"Oh." Jack tried not to make a face. Funny, he'd never heard Aunt Linda mention anything about genealogy before.

"That should be fun," Becka said enthusiastically. She loved wading through dusty old records, legal and otherwise. "I wish I could go. Jack and I went down there once, but we didn't find much. Maybe you two will be more successful."

"Ri-i-i-ght," Jack said skeptically.

Linda grinned. "Look," she said. "What I really need is some muscle to dig up the bodies. Why don't you invite a couple of friends? What about Will? Isn't that his name? Or maybe Harmon Fitch."

How could she remember their names? She didn't visit all that often, and her last visit had been over a year ago. "I'm sure traveling to southern Ohio to do gene-alogy on my family will sound even more appealing to *them*." Now he did make a face.

"Come on," Linda pleaded. "We'll have fun. We'll stay at a hotel with a pool. You guys can eat junk food and stay up late. My treat." They both knew the entire dialogue was just a formality, a ritual they had to go through. He had never been able to say no to her.

"Call your friends now," Linda said, pushing back her plate. "I'd like to be on our way by ten."

"You want to leave now?" Becka shook her head. "Then Jack can't go with you. He has to go to school."

"He does?" Aunt Linda looked nonplussed, as if the idea of school being in session had never occurred to her. "How inconvenient. I wanted to go to the courthouse today. I don't think they're open on the weekend." She spooned three or four teaspoons of sugar into her tea, and stirred. "Never mind," she declared suddenly. "We'll go after school. It's all settled. Jack—ask the boys about it this morning."

To Jack's surprise, Will seemed up for a road trip. For one thing, Will's parents were having six yards of leaf humus mulch delivered that afternoon. It seemed like a good weekend to get out of town. But Linda Downey's involvement was the deciding factor. Will was ordinarily shy around girls, but he was absolutely tongue-tied around Linda. "You know your aunt is gorgeous, Jack," he'd once said solemnly, almost apologetically. And Jack had to admit, she was.

Jack and Will lingered in the foyer by the school office, hoping Fitch would make an appearance before the last bell rang.

Penworthy was at his usual post by the front door. He was deep in conversation with a man Jack had never seen before. The man was dressed all in black, and towered over Penworthy.

"Hey! You! Swift!"

Jack pivoted to see Garrett Lobeck emerging from the principal's office, flanked by his friends, Jay Harkness and Bruce Leonard. Probably serving detention before school. Any one of them were bigger than two of Jack.

Lobeck kept coming until he was heavily into Jack's personal space. "We need to talk about that scumbag play you made yesterday," Lobeck said. Only, it sounded more like "thumbag" and "yethterday" because Lobeck's lips were swollen to twice their usual size.

"Look," said Jack. "I took a goal shot. That's all. It's not my fault if you got in the way. Get over it."

"I'm going to hurt you, *Jack*, and that's a promise. You'll just have to wonder when." Lobeck attempted a sneer, but gave it up. Apparently too painful. Leonard and Harkness were grinning, though. Lobeck was playing to his audience. He had to do something, after all. The soccer story would be all over school by day's end, what with Garrett walking around with the evidence displayed all over his face.

Jack couldn't say what made him do it. Some sort of death wish, probably. He leaned in so he was inches from Lobeck's face. He was as tall as Lobeck, if not so big around. "Fine. You do that," Jack said, smiling pleasantly. "Next time, I'll break your nose, and there goes the modeling career."

Lobeck squinted at Jack as if he couldn't believe what he was hearing. He extended a hand with the apparent intention of grabbing Jack's shirtfront. Then seemed to think better of it and flipped him the finger instead.

"MISTER LOBECK!"

They all jumped.

It was Penworthy, accompanied by the tall stranger Jack had noticed earlier.

Penworthy stuffed a detention slip into Lobeck's hand.

"Mr. Lobeck, it seems you have not spent enough time in detention this week. You of all people should know that obscene hand gestures are expressly forbidden on school property."

Lobeck vibrated like a boiler about to blow. When he finally got his mouth working, he let go a string of obscenities. Penworthy just kept peeling off the detention slips until Lobeck ran dry.

"Uh, Mr. Penworthy," said Will, obviously wary of getting in the way of flying detentions. "We were just heading to homeroom." Lobeck and his friends seemed anxious to leave also.

Jack looked up to see the stranger staring at him. Against his will, Jack found himself rooted to the spot, staring back. The man had high cheekbones and chiseled, aristocratic features that were marred only by a somewhat overlarge nose. His complexion had the pale cast of a scholar or someone whose skin doesn't react to the sun. Startling green eyes were sheltered under brows unusually heavy and black for someone of such fair complexion. Jack had a quick impression of a searing intelligence, of physical power, and then Penworthy broke in.

"Before you go, gentlemen, I'd like you to meet Mr. Leander Hastings, our new assistant principal," he said briskly. "He's replacing Mr. Brumfield." He put a hand on each boy's shoulder in turn. "Mr. Lobeck. Mr. Harkness. Mr. Leonard. Mr. Childers. Mr. Swift." Hastings's gaze swept briefly over each of them. "Mr. Hastings will head our student discipline team, and will be in charge of enforcing the attendance policy."

"I won't be spending all my time issuing detentions." Hastings's lips quirked, as if at a private joke. "In fact, I'll be developing programming for some of your . . ." he paused, trying to choose the right words. "For some of your . . . more gifted students." Hastings had a presence about him that seemed inconsistent with school administration. Rather . . . wolflike.

"Yes, well . . . gifted education . . ." Penworthy sputtered, as if this were a complete and unwelcome surprise. "An excellent idea, assuming you have the time."

"But of course. I'll make the time," Hastings replied. "Nothing is more important than seizing talent where you find it and putting it to its highest use." His gaze settled on Jack.

Jack hadn't heard that Brumfield was leaving. He wanted to ask a question about it, but couldn't. A deep chill had settled somewhere behind his breastbone, making it difficult to breathe, let alone speak. He felt a strong sense of onrushing danger. Once, when he was a child, he and Will had been playing on the railroad tracks, when he realized a train was coming. He could feel the rails vibrating through the soles of his shoes, hear the shriek of the whistle, but he couldn't move. Then Will had grabbed his arm and yanked him into the cinders beside the right-of-way.

"Uh, we have to get to homeroom before last bell," Will said, again tugging at Jack's arm.

But Hastings was speaking again, and nobody moved. "Do you boys play soccer? Are any of you on the team?"

"We all tried out for the team this week." Will gestured, including the other four. "We don't know yet if we made it or not."

"Where I came from, I was the assistant coach," Hastings said. "I mean to get involved with the program here."

Jack had no doubt it would happen, whether Coach Slansky liked it or not.

The last bell rang, and it was as if some kind of spell had been broken. The group spun out in three different directions, Will and Jack into the tenth-grade wing, Lobeck and his friends heading into the eleventh-grade hallway, and Penworthy and Hastings back to the office.

Fitch was in Jack's calculus class, so Jack was able to ask about the road trip before lunchtime. Fitch nodded gravely, as if the prospect of traveling hundreds of miles to look at old court records about Jack's dead relatives was natural recreation. Fitch never cared much what other people thought, and he had a way of finding the interesting angle to any situation. During lunch period, he called his mother at work. She said he could go as long as it didn't cost any money.

Will had a harder time getting out of shoveling mulch. "But it will be *educational*," he pleaded into the phone. "Jack's aunt is a geologist. Uh, I mean genealogist. And I'm going to write a paper about it for school," he added. That must have been enough to clinch it, because he was smiling when he put the receiver down.

When Jack arrived home, an unfamiliar white Land Rover was parked at the end of the driveway. A surprising choice for Aunt Linda, who usually leased a sports car when she came to visit. He found Becka in the kitchen, loading sandwiches into a cooler.

"Linda is visiting with Nick," she explained. "She said to tell you to go ahead and get packed."

Jack's duffle sat open on his bed. Next to it was a small parcel wrapped in butcher paper with a bright blue block print design. He picked up the package and examined it curiously. It was almost weightless in his hands.

"Mercedes left that for you," Aunt Linda said from the doorway, making him jump. "She said it might come in handy on the trip."

How did Mercedes get involved? Were their travel plans posted on the town Web site? Or displayed on the magnetic sign in the university commons? Jack made a noise of disgust. Sometimes he hated living in a small town.

He ripped the paper away. It was a sleeveless vest, woven in a lightweight gray fiber that seemed familiar. Three silver buttons decorated the front. When Jack looked more closely, he saw they were the faces of three different bears, in silver, gold, and copper.

"Not exactly my style," he muttered, tossing it onto the bed. "And it's not even my birthday. But tell her thanks anyway."

What had gotten into Mercedes? She knew what kind of clothes he wore. Nothing more exotic than jeans and T-shirts. She saw him practically every day of the week.

Linda remained in the doorway, her arms folded. "Try it on," she said. Jack looked up, startled. He wanted to argue, but knew that if Linda meant for him to put the thing on, there was no point in fighting it.

"I feel stupid," he growled, snatching it up off the bed and pulling it on over his T-shirt. It fit perfectly. He finally realized what it reminded him of. It was made of the same yarn as the baby blanket Mercedes had made for him years ago, now packed away in a box under his bed.

"Looks good," Linda said. She twisted a lock of her hair between her finger and thumb. There was a tension about her that he hadn't noticed in the morning. She had just come from Nick's. Could the old caretaker have said something to upset her?

When he went to take the vest off, she put up her hand. "Leave it on."

He supposed he should be glad it wasn't pink with purple polka dots. Will and Fitch would have plenty to say about it.

"Thanks a lot, Aunt Linda. I hear this is what all the guys are wearing." Grumbling under his breath, he yanked open his bottom drawer and started packing.

Linda took in his sullen expression. "Look, I'm not out to embarrass you. It would just mean so much to . . . to Mercedes if you would wear it. Why don't you put a sweatshirt over it, if it makes you happier? It's chilly out anyway." And she smiled that smile that always made you want to please her.

Jack wondered how flattered Mercedes would be to know he was wearing her precious vest like underwear. He found his Ohio State sweatshirt on the floor, pulled it over his head, and zipped up the duffle. Then he remembered what he'd meant to tell her. "Oh, yeah. Will and Fitch are both coming," he said.

He thought she'd be pleased, but she frowned and said, "Oh," like she'd completely forgotten she'd invited them. "Maybe we should just go by ourselves," she suggested, after a pause.

Jack stared at her in disbelief. "You can't be serious. You were the one who told me to invite them in the first place."

She wrapped her arms around herself, shifting from one foot to the other. "I . . . it's just that—"

"Mom's packing enough food for an army. She even made brownies, for once, instead of those disgusting bran applesauce carrot bars."

"All right. Never mind. I just hope they get here soon. I'd like to get out of here as soon as possible."

She's moodier than I remember, Jack thought.

Back in the kitchen, Becka was just closing up the cooler. "This should tide you boys over if Linda won't stop to eat. She really does seem to be on a mission. I'll put your medicine in your duffel," she added pointedly, sliding the big blue bottle in with Jack's clothes. "Don't get so involved in family history that you forget to take it."

And then Will and Fitch arrived, seeming to fill up the kitchen. Will was wearing his varsity jacket, T-shirt, and blue jeans. Fitch wore an army issue camouflage jacket, a bright yellow sweatshirt with the logo of a country music station emblazoned on the front, and gray-green climbing pants with a red necktie threaded through for a belt.

Jack realized that no matter what he wore, he could never match Fitch's display. Fitch played by his own rules, and it never bothered him that the preps called him weird. "Weird is good, strange is bad," Fitch always said. Jack felt a little better.

⊗ CHAPTER THREE ⊗
DIGGING UP DEAD RELATIVES

Linda had a heavy foot. She seemed determined to make up at least part of the time they had wasted at school. Whenever Jack, who was riding shotgun, stole a look at the speedometer, it hovered around eighty-five. He had been hoping she might ask him to drive, but realized they would only lose time with him at the wheel.

They passed through a series of tired little towns: a traffic light, a gas station or two. As darkness fell, they began to see the debris of strip mining: heaps of slag and mine tailings. Iron oil rigs crouched like giant mosquitoes in the dusk, sucking the black blood out of the land.

"Have either of you ever been here before?" Will asked.

"My mom brought me down here a few years ago," Jack admitted. *Dragged* was more accurate. Becka had made him walk all over those hills, looking for the family homestead. They never did find it. "My great-great grandmother Susannah lived here. She was quite a character, I guess. She played banjo and fiddle and made killer black cherry wine."

Linda took up the tale without taking her eyes from the road. "Susannah is the one we're looking for. She had the Second Sight, they say. She communed with spirits, read the cards, and had prophetic dreams."

"She sounds like some kind of witch," Fitch remarked.

"Mom's always been into that kind of thing," Jack said, grinning. "It's been rumored that magic runs in our family, you know."

"I'd prefer that to allergies," Fitch said, sneezing.

"Susannah had quite a following around here, mostly women." Linda swerved to miss a groundhog. "In those days, it always seemed to be men who made the future, and women who needed to protect themselves against it."

Jack stared out the window. This home of his ancestors was on the way to nowhere; a place of graveyards, where they dug up the coal and buried the people.

It was fully dark when they reached Coal Grove, the county seat, a town without a traffic light. An ornate old courthouse anchored one end of the square. The stores were all closed, although several cars littered the parking lot next to the movie theatre; light and music spilled from a place called the Bluebird Cafe diagonally across from the courthouse. Friday night in Coal Grove, Jack thought. Even slower than Trinity.

Linda turned the Land Rover down one of the side

streets off the square and parked along the curb under a huge maple tree. There were no streetlights, and it was pitch black in the shadow of the great tree.

"Where are we?" asked Will, puzzled. "Aren't we going to the motel?"

"I need to go to the courthouse first," Linda replied, climbing down out of the front seat. She slung a backpack over her shoulder and slammed the car door. It seemed unnaturally loud on the quiet street.

Jack unfolded himself out of the car, feeling a little unsteady on his legs after the long ride. The night air was cool and fragrant, and there was a soft sound of spring peepers from somewhere in the distance. A small dog began barking madly behind a screen door in a nearby house. The porch light went on, and they could see a figure silhouetted behind the screen.

Linda led them across the street and into the parking lot behind the courthouse. A modern brick building crouched on the other side of the parking lot, away from the square. Two police cars were parked next to the building. A mercury vapor light cast a sallow light over the scene.

"But isn't the courthouse closed?" Will persisted.

"Oh, I'm sure it's open late on Friday nights," Linda said. She led the trio along the back of the building, between army green trash Dumpsters and into the shadows of an alley on the far side. She followed the side of the building back until she found what she was looking for: a concrete stairwell with an ancient iron railing that descended below ground level. There was a door at the bottom.

Linda looked up and down the alleyway, then

descended the stairs, motioning for Jack and his friends to follow her. She fumbled with the door for a moment before it swung open on loudly protesting hinges. She looked back over her shoulder at them. "I told you it was open!" she said, then disappeared inside.

"I have a bad feeling about this!" Jack whispered to Fitch. Fitch shrugged. With Linda in charge, there was nothing to do but follow.

The doorway led into an ancient cellar. The smell of old paper and mildew and damp earth was overwhelming. Aunt Linda produced three powerful flashlights from her backpack. Only, just a little late. "Ouch!" Will had already banged his head on a low ceiling joist.

Jack let the beam of his flashlight play over the walls. They were lined with shelves filled with huge ledgers stamped with gold lettering. Everything seemed to be the same matte gray color, because it was all covered with a thick layer of dust. Fitch was already beginning to sneeze. High on the walls, above the ledger books, were rows and rows of numbered metal boxes.

An ancient wooden staircase provided access to the main floor of the building. Boxes of records were stacked on nearly every step, leaving only a narrow path to the top. Linda found a light switch on the wall by the steps, and the room was suddenly flooded with light.

"What are we looking for?" Jack asked his aunt. "And why can't we come back tomorrow?"

Linda was already lifting a ledger from the wall. She was surprisingly strong, considering her size, and manhandled the huge book onto the sloping reading table in the center of the room. She had a smudge of dirt across the bridge of her nose.

"We're looking for death records," she explained. "We need to find one for your great-great grandmother Downey. I estimate she died between 1900 and 1920. The courthouse won't be open tomorrow, so we'd better do this tonight."

The book on the table was labeled Death Book A. Jack looked over Linda's shoulder. The pages were covered with long columns of spidery writing. *Name. Date of Death. Place of Death. Where Born.* The dates at the front of the book were all in the late 1860s. Linda quickly turned over the yellowing pages, scanning them from top to bottom until she reached the back of the book. It ended about 1875. Too early.

"Couldn't you just write to Columbus to get this information?" Fitch asked, sneezing again. "Or look it up online?"

"They don't have electronic records back this far," Linda replied, lifting the book with Jack's help and replacing it in its slot. "Besides, I'm in a hurry. Now we need to look for Death Book B or C."

The ledgers on the shelves seemed to be in no particular order. The volume next to Book A was labeled BB and was dated 1950s. They split up to scan the spines of the books on all sides of the room. It was a real mixture. Common Pleas Court proceedings. Will books. Land records.

Jack's eyes kept straying to the staircase that led to the main floor. That was the police station he'd seen across the parking lot; he was sure of it. Would a passion for genealogy be considered justification for breaking and entering? Aunt Linda had always seemed to make up rules as she went along, but he'd never known her to break the law.

Then again, perhaps he didn't know her very well.

Will was methodically working his way through a stack of ledgers, no doubt motivated by the fading prospect of a late dinner. "Hey!" he said suddenly. "What dates were you looking for?"

"Early 1900s," Linda replied, moving to look over the book he was examining. "This might be it." She ran her finger down the page, then flipped several pages back. "This is the right time frame." These later entries included information about cause of death, mostly ailments Jack had never heard of: scrofula, dropsy, brain fever. Some he had seen only in history books: consumption, typhoid fever, smallpox. Some deaths were accidental, the descriptions flat: *Drowned. Fell from roof. Kicked by a horse.*

Linda's lips moved silently as she turned the brittle pages over. "Here it is!" she said tersely. " 'Susannah Downey born 1868; farmer's wife; died 12 May 1900; cause of death: accident.' "

They all gathered around so they could read the scrawled entry.

"She was pretty young," Jack observed. "Any idea how she died?" He was interested in spite of himself.

"No," Linda replied, transcribing the entry into a notebook she had pulled out of her backpack. "It doesn't say where she lived or where she was buried." She sounded disappointed.

"None of them do," Fitch said. "Is that important?"

"I need to find her grave," Aunt Linda said. "So we have to figure out what cemetery she's buried in. Unless they buried her on their own property. In which case we'd need to check the land records."

They were all concentrating so hard on their find that it took Jack a few seconds to process what he was hearing. He held up his hand for silence, then jerked his head toward the ceiling. There was the unmistakable sound of footsteps on the floor above.

They all froze. There was a bitter, metallic taste in the back of Jack's mouth, and his heart felt like a desperate fish flopping about in his chest. Linda tilted her head back as if she could look through the rough planking into the room above. She let out her breath, a small, animal sound of fear. Then she quickly shut the ledger book and lifted it back into its niche. Almost simultaneously, a door opened at the top of the stairs and a pale rectangle of light appeared in the dark stairwell.

The staircase was between them and the door to the outside. "Go!" Aunt Linda hissed as she made a leap for the light switch. The room was plunged into darkness. Jack stumbled against the center table as he desperately felt his way to the outline of the outside door. Aunt Linda was crashing around behind him, making an unholy racket. What the hell was she doing? He could hear Will and Fitch somewhere ahead of him. He stole a quick look over his shoulder and saw a tall black silhouette at the top of the stairs, framed in the dirty yellow of the mercury vapor lights. He could make out no face or feature. As he watched, it turned to him.

Jack felt the touch of its attention like a physical blow. He staggered, grabbing a filing cabinet for support.

Suddenly Linda was beside him, fiercely pushing him forward. "You! Get moving! I'll meet you at the Bluebird Cafe in half an hour!"

Behind them, Jack heard a muffled exclamation, the sound of something heavy falling, then a string of curses. Will and Fitch must have reached the outside door, because gray light poured in from the stairwell. He scrambled after his friends. Just as he reached the doorway, he heard an explosion. There was a blinding flash of light, then something hit him square in the back, knocking him sprawling onto the concrete pad just outside the door. He came down on his hands and knees, and bit his tongue, hard. Blood tasted salty in his mouth. Then Will and Fitch each grabbed an arm and dragged him up the stairs and down the alleyway. When he finally found his feet, Jack twisted around to see if Linda was behind them, but the alley was empty.

The alley led back to the main square at the front of the courthouse. The street was still deserted. They sprinted across the green and squeezed between the bushes planted around the gazebo. There were three or four feet of space between the evergreens and the cinder block foundation of the building. They crouched there, breathing hard, looking back toward the courthouse, then wide-eyed at each other.

Finally Will spoke. "What the hell was that?"

"What was what?" Jack snapped. He had too many questions of his own to be answering theirs.

"That spooky dude on the stairs, for a start," Fitch replied. "The one with the cool light saber."

"Light saber? Be serious." Jack peered out at the courthouse again.

"Light saber. Flame thrower. Phaser. Electromagnetic de-atomizer. What he shot you with, dude." Fitch swiped at the blood on his face with the back of his hand and attempted a smile.

"Why aren't you dead?" Will demanded. "It should have killed you, so I don't understand why you aren't dead. You're sure you're not hurt?"

"No," Jack said slowly. "A little bruised, maybe." There was a painful area between his shoulder blades, like he'd been hit in the back by a fast pitch. The only other sensation was a kind of tingling all over his body.

Fitch reached around behind Jack and tugged at his hoodie. It disintegrated in his hand. "Nice shirt," he said, handing the charred shards of cloth to Jack. They had a gunpowder smell, like bottle rockets after a launch. Jack pulled the remains of the sweatshirt off over his head. The entire back was gone. Underneath, his new vest seemed to be in one piece. As a matter of fact, it didn't seem to be damaged at all.

"Good thing you wore your bulletproof vest," Will observed dryly. "Guess me and Fitch didn't get the memo."

Jack looked back at the courthouse, still lit only by the

sallow glow of the security light. If an alarm had been raised, why hadn't anyone turned on the lights? And why hadn't the man at the top of the stairs said anything, identified himself?

There was no sign of pursuit. The square and the courthouse were quiet.

"Look," Jack said, swallowing hard. "I'm really sorry. When I asked you to come along on this trip, I never thought . . . I don't know who that was or what Aunt Linda is up to, but—"

Fitch interrupted him. "Where *is* she?"

No one had an answer for that. Jack imagined explaining to his mother that they'd lost her sister during the commission of a burglary, and shoved the image away.

Fitch leaned wearily back against the stone foundation of the gazebo and closed his eyes. His pale hair lifted off his forehead as a breeze sprang up. "It's funny that he didn't set off an alarm."

Jack shrugged. He'd heard of pitched battles over archaeological sites. But *genealogy*? What had they gotten into? Nervously, he checked his watch.

"Aunt Linda said to meet her at the Bluebird in a half hour. It's about time." He prayed she would show up as promised. He wasn't sure what he would do if she didn't.

Still wary of the courthouse, they slipped straight back from the gazebo to the far side of the square, then cut between the buildings to the next street. They traced a wide circle around to the Bluebird. It was a few minutes after nine when they walked into the bar.

Loud music overwhelmed them as they stepped

inside, followed by the scent of stale tobacco and beer. It took a few minutes for their eyes to adjust to the light. The only illumination came from neon beer signs. The place was crowded and there was a mix of patrons, young people, older people, those who were dressed up a bit and those who had obviously come straight from working a shift. It was, after all, a Friday night. Jack had the feeling that everyone in the place knew each other, and he and his friends were clearly outsiders. And they were underage, which was pointed out immediately.

"Can I help you boys?" The girl wore an air of authority, although she didn't look much older than they were. A grinning, toothy bluebird hoisting a beer was embroidered on the pocket of her shirt. "I need to see some ID."

"We're not drinking," Will explained. "Couldn't we just sit back in the restaurant part?" he asked. "We're waiting for someone."

The waitress studied them for a moment, her gaze lingering longest on Will. Then she shrugged. "Sure, why not?" She nodded at an empty table in the back. "Seat yourselves. I'll bring you some menus if you like."

"That'd be great," Will replied.

"You look like *you* have a good appetite," the waitress replied, smiling at Will and fixing her ponytail. "Do you work out?"

It turned out the waitress was into bodybuilding. She and Will quickly progressed to flexing and feeling each other's biceps before she finally left to fetch their sodas.

Jack glared at Will. "You can't possibly be hungry." A great hard stone of apprehension at his center made it impossible for him to think of eating. Or of anything else.

"Well, why not?" Will said, unperturbed, scanning the menu. "They aren't going to serve us beer, and we can't just sit here."

"How do we know that guy isn't in here?" Fitch was hunched over, as if to make his lanky frame smaller.

Jack looked around. He saw no tall men in long coats, felt no cold, threatening presence, but it wouldn't be hard to hide in this crowd.

"Do you mind if I join you?"

Jack looked up, startled, into blue and gold eyes. Aunt Linda's spiky gold-and-silver hair was disheveled, and there was the shadow of a bruise over one cheekbone. Her blue jean jacket looked like it had been used to wipe up the floor.

All three of them started talking at once. Linda shook her head, her lips pressed tightly together. The waitress had returned.

"I see you found your friend," she said, clunking glasses down in front of them, eying Linda jealously. "You all ready to order?"

Jack ordered something at random, watching Linda. She sat, facing the door, looking up each time it opened.

She's scared to death, Jack thought.

Linda leaned forward. "Are you three all right?" She studied each of them in turn as if she feared there might be parts missing, looking so guilty and miserable that Jack found himself wishing he could make her feel better somehow. "Jack, I saw you fall—"

"I'm okay," Jack said quickly. He looked around at the others. "You guys are all right, aren't you?"

"Well . . ." Will shrugged. "I about wet my pants when that freak opened the door."

"Why would he shoot at us?" Fitch asked. "If it wasn't the police, or a night watchman, why would he be sneaking around in there at night? There's nothing but a bunch of old court records." He swirled the ice in his glass and looked at Linda. "Unless he was looking for the same thing we are. Like in Tomb Raider."

Linda said nothing. The waitress circled the table, setting their plates before them.

"All he had to do was ask," Will said. "I would've given him Death Book A, for sure."

Jack studied his steak sandwich as if it were something unfamiliar and inedible. Fitch picked at his food, and Linda ignored what was on her plate and drank her second beer straight from the bottle. Will was the only one who seemed hungry.

"Do you think he was just trying to scare us off?" Jack asked, conscious of the bruised spot in the middle of his back. "Or would he come after us in here?"

"He won't come in here," Linda said, picking absently at a broken nail. "He knows we haven't found anything yet. And now he knows all he has to do is follow me." With that, she shut her mouth, as if she realized she had already said too much.

Jack dropped his silverware onto his plate with a clatter. "So you know who that guy is?" More and more he was asking questions he already knew the answers to.

"Yes," she said. "I know who he is. I just never expected to meet up with him here." She looked at Fitch and Will. "If I had, I never would have brought you two along."

What about me? Am I, like, expendable, then? Jack thought, careening between anger and bewilderment.

Rock music pounded from the speakers as people crowded into the Bluebird Cafe. Someone propped the front door open as the room heated up. Linda's gaze flickered to the open door.

"Is he out there?" Jack asked.

Linda nodded. "Not far away, anyway. The thing is," she said as if continuing their earlier conversation. "I'm looking for a . . . a family heirloom. I was hoping to find it this weekend. He must be looking for it, too. Either he traced it to Coal Grove through Susannah's genealogy or he followed me down here. And if he followed me here . . ." Her voice trailed off. She was looking at Jack. He shifted uncomfortably in his seat.

Will scarfed down the last of his sandwich. "So what was that weapon he used?"

"I don't know," Linda said. "I . . . I didn't really see anything."

She's lying, Jack thought.

"Why don't we just go back home?" Fitch suggested. "He can't hang around here forever. We can always come back another time."

Linda shook her head. "The fact that he's here may mean it's already too late. We can't take the chance that he might find it before we do." She looked at each of them in turn. "I'm going to have to find it this weekend or risk losing everything."

"Then, what's our next step?" Fitch asked.

"There's no next step for you two boys," Linda said. "I'm going to take you to the hotel and leave you there until this is over. I . . . I don't always think things through, I'm afraid." She looked down at her hands. "It was a mistake to get you involved. I'm not putting you at risk again."

"What about me?" Jack asked, realizing that once again he'd been intentionally excluded.

She wouldn't look at him. "If I can find it, I'll need your help to retrieve it, Jack. I have some inside information that will help us. Only . . . I don't know how we'll manage to lose him. And if he sees us together . . ."

Fitch rested his chin on his hands. "Maybe we can help."

Linda leaned into the center of the table. "You don't know them," she whispered. "This is not a game." Jack had never seen his irreverent aunt look so serious.

"Just listen," Fitch persisted. "You said this guy would be following you. You're not going to find anything without his knowing it." Aunt Linda nodded warily. "But he probably didn't get a good look at us at the courthouse," he went on. "And there's only one of him. I'll bet if he has to make a choice, he'll follow you. I would," he admitted, blushing a little.

"What are you thinking?"

"What if you lead him away from here while the three of us look for the . . . thing," Will said. "If he's following you, we won't be in danger."

"Well, maybe we should split up now anyway," Linda said, wavering. "If I take you to the motel, we might be followed. The next place we need to go is the library. That should be safe enough."

Jack didn't like it. Linda knew the man in the courthouse, and she was frightened of him. "I don't want that guy following you around. I think we should stick together."

She shrugged. "He'll be following me anyway. There's nothing I can do about that. And if you're with me, you'll be in danger." It was plain that she didn't consider them much protection against whatever waited outside.

"How important is it that you . . . win?" Jack asked.

"Winning is everything." She looked up at him and said again, "Everything." Something in the way she said it made Jack wonder if this desperate quest had something to do with him.

The plan was hatched over the battered table in the back of the Bluebird Cafe. Aunt Linda handed Jack a wad of bills and a credit card, along with the confirmation number for the hotel reservation. The hotel was back by the highway, and they would have to get there on their own. Linda didn't think it wise for the boys to return to the Land Rover if they wanted to avoid the attention of the stranger outside. Will put Aunt Linda's cell phone and her notebook in the inside pocket of his jacket. She had scrawled some instructions inside. Fitch carried two of the flashlights. When all was set, she called the bartender over. Her voice took on a distinctly local accent.

"You know what," she said to the bartender in a voice dripping with charm. "My ex-husband's out there waiting in the parking lot, and I'm afraid there might be trouble. He's been following us around all night. I'm scared we might have words, and I don't want my boys getting mixed up in this."

The bartender nodded sympathetically. He was a huge man with a florid complexion, massive shoulders, and beefy hands. If he thought she had a peculiar-looking family, he didn't say so.

"I wonder if they could just slip out the back," Linda went on. "Do you have a kitchen door?"

The man nodded again. "No problem. I understand how it is sometimes with exes. I have one myself." He jerked his head at a door at the back labeled RESTROOMS. "Just go through there and keep heading straight back. There's a door that lets out to the alley."

"I really appreciate it," Linda said. "If it's okay with you, I think I'll sit here a bit until I know they're safe away."

"No problem," the bartender said solicitously.

Jack and his friends pushed back their chairs.

"Be careful!" Linda called after them. Jack looked back. His aunt seemed small and vulnerable sitting alone at the table.

They pushed through the swinging door at the back of the restaurant and found themselves in a shabby hallway with a linoleum floor and restrooms to either side. There was another door at the far end, under an exit sign.

The door let out into an alley between two huge Dumpsters. The music from the bar seemed distressingly loud when they opened the door. They jerked it shut quickly behind them and lingered between the Dumpsters for a moment. No one appeared. Then, like ghosts, the boys slipped down the alley and into the street beyond.

"Excuse me."

The night clerk was perched on a stool behind the counter, immersed in a handheld video game. He looked to be in his mid twenties, scrawny, with a generous supply of post-adolescent acne. After briefly surveying Jack and his companions without interest or curiosity, he returned to his game, which played a little tune as he advanced to the next level.

Jack cleared his throat. "Excuse me," he repeated.

"Mmmm?" This time he didn't lift his eyes from the screen. His name badge said "Stan."

"We have reservations. Name of O'Herron," Jack persisted. Finally, Stan ran out of lives and the game came to a sudden and tragic end. Reluctantly, he shut it off and turned his attention to Jack.

"We don't rent to teenagers," he said abruptly. He took a long drink from a can of Mountain Dew. "You boys better go back home."

"The reservation's in the name of my aunt," Jack continued, pushing a credit card and the slip of paper with the confirmation number on it across the counter to Stan. "She'll be here later."

Why does Aunt Linda have a credit card in the name of O'Herron? Somehow, he hadn't thought to ask her.

Stan eyed the credit card suspiciously. "Well, where's your aunt right now?"

"She, uh, she met someone at a bar in town. She said she was going to stay a while longer, but me and my cousins were . . . were getting tired." Jack stifled a yawn. "So she told us to come ahead." Will and Fitch yawned also.

Stan rocked back on his stool, folding his arms across his chest, the picture of stubbornness. Just then the phone buzzed. Now keeping his full attention on the trio in front of him, Stan picked it up and listened for a moment.

"Well, they're here," Stan replied to something the caller said, "but I don't think I can let them check in without your being here." He sounded suddenly less sure of himself.

He listened for a moment, shaking his head as if she were there to see it, then launched a weak protest. "Miss O'Herron, I really think you'd better get over here and check in yourself—" he began, but then stopped, listening again. "Well, I suppose, if you'll be here in a few hours—" He listened some more, swallowing rapidly, his Adam's apple bobbing up and down. "Well, 'course, whatever I can do to help, honey, you know." Finally, reluctantly, he hung up the phone, another victim of Aunt Linda's uncanny charm.

"Well, okay, I guess there's no harm in letting you wait for your aunt in your room," Stan said, suddenly gracious. Jack had a feeling Stan would stay past quitting time, waiting for Linda to arrive. "You all got any luggage?"

"Our aunt has the rest of our things," Fitch explained. They were directed up a flight of open stairs to a concrete walkway on the second floor, on the far side of the motel from the office. The room had the cozy feel of public housing: two double beds with imitation wood headboards, plastic cups in the bathroom. There was a lingering stench of tobacco smoke, and cigarette burns in the carpet. They tried the television, but the cable was out and the reception was poor. There was little else to do, so they undressed and slid into bed.

"What d'you think your aunt is looking for?" It was Will's voice in the darkness.

"I have no idea," Jack said. Aunt Linda was sharing information in small, miserly installments. He wondered where she was at that moment, and if the man from the courthouse was following her. He realized his hands were clenched under the sheet, and he forced himself to relax his fingers. Now that he had stopped moving, his back had stiffened up. He shifted, trying to get comfortable on the unforgiving mattress. "I don't get it. Why do you guys want to get involved in this?"

"We're already involved, aren't we?" Fitch pointed out.

"I could go to the library by myself," Jack suggested. "I know the family names. You could hang out here. It might be better if we aren't seen together."

"Maybe there's safety in numbers," Will said.

Jack propped up on his elbows. "Look, I could call my mom. She could pick us up in a few hours. We could step out of this thing right now."

The thought of explaining all this to Becka depressed him. He might never see Linda again, except in small, supervised doses.

"You'd leave Linda here on her own?" Will sounded scandalized.

"That man is after her," Fitch added. "She's scared. We should help her if we can."

She's charmed them, Jack thought. Just like she's done me, all my life. "Look, I know you want to help a maiden in distress, but did you consider the fact that you might get hurt? And if she's innocent, then why won't she tell us what's going on? Why doesn't she call the police?"

"Maybe the police can't help her." Fitch was picking his way, trying to make sense out of disorder. "I wouldn't want to try to fight that flamethrower dude."

"At least the police have guns. What do you think he'll do when he finds out what we're up to?"

They didn't have much to say to that. There was a long, uncomfortable silence that wasn't broken until their regular breathing told him they were asleep.

Jack lay on his back, staring up at the fake stucco ceiling. Sleep seemed far away. Aunt Linda was his godmother, but there was something stronger between the two of them, some genetic and spiritual linkage that went beyond ceremony. He couldn't shake the idea that she'd brought him along for a reason, that this artifact she was hunting had something to do with him.

But it wasn't just that. He felt danger closing in, drawing closer with every breath he took. He pulled the thin sheet up to his chin. The motel felt like a frail eggshell, a feeble shield against the dark. And he worried that all his relatives and friends together would not be enough to save him.

❧ CHAPTER FOUR ❧
SHADOWSLAYER

The house had good bones. It was built of rough-hewn rock quarried on the property, still standing stone on stone after years of neglect. But the skeleton was all that remained. The roof and porch and wooden parts had rotted away to reveal a stark and decaying beauty. A stone set into the wall next to the entry was engraved *A. Hastynges, 1850*. The footprints of other buildings were nearly obscured by the undergrowth: a barn, perhaps, a shed, the remains of a stone wall.

Linda shivered, wrapping her arms around herself. She'd had no difficulty finding it again, this site of long-ago tragedies. Lee had brought her here once, when he was trying to explain who he was. She ran her hands over the cool stones, velveted with moss, and stood where the porch had been, looking down on the great river. She could see it glinting in the early-morning sunlight, several miles to the south.

She'd led the wizard on quite a chase, along narrow, twisting mountain roads, back onto the interstates, making a great circle around Coalton County so she never put too much distance between herself and Jack. She knew the area better than her pursuer and had avoided any traps he'd laid for her. Until now.

She circled the ruins, cut through the new growth behind the house, picking out the remnants of an elaborate garden, the winter-burned canes of old roses against the foundations of old walls. The leaves of red maples still lay like blood on the ground. She walked back to the front of the house.

"A delicate flower amid the ruins." The voice was like the rustle of dead leaves. She froze in place like a startled animal, a scream caught in her throat.

He was there at the edge of the yard in front of the porch, tall and spare in a long coat, bearded, hatless, shimmering with power. *Wylie*, she thought, the name coming back to her as if from a former life. She had never met him, but she had known too many like him. She tried to draw inward, to hide what she was, knowing it was already too late. Although his appearance was not unexpected, he'd still taken her by surprise.

He smiled, a slow and suggestive rearrangement of his face. She said nothing, fearful that her voice would give her away.

"Tell me, who sends an enchanter to do a wizard's work?"

She shook her head wordlessly. He would be on top of her in three strides if he didn't knock her senseless first.

"What is your name? Who is your guarantor? Is he with the White Rose?"

One question followed another, too quickly for her to answer, even if she wanted to. He didn't expect her to answer. If she were under the control of a wizard, he would have to force the information from her.

So Wylie didn't know who she was. He must have tracked the blade another way. That was something, but it would be nothing if he got his hands on her.

"Is the blade here somewhere?" he demanded. "Is this the Downey property?"

She shook her head mutely. Telling the truth, in fact.

"I asked you about the blade," he whispered. "Cooperate now, and it will go easier with you. If not . . ." He flexed his fingers, and flames bristled about his hands and arms. "I will pull your feathers, little bird. I will remove your petals, one by one, and leave you screaming." *Wizard endearments.*

She said nothing.

"First we'll talk, and then we'll play. It's been a long time since I've had . . . the pleasure." He moved smoothly toward her, an experienced predator. But as soon as his boot came down in the yard, he stiffened and spasmed backward, clawing at his face. He landed on his back in the brush, writhing in pain, shrieking as if he were being flayed alive. She watched as he rolled helplessly in the dirt, and finally made out what he was saying. "Help me, Enchanter! It's warded! Get me out!"

"Burn in hell, Wizard," she replied.

She didn't dare stay to see the outcome of the trap

she'd laid. She had no idea how long the old magic would hold. She turned and ran down the slope toward the dirt track where the Land Rover waited, just beyond the shell of the trailer. Another car, a plain gray coupe, stood next to it.

She threw herself into the front seat of the Rover and poked the key into the lock with shaking hands. It took several tries. Once she succeeded, she threw it into forward, spun the wheel, and then was bumping wildly down the rutted road that led to the highway. When she looked in her rearview mirror, she could see no one following.

The Coal Grove Regional Library was housed in an imposing red brick building that had been a schoolhouse at one time. It stood on the square across from the courthouse, a half hour walk from Dave's Slumbre Inn. Since it was a Saturday morning, the library was already busy when they arrived. A motherly-looking woman at the front desk directed them to the genealogy section in the rear.

A man clad in a blue work shirt, jeans, and cowboy boots was seated at the large table closest to the genealogy collection. He had a huge stack of books spread out across the table, and was busily typing notes into a laptop. A bright orange extension cord snaked its way across the floor and behind a bookcase.

"Mind the cord, boys," he said, shoving his books to one side of the table to free up space for them to sit down.

Jack pulled Aunt Linda's notebook from his duffle and dropped it onto the table. Then the three of them looked at each other, at a loss.

The stranger looked up from his keyboard. "What's the matter? Don't know where to start?"

"No," the three said together.

"Well, I think it's great to see young people taking an interest in genealogy," the man said, beaming. "Me, I didn't get started until four or five years ago. What names are you looking for?"

"Uh, Taylor," Jack said quickly.

"Mmmm, Taylor, Taylor . . ." His fingers flew over the keyboard. "I got a Ransom Taylor here, born in 1830. That your Taylor?"

"We don't know," Fitch replied, shrugging. "We're pretty new at this. Uh, maybe you could tell us about the books in here?"

"Sure." The man rose heavily to his feet, seemingly eager to share what he knew. "Where you all from?"

"Erie, Pennsylvania," Fitch spoke up again.

The man nodded. "Well, over here you got your county histories, most of the counties in southern Ohio and a few in West Virginia. This part of Ohio used to be part of Virginia, you know. Over here"—he waved his arm vaguely down the stacks—"you got your census indexes. They have census records on microfilm from 1830 to 1920 in these cabinets. The vital statistics are on these metal shelves—marriages, births, deaths, and cemetery records."

"Cemetery records?" Will repeated, with interest.

"Yep, the county genealogical society has been canvasing the graveyards, copying stones for years. They have them about done. Only thing is, they aren't indexed yet."

"Do they have any old newspapers here?" Jack asked, running his hands across the books of cemetery records. There were three fat volumes. It looked like they had their work cut out for them.

Their benefactor nodded. "We have the *Post-Telegram* and the *Coal Grove Democrat* on microfilm, back to the mid 1850s. Those ain't indexed, either, but it makes for some interesting reading."

Fitch had a plan. "Okay," he said, nodding to Jack and Will. "Will and I will each take one of those cemetery books and start looking for your . . . uh . . . our dead relatives. Jack, you go through the newspaper microfilm and see if you can find an obituary or something."

Jack chose a reel of microfilm for the *Post-Telegram*. Susannah Downey had died in May, 1900. He rolled forward through the film until he found May, 1900, then carefully scanned each page of the paper for any reference to her passing. After nearly an hour of reading stories about who visited whom, and who was under the weather, Jack switched from the *Post-Telegram* to the *Coal Grove Democrat*. And there it was.

"Look at this!" The boys crowded around Jack, reading over his shoulder. It was a news story: "'MRS. DOWNEY DIES IN FALL FROM HORSE. Neighbors in Coal Grove were shocked to hear of the untimely death of Mrs. Susannah Downey, late of Munroe Township, who died when she was thrown from a horse last Sunday. Lee Hastens, a visitor in the township, found her lying in the woods near the back of the family farm in the late evening. Her horse was standing nearby, all lathered up, as if he'd been ridden hard for a distance. Although known to be a capable horsewoman, Mrs. Downey took a fall onto a fence post. A severe gash to the chest was the cause of death. Reverend Eugene Carter presided over the funeral service from First Methodist. She leaves a husband and infant son to mourn.'"

"Wow," Will breathed. "What a way to go."

Jack had seen hand-colored pictures of his great-great grandmother from the old trunk in the attic. She had been photographed with her husband, who looked stiff and solemn. Susannah, though, looked as if she were just about to break into laughter. She was beautiful, with heavy strawberry blond hair twisted up onto her head, small graceful hands, and fine features. There was a strong resemblance between the woman in the photograph and her great-granddaughter Becka.

Fitch hit the print button on the microfilm machine.

"Does it say where she was buried?" Jack asked.

"No," said Fitch, "but it says she lived in Munroe Township. Aren't those cemeteries listed by township?"

Will checked the table of contents of the book he was reviewing, and turned to the back. "There are eight or ten cemeteries in Munroe Township," he reported. "Most of them seem to be small." He ran his finger down the page. "Here! Susannah Downey, wife of Abraham. 1868 to 1900. It's in the old Methodist cemetery."

Their voices had grown louder and louder, and Jack suddenly realized that the man in the cowboy boots had looked up from his microfilm machine and was listening with interest to everything they said. Jack shot a warning look at his friends and turned back to the book. "Wait a minute!" he said. "That can't be her. The dates are all wrong. She would have been alive much earlier." He turned suddenly to the man with the laptop. "What if a person isn't in the cemetery book? How far back do the death records go?"

The man shook his head. "Not earlier than 1867, which is when the state began requiring the counties to keep records. There might be an estate record up at the courthouse, though that would be uncommon for a woman. Have you all been up there?"

Was there sharp interest in the man's eyes as he asked that question?

"No," Fitch said. "We thought anything that old would be in the library."

"No original records in here," the man pointed out. "Only indexes and extracted records. You might want to try the courthouse, though they won't be open over the weekend. Are you boys here through Monday?"

"Probably not," Fitch replied. "We have to be back at school, unless we can convince our mom to let us ditch on Monday. She's at our Aunt Fran's," he added. "Do you know Frances Dunlevy, who works at the dry cleaners by the grocery in the plaza?"

Jack stared at Fitch in amazement.

"Sure, I know Fran," the man replied, nodding. "Went to high school with her, in fact."

By now, Will had copied the information from the cemetery book into his notebook. Fitch stood up abruptly. "We'd better go. We told Mom we'd be back by three," he said. "Let's bring her back here tomorrow. We're not getting anywhere." He rewound the newspaper microfilm, lifted it off the machine, and placed it in its box. Will and Jack hesitated, but Fitch continued packing up at a rapid pace. Now fully aware of the surveillance of the man in the cowboy boots. Jack reshelved the cemetery books, and Will returned the notebook to his duffle.

"My name's Sam Hadley," the cowboy said, handing them a card. "I'm a certified genealogist, and I do research for hire. Tell your mom she can reach me through the library if she decides she'd like some help."

"We'll do that," Jack replied. "Thanks for your help. And good luck with your research."

They paid for their copy at the front desk. Fitch jerked his head toward the men's room, which was just inside the front door. The three of them filed into the restroom. Both stalls were empty.

"What do you think you're doing?" Will demanded, as soon as the door closed. "Why'd we have to leave in such a hurry? We could've asked that man Hadley how to get to the Methodist cemetery. And why were you spinning all those stories? I was afraid there was going to be a quiz."

Fitch calmly removed his glasses and wiped them with a paper towel. "Look," he said. "Something wasn't right. The dude claimed he knows our Aunt Fran. There is no Frances Dunlevy. Why would he say he knows her when he doesn't?"

Will shrugged. "Maybe he's just one of those people who likes to make you think he knows about everything and everybody."

"What if he was the guy from the courthouse?" Fitch suggested.

Jack compared the tall, spare, deadly figure on the staircase with Sam Hadley's portly build. "No. Not unless he's some kind of shape-shifter." They all laughed uneasily.

"He sure seemed interested in what we were doing," Fitch mused. "Though I think those genealogy people love to talk about this stuff. I wonder how much he overheard."

Jack shrugged. "Nothing we can do about it now. Let's see if we can find out where the cemetery is from someone else."

"It gave a location for each graveyard in the book," Will reminded them. He pulled the notebook from his duffle and paged quickly through it. "It's on Methodist Chapel Road." He nodded wisely. "Makes sense."

"Let's get going." Jack nodded toward the restroom door. They pushed it open just in time to see the man in the cowboy boots walk briskly past, his laptop swinging from his shoulder. They shrank back into the restroom doorway and watched him exit through the front door of the library. Jack sprinted to one of the front windows. A black Mercedes was pulled into one of the angle parking spaces in front of the library. The man opened the rear passenger door, tossed his laptop into the backseat, and then climbed behind the wheel. The car backed out of the space and sped off down the street, disappearing around a corner.

Fitch and Will were right behind him. "Not a local ride, I'm guessing," Fitch observed. "He sure took off in a hurry. What if the dude overheard everything, and he's heading out to the cemetery right now?"

"Aunt Linda told us to find out where Susannah Downey was buried and then she would call with further instructions," Jack replied. "He'd have to know more than we do."

"Well, that's certainly possible, since we don't know much," Will muttered. They looked at each other miserably. Fitch turned without a word and headed back into the library. He stopped at the front desk and spoke to the elderly woman behind the counter. He returned carrying a piece of paper. "I got directions to the Methodist cemetery," he announced. "I don't think it's too far."

Will grinned. "The librarian's probably conspiring with the cowboy," he said. "Her and the whole town. They'll all meet us at the graveyard with chain saws. Like in a horror movie."

"Maybe." Fitch stuffed the paper into his pants pocket. "But it might take them a while. I asked about five different cemeteries. That ought to slow them down or split them up, at least. We'll have to wait for dark anyway, if we're going to be digging up bodies." He smiled, but there was little joy in it, only that famous Fitch persistence.

Who knows? Jack thought. With all that's happened already, that might turn out to be our assignment.

The sun had disappeared while they were in the library, and it was noticeably cooler. The wind had picked up as well. Jack thought wistfully of the warm jacket he had left in Aunt Linda's car. Which reminded him of something else.

His medicine was still in the back of the Land Rover. He'd missed his dose again that morning. Jack rolled his eyes. Becka would be all over him if she knew he'd messed up twice in one week.

It doesn't matter, he told himself. Wasn't a problem last time, wouldn't be a problem this time. He couldn't help it. Life seemed to be getting more complicated.

Anyway, he felt good. Incredibly good, like he'd been looking at the world through a cloudy lens and the film had been stripped away. The day seemed rife with possibilities, a gift about to be opened. He couldn't help grinning.

Will's voice broke into his thoughts. "What do we do now?"

Jack looked at his watch. They had several hours of daylight left. "We're going to need some things. Shovels, flashlights, sweatshirts, like that."

"Let's go there." Fitch pointed across the square to a storefront. A weathered sign proclaimed, BICK'S ARMY-NAVY, and underneath, WEAPONS, AMMO, CAMO, CLOTHING, BAIT, HUNTING LICENSES.

It seemed totally fitting. "Let's go shopping," Jack said.

The boys were killing time in the Bluebird Cafe, feeding the jukebox and flirting with the waitress over second desserts. They were fortified with tavern food and dressed for battle. Jack wore a long-sleeved T-shirt and dark hoodie over Mercedes's vest. Will had chosen an insulated vest with lots of pockets, and Fitch looked like a punk urban commando with a camo jacket, dog tags, and heavy boots.

The duffel bags at their feet contained flashlights and spades.

The cell phone rang, and Jack fumbled for it, flipped it open.

Linda didn't waste any time on pleasantries. "Are you all right? Did you find out anything today?"

"Yeah," Jack replied to both questions, his eyes on the other two. "We have a location. The old Methodist cemetery." Automatically he looked around him. No one was in earshot, especially given the volume of the music. "Don't know where in the cemetery, but it seems to be a small one. We got directions."

"Good." She sounded relieved. "Have you seen anybody suspicious? Anyone seem to be following you?"

Jack hesitated. After all, they had no hard evidence that the cowboy was up to anything at all. They were probably just being paranoid. Only . . . "There was a . . . a genealogist in the library who might have overheard us talking about the cemetery."

Linda made a noise of irritation and dismay. "What did he look like?"

"Fat. Bald. Cowboy boots. Western shirt. He did seem to know quite a bit about genealogy. Had a business card and all. He helped us find stuff in the library."

There was a brief silence. "Okay," she said finally, as if reassured by this description. "But you haven't seen the man from the courthouse? Or anyone . . . like him?" It was an odd thing to say, but somehow Jack knew exactly what she meant. No, Sam Hadley was not like the man in the courthouse.

"No," he said. "Haven't seen him. What have you been doing?" He had already decided not to mention the medicine. It wouldn't do any good to worry her.

"I've been traveling around," Linda said evasively. Her voice sounded brittle, breathless, barely controlled.

"What's the matter?" Jack demanded. "Did something happen?"

"I'm just tired. I've been up all night, driving all over southern Ohio. Our friend has been following me."

"Can't you just find a motel room and hole up there, get some sleep? He won't bother you if there are a lot of people around. Isn't that what you told us?"

He was looking for reassurance, and she provided it, but not quickly enough to be convincing. "That's a good idea," she said hesitantly. "Maybe I'll do that. Where are you?"

"We're at the Bluebird," Jack said. "Waiting for dark."

"You need to be careful. I . . . I would like to come with you to the cemetery, but I'm still a couple of hours away, down by the river. I . . . may have lost him, but I'm not sure." She paused. "If he can't find me, he might come looking for you. If you have even a hint that there's a problem, I want you three to go back to the motel and stay there until I come. If I don't come by noon tomorrow, call Becka."

Jack didn't like the sound of that.

There was another long pause, but when she spoke again, her voice was businesslike. "Now listen carefully. I'm only going to tell you what you need to know, because the man we saw could easily force things out of you. Don't share any more with Will and Fitch than you have to."

"Okay," Jack said cautiously.

"The piece you are looking for is a weapon. A sword. It once belonged to Susannah. Now it belongs to you."

"A . . . uh . . . okay." With some effort, he stopped himself from repeating her words, from asking the questions that crowded in. Why would Susannah have a sword? Could it be a Civil War piece, perhaps? And why would it belong to him? Susannah had died long before he was born. It seemed that his mother or Linda would have a better claim.

"It will be buried behind her gravestone in a case of some kind. Now, this is important. *You* must be the one who opens the case. No one else. I'll give you the charm you'll need to open it." She paused, as if expecting a question, but he didn't ask it. "Are you listening, Jack?"

He nodded without thinking, and then said, "Yes."

The words sounded like Latin, a soft and familiar music, the truth that lay under all the languages that he knew. He repeated them back to her several times, until she was satisfied, ignoring Will and Fitch, who were staring at him as he memorized the phrase.

"You won't forget?"

"No."

"Make sure the sword is in the case, then close it up and carry it back to the motel. I'll pick you up there."

"Uh, Aunt Linda?" He looked across the table at his friends. "Maybe I should just go by myself." It was half statement, half question.

There was another long silence. "Maybe you should."

"They won't like it."

"Let me talk to them."

Wordlessly, Jack extended the cell phone toward Fitch, who put up both hands and shook his head. "Forget it, Jack. I'm not going to let her talk me out of it. I'm coming with you whether you like it or not." Will had his arms crossed over his chest, looking scared and yet stubborn as stone.

"They won't talk to you, Aunt Linda."

She sighed. "I'm so sorry, Jack. I should not have brought them into this." She paused. "All right. They can help dig. Just get in and get out quickly. Go back to the motel and wait. I'll be there as soon as I can. I'll call you a little later."

It was definitely colder when they left the Bluebird, but Jack hardly noticed. His lingering worries were overshadowed by a kind of euphoria. He felt taut and catlike, full of power, barely contained within his skin. His fears of the day before were forgotten. Something ancient had kindled deep within him, a bright and powerful thirst for adventure. He felt invulnerable, as if the strangers and their agenda were irrelevant. He looked at his two companions and grinned. Anything could happen. And that seemed like a good thing.

The church was a modest white structure on a narrow strip of flat ground along the road, perhaps two miles out of town. The hills rose up behind, a dense black nothingness against the brighter sky. The building was in the plain Methodist style, with a traditional steeple and a large double front door. A simple sanctuary and little else. A white wood framed sign with magnetic letters stood off to one side. PASTOR: WILLARD F. GUFFEY. SUNDAY SERMON: ASHES TO ASHES, DUST TO DUST.

There was a small gravel parking lot between the road and the church. It was empty. There were no lights anywhere around the building.

They cut away from the roadside and approached the front of the church. Jack shone the beam of his flashlight over a brass plate above the double doors. FIRST METHODIST CHURCH. FOUNDED 1850.

The cemetery was marked off from the rest of the churchyard by two brick pillars about twenty feet behind the building, probably gateposts of a fence that had long since gone. The first grave markers clustered just on the other side of the posts.

Jack looked back at Methodist Chapel Road. They had seen very little traffic, and the church was surrounded by dense forest. As far as he could tell, they had not been followed. There were no houses in sight. Once they moved to the back of the church, it seemed unlikely they could be seen from the road.

They passed between the pillars into the cemetery beyond. Jack soon realized there were many more grave sites than were listed in the book. Some of the stones were broken, worn away, and unreadable. Grass was growing over some of the markers, and others had toppled over. The oldest, most dilapidated stones seemed to be closest to the church.

He found a legible one just inside the old wall. He

knelt, shining his light over its surface. BRAM WHALEY, 1863. DIED AT CHANCELLORSVILLE. A metal GAR marker stood alongside. "Susannah died in 1900," he said. "Do you think that her grave would be farther back, because it's later?"

"Maybe," Fitch said. "But families tended to be buried together. So you might find early and late markers in the same plot."

"How do you know this stuff?" Jack demanded. The three of them divided the graveyard into three sections and proceeded to move methodically through, shining their lights over the cold stone surfaces, scraping moss away with their fingernails, yanking weeds that obscured the base of the stones, sometimes digging in the dirt with a stick to expose the lowest row of lettering.

They worked their way back from the church to the hill, in line with each other, afraid of missing something. The trees grew closer together at the rear of the property, and in some cases their roots had heaved stones completely out of the ground, dividing families. The moon had risen, but it burned dimly behind a thin curtain of clouds. They could see nothing outside the circle of their flashlights. Soon they were almost in the shadow of the cliff.

"Here's a Downey," Jack said quietly. He was in a small grove of trees, to the far left of the cemetery. Will and Fitch came to see. It was a small white marker with a death's head at the top. JOSEPH DOWNEY, 1823–1872.

"Here's another," said Will. It was close to the one Jack had found, for a child, JEREMIAH DOWNEY, AGE 18 MONTHS, S.O. JOSEPH AND MARTHA. DIED 1860.

They crept farther under the trees, scanning stone by stone.

It was Will who found it. A large stone, set a little apart from the others, almost up against a wire fence that marked the edge of the property. SUSANNAH HALE DOWNEY, 1868–1900, BELOVED WIFE OF ABRAHAM, GONE BUT NOT FORGOTTEN.

"Look at this!" Fitch scuffed his foot across the neatly clipped grass that surrounded the gravestone. "This whole place is grown up in weeds, but your grandmother's grave looks like somebody's garden." The stone had been cleared of moss and debris, and spring bulbs were pushing their way through the turf. A small dogwood tree had been planted behind the stone.

"Where's my great-great grandfather?" Susannah's was the only name on the stone. Maybe Abraham had remarried. If so, Jack had never heard about it.

"Look at this!" Will gathered up the remains of several long-stemmed roses that had been scattered over the plot. The blackened petals spiraled gently back to the ground as he lifted them. "Is there still family around here?" Will asked, looking over his shoulder as if one of them might appear at any moment to challenge him.

"I don't know." Jack shook his head. Even if there were, Susannah had died a long time ago. There couldn't possibly be anyone still alive who would remember her. He thought of the laughing young woman in the photographs. GONE BUT NOT FORGOTTEN. She looked like someone who would be hard to forget.

"Now what?" Fitch shivered and stuffed his hands

in his jacket pockets. "I feel like a grave robber."

Jack knelt and unzipped the duffle bag. He pulled out the two short spades. "Now we dig. Aunt Linda said we should look for something buried behind the stone."

Will took one of the spades from Jack and chose a spot about a foot in back of the marker, far enough away to keep the stone from toppling.

"Couldn't your grandmother have kept her heirlooms in the attic like everyone else?" Fitch asked, leaning against Susannah's stone. "And how does your Aunt Linda know there's something here?"

"I don't know," Jack replied, sinking his spade into the dirt a few feet away from Will. "But I guess this was something that my grandmother didn't want falling into the wrong hands."

"Like ours, maybe," Fitch said dryly. It felt like the earth behind the stone had not been disturbed for a century. Or ever. It was clay and shale and full of tree roots. Fitch kept watch while the other two handled the shovels. Once in awhile they could see the lights of a car along the chapel road. The trees in the woods on either side complained as the wind moved through them. Otherwise the only sound was the clink of shovels against stone and the labored breathing of the diggers.

Eventually they'd dug a fairly large hole, three feet long and perhaps three feet deep. Despite the cold air, Jack was sweating from the exertion. And then his shovel hit something with a dull clunking sound that was different than before. And then again. He continued to dig, lifting away smaller amounts of dirt until they could see a rough rectangular outline. Will dug with renewed energy, enlarging the hole, trying to find the other end of the box, if that was what it was.

Jack cleared the earth away from the sides, so they could see how deep it was. Now they had all four of the top corners exposed. It was about three feet long, and narrow.

Jack leaned wearily on his shovel. Something strange was going on. His head was spinning, and there was a murmuring in his ears, the sound of a thousand urgent voices. He sat down heavily on the edge of the hole, his legs dangling, and put his hands over his ears.

"Hey, are you all right?" Fitch shone his flashlight in Jack's face. "Why don't you just sit there a minute? You've been doing most of the work." He turned and fumbled in his backpack, and pulled out two water bottles. He tossed one to Jack and the other to Will. "Drink that." Fitch picked up the shovel and set to work with a vengeance, making the dirt fly. Will drained his water bottle noisily and threw it aside, continuing to work, motivated by the prize that seemed almost within their grasp.

Now Jack could make out some of what the voices were saying. "Who comes to claim the blade?" There was a rumble of drums, at first far away, and then growing louder, coming closer, pounding inside his head. Jack closed his eyes and leaned back against Susannah's stone, his breath coming in short, shallow gasps, his heart beating wildly. Sweat poured from him. He thought of the forgotten medicine. Maybe he was having a heart attack.

"Do you hear something? People talking? Drums?

Anything?" Will and Fitch stopped digging to stare at Jack. "Never mind," he said hastily.

The drums and voices grew to a crescendo. And then a woman's voice, cool and quiet, broke through the din. "Be at ease. He is the heir," she said. The voices and the drums fell silent. Jack wiped sweat from his face with his sleeve and breathed easier.

The box itself was only about eight inches deep, and Fitch and Will soon cleared the dirt from three sides. Will worked the tip of his shovel under it, and attempted to pry the box out of the dirt. The earth was reluctant to yield what it had held for so many years. It took several tries, but at last one corner came up, and Will carefully propped it against one side of the hole. It didn't seem too heavy. He climbed down in the hole and pushed the box over the rim. Fitch grabbed the leading edge and hauled it out onto the grass.

"They must have buried it in a leather bag," Will said. The bag had nearly disintegrated, and the leather fell away when they turned the box over. It was encrusted with dirt and sand. Will spat into his hand and wiped some of it away.

"It's covered in jewels!" he exclaimed as the light reflected back. "You don't think they're real, do you?"

Jack had recovered enough to lift himself away from the gravestone and lean forward to look.

"Who would bury valuable jewels in a graveyard?" Fitch ran his fingernail over one of the stones. It was bloodred and faceted and about the size of his thumb. "This is probably the closest I'll ever come to buried treasure." He leaned down, fumbling along the side of the case. It took Jack a moment to realize what he was doing.

"Fitch, no, don't!"

Too late. There was a bright flash and a *boom*. Fitch flew backward, landing flat on his back several yards away on the grass. A pale cloud of smoke drifted skyward.

Will leaped after him, but Fitch was already sitting up, shaking his head. "What the hell was that?" His face was smudged with soot, and he spat blood out of his mouth.

Will and Fitch regarded the case with grudging respect. Somewhere close by, a dog was barking. Jack wondered if the noise would bring any curious neighbors. Or worse.

"Maybe we should take it to a safer place," Will suggested.

"Maybe we'll be blown to smithereens if we try," Fitch replied warily.

"Let me do it," Jack said. The other two stared at him. Scrambling to his feet, he stumbled over to where the box lay, and cradled it carefully in his arms. He carried it a safe distance away and set it on the ground. "Why don't you two fill in the hole, and clean up this area as much as you can, and I'll try to figure out this locking mechanism."

"Be careful, Jack," Fitch warned him. He and Will grabbed the spades and began pushing dirt back into the hole. It was hard to tell in the darkness how much of a mess they'd made. Jack suspected it would be pretty obvious in the morning that someone had been digging.

Jack ran his hands over the ornate lid until he found the tiny latch, right where he knew it would be, as if he'd opened the case a hundred times before. The words of the old speech came back to him, and he whispered them as he pressed his fingers against the lock. The case snapped smoothly open.

Inside the velvet-lined case was a sword in a scabbard. The scabbard was ornate, worked in gold and silver, and the hilt that protruded from it was cast in an elaborate, swirling gold design. A brilliant ruby was set in the end of the pommel. When Jack brought the flashlight close, he could see inscriptions faint against the burnished metal, symbols and words he didn't understand.

He set the flashlight on the ground, gingerly grasped the hilt, and drew it out, noticing how the grip fit his hand without slipping. The sword created its own light as it emerged, a silver flame that ran along the blade. It was double-edged, and the metal appeared rippled in a way that meant the steel had been folded and refolded to strengthen it. How he knew this, he couldn't say. After a century in the ground, it bore no trace of rust, but seemed ready for immediate use.

Will and Fitch, drawn by the light, looked over Jack's shoulder. "Wicked," breathed Fitch.

"No," said Jack. "Not wicked at all." He lifted the weapon before him with two hands and knew that it was his, although it had been forged long before he was born. It was lighter in his hands than he expected, lighter than one would expect from the size of it. "Shadowslayer," he whispered, as if the weapon spoke to him. And the power in the blade ran into his hands and up his arms as if, somehow, the sword were wielding *him*.

"Jack . . ." It was Will, sounding dismayed, uncertain. The sword flamed in Jack's hand as he brandished it, a marriage of man and metal, flesh and steel. Fierce and primitive. He grew, extended himself through the reach of the blade, and the sword sent light and shadow racing across the grass, illuminating the leaning stones. The blade sang as it sliced the darkness, once, twice, three times, dividing it, trailing light. *Shadowslayer.* He pivoted, seized the hilt with both hands, and swung the blade, severing a two-inch sapling with a whisper of effort. He saw blood before his eyes and it was not the blood of trees. It took considerable self-discipline to end the dance. When he lowered the blade, its light subsided to a soft brilliance.

"It's so sweet," he said, swallowing, trying to control his voice. "I . . . I had no idea. . . ."

"Be careful with that. I mean, don't go weird on us." Something in Fitch's voice said he sensed something more dangerous here than the edge of an ancient blade.

Will eyed the scabbard in the case, as if half afraid to approach it. "Is that some kind of belt?"

Jack thrust the blade into the ground momentarily and lifted the scabbard with two hands. It was mounted on a light belt of cleverly wrought linked metal. It was designed to fit two ways, about the waist or over his shoulder, as a baldric. *Baldric.* Where had the word come from? Somewhere inside him, a door to knowledge had opened. He put it about his waist and clasped it tight, positioning the scabbard on his left hip so he could draw across his body with his right hand. It lay comfortably across his hipbones. Aunt Linda had said to put the sword back in its case, but . . .

"What's that?" Fitch spoke quietly, but in a way that got Jack's attention. He was staring back toward the church, hands on hips. Jack followed his gaze. A strange glow bled through the back windows of the building, spinning out crazy shadows. Someone was walking along the far side of the church with a light, and it was reflecting through the back windows.

"Hey," Fitch whispered. "Someone's here!"

With a quick movement, Jack picked up the case and tossed it to Will. "Here! Hang on to this. We'll need it." He pulled the sword from the dirt with his right hand and held it, point downward, close to his side. They faded back into the shadows behind Susannah's stone, careful to avoid stepping into the half-filled hole.

Someone rounded the corner of the church, carrying a powerful flashlight. At first, they could make out only a bulky outline, because of the glare. The figure advanced rapidly toward their hiding place, running the light over the gravestones in his path. He stopped about ten feet away, shining the light over Susannah Downey's stone. They heard a grunt of satisfaction. Then a voice.

"What are you boys doing out here in the dark?" It was the cowboy, Sam Hadley.

It was no use staying hidden. Fitch stepped out from behind the stone, shielding his eyes against the flashlight. "We decided to come see if any of our relatives are buried here. But I guess we got too late a start. It's no use trying to find anything in the dark. I suppose we'll have to come back tomorrow." He shrugged his shoulders in an exaggerated fashion.

When Hadley spoke again, there was an edge to his voice. "Wasn't Susannah Downey the person you were looking for?"

"No, it was Taylor," Fitch replied, sticking his hands into his jacket pockets disarmingly. "But we think she married a Downey. Like we said, this seems to be the wrong person. Our Susannah was earlier, and it looks like this one was a Hale. We just thought we'd come look in the graveyard to see if some of the surrounding stones might give us a clue." Jack could tell Fitch was nervous from the way the words poured out of him like marbles from a bag.

"So we're just about to head back," Will added, moving up to stand by Fitch. He'd picked up his duffle bag, and he held the case horizontally under his arm, as casually as he could, hoping Hadley couldn't get a good look at it in the darkness.

Jack remained back in the shadows, behind Susannah's stone. He was acutely aware of another presence, following after the cowboy, something menacing, something greedy, coming closer. He tightened his grip on the hilt of the sword and his arm tingled all the way to the shoulder.

"You boys want a ride back to town?" the cowboy asked.

"No, thanks," said Will. At this, Jack moved out of the shadows to join his friends, standing just behind them.

"What've you got there?" Hadley's voice had a nasty undercurrent. He was speaking to Jack, who was trying to keep his body between the cowboy and the sword, but the glow of the blade stood out like a beacon in the dark.

"He has the blade." The new voice was dreadfully cold and uncomfortably close. A deeper shadow detached itself from the side of the church and approached them with an odd, floating gait. It was a man, tall and angular, his garments kiting about him as he advanced. He lifted a skeletal arm and pointed at the sword in Jack's hand. The blade flared red, as if it ran with blood. It was the stranger from the courthouse. *Wizard!* The thought arose, fully formed, in Jack's mind, a warning. An ancient terror kindled inside him.

Hadley's eyes flicked nervously to the wizard, then back to Jack. "Looks like y'all been doing some digging," he said, gesturing at Susannah's stone. "Looks like you stole something that don't belong to you." He took a step closer to the boys. "You'd best give it to the man and go on home."

"No," Jack replied, broadening his stance. "If you want the sword, come and take it." It was as if a stranger spoke through him. Hadley didn't scare him. It was the wizard that compelled his attention. If not for the vest, the wizard would have killed him at the courthouse. Linda had insisted he wear it. How had she known he would need it?

The wizard came closer, moving like a man in pain. Jack watched him warily. A beard covered the lower half of his face, but the upper half was red and blistered, as though he'd been burned. His voice was dry and devoid of emotion, like scales sliding over rock. "No doubt this has been an exciting adventure for the three of you, but it's over. Now give me the weapon." He smiled, an awful reshaping of the ruined face. "I'm sure we can devise a *suitable* reward for your trouble."

He's going to kill us, Jack thought. Once he has the blade. He looked over at Will and Fitch, wondering if they understood. I shouldn't have let them come. As if he were in charge.

"Where's the enchanter?" It was the wizard again. "I have unfinished business with her." And the way he said *business*, it was clear he meant pain and something else. What was he talking about? *Who* was he talking about?

Although he was frightened, Jack also felt reckless, wild, and rebellious. He had possession of the sword; he'd felt the power in it, and he didn't intend to give it up without a fight.

He wavered, unsure what to do, standing astride his great-great grandmother's bones, his back up against her marker. A sudden breeze moved the leaves overhead, whispering to him.

And then he knew where they would be safe. He stepped between his friends and the wizard and shouted, "Run for the church!"

Will and Fitch needed no encouragement. They turned and charged to the building, leaping over grave markers as if they were hurdles. Jack backed up rapidly, always keeping his face to the wizard. He held the sword up with both hands, flat side facing him. It responded, blazing, illuminating the scene.

He couldn't see a weapon in the wizard's hands, but suddenly a cascade of blue-green flames rolled at him. Instinctively, he used the sword to parry the volley, which exploded into a shower of sparks that fell harmlessly about his shoulders. Twice more he deflected similar attacks. The heat of the flames dried the sweat from his face. The wizard fire had an unfamiliar, acrid scent, like the taste of blood in his mouth.

The wizard with the horrible charred face extended his hands toward him and began to speak, the same time-worn Latin that Linda had used, the language of charms. Jack knew he had to stop him, that the words had power in them. Desperately, he swung Shadowslayer with both hands in a broad, flat arc. Flames roared from the honed edge of the blade, and the spell died unfinished as the wizard threw himself to the ground. The flames screamed past him and sliced into the trees behind. The trees stood momentarily, then toppled, sliced off neatly at chest height. And somehow Jack had arrived at the door of the church.

A sagging wooden stairway led up a few steps to the back door of the building. Fitch and Will were already at the top of the stairs, unsure what to do next. Jack pointed his sword at the back door and thrust it forward. There was a loud concussion, and it flew open, hanging crookedly on its broken hinges. Will and Fitch ducked inside. Jack leaped through the doorway and turned to face his attackers.

They were in some disarray, as if resistance were totally unexpected. The wizard was back on his feet, staring up at Jack. The cowboy looked back at the shorn trees, up at the ragged opening in the canopy overhead, then back at Jack. His mouth was hanging open and his round face was slick with sweat.

"The boy's a demon," he wailed. "I was hired to do research. I never signed on to deal with demons."

"There is no *magic* about this boy," the wizard said contemptuously. "The power is in the blade. This is just a foolish Anaweir adventurer who is in more trouble than he can imagine." Jack thought he said *unaware*. It seemed an odd choice of words. "Now go fetch me the sword."

"I ain't going in there," Hadley protested. "He'll fry me alive."

"Magic is ineffective in the sanctuary. The sword has no special power in there."

And, indeed, now that Jack was inside the church, the blade had dimmed, grown heavier, so it took both hands to lift it. Its power no longer burned through him. It was nothing more than metal in his hands.

Something the wizard had said lingered. *Magic?*

Fitch stood next to him, armed with a candelabra. "Why aren't they coming after us?" he whispered, glancing around uneasily. "Are they warlocks or vampires or something, so they can't set foot in a church?"

Wizards, Jack almost murmured. "I don't know," he said aloud. He didn't know whether the wizard couldn't come in, or if he just preferred to send Hadley against the sword in a situation where magic would do no good.

"That sword'll still cut well enough," the cowboy persisted. "And there's three of them. I never agreed to go unarmed against a sword." He looked as though he wanted nothing more than to escape.

"Is that so?" The wizard's voice dripped contempt. "Then we shall have to . . . renegotiate." He put his hand on Hadley's shoulder and the cowboy screamed, at first arching away, and then sinking helplessly to his knees under the wizard's touch. The wizard kept it up, and the cowboy shrieked like he was being flayed alive; he pleaded for mercy and begged for a chance to change his mind. When it finally stopped, Hadley lay trembling and whimpering on the ground. Jack was sick with the knowledge that the demonstration was for his benefit.

As if to confirm it, the wizard spoke to Jack. "You see that resistance has consequences," he said coldly. "Give up the blade or all three of you will die tonight. And by the time I'm done with you, you'll beg for it."

Jack was shaken for a moment by the image of himself standing in the doorway like some movie hero, wielding a sword, ready to fight a man who could lob flames with his bare hands, could torture and kill with a touch. He looked over his shoulder at Will and Fitch. Their faces were pale as parchment in the gloom of the church. If they hadn't understood the stakes before, they did now.

He stared down at the blade in his hand and then out at the wizard. Where was this coming from? He'd never been particularly foolhardy in the past. There must be something about the sword that was interfering with his judgement. He swiped sweat from his face and shook his head.

It was an impasse. If they left the building, the wizard

would kill them. He'll take Shadowslayer, he thought. I can't let that happen.

Fitch had left his side momentarily, and now he was back. "The Mercedes is in the parking lot," he whispered. Jack looked over his shoulder again. The back door led directly into the sanctuary. They were standing just behind the pulpit, in the tiny choir area. It was a plain, white-washed room with rows of wooden pews lined up on either side of a central aisle. Large double doors opened to the parking lot at the other end.

"Look," Jack said quietly, turning to face Fitch. "We can probably lose them in the woods." *They'll follow the sword.* "You and Will slide out through the front doors while I keep them occupied. Stick to the woods and stay off the road. When I know you're away, I'll make a run for it."

"Are you crazy? The dude is shooting flames, Jack. If we know they won't come in here, let's just wait it out. They can't hang around forever."

He won't wait forever, Jack thought. And if he gets his hands on us . . .

Hadley had lurched to his feet and was moving closer, driven by the wizard behind him. Now Jack had no inclination to hurt Hadley. He felt sorry for him.

"Don't you see?" The wizard was speaking to Jack. "The enchanter has bewitched you, and you're the ones who will pay the price. She doesn't mind sacrificing you to get what she wants."

Just then the cell phone buzzed, startlingly loud. With one hand, Jack fished it out of his pocket, keeping the sword pointed through the doorway.

It was Aunt Linda. "Where are you?"

"We're in the church at the old Methodist cemetery on Methodist Chapel Road. I have the sword, but we're under attack."

Linda was silent for a moment. "I'm close," she said. "Hold them off for five minutes. Keep the phone on."

The cowboy had advanced to the second step. Jack stepped over the threshold to free his swing, and swept the blade from left to right, bleeding flames, enough to move the man away without cutting him. Hadley leaped backward, nearly falling. The magic of the sword flooded into Jack like a drug. Exultant, he descended another step. The cowboy disappeared into the dark, and there was only the wizard, launching volley after volley of fireballs, as in some kind of frenzied video game. Jack sent flames spiraling back at him, and his adversary retreated. Jack moved forward, into the duel, pursuing. He was on the last step and ready to step off, when he heard someone shouting behind him.

"Jack! Are you crazy? Get in here!" It was Will, and the spell was somehow broken. He launched himself backward as a thick wall of wizard flame roared toward him, too broad to stop with a sword. Will grasped his shoulders and half lifted him inside, away from the dreadful heat. His face was burning, vision blurred by tears, his lungs scorched from the near miss. He leaned on his sword, gasping, Will still supporting him on the other side.

"I am an idiot," he whispered. "An idiot."

He heard his aunt's voice over the cell phone. "I'm in the parking lot. Come out the front doors. Hurry!"

Jack straightened, lifted his weight off Will and Shadowslayer, and took a painful breath that told him he was still alive. "Aunt Linda's outside," he said. "Time to go." They stampeded to the rear of the church.

"Look out!" Linda cried as Will and Fitch threw open the front door and came face-to-face with the cowboy. It was hard to say who was more surprised. He made a grab for Will, which turned out to be a mistake. Will had been spending considerable time in the gym. He peeled Hadley off him and, despite the man's size, lifted him off the porch and flung him into the parking lot. Hadley slid on his stomach, arms and legs splayed like a jellyfish. Fitch retrieved the case that Will had dropped.

The Land Rover was pulled up alongside the Mercedes. They sprinted for it. Will skidded to a stop next to the Mercedes, reached through the open window, and yanked the keys from the ignition. He hurled them as far as he could out into the darkness.

They flung themselves into the backseat of the Rover, Jack with the sword, and Fitch with the case. The Rover kicked up gravel as they pulled out of the lot. Behind them, the cowboy had risen to his hands and knees. And then the church was out of sight, and they were speeding down Methodist Chapel Road.

Linda was calm, businesslike, even, handing the phone to Fitch to make reservations at a hotel in Columbus under a new name, asking Will to find the map in the glove compartment and navigate, even though she knew the county well. Her voice washed over them, soothed and relaxed them, blunted their terror and curiosity. As if flaming swords and wizards were everyday events. She spoke no charms aloud, but now Jack could hear the sorcery in her voice. Why had he never noticed it before?

She gave no tasks to Jack. Once she had wrung every detail about the cemetery from him, she let him be. He sat slumped in the seat, head thrown back, eyes half closed. His entire body ached, and the whole front of him burned, save under the vest. Shadowslayer was back in its case, resting comfortably under his feet.

Sometimes he caught Linda watching him in the rearview mirror.

She is the enchanter. She is the one the wizard was talking about. Maybe what he said was true. Maybe she was just using me to get the sword.

She said it was mine, didn't she?

What would he do if she tried to take it away? That was a question he couldn't answer. It seemed to fill a need in him that he didn't know was there before.

He squirmed uncomfortably, then turned and leaned over the backseat to see if there was something he could use for a pillow. He saw his duffle bag and remembered. His medicine! He tugged open the zipper and slid his hand inside, feeling for the familiar shape, the cool glass amid the clothing.

I don't want to take it, he thought. Ever again.

He pulled it out anyway, turning the blue bottle between his hands. He looked up, saw Aunt Linda watching him again.

"Never mind, Jack," she said softly. "You don't have to anymore. We'll talk about that later."

They stayed at a chain hotel north of Columbus, complete with the promised swimming pool and hot tub. She ordered several platters of room-service sandwiches and appetizers, and talked the fitness club manager into allowing them to use the facilities until midnight. The man returned at intervals during the evening to see if they needed anything and to let Linda know he got off at eleven if she would like to have a drink. She declined. Several times.

He doesn't know who he's dealing with, Jack thought. Just like the wizard said.

Jack looked and felt like he'd laid out too long in the sun. The pool was soothing, but he couldn't tolerate the hot tub. He lay on his back, dozing by the pool, half awakening to hear the others talking.

"Do you think those men will try to find us?" Fitch was asking. "Do you think they'll try to get the sword back?"

"He's looking for us now," Linda said.

Jack noticed she used the singular. *The cowboy doesn't count. He's probably dead.*

Linda's voice continued to wind through his thoughts. "If we're lucky, he has no idea who we are or where we're from. Nothing is in my name: the car, the hotel, nothing can be connected to me. He'll assume I have the sword. That's your best protection. And this." As Jack watched through slitted eyes, she reached out and seized Will and Fitch each by a hand.

"You mustn't say anything about what happened this weekend to anyone, do you understand? Not a hint, not a whisper, not a boast or complaint." She looked from one to the other, looked them in the eyes. "It's over and done. It will be our secret, a memory shared among the four of us alone. Do you understand?"

They nodded solemnly, eyes stretched open, like acolytes of a new religion.

Great, Jack said to himself. *My aunt's a witch. What am I going to do?* He abandoned his friends to her tender mercies, knowing they were beyond his help. He stood and stumbled his way to his room and fell exhausted into bed, welcoming the temporary escape of sleep. The sword lay in its case under his arm.

Jack slept late, and when he awoke, Will and Fitch seemed normal enough. Too normal to be normal, in fact, because they were relaxed and joking about the chores awaiting them at home. They didn't say a word about the events in the graveyard.

Linda didn't check out until after lunch, and when they carried their duffles outside, Jack was surprised to find her loading her things into a different car, a rather nondescript sedan. It seemed routine for her: using fake IDs, swapping cars.

It was nearly four P.M. when they pulled up in front of the Fitch house. Fitch lived in a tired-looking shotgun ranch that didn't seem nearly large enough to accommodate all the Fitch children. When Aunt Linda tapped the horn, it was like stirring an anthill. He was quickly immersed, waist-deep, in a sea of younger Fitches. Fitch waved ruefully and disappeared into the house with his retinue.

At the Childers house, a fair-sized pile of mulch still remained on the driveway apron. "Can you drive around the block a few times?" Will pleaded with mock desperation. He reluctantly exited the car, pulling his bag after him. "See you tomorrow."

And then it was just the two of them. When Will was well away, Aunt Linda turned her car back toward downtown.

"Where are we going?" Jack asked warily.

"I think we should talk before I take you home," his aunt replied, not looking at him. "I hope you have a little time."

The Legends Coffeehouse occupied the first floor of a Victorian mansion that stood next to the lake a block from the university. Linda chose a table in the solarium with a view of the water. The late-afternoon sun streamed in through the windows. She sat with her back to the lake, facing the door.

Jack ordered a cinnamon roll and hot cocoa. Linda ordered orange spiced tea. She said little until the waitress had served them and disappeared. Then she turned to Jack.

"So what do you think of the sword?"

"It's . . . it's . . ." Jack recalled the rush of power, searched for the appropriate adjective. "I've never seen . . . felt . . . anything like it." He'd brought it into the restaurant and leaned it against the wall, unwilling to leave it in the car.

"I didn't think you'd have to try it out." Linda smiled ruefully. "You did well. I don't think our friend knew what hit him. At least I hope he didn't."

"If you're going to keep talking in riddles, just forget it," Jack snapped. "Why'd you involve us in this, anyway? Either I'm going crazy, or I'm not, and either way I don't like it. We could have been killed. And now you've done something to my friends, bewitched them so they don't even know enough to be scared."

"I'm an enchanter, Jack. Not a witch." Linda's face held not a trace of humor. "What most people think of as witches are usually sorcerers. They specialize in material magic: poisons, potions, amulets. Unfortunately, they're not very good with people, so . . ."

"Okay, you *enchanted* them," Jack broke in. He felt like putting his hands over his ears. "Just stop it. The less I know about this, the better. That guy in the graveyard scared the hell out of me."

"They scare me, too, Jack," Linda said quietly. She regarded him with a sympathy that was altogether too inclusive.

"Who are they?" he asked, after a minute. He couldn't help himself.

Linda frowned and tapped her fingernails on the teacup. "I can't tell you everything. And you're going to have to be satisfied for the time being with what I can tell you."

Jack licked icing off his fingers and pulled another section away from the cinnamon roll. "What if I'm not satisfied?"

"Then you'll still have to wait." When Jack looked up, she was gazing out over the water, her jaw set firmly.

"Whatever," he said grudgingly.

Linda studied him for a moment. "There is something that you should know about our family. The Downeys and Hales have a history of magical gifts that goes back hundreds of years. Had you heard that?"

Jack thought about it. "Well, there's Susannah."

Linda nodded. "She had the gift of reading the future in the cards. That talent is common in our family. But it is not the only gift. Originally the line was very pure. People of our kind tended to marry each other and bear children who were true to their lineage. Our ancestors came from Britain, which at one time was heavily peopled with the Weir."

"The Weir?" It sounded like she was saying *ware*.

"The magical guilds. Our ancestors." Aunt Linda picked up her teacup, then set it down again without drinking from it. "We include our share of poets, writers, revolutionaries, and visionaries. But the Weir inherit unusual abilities."

Jack shrugged. "Such as . . . ?"

Linda reached across the table, gripped his hands, and looked him in the eyes. "We inherit a gift of power. Our ancestors include wizards, enchanters, soothsayers, sorcerers, and warriors."

Jack sat without moving, waiting for the punchline. It never came. Linda watched him as if he were a bomb that might go off at any minute.

She really believes this stuff, he thought. His mother and his aunt had always been interested in what Linda called "hedge magic": astrology, card reading, palmistry, and the like. But he'd always been under the impression it was more entertainment than anything else.

Jack licked his lips. "So. Wizardry in the family. What does that have to do with us?"

"We are heirs, you and I," replied Aunt Linda. "As I said, I am an enchanter."

"An enchanter," Jack repeated. He remembered what the wizard in the graveyard had said. *The enchanter has bewitched you, and you're going to pay the price.* "And what

. . . is your gift . . . supposed to be?" he asked.

She colored a little, twisted a napkin in her hands. "We, uh, we have personal power over people," she said finally. "We are persuasive. People are drawn to us, whether they like it or not. We are . . . irresistible, I guess you might say." She slid a look at him as if to assess his reaction.

It was true. He'd never in his life been able to resist her, but he'd always assumed it was just . . . the way she was. He remembered Will and Fitch back at the hotel. "Okay. What about me?"

Linda hesitated. "You are a warrior, one of the Weirlind, they're called."

"Warrior?" If Linda's gift seemed appropriate, his wasn't a good fit at all, he decided. "That doesn't sound magical to me."

Aunt Linda sighed. "Relations have never been peaceful among the different branches of the Weir. Wars have broken out periodically as one faction tries to win supremacy over the others. Wars require warriors, who have . . . appropriate gifts." She paused. "There are really wars among wizards. Because they are the most powerful of the guilds, they control the others. Many of the wars through British history originated with our family disputes. In recent years, the battles have continued, virtually unnoticed by those outside the family."

"They're still fighting in Britain," Jack said. "What about over here?"

"One of our ancestors, a Hale, came to this country in the 1600s to avoid the European wars. He brought several hundred gifted emigrants with him who sought peace in the New World. We were forgotten. For a while." She looked away.

Jack was spinning between past and present. He thought of his mother, so different from Linda. "If you're an enchanter, does that mean Mom . . ."

"Becka is not an heir. She and your father know nothing about this. The Weir in the New World have intermarried with Anaweir, those without the gift. Not everyone inherits."

Anaweir. The wizard in the graveyard had called him that. But *unaware* was certainly appropriate, too. "Why haven't you told my mother about this talent of yours?" He stared out at the sunset.

"Jack, believe it or not, when I was your age, I thought I knew everything. But I didn't understand about my gift. So I was unprepared when I encountered my first wizard."

He couldn't help it. He turned to look at her. But she looked away. "I was sixteen. My parents couldn't help me. Becka couldn't help me. The Anaweir have no chance against the gifted. But they would have thrown their lives away trying. So it's better if they don't know." She half smiled. "You'll see. Telling this secret to Anaweir is like pulling on a loose thread. Everything comes unraveled."

"What does Susannah have to do with this?" Jack asked.

"She was a warrior. Like you."

"A woman warrior?"

Aunt Linda shrugged. "Men and women can be warriors, wizards, or enchanters. They say she had the gift. I don't know if she used it."

"If I have some kind of special power, why haven't I noticed anything?" Jack did a quick personal survey just to be sure. He ached as though he'd been beaten, and he was conscious of the weight of his clothing on his burned skin. Beyond that, he felt different than before: edgy, impatient, euphoric, *alive*. A mercurial stranger now lived under his skin. What was going on?

"Your powers have been suppressed. That medication you've been taking since your surgery keeps your powers from becoming manifest."

It took him a moment to realize what it meant. "Dr. Longbranch knows about this?" He was beginning to wonder if he were the only one in the dark.

Linda leaned forward. "The gift is passed from generation to generation in a kind of stone or crystal that sits behind the heart. Wizards carry wizard stones, enchanters enchanter stones. You were *Weirflesh*, a designated heir, but . . . something went wrong. There was no crystal. Without it, you were dying."

"Why didn't I have a crystal?"

"Maybe it has to do with the mixing of blood. I don't know. But you were dying. So I contacted Dr. Longbranch. I . . . I had met her through some people I knew in England."

"What did you tell Mom?"

"As far as she and Thomas know, you were born with a heart defect, and Dr. Longbranch was your heart surgeon. Which she is," Linda added.

"A heart surgeon," Jack repeated. "And?" He leaned back, waiting for the rest.

"Jessamine Longbranch is a wizard. She brought a stone and implanted it. You recovered. Only . . ." She looked away. "Only, you were meant to be a wizard."

Jack pressed his fingers against his temples. "I was born a wizard, and she put in a warrior stone?" Linda nodded. "Why would she do that?"

Linda stared down at the table, a muscle working in her jaw. "It . . . it was an experiment. She wanted to see what would happen."

She's angry, Jack thought, but she doesn't want me to know it. "So where does that leave me? Wizard or warrior?"

Linda looked up at him, her eyes swimming with unshed tears. "I don't know, Jack," she said, swallowing hard. "You're a warrior, I suppose."

Jack shrugged, unsure why that was bad news. "So why would Dr. Longbranch want to suppress these warrior powers, whatever they are?"

"It was important to keep your secret hidden."

"Hidden from whom?" Although Linda had initiated this strange conversation, he felt like he was dragging information out of her, bit by precious bit.

"People could be looking for you, Jack," she said quietly.

"What people? And why?" Jack was bewildered.

"Wizards. Like the man in the courthouse. They are always looking for warriors to fight for them, or trying to kill warriors who fight for their opponents. They don't want the other side to gain an advantage. The best time to recruit or attack a warrior is when he is untrained, before he comes of age."

Jack shivered and looked around the room. The waitress had lit candles on each table as the daylight died. Shadows flickered and danced on the walls. The lake had turned a slate gray color as darkness fell. Suddenly, the world seemed like a dangerous place.

"But I'm not on a side," Jack pointed out. "I don't want to fight anybody."

"It doesn't matter. They'll come after you anyway."

She's not telling me everything, Jack thought. He felt as though he were peering through a keyhole into a room full of demons and he could only see the one nearest the door. It was quite possible the rest were even bigger and uglier.

"Can't I get rid of this crystal somehow?"

"You'd die," Aunt Linda said simply. The two sat in silence for a time.

"So what are the chances anyone would find me in Trinity?" Jack asked.

She released a soft breath. "There are wizards in Trinity now, looking for you. I don't know how they tracked you here. We didn't know about them until the soccer tryouts. When you blew Garrett Lobeck into the net. You forgot to take your medicine, and you were leaking magic." She hesitated. "Your powers are beginning to manifest. In warriors, that usually happens at about your age." Her voice shook a little. In fact, there was considerable unexplained emotion in the whole conversation.

"They came after you that afternoon, but you'd already left practice." Linda shivered. "Wizards can detect

use of power and link it to a stone. Nick managed to . . .
to distract them."

"Nick!" He said it louder than he intended, and
looked around guiltily. The room was still empty. Nick.
Even Nick. One of them. One of us? "So who is he,
really?" Jack demanded.

"His name is Nicodemus Snowbeard. He's a wizard,"
Linda replied. "He's looked after you ever since you were
born."

Somewhere in the back of his mind, Jack had always
wondered why a man as intelligent as Nick was working
as a handyman in a small Ohio town. But what hold could
Linda have on the wizard, to persuade him to take on this
job?

"Can an enchanter charm a wizard?"

She thought a moment, cleared her throat. "We are
masters of mind magic. Wizards are more powerful than
enchanters, because of their use of spoken charms. But
they are vulnerable to us, also, particularly if we take them
unawares. They cannot always detect our use of power. We
can change appearance, seduce them, make them act fool-
ishly."

She'd slipped in that part about seduction along with
the rest. *I don't even want to know this*, Jack told himself. *So
why am I asking so many questions?*

"Each of the other guilds has some specific advantage
over wizards. For example, a warrior can defeat a wizard
in a physical fight, if he can keep the wizard from casting
a charm. As you found out in the graveyard. Sorcerers are
experts in material magic, potions, talismans, magical

tools, and so on. Small magics. A sorcerer may produce an artifact that either enhances or limits a wizard's magic. An enchanter may bewitch him. Most Anawizard Weir, once they are alert to it, can sense a wizard's stone, while wizards cannot detect the other stones unless there is a release of power. But wizards can use spoken charms, physical *and* mind magic, which makes them most powerful overall."

Jack wondered if he should be taking notes. "So the wizard in the graveyard followed us to Coal Grove from Trinity?"

She shook her head. "No. Thank God. I know him by reputation. His name is Geoffrey Wylie. But it seems he doesn't know who I am, and based on what happened in the graveyard, he doesn't know who you are, either. He was after the sword, and the fact that you crossed paths was a coincidence. We have to hope he doesn't follow the genealogy any further. If they find out who you are, you'll have to leave Trinity."

Jack stared at her. Linda leaned over the table, speaking softly. "We have to either suppress your powers, or hide them. That's where your new vest comes in. It prevents them from detecting your stone, even if there is a release. Along with some other advantages that I'm sure you've noticed."

The import of this penetrated slowly. "So Mercedes is in on this, too?" Eccentric Mercedes Foster, with her clouds of wiry gray hair and wild handwoven clothing. Mercedes with her garden full of exotic plants, some too poisonous to touch.

"Mercedes is a sorcerer," Linda said matter-of-factly.

Jack reviewed a mental map of his neighborhood. "Blaise and Richard?"

"Blaise is a soothsayer," said Aunt Linda, laughing in spite of herself at the look on his face. "Richard is Anaweir. A non-heir," she added.

"Iris?"

"A wizard."

"Hanson and Sarah?"

"Anaweir. A nice old couple that loves babies."

"There goes the neighborhood," Jack growled. He massaged his forehead with his fingertips. What had started as pressure was now a really bad headache. He felt like his world had been turned inside out. He wanted to sit and review every little detail of his life so far, sift for the little clues that might have warned him. "So these are all my relatives?"

"So to speak," Linda replied. "You all carry the same ancient blood."

Jack shoved back from the table, sloshing the tea out of Linda's cup. "Well, thanks so much for sharing this with me. Finally. So what now? Do I go home and hide under the bed? Wait and see if someone comes after me?"

"No," she said. "It's too late for that. They're relentless. It's only a matter of time before they discover your where-abouts." Apparently not liking what she saw in his face, Linda rushed on. "That's why we . . . ah . . . I decided to retrieve your grandmother's sword. We . . . that is . . . I thought that perhaps, with some training . . ."

"Training?" This was all crazy, but there was something about his aunt's manner that was absolutely compelling, impossible to turn away from. Maybe that was her gift. This ability to capture a person and work them until they suspended the rules of common sense. *The enchanter has bewitched you.* He looked into Linda's blue-gold eyes and knew it was true. He was helpless to resist. "Training for what?"

"We're going to teach you how to fight, Jack. In a physical fight, at least, you could be a match for a wizard." She gestured toward the case leaning against the wall. "Shadowslayer is . . . a legendary weapon. We want to make sure that when they come for you they will encounter a more dangerous adversary than the boy in the graveyard."

Jack thought he'd done all right, under the circumstances. "Who is we? Are *you* going to teach me how to fight with a sword?" He found that hard to imagine, although at this point nothing would surprise him.

Linda shook her head. "I've found a trainer for you. A wizard. Unfortunately, I'm not going to be here."

"What? You're leaving?"

"Jack." She put her hand over his. Power flooded into him like a highly potent drug.

He jerked his hand back as if he'd been scalded. "Don't try that with me."

He might as well have slapped her. "All right. No magic. Right now you're well hidden in an Anaweir family with no sorcery about it. I plan to lead Wylie away from you."

"What do you mean?"

She shook the hair back from her face. "He'll follow

me. He won't have any choice. He'll enjoy the chase, but he'll never catch me."

Jack thought of the cowboy, screaming under Wylie's hands, remembered the wizard and what he'd said about *unfinished business*, and shivered. "Aunt Linda. Please don't mess with him. Stay away from him."

"Don't worry, Jack. I know all about wizards." From the way she said it, she knew things he didn't want to know.

"Now, listen to me." It was like she was going down a checklist. "You need to keep the vest on at all times. It will make it more difficult for them to detect your stone. You must resist the temptation to use your powers except during training. It won't be easy. But each time you use them, it sends up a signal for unfriendly eyes." Linda paused. "Take the sword with you. Keep it in its case when you're not using it. The box will keep it from anyone but the rightful heir." Linda pulled three glass bottles from her backpack. Jack realized with a start that they were some of the ones Iris had made for him when he was just a baby. The ones for dreams and potions, as the story went.

"Discontinue Dr. Longbranch's medicine and start taking these." She handed them over. Jack unstoppered one of the bottles. The aroma struck an almost physical blow. It was potent and intoxicating, like strong liquor. He wrinkled his nose and replaced the stopper. "One teaspoon of each, once a day. You can't tell your mom or dad about the switch, and you absolutely must not tell Dr. Longbranch, either."

"Longbranch?" Jack was puzzled. "Isn't she in on this?"

"Not exactly," she said. "Don't trust anyone. Except Nick."

Which made him think of something else.

"Why'd you get Will and Fitch involved in this? They could have been killed."

Linda stared down at the table, her cheeks pink with remorse. "I never meant to put them in danger. Sometimes we in the guilds are careless of Anaweir. I had no idea there were wizards around until I spoke to Nick. By then it was too late." Jack remembered that she had tried to change her mind, and he had resisted. "I planned to leave them at the hotel and go get the sword on our own. I knew they would never say anything . . . if I asked them not to."

"If you bewitched them, you mean."

"I don't apologize for who I am," she said softly. "I want you to be proud of who you are, also. I know this isn't easy to hear, but I'm glad I can finally tell you the truth."

"Really? What's been stopping you all this time?"

Linda flinched but did not reply. She fished in her jacket pocket and handed over a sealed envelope. "The information about your trainer is in there," she said. "Do you have any questions?"

He shook his head. He was angry and scared, nerves jittering, the hot blood flowing to muscle and bone. He closed his eyes, remembering the weight of Shadowslayer in his hands.

"Like I said. I can't tell you everything today. But this is enough to get started." She looked at her watch. "We'd better go, or your mother will send out a search party."

Linda threw some money on the table and they left the coffee shop. It was dark now, and Jack could see lights far out over the water. They drove back to Jefferson Street in silence, each occupied with private thoughts. The porch light was on when they pulled up in front of the Swift house. Aunt Linda wouldn't come in. "Tell Becka thanks for loaning you out this weekend."

Jack climbed out of the car and pulled his duffle bag out of the backseat. The three glass bottles were tucked safely inside. Linda passed the box with the sword in it through the window. A look passed between them, sympathetic on the one side, angry and rather desperate on the other.

"Keep the phone," Aunt Linda instructed. "I'll be in touch."

"Sure. Fine." If what she had said was true, then he was in deep trouble, and his aunt was the only lifeline he had. She'd dumped this load on him, and now she was going away. Jack turned to go, but she gripped his arm, pulled him close, and kissed him on the cheek.

Fortunately, Becka didn't ask many questions. She had legal briefs spread out over the kitchen table. When she saw Jack's face under the overhead light, she exclaimed, "Oh, no! Did you forget your sunscreen?" He reached up, touched his burned face, and nodded. She asked if he and Linda had found any new relatives, and Jack said, "A couple." She asked if the road trip was boring after all, and he said, truthfully, "No." That seemed to satisfy her.

He thought about going out to the garage to talk to Nick, but decided against it. He'd seen enough of wizards for one weekend.

Later, up in his room, Jack stowed the glass bottles in the back of his underwear drawer. He pushed the box with the sword in it under his bed.

The note with the information about his trainer was in his jeans pocket. He tore open the envelope and unfolded the paper inside.

The name on the paper was Leander Hastings. Trinity High School's new assistant principal.

❧ CHAPTER SIX ☙
DANGEROUS GAMES

The next morning, Jack moved his blue bottle of medicine into the upstairs bathroom, along with a measuring spoon. "It'll be easier to remember if I take it before I brush my teeth," he explained to Becka. After his shower, he carefully measured out a tablespoon of Longbranch's medicine and poured it down the sink. Then he carried the potion bottles in from his bedroom. He opened each in turn and swallowed down a measured teaspoon. Two of them were strong-tasting. The third was milder, almost pleasant. He carefully returned the bottles to his drawer. Then he pulled Mercedes's vest on over his head. He was already feeling vulnerable without it. He wondered if wizards might charge in on him while he had it off, when he was in the shower, say. He followed with a flannel shirt. He still looked like he'd had a bad day in the tanning salon.

The kitchen was empty, but a bowl of cereal waited at his place, along with a note: "Gone to the university. Have a good day. Take your medicine. Love, Mom."

Jack poured milk over his cereal and sat down to eat. A moment later Will tapped at the kitchen door.

"Come on in," said Jack. "I'm just finishing."

Will let himself in. Jack wondered if he should lock the door now that he knew he was being hunted. He sighed.

"Is your aunt gone?" Will asked, looking around as if she might appear at any moment.

"She's gone."

"I guess that's good," said Will, looking a little wistful nevertheless. "Don't get me wrong. I like her, but she seems to attract trouble."

Is it Aunt Linda or me? Jack wondered. He waited for Will to bring up the sword, or the graveyard, or the wizard, but he didn't.

Instead, he said, "Do you have your soccer gear? If we're lucky, we might have practice tonight." Meaning, if they made the team.

"Yeah." Jack pointed out his gym bag by the door.

"Well, we'd better get going," said Will. "Penworthy awaits." He hoisted his book bag to his shoulder and winced.

"You sore, too?" Jack asked.

"Yeah," Will replied. "Must be from digging up graves." He grinned. And that was all that was said between them.

Jack was at a loss for how to initiate his training. Was

he supposed to approach Leander Hastings at school and say, "I understand you're supposed to teach me how to be a warrior and use my magic sword. What's your schedule like?" He wished Aunt Linda had remained to act as go-between. It hardly seemed real, now that she was gone and he was back in school. And Hastings was definitely intimidating.

Aside from his worries, Jack felt great. It was hard to explain. He felt clear and focused, emancipated, as if someone had swept out the old and dusty corners of his soul. He could only assume that Dr. Longbranch's medicine had a kind of sedative effect.

Once at school, worries about wizards and warriors seemed overblown and insubstantial, like a bad dream. Penworthy was at his usual post, but there was no sign of Hastings. Jack and Will had a little time to kill before the first bell, so they walked back to the athletic office to see if the soccer team roster was posted. It was, and Jack, Will, and Fitch had all made varsity. Even better, Garrett Lobeck had been bumped back to JV.

"He'll be pissed," Jack predicted, knowing that somehow it would turn out to be his fault, and not really caring. The first practice was scheduled for that afternoon.

There was still no sign of Hastings when they walked back to their classrooms. Maybe it'd be best to wait a few days and see if the assistant principal contacted him.

After school, Jack and Will carried their gym bags into the boys' locker room to change for practice. The day was cold, so they pulled sweatpants over their shin guards and socks. Jack glanced around before he took off his flannel shirt. It was still early, and he and Will were the only ones in the locker room. Jack slid a long-sleeved T-shirt over his vest.

Will was looking on curiously. "Expecting trouble?" he asked.

"You never know," Jack replied.

As they assembled on the practice field, the players slapped hands, grinning, happy to have made either team, given the competition. The notable exception was Garrett Lobeck, who, of course, had expected to play varsity. His friends Harkness and Leonard had made the first team. Lobeck looked like an assault waiting to happen, but for once he was heckling some other player. No doubt he was gun-shy after their previous encounter. Which was fine with Jack.

After fifteen minutes of warm-ups, Jack found he wasn't even breathing hard. *I must be in better shape than I thought*, he told himself. Then they started a scrimmage game between the varsity and JV teams.

The varsity team scored first, but after that the JV team managed to keep them from scoring until the five-minute quarter was called. Jack played midfielder during the second quarter. His team took possession near the JV goal, and one of the fullbacks passed the ball to Jack. Jack began to dribble it down the field, dodging effortlessly around defenders. As he approached the goal, the JV players parted before him as if they couldn't get out of his way fast enough. He took his shot from just outside the box. The goalie practically jumped out of the way, and the shot sizzled in. The varsity team cheered. Will and Fitch slapped him high fives.

Jack felt a trickle of fear, like a cold finger down his spine. There was something supernatural at work. Now that he was off Longbranch's medicine, keeping his powers under wraps was going to be easier said than done. Instinctively, he scanned the crowd. It was sparse: a few parents and assorted girlfriends. Ellen Stephenson was sitting in the bleachers, leaning forward, intent on the field. Looking everywhere but at Jack.

"Nice going, Swift," Coach Slansky said. "You've really improved since last year." Jack was swapped out right after the goal. He stood miserably on the sidelines. How was he going to get through the season without drawing attention to himself?

"The first thing you need to do is work on your control." The voice was practically in his ear. Jack jumped and spun around. It was Leander Hastings, wearing a red Harvard sweatshirt and khakis, hands thrust into his pockets. He was standing close enough so that he didn't have to speak loudly to be heard. "I can help you with that."

"Can you?" Jack spoke in the same code. "That would be great. What would you suggest?"

"Let's see." Hastings ran his hand through his hair. "You'll have soccer practice every afternoon this week, three to five. Let's plan on Wednesday afternoon, right after your regular practice. Tell your mom you'll be home by eight." Hastings had the manner of a man who was used to issuing commands and having them obeyed.

Jack nodded. "Will we practice here?"

"No," the wizard replied. "I'll find a place."

Jack hesitated. "What about . . . will I need to bring anything?" He might have difficulty storing Shadowslayer in his locker. Besides, he was pretty sure swords were forbidden under Trinity's zero tolerance weapons policy.

There was a trace of a smile on Hastings's face, as if he'd read Jack's thoughts. "No. Not this time."

"Swift!" It was the coach. "You're in!"

Jack nodded to Hastings, and ran back out onto the field. Well, for better or worse, he had a plan. He would have to hope for the best. Hastings made him uneasy. Still, his aunt had chosen him, and he had to assume she knew what she was doing.

But there was that other thing she'd said. She'd told him he could trust no one. And now he was putting himself into the hands of a stranger.

When he glanced back at the sidelines, Hastings was gone.

Many of Jessamine's guests chose to come by water; not that it was necessary, but because it was reminiscent of a more elegant age. They disembarked at the Thameside docks and promenaded through the birch allee to the manor's south terrace. It was lit by torchlight, bordered by beds of white roses: Glamis Castle, Honor, Penelope, Iceberg, and Fair Bianca, among others. Old roses, hybrid teas, floribundas, and shrub roses. The blossoms appeared as white smudges in the darkness, their fragrance a subtle reminder of who held power over the guilds.

Servants in White Rose livery circulated through the

crowd, bearing trays of wine and canapés. Each of the gifted brought a party of servants: members of the lesser guilds to serve as a guard of sorts. A few of the very fortunate had enchanters on their arms. They were the focus of envious eyes and not a few malevolent gestures.

Jessamine Longbranch received her guests where the allee met the terrace. She had chosen them purposefully; entertaining was an essential element of wizard politics, meant to extract information, intimidate, even draw blood on occasion. One could risk coming, or one could risk staying away. Neither was a safe choice.

Jessamine's hair flowed over her shoulders, confined by a net of seed pearls. Her gown was a confection of diaphanous silk, embroidered over with white roses in strategic locations. The hands she extended for kissing glittered with jewels.

Geoffrey Wylie bowed over her hand. He was dressed in subdued fashion, suitable to a declining House. His coat was a red so deep as to be almost black; he wore a ruby in one earlobe. "Jessamine." A whisper of power touched her skin. A gesture, only, to let her know he was at home. He kept his head slightly turned so one side of his face was illuminated by torchlight, the other in shadow.

"Geoffrey! You poor thing! Whatever happened to your face?" She grasped his chin, turning his head so she could see better. His face looked to have been badly burned from chin line to brow on the right side. He'd applied a magical glamour that might have fooled someone less perceptive.

She *tch*ed. "Did you run into an angry Dragon?" That

was the name taken by one of the rabble-rousing leaders of the Servant Guild.

The wizard's breath hissed out. So he'd hoped she wouldn't notice. She knew Wylie was vain. They'd been together once.

"It's nothing. An accident." But the fury in his eyes said he'd found someone else to blame, and that someone was not yet dead. Wylie was powerful, the procuror of warriors for the Red Rose. Not many would choose to cross him. She filed that away.

Jessamine looked over his shoulder. "Where's that handsome Mr. Paige? I was looking forward to seeing him again."

"Simon sends his regrets." The fury had drained away, to be replaced by an impassive calm. Simon Paige was Master of Warriors for the Red Rose. A rather empty title, as he'd had little to do for several years.

He must have something rather important to do now, to have missed this affair. Could it be the Red Rose had finally found a warrior? If so, there was too much at stake to play at guessing.

She surveyed Wylie's escort and found what she was looking for. A handsome young man in Red Rose livery who ducked his head when she looked at him. An apprentice sorcerer, perhaps (they were a penny a dozen.) A servant who knew enough to be afraid of her might know other secrets as well. Still smiling, Jess gestured to one of the bodyguards that stood unobtrusively along the wall.

The sun was up before she finished with the boy. Not because he'd had that much to say, but because the work was so appealing. He'd been very eager to please, at the end. She was confident she'd wrung every scrap of truth from him, the little hints and clues that suggested the Red Rose might issue a challenge one day soon.

Jess showered and changed clothes and carried her tea out onto the terrace. The morning was cool and clear. The river rolled by, ancient roadway of the Britons.

Wylie had threatened and blustered, of course, when his servant turned up missing. But that was the risk one took in bringing an entourage to a gathering of wizards. If the Houses couldn't attack each other directly, servants could be picked off at need. Could she help it if Wylie's young man had drunk too much and fallen unseen into the Thames, where his body would be found one day soon, dreadfully decomposed?

She thought of the young warrior she'd left in America. Her most closely held secret. She'd been extraordinarily careful, had minimized her contact with him. But she had planted eyes and ears in that drab little town to watch the boy, though they didn't know why he was important. They could not betray what they didn't know.

He was old enough to manifest, but she'd kept him suppressed. She chewed her lower lip thoughtfully. She had to weigh the boy's need for training against her desire to keep him alive a little longer. Perhaps it was time to claim him, to contact the Warriormasters and tell them to ready their tools.

That night after supper, Jack couldn't seem to focus on his math homework. After struggling for half an hour, he packed up his papers and supplies and headed for the garage.

Nick was busy painting a bluebird house when Jack knocked, but he pushed the project to one side to make room on the table for Jack's homework. It was a familiar pattern. Somehow it was always easier to concentrate in Nick's kitchen. But today, Jack meant to pick a fight.

Nick removed a paint-splattered green apron and slung it over the back of a chair. Jack refused his offer of a beverage and sat glaring at the battered tabletop while Nick made himself a cup of tea.

"So," Nick said, settling himself into the chair across the table from Jack. He glanced down at the untouched homework. "You look like a boy who has eaten the fruit of the tree of knowledge and doesn't like the taste."

Jack studied the old man, hunting for any sign of wizardry. He was aware of a bright intelligence, nothing more.

Nick was watching him keenly. "How are you, Jack?"

"Just great," Jack snapped. "I'm lying to my mother, going against doctor's orders, and being hunted by wizards. Matter of fact, when I'm not being hunted by wizards, I'm hanging out with them."

Nick sat back in his chair. "But you have the sword."

Jack nodded sullenly. "Yes."

"You should be pleased, considering what you came up against," the old man said. "In a contest between warriors and wizards, it usually goes the other way."

"What's to keep them from taking it back?"

"They cannot sense its presence, and they will not breach these walls. I've seen to that." For a moment, he looked *scary* again, and then his face settled into its usual pattern of laugh lines and history. "Before, wizards were hunting you and you had no clue. Not only that, you were unarmed. You are better off than before."

"I think I was better off not knowing."

"Don't be foolish!" Nick's tone was brusque. "Ignorance can get you killed. Or worse."

"Then why didn't you tell me all this before? You've kept me in the dark for years, watching me, dosing me with potions, talking behind my back. The whole neighborhood, practically. You must've thought I was pretty stupid."

"You were a child, Jack," Nick said gently. "It wasn't necessary for you to know. The situation was stable, and there wasn't any reason for you to worry about such things. Children have enough to be afraid of, what with monsters under the bed and so on."

Jack had to admit his childhood had been relatively carefree. Worrying about wizards would not have improved it. But he wasn't feeling charitable just then. "Well, now I'm worried. And even Aunt Linda hasn't really explained what's going on."

Nick sighed, looking unaccountably sad. "I don't know how this will all turn out. Just remember that your Aunt Linda has done everything in her power to protect you, from the time you were born. She is absolutely committed to you. Never doubt that."

"I still don't get it. If you're a wizard, how come you took on this job?" Jack indicated their surroundings with a wave of his hand. "This can't be too exciting next to the world of spells and incantations."

Nick smiled. "Sometimes, as you get older, excitement loses its appeal. Let's just say I have a special interest in you and your aunt. *You* are important. That makes this important work. Besides, now that you know who and what you are, it opens many doors. So much material has been off-limits up to now. I've been putting stuff by for years against this day." Nick stood, leaning on his staff, and then disappeared into the room Jack thought of as the library. A moment later he returned with a thick leather-bound book. "You can start with this," the old wizard suggested, handing it to him.

The cover was embossed with gold. "Weir Hale," and underneath, "Jackson Downey Swift." He opened it.

A large part of the book was taken up with a genealogy: pages and pages of names of people joined together and their children. Some of the names in the family tree were outlined in bright, metallic colors: blue, red, gold, green, and purple. The rest were in plain black text.

He looked up at Snowbeard. "What is this?"

"This is your Weirbook, Jack. It was created when you were born. All of the Weir have them. Look on the back page." There Jack saw his own name, Jackson Downey Swift, and the names of his parents, Thomas Swift and Rebecca Downey. All of it written in the same flowing hand.

"The illuminated names are heirs, and the colors indicate what kind—wizards, warriors, and so on. Wizards are in gold."

Jack noted that his own name was in gold. The warrior who was meant to be a wizard.

"Traditionally, the book is commissioned from the Sorcerer Guild by the child's parents, using the family Weirbook as a template. In this country, things have become rather muddled due to the mixing of blood. The nearest Weir relation stands as godparent. That's your Aunt Linda, as you know. She asked Mercedes Foster to do the work."

"I don't get it," Jack said slowly. "Why are wizards so much more powerful than the other guilds?"

"Wizards are singular among the Weir because they shape magic with words. They can do much more powerful and sophisticated tasks through charms. They are limited only by the extent of this knowledge of magical language, and the power of the stone they carry."

He waved his hand at the book in Jack's hands. "Spend some time reading through this. Study it. Especially the part about charms and incantations. Then we'll try a few things." He gave Jack an appraising look. "I think it's worth testing you to see if you have any talent for wizardry. Despite your warrior stone."

Great. He didn't know how to be a warrior, and now Nick Snowbeard was going to teach him to be a wizard, too.

"But right now you'd better finish up your homework," Nick added.

Wizardry and calculus. Jack sighed, stood, and picked up the book and his homework. "I can do the math in study hall," he said. "I'll look this over. Thanks, Nick."

Later, in his room, Jack switched on the reading light over his bed. It was already getting late. He pulled the heavy volume onto his lap and flipped to the first page—heavy stock embossed with the stylized figure of a bear.

JACKSON DOWNEY SWIFT
A WIZARD HEIR
A WARRIOR MAYDE

Under *Founding of the Guilds*, he read:

The Guilds were founded by five cousins who wandered into an enchanted valley in the North of England. There dwelt an immense dragon. The dragon slept atop a mountain made of precious jewels. The wanderers, upon discovering the treasure, and being unaware of the dragon, began chipping pieces from it to carry away with them. The dragon awakened with a roar, demanding to know who dared steal his treasure. To save themselves, the cousins swallowed the stones they'd stolen. They were magical stones that conferred on them amazing powers, but also made them slaves to the dragon and tied them to the high valley known as Raven's Ghyll.

The cousins served the dragon for seven long years. At night, they conspired together, even though the dragon slept with one eye open. The wizard wrote a covenant of mutual protection that they all signed in blood. The sooth-sayer warned them that they must not kill the dragon, but only put it to sleep, or they would lose the powers they had acquired from the magical stones. The enchanter sang to the dragon, distracting it while the sorcerer brewed a pow-erful sleeping potion. To the warrior fell the task of pour-ing it in the dragon's ear.

The plan worked perfectly. It wasn't until the cousins were celebrating their victory over their erstwhile master that the wizard revealed that the covenant they had signed made wizards masters over the other guilds. If the covenant were broken, the dragon would wake and exact terrible vengeance on all of them.

Thus were founded the Five Guilds.

Jack felt as though he'd wandered into a fairy tale. He opened to the middle of the book and read the following verse:

In heighe midsummer Gareth came forth in faire array
For werre, with horse and horsemen, all verray,
His lust for battle was his fortune and his bane,
For a thousand spears rode out against the Weirlind
His haire shown brilliant as the dying sun
His cause was lost before he'd e'er begun
Forever bound to do a wizard's will
His sweet blood would water Raven's Ghyll.

Well. That was clear enough.

In the back of the book was a compendium of charms, recipes, and incantations. He settled back to read.

It was after two A.M. when he finally turned off the light, his head filled with the spark and mystery of his ancestry. And when he slept, a warrior with red-gold hair charged through his dreams.

The next morning in homeroom, Jack was more lethargic than usual. He felt as if he had been up and fighting all night. He drowsed, waiting for morning announcements. High school is incompatible with a secret life, he thought as he shook himself awake for the third or fourth time.

He looked up to see Ellen Stephenson twisted around in her seat watching him. His stomach did a kind of complicated gymnastic backflip, and he sat up straighter, trying to look alive, if not alert.

"You look beat," she said.

She, in fact, looked great in a white tank top and jeans.

"Were you up late last night working on that math homework?"

"Math homework!" He groaned. "Right. I need to finish that!" *Start it, more like.* He pulled out his math folder. Maybe he could get a few problems done before homeroom was over.

"Would it help to look over what I've done?" Ellen extended her math folder.

"That's okay. I guess I'd better figure it out on my own. But, thanks."

"Okay." She returned the folder to her book bag and rested her arms on the back of her chair. She'd been out in the sun; the skin on her arms had turned pale gold, and a few freckles had surfaced on her shoulders. "So you weren't working on math, then. You have a part-time job or something?"

"No." Jack shook his head. "I've had some other things I've been working on. Special projects," he added, when Ellen frowned. She was an honors student, so she was in most of his classes. All of his classes, he realized suddenly.

"I've been watching you in soccer practice," she said, the words coming out in a rush. "I mean, watching the team. You're pretty good, especially at midfield. But don't let them put you in at fullback, is my advice."

Jack rummaged for a mechanical pencil and a halfway intelligent response. "Thanks. You seem to know a lot about soccer."

"I used to play forward and goalie at my old school," Ellen replied. "But I couldn't go out this year. By the time I moved here, tryouts were already over." Girls' soccer was a fall sport at Trinity.

"Well, maybe you can try again in the fall." *Brilliant. Bet she never thought of that.*

Jack pulled out his math assignment sheet. He hesitated, tapping the pencil against the page. "Listen, would you want to stay through practice tonight and go to Corcoran's afterward?"

She bit her lip, then smiled. "That'd be great. Only . . . do you mind if Will comes along?"

"Will?" Jack hadn't realized Ellen and Will even knew each other.

"Well, I was talking to Coach Slansky, and offered to help with the soccer team, and he said Will was planning to do some drills with the JV team, and so we were going to get together after practice and talk about it." She shrugged. "We could probably do it another time, but . . ."

"No, that's okay. We'll all go." A threesome wasn't exactly what Jack had in mind, but if Will and Ellen already had plans, then . . .

At practice, Jack was less than impressive. He was over-conscious of Ellen's presence and fearful of unleashing some kind of magical display. "You feeling okay, Jack?" Fitch asked, during one of the breaks. "You look like you're kind of stiff or something."

"I think maybe I pulled a muscle at practice yesterday," Jack said. "It'll work itself out." It was a relief when practice was over.

He looked for Ellen, wondering if she'd noticed how badly he'd played. In fact, she was standing by the concession stand talking to Will, absently juggling a soccer ball with her feet. She obviously knew what she was doing.

They took a corner booth at Corcoran's, ordering sandwiches and milk shakes. Fitch was sitting by the front window with Alison, his on-again, off-again Goth girlfriend from St. Catherine's, the Catholic high school. She broke up with him whenever Mars was in retrograde. Something like that.

Ellen and Will launched into a discussion of soccer strategy and players and possible dates and places for drills. Ellen kept trying to draw Jack into the conversation, but he contented himself with watching her.

When she talked to Jack one on one, she seemed awkward and self-conscious, as if she were navigating by unfamiliar stars. But now that the topic was soccer, she lit up with enthusiasm, sketching out ideas on a piece of notebook paper, teasing Will about his size and athletic prowess.

"Has he always been this big?" she asked Jack, nodding at Will. "I mean, he doesn't exactly have the body for soccer."

Jack squinted at Will appraisingly. "I guess he was a little smaller in preschool. But he's good at any sport. He'd be named captain, or his dad would be coach, and pick me for his team." He grinned. "And then, of course, we'd win."

Ellen was scanning the menu again. "Let's get ice cream," she said.

Will stood and picked up his check. "I've gotta go. My mom'll have supper on the table." He nodded at Ellen. "We'll try for Tuesdays, then, unless it conflicts with Mr. Hastings's schedule. See you, Jack."

Ellen looked from the menu to Jack inquiringly.

"I've got no plans," Jack said, grinning, knowing Becka would be late. "When do you have to be home?"

She shrugged, smiling back. More at ease than he'd seen her before.

Their ice cream came, along with Corcoran's trademark caddy of sundae toppings. Ellen poured on hot fudge and caramel sauce, nuts, and whipped cream. Jack did the same.

Someone slid into the seat next to Jack. "Hi, Jackson." It was Leesha Middleton in a fuzzy white sweater and tight pink jeans.

Jack moved over reluctantly, trying to put space between them. "What do you want, Leesha?"

Leesha looked around, surveying her audience. "I wondered if you wanted to hang out later."

"I'm kind of busy."

"You're not going to be busy all night, are you?" She smiled at Ellen patronizingly and put her hand on Jack's thigh.

He looked down at it, back up at her. "Lobeck have the flu or what?"

"*You* should talk. No offense, but I don't think you want people to see you with your rebound, here. Talk about pathetic."

Ellen rose to her feet. Jack thought for a moment she was going to storm out. Instead, she picked up the pitcher of hot fudge and poured the contents onto Leesha Middleton's pink jeans and white fuzzy sweater.

"Oops." Ellen sat down again and went back to eating her ice cream.

Leesha screamed, a sound that could have been heard in Canada. Every eye in Corcoran's was on her. She slid out of the booth and swiped ineffectively at her jeans with a paper napkin. Then plucked at her ruined sweater with her thumb and forefinger. "You . . . you . . . I can't believe you did that!"

Ellen licked whipped cream from the back of her spoon and looked back at Leesha calmly.

Leesha was tiny, but she appeared to expand, like an amphibian taking on air, then she drew herself up and retrieved her pink leather purse from the bench next to

Jack. It was smeared with fudge, too. "You'll pay for that, I promise you," she said to Ellen in a voice that raised gooseflesh on the back of Jack's neck. Then she turned and walked out of the restaurant.

For a moment, Corcoran's was totally silent.

Ellen looked across the table at Jack's sundae. "Are you going to finish that?"

⊛ CHAPTER SEVEN ⊗
BEGINNER WARRIORING

The next day was Wednesday, the day of Jack's first warrior training session. That in itself made him apprehensive. Plus, news of the events in Corcoran's had spread like wildfire. Ellen was Fitch's new hero. Will couldn't believe he'd missed it by mere minutes. Lobeck careened about the campus, taking out freshmen and other small objects. Leesha looked positively combustible. But Ellen herself was out sick.

After practice that afternoon, Jack was helping collect the balls for Coach Slansky, when he noticed Hastings on the sidelines. He was dressed to play, in a windbreaker, soccer shorts, and athletic shoes. Jack gathered up his water bottle and gym bag and was headed in his direction, when someone touched his arm. It was Ellen.

He blinked at her. "I thought you were sick." She did look rather pale.

"Well . . . ah . . . I'm better, I guess," she said, as if the question had taken her completely by surprise. "Look, could we go somewhere and talk?"

Jack looked across the field to where Hastings stood waiting, then back at Ellen. "I'm sorry, I can't right now. I'm supposed to work out with Mr. Hastings."

"With Hastings?" She looked from Jack to the wizard and back. "I didn't know you were working with him."

"This'll be the first time." He shrugged apologetically. "Listen, I could stop by later if you want. I don't know how late I would be, but . . ."

She shook her head. "No, that's all right. I . . . I just had some questions about the homework I missed. I can get it from the hotline." She turned and walked away quickly, shoulders hunched, as if against bad weather.

He watched her cross the soccer field toward the parking lot, then walked on to where the wizard was waiting for him, having no doubt watched the entire performance.

"Who was that?" Hastings asked, nodding toward Ellen's retreating back.

"Ellen Stephenson. She's in my homeroom," Jack said stupidly, still wondering what had just happened.

Hastings frowned, looking after her. Then he turned his attention to Jack. "Are you ready to go? Your mom okay with this?"

Jack nodded. His mother would not be home from the office until late anyway.

Hastings directed Jack to a black Volvo with New York plates in the parking lot. Jack threw his gym bag in the back and climbed into the shotgun position. The interior was pristine. Not a sports sticker or scrap of paper, no fast-food debris in the backseat. Not one clue to chip away at the mystery of the man. Hastings pulled out of the lot and headed back into town.

"Are you from New York originally?" Jack asked politely.

"I've moved around a lot," he replied. "Most recently I've been in New York."

"Have you always been a teacher?"

"Teaching has been one of my roles, though not in what you might call traditional settings."

"How do you know my aunt?"

They were stopped at a light, and Hastings turned and frankly studied him for a moment, as if judging how much Jack already knew. "Linda and I are old friends," he said.

"And you came to Trinity to take Mr. Brumfield's job?" Jack persisted. He was finding it hard to reconcile workaday jobs with the role of wizard. He thought of the wizard in the graveyard, and couldn't imagine him working as an accountant, say, during the week.

"I came to Trinity to teach you, Jack," Hastings said. "My work at the high school provides access and a convenient cover. That's all."

Jack stared at him. This deadly-looking man had come all the way to Ohio from New York to teach beginner warrioring? "But why would you do that?" he demanded, before he realized how rude it sounded.

To his surprise, Hastings colored a little, as if he were embarrassed. "If you must know, I suppose it was because

I couldn't say no," he replied, staring straight ahead.

"Oh." Had Linda bewitched him? That seemed unlikely. Jack decided it was time to move to safer ground. "Where are we going?"

"I've joined a health club. I've arranged for some private court time."

The fitness club was in a complex of office buildings close to the interchange. Jack could see people running around a track through a wall of glass windows on the second floor.

The reception area was crowded with people coming in to exercise after work. Hastings keyed in a code on a keypad on the counter. They walked past a large gymnasium, into a back hallway lined with racquetball courts, aerobics studios, and workout rooms. Hastings produced a key and opened one of the doors.

It looked like a racquetball court with a highly polished wood floor, but it had one mirrored wall. Jack dropped his gym bag by the door.

"What's this room used for?" he asked.

Hastings smiled. "Fencing. Appropriate for us, wouldn't you say?"

Jack shrugged. "I wouldn't know. I'm not at all sure what kind of material we're going to be covering." He knew he sounded irritable, and he didn't care. All of this intrigue was beginning to get on his nerves.

"You warriors are impulsive people," Hastings replied with just a bit of an edge to his voice. "You're going to have to learn patience, among other things. We're going to take care of your control problem today." He shed the windbreaker to reveal a T-shirt underneath. Hastings had appeared tall and angular when Jack had seen him at school. He was surprised to find that the assistant principal was layered in muscle, despite his lean build.

"I understand you've had no schooling whatsoever." It was not really a question.

"Right. No schooling." Jack removed his sweatshirt, revealing the vest underneath. Hastings gestured impatiently, and Jack shed the vest, also, leaving his T-shirt.

The wizard walked around him, studying him from all angles. "How long since you've taken the Weirsbane?"

"What?"

"The preparation Dr. Longbranch gave you."

"Oh. A week, maybe."

Hastings grunted. "Have you used your powers in the past?"

"Well . . ." Jack hesitated. "Whenever it's happened, it's been . . . accidental."

Hastings nodded. "When you were angry? Out of control?"

Jack thought of the episode in the graveyard. It was hard to say how much magic had been involved there. "Well, angry or scared, I guess," he admitted.

Hastings drew a small object from his shorts pocket and held it up for Jack to see. It appeared to be a top, finely enameled and decorated with an intricate pattern of symbols and pictographs. Hastings set it on the bench before the mirror. "Set that spinning," he ordered, standing aside, hands on hips. Apparently Jack was to do it from where he stood.

"What's that got to do with—"

Hastings's breath hissed out in frustration. "Look, our time together is limited, and you are getting a rather late start as it is. Just do it."

Jack regarded the top doubtfully. "*Right*," he mumbled. He tried to focus all of his attention on the target, tensing up and gritting his teeth with no particular strategy. "Move!" he whispered to himself. The top sat stubbornly motionless. Jack shrugged. "It's not working."

"Try to relax. Don't hold your breath. Picture the top spinning."

Jack tried again, acutely aware of his teacher's scrutiny. The top didn't move.

"Let's try this." Hastings unzipped his bag and pulled from it two lightweight foils, corked at the ends. He handed one to Jack. "Just do your best to keep my point away from you." With no further instruction, he poked Jack, hard, beneath the rib cage.

Jack brought his point up and tried to parry the blows that now came thick and fast. Again and again, Hastings hit home—shoulder, chest, back, stomach—effortlessly. Despite his best efforts, Jack could not seem to protect himself or land a blow. Gradually, Hastings drove him backward until he was defending himself from a corner.

Jack grew more and more annoyed. This man was supposed to be a teacher, wasn't he? He knew he needed training, so why humiliate him? He took another hard poke in his rib cage, and something in Jack uncoiled itself. It was as if hot energy had been collecting unnoticed in his arms and fingertips. His sword arm came up, and flames erupted from the end of his blade. Hastings's foil clattered to the floor.

Instantly Hastings's other hand came up, flinging an arc of what looked like powdered gold. It hung, glittering, in the air. "Now look!" Hastings commanded. He caught Jack's elbow and turned him until he was facing the mirror.

Jack was at the center of a radiant star described in glitter, his body surrounded by a shimmering outline.

"Now shut it down," Hastings said.

Keeping his attention focused on the image in the mirror, Jack began to draw inward, as if he were inhaling a dream. Slowly the star dissolved before his eyes until only traces of glitter caught the light, and then went out.

"That's the process we want." The wizard looked amused. "Now you have to learn to access the energy without the provocation. And control it when you are provoked. Use your sword arm, if it's helpful. You must perceive the flow of energy in order to manage it. It's like steam building in a boiler. You need to release it before it explodes." He nodded again at the top on the bench. "Try again. Now you know what it feels like. Locate the energy. It won't take much. Then direct it through your fingertips."

Jack closed his eyes and sketched a small picture of the top in the vacancy before his eyes. He painted in the colors, the mysterious lettering on the side. Then he set it spinning in his mind, faster and faster, until the colors bled together into an exotic blur. He felt a tingle in his hands, like blood returning, energy bleeding from his fingers.

When he opened his eyes, the top was spinning prettily about a foot above the bench.

"Now stop it," his teacher directed.

Without closing his eyes this time, Jack drew back, allowing the top to settle gently onto the scarred wooden surface of the bench. It spun silently for a moment and then coasted to a stop. Hastings flung up his fistful of gold again. There was a soft brilliance about Jack this time, less distinctive than before. Jack consciously re-sheathed his weapons, and the image dissipated as before.

There followed several similar exercises, where Jack raised magical energy, then dispersed it. Finally, they spent some time working with the foil, beginning with classic fencing moves, then adding the element of magic. Jack learned to hold on to the power, then channel it into the blade and send flames spinning from its tip at will. This raised a question: he remembered the way he had felt in the graveyard, the marriage of flesh and metal, recalled his successful attack on the wizard, and wondered how much he had contributed to it.

"I have a sword. The Shadowslayer, it's called. What I'm wondering is, how much magic is in me, and how much is in the sword?"

At first it seemed there would be no answer to his question. Hastings frowned and passed the two foils to Jack without comment, indicating that he should return them to the bag. He also handed over the top and a soft suede pouch.

"The top's a wizard's toy," Hastings said. "You can use it to practice control at home. There's more of the shimmer powder in the bag." Jack put both items into his gym bag. "Self-awareness is the first step. Practice is the key. Soon you will manage your power intuitively, and that more than anything will keep you safe. Then we'll move on to other things."

"Aunt Linda told me not to use my powers, that it would send up some kind of a signal."

"She means you should not use them for entertainment. Of course you must practice, or you'll never get any better. Magic isn't a tool to be used recklessly or thoughtlessly. It must be harnessed to an intellect strong enough to control it. Talk to Snowbeard. If your house is not already warded, he can make an arrangement." Hastings studied him, hands on hips. "Do you know who you're hiding from, Jack?"

Embarrassed, Jack shook his head.

Hastings frowned and rubbed his chin with his thumb. "We'll continue to meet to work on your skills, Mondays, Wednesdays, and Fridays. I'll be working with some of the other soccer players as well, so it will be perceived as nothing unusual." The wizard was issuing orders again, almost unconsciously.

Hastings turned to the door, but stopped, his tall frame filling the doorway. "The Shadowslayer is one of the Seven Great Blades, forged by the sorcerer Althis Mac at Raven's Ghyll more than five centuries ago. The other six have been lost. The pommel is a piece of the Ravenshead. There is tremendous power in it, and it was made for your hand. Others can wield it, but none so capably as the heir, properly trained." He paused. "There is considerable power in you, too, Jack, despite your unusual history. With the weapon you have, and the proper training, you could be . . . impressive.

"Let's go."

The lesson was over.

❧ CHAPTER EIGHT ❧
THE APPRENTICE

Jack grimly advanced on Hastings, body angled to present a smaller target, elbow up and blade extended to prevent escape to the right, his small shield protecting his chest. The wizard kept him honest, made him work for every forward step. Steel came together, shrieking and sparking, and when Jack thought he had his teacher trapped in the corner, Hastings spun away from the wall, blade hissing toward Jack at waist level. Jack had to leap backward to avoid it, and Hastings was on the outside again, with the room at his back, and Jack against the wall.

"This . . . room's . . . too . . . small!" Jack gasped, forcing him away once again.

"You'd never get near me in a bigger room," the wizard replied, teeth flashing in a smile, although they had been at it for more than an hour. "You can't always pick *where* you fight, or *who* you fight . . . or even . . . *how* you fight. But do the picking . . . whenever you can." Still teaching, but his breathing was noticeable now, and perhaps he was slower in blocking blows, parrying the flames. So maybe he *was* winded, just a little. "We're going to have to end this . . . you know. Your mother . . . is expecting you."

"Do you yield?" Jack's shoulder was numb from the hundred collisions it had already absorbed. He was feeling the weights on his wrists and ankles, designed to build muscle and ready him for a heavier blade. Even the foil was growing heavy, or maybe it was his arm, almost too heavy now to lift.

"Your mother . . . can wait a little longer."

Slowly, Jack drove Hastings across the room until he was once again in a corner. Jack thrust forward with his sword hand, and Hastings moved to parry it. At that moment, Jack straightened his shield arm, which exposed his chest but freed his nondominant hand. Flames spiraled out from his fingertips, and Hastings's foil hit the floor. Hastings raised his hands in surrender. "I yield, Warrior," he said, smiling.

Jack let his point drift to the floor. "Thank God," he said. He snatched up a towel and swabbed off his face. His hair was plastered to his head and his shirt was soaked. The floor was slick with sweat. The room stank of it.

"Next time we'll work some more with the axe," the wizard promised. "I think you're beginning to master two-handed play."

"We were playing, were we?" Jack grinned. "That's the

first *plaisance* I've won." He felt the need to point it out, in case Hastings hadn't noticed.

"You've come a long way, Jack." Hastings was always sparing with compliments, and followed with a demand. "How are you coming with your reading?"

"I've been trying."

"I didn't ask you to *try*."

Jack scowled. "It's like Shakespearean English without the poetry," he complained. The work with the wizard was mostly physical, but Hastings had recently given him a slim volume called *Rules of Engagement*. It was the bible, where Weir tournament warfare was concerned, addressing elements of garb, weaponry, and battle etiquette. The weaponry was explicitly limited to medieval hand weapons, such as swords, slings, maces, and so on.

Hastings didn't respond, so Jack persisted. "I don't understand why they haven't updated them."

"The rules are intended for tournaments," Hastings said patiently, wiping off the foils, returning them to their case. "They are not meant to be modern. Weapons are not allowed to overshadow the skills of the warriors."

"But aren't some weapons better than others? What about Shadowslayer? What's fair about that?"

Hastings shrugged. "That's a special piece. But still within the rules."

"What about the rest of it? You can't deny that's out of date." He pulled the book out of his gym bag and thumbed through it. "Listen to this: 'Enchanters were created for the entertainment of wizards.' And, here: 'A wizard guarantor may choose to keep and protect an enchanter in exchange for service rendered.' That can't be right. And the rules governing the relationships among the guilds are unfair. They all favor wizards." He'd heard of things like that, obsolete city ordinances that were still on the books. Rules that prohibited interracial marriages or riding horses into church, for instance.

"You don't have to like the rules," Hastings pointed out. "They were written by wizards, so of course they are biased. And I didn't ask you to read the whole thing. Only the tournament regulations."

"Those are bad enough. What's all this about calling up dead warriors for practice bouts? Why is it necessary to have a rule that only live warriors can be used in battle?"

"We'll talk about that when the time comes." By now everything was packed up. "We'd better get going. You're late already."

Jack could tell Hastings was losing patience, but somehow he couldn't stop himself. "I don't understand why I have to learn about tournaments, anyway. Do you think a wizard is going to challenge me to some kind of duel? I'm more likely to be taken by surprise. Maybe you should be teaching me weaponless warfare, like tai chi."

"Maybe I should. Perhaps I shall. But I didn't come here to debate with you. Let's go." Hastings laid a hot hand on his shoulder, pushing him out the door.

It was always this way. The wizard never answered his questions. Hastings was relentless in coaching him about every aspect of his new trade: weapons, equipment, conditioning, and strength training, but shared nothing about his own background.

Jack had tried to ask questions early on about Hastings's family, about where he'd received his training. He'd been met with a stone wall. The focus was always on Jack. He sometimes had the feeling that Hastings was working him like a problem, gradually peeling layers away until he was entirely revealed. Or maybe whoever he used to be was being stripped away. He just wasn't sure who had taken his place.

He hadn't heard from Aunt Linda since their trip to Coal Grove. She'd abandoned him to Hastings. Was she still running from Wylie? What if he had caught her?

He wished she would call. He felt lonely and ill at ease. Even his relationship with Nick had changed. In the old days, the apartment over the garage had been a sanctuary. Now, some nights he went directly from lessons in warrioring to lessons in wizardry without a break. Like this evening.

Nick's voice broke into his thoughts. "Remember, of all the Weir, only wizards can use charms to harness and control magic. For the other guilds, magic is personal and hands-on. More of a physical power. Less versatile. Are you listening, Jack?"

"Less versatile," he repeated dutifully, biting into another chocolate chip cookie. It seemed he was always starving lately.

"Wizards are sophisticated crafters of magic, which is why they have been able to dominate the other Weir for centuries." Nick found a marked passage in Jack's Weirbook. "Now, let's go over what we covered last week. *Transformare:* the art of turning one thing into another."

They were working their way through the Weirbook, chapter by chapter. Spoken charms for moving objects about, confusing the enemy, barriers, and attack charms. Charms small enough to try out in the apartment over the garage.

"When are you going to teach me some love charms?" Jack asked, thinking about Ellen.

"We'll save that for when you're older and more responsible," Nick observed dryly. "Charms of ensnarement are entirely too tempting for the average adolescent. You'll just have to rely on your own *personal* charm for the time being."

"I'm just trying to be efficient," Jack growled. "Between soccer and school, and warrior and wizardry training, plus reading all the books you give me, there's no time for anything else." It seemed that Nick had new books for him every week—treatises on magic, potions, and philosophy—dusty volumes that must have lain unopened for years.

"There's always time for the most important things," Nick said mildly.

"Don't give me that time management crap." Jack sighed and put his face in his hands. "All I do is study and work out with Hastings. I never sleep. My grades are slipping. I mean, am I going to have to study like this forever?"

"Wizardry manifests early, remember," Nick replied. "Most apprentices begin working with this when they are very young. You have a lot of catching up to do. And because of your warrior stone, your powers of wizardry are relatively weak."

"Maybe I should just quit school, now that I'm learning a trade." When Nick didn't respond to this, Jack rose and began pacing the room. "I don't understand why I have to do it at all. Aunt Linda told me I have to be ready to defend myself against someone who might attack me. I don't know who and I don't know when. Frankly, I don't think anyone is after me at all. Maybe Wylie was after the Shadowslayer and I just happened to be in the way. I'm only sixteen, and I've only been in training for a couple of months. Any wizard would be stupid to think I was a threat, or much of an asset, either."

He paused. "Mom says any time you buy weapons, or build an army, you begin to look for an excuse to use them. Plus, you pose more of a threat to others. The more training I get, the more likely it is that someone will come after me. That's what I think." He looked sideways at Nick, to assess his reaction to that theory. He'd been working on it for some time.

"So. Linda hasn't told you about the Game," Snowbeard said. "Sit down, Jack." Jack sat down in the chair opposite the old wizard. He had a strong premonition of bad news coming.

"Conflict among wizards is highly ritualized, of necessity," Nick began. "Otherwise we would destroy each other, no? In fact, we almost did. Fighting is used to allocate power, in particular, control of magical artifacts. The Wizard Houses gain power through a win. Originally, there were actual battles between armies raised and led by wizards. But it has evolved into a series of tournaments. They use warriors as surrogates. They call it the Game.

Only, for warriors, it's no game at all. It's a fight to the death.

"These days warriors are hard to come by. They are the rarest of the Weir, and getting rarer, because they are killed off so quickly. Fewer tournaments are held these days due to lack of players. And when one side locates a warrior, the other side does its best to kill him off."

Jack shook his head in disbelief as Snowbeard continued. "There is actually a black market in warriors and other nonwizard Weir. They call it the Trade. Warriors fetch the highest prices. There are traders who work full time reading genealogies, following up leads, hunting warriors down, and kidnapping them to sell for profit. They try to find young warriors like yourself who are just beginning to manifest, who don't yet realize who they are."

"They buy and sell people?" Jack was appalled. "They can't do that!" he said. "It's illegal."

Snowbeard smiled ruefully. "I wish that were true. But anyone with enough power can do whatever they want. And wizards are a powerful and arrogant lot. From a wizard perspective, the other guilds are a servant class with specific talents. Those who believe that look on them as property, and therefore a tradable commodity."

"About how many warriors are left?"

Nick looked him in the eyes. "Well, at the moment, there's you, that I know of," he said gently. "There may be others that I don't know about."

Jack opened his mouth, but no sound came out. He was suddenly aware of sweat trickling down between his shoulder blades, despite a pleasant breeze through the window.

Now things were coming clear to him. Why his aunt was convinced wizards would eventually come after him. Why Leander Hastings would come all the way to Trinity to train him. Why Nick Snowbeard was living over his garage. Why Dr. Longbranch would . . . A shudder passed through him.

"Aunt Linda said Dr. Longbranch implanted the warrior stone in me because she wanted to see what would happen." Jack leaned forward, his hands gripping the arms of the chair. "She was trying to create a warrior, wasn't she?"

"I suspect she was," Nick said quietly.

"So I'm some kind of freak. The Frankenstein of the wizard world. Why didn't Aunt Linda tell me?" Jack demanded.

The old wizard stroked his beard. "Linda feels . . . responsible for you. She is the one who got Dr. Long-branch involved in the first place. She did it to save your life. But your situation has been very difficult for her."

"Difficult for her?" Jack was on his feet again. "Difficult for her? Is that why you're all hanging around, you and Mercedes, and Iris and . . . and all the rest? Because I'm so damn *valuable*? Are you all hoping to cash in?"

Nick sat, his gaze steady and kind, until Jack finally dropped back into his seat, flushed and embarrassed. "Although we are not warriors, we are all people who disapprove of this system. Rather like conductors on the Underground Railroad. We're here because you're in danger.

"That's why we started the training. It was the best plan we could come up with. Believe me, it's a tremendous advantage that you can do some wizardry. It can't hurt to have a few surprises up your sleeve. If you are to survive, you must have weapons at your disposal beyond those that Hastings will provide."

Jack covered his face with his hands. When he closed his eyes, he saw an image of himself in shackles, being auctioned off at a slave market. An image of himself as a gladiator before a bloodthirsty crowd. "What do you know about Leander Hastings?" he asked abruptly.

If Snowbeard was surprised by the question, he didn't show it. "Hastings is what we call a Master, meaning he has expertise in a number of the magical arts. They are the best teachers, because they can develop students in a number of areas. Of course, most Masters have their specialties. Hastings specializes in warfare. But he is first and foremost a wizard. An unusual combination of talents perfectly suited to your situation," he added.

"How do we know we can trust him?"

"Leander Hastings is the best. He has an international reputation, though he has made a lot of enemies along the way." The old man cleared his throat. "I don't think it was easy for her to make that choice. You see, your Aunt Linda and Leander Hastings were . . . ah . . . *involved*, years ago."

Jack was stunned. He tried to picture the two of them together, his tiny, shimmering aunt with the tall, dark, and dangerous Leander Hastings.

"They're not still . . ." Jack didn't complete the sentence, but didn't have to.

"No." The old man replied quickly. "They haven't seen each other in years."

"Oh." Jack's anger was dissipating, and he was left with an overwhelming sense of hopelessness. "I asked Mr. Hastings why he was doing this, and he said something about not being able to say no. I'm not sure he wants to be here."

"Hastings wouldn't be here if he didn't want to be," Nick said bluntly. "Jack, don't try to understand the whole of it. It's too hard to deal with. Narrow your focus. Your job is to learn to use all the tools at your disposal. For instance—" Once again, the wizard pushed himself stiffly to his feet and shuffled into the next room. He returned a few minutes later with a package wrapped in soft leather. He handed it to Jack.

Jack unwrapped it. It was a mirror, framed in silver, decorated with dragons and wizards. It was familiar. Blaise Highbourne had given it to him as a baby present. It had been stowed away in the trunk under his bed for years.

Jack turned it over in his hands. "Where did you get this?"

"This may help you, now that you've been off the Weirsbane for a while. Blaise is a soothsayer. This is a mirror that shows the truth: in the past, the present, and sometimes the future. And sometimes the future."

"There's enough scary stuff in the present," Jack said. "I don't want to know about the future." He didn't look at the mirror.

"Take a look," Nick suggested. "Just keep in mind

that the meaning of the image is not always clear. That's the curse of prophecy."

Cautiously, Jack drew the mirror toward him, tilting it so he could look into the glass.

The image cleared, revealing two figures standing on a high bluff overlooking a river. Jack rubbed his eyes in astonishment, then turned his gaze back to the mirror.

He saw a young woman in a long dress, her red-gold hair flying free, and a tall, spare man facing her, his back to Jack. They were arguing furiously. The woman turned and tried to leap from the cliff, but the man pulled her back and forced her to the ground, pinning her. Jack wanted to look away, but was riveted.

The image changed, focused over the man's shoulder on the woman's face, her frightened blue eyes, her flaming hair spread across the rock. "No," Jack whispered, but still he could not look away.

The man in the mirror leaned forward and gripped the woman's shoulders. "Listen to me now. You're going to tell me where you've hidden the boy, and we're going to go and get him. And then I'm going to take you away from here." The voice was eerily familiar, but all Jack could see was the back of the man's head. Suddenly, the woman had a knife in her hands, as if plucked from the air. Turning the blade, she stabbed herself with it. The man gathered her into his arms, cradling her, rocking back and forth.

"Aaaaaaah!" Jack flung the mirror against the wall. It did not break, but slid down behind the bookcase.

"What did you see?"

"I saw some guy attack my mother, demanding to know where I was. Then she killed herself."

"Are you sure it was your mother?"

"Don't you think I'd know?" Jack shuddered. He retrieved the mirror from behind the bookcase and set it facedown on the table. "It's not even safe to look in the mirror anymore."

"How was she dressed?"

Jack considered. "Like . . . well, in some kind of period costume."

"So. Perhaps an ancestor then, who only resembles your mother. The mirror will try to tell you the things you need to know. But you have to interpret what you see."

"Look. I don't need to see that, okay?"

"All right, Jack. We'll let it be for now."

Jack tried to follow Snowbeard's advice in the days that followed, the part about focusing on the job he had to do. He didn't see that he had much choice but to press on. The worst part was the dreams. Jack began to put off going to bed until he was absolutely exhausted. Every night he struggled through battles with traders and monsters, friends and family who turned on him and sold him to the highest bidder. His friends, his teachers, relatives, neighbors, all circulated through his nightmares, playing different roles. During the day he felt jumpy and irritable, always watching his back.

His relationship with his neighbors had changed. He had begun to realize that all of Jefferson Street had a stake in him. When Mercedes waved at him from her front garden, he thought of the soft-spun vest next to his skin. When Iris brought snow peas to Becka, she smiled at him encouragingly, asked how he was doing, if he needed anything. Blaise made him a pair of gauntlets, trimmed in silver, engraved with the words STRENGTH THROUGH VIRTUE. He felt alternately safe and smothered in the fortress of Jefferson Street.

Something peculiar was happening to Jack's body. His shirts became tight across the chest and arms, and his jeans snug in the thighs. He told his mother he had begun a weightlifting program at school. She took him out to buy new clothes twice in as many months. Sometimes he would stare at himself in the mirror after his shower, transfixed. Jack had always been lean and physically fit, but now he was confronted with a muscular stranger.

He took to wearing flannel shirts and baggy jeans to hide the metamorphosis, which worked as long as the weather was cool. It didn't help when he was out on the soccer field, or in the locker room. It would have been funny if Jack weren't so apprehensive. Here he was trying to hide what most boys his age would be happy to show off. I look like a poster boy for steroids, he thought. He considered all the potions he was taking and wondered if he could pass a urine test.

Soccer, at least, was definitely going better, now that he didn't have to worry about blowing anyone off the field. Not that, it wasn't tempting sometimes. Garrett Lobeck seemed to be regaining his old arrogance where Jack was concerned. He still blamed Jack for his failure to make varsity. And Leesha's continuing interest in Jack didn't help. Wary of losing control, Jack did his best to avoid a confrontation. Naturally, Lobeck saw this as a sign of weakness.

Jack was playing better than he ever had. He was stronger, more aggressive, and quicker on his feet—more willing to take risks. It seemed the qualities that went into warrioring were just as useful in playing less deadly games. Jack's success didn't improve Lobeck's mood any.

Ironically, Jack's star seemed to be tracking upward on the Trinity High School social chart. These days, his locker was decorated before every game, and Jack had his own private cheering section. Girls Jack had known all his life found him suddenly and totally fascinating.

He was seeing a lot of Ellen, but always in a crowd. On the days he didn't meet with Hastings, he often stopped in at Corcoran's after practice. Ellen had become a regular there since she and Will began drilling the JV team.

Will and Ellen were good foils for each other. Will was endlessly patient with the least competent players, while Ellen played an aggressive, European-style, in-your-face game. Under their tutelage, team play improved dramatically. Even some of the varsity players had begun participating.

Will, Fitch, and Ellen had joined the Chaucerian Society, a medieval culture club Hastings had founded. They were planning a medieval banquet in an old theater downtown before school ended. Jack didn't participate. He was spending enough time with Leander Hastings as it was.

Jack was feeling more and more isolated by the burdens he carried and the secrets he kept, by mental and physical exhaustion and the unrelenting fear of exposure.

One afternoon, Jack and Will and Fitch lingered at Corcoran's after a win over McKinley. Ellen had been absent from school again, and Jack found himself worrying about her health. She'd seemed fine the day before.

Leesha had just left, having distributed invitations to her birthday party.

"Leesha still lusts after you, Jack," Fitch commented. "The princess wants whatever she can't have."

"Well, she'll have to get in line if she wants to make time with our Jack," Will drawled. "I can't count the girls who have come to me asking who he likes. And I just don't know what to tell them." He was sprawled back in his chair, long legs extended out in front of him. "You know Ellen's crazy about you."

Jack sat up straighter. "What do you mean? Did she say something? She hasn't said anything to me. Seems like I never even get to talk to her."

Will rolled his eyes. "She just can't deal with the competition. But seriously, Jack, we're just wondering what's going on." He leaned forward. "There's something really different about you. Physically, you look great. You've put on a lot of muscle. And you're playing great—better than I can ever remember."

Jack flinched and glanced around the restaurant. It was getting late, and the place was nearly empty. No one was sitting in a position to overhear.

"But it's like you're on another planet," Will continued. "You don't even hear us half the time. And you're constantly studying or working out."

Fitch had his pencil out and was sketching on a napkin. "You're never online at night anymore. One minute you're wired and the next you're falling asleep in class. I'd say you were in love, but girls throw themselves at you and you hardly notice. I wish you'd send some my way," he added. Apparently he and Alison were on the outs again, and Jack hadn't known.

"We're wondering if this has anything to do with the graveyard thing," Will said quietly.

Jack slumped down in his seat, resting his elbows on the table in front of him. He'd underestimated his two friends and their ability to strike so near the truth. *Don't trust anybody*, Aunt Linda had said. But she was the one who had involved Will and Fitch in the first place. As it turned out, he didn't have to say much.

Fitch nodded at Jack's lack of response, as if he'd confirmed it. He leaned back in his chair. "Has your aunt been back?"

Jack shook his head, not speaking.

"And you're not sleeping very well, I bet," Will said.

"I guess this isn't something you can talk to your mother about," Fitch said slowly.

Jack looked up sharply. Fitch's face was expressionless. Jack's friends were already in danger because of the episode at the graveyard and their relationship with him. And they had inherited no special gift. They had no magical weapons at their disposal. The less they knew, the better—for his sake as well as theirs.

"Look," he said wearily. "I appreciate your concern. I

really do. But it's a problem I'm going to have to work out on my own."

"I can't understand why we can't help you out with this," Will said stubbornly. He was always confident that his size and good will and skills of diplomacy could solve any problem.

Fitch pulled out a handful of dollars and scooped up his check. "We're not matchmakers, and I have my own love life to worry about. But seems to me you're not particularly happy. Why don't you try to have a little fun for a change?" He pushed his chair back. "Couldn't hurt."

❧ CHAPTER NINE ❧
THE BOUT

The next night Hastings drove Jack home from soccer practice to pick up his sword. He had the feeling that all of Jefferson Street was watching as they pulled up in the Volvo. To his surprise, Hastings turned off the ignition and followed Jack into the house. Becka looked up from her desk in the front parlor as they came in. She was barefoot, in jeans and a T-shirt, with her hair twisted into a clip on top of her head. She was working on her laptop with piles of papers all over the floor. She rose and came into the front hallway. "Hi, sweetheart. I didn't think you would be home so soon." She gave Jack a quick kiss, looking over his shoulder at his tall companion.

Jack had hoped to be in and out of the house without being noticed. "Uh, this is Mr. Hastings. He is the new assistant principal I was telling you about. He's the one who's been helping me out with soccer."

"Well, it's so nice to finally meet you," Becka said graciously. "It has been kind of you to spend so much time working with Jack. I've been to some of the games, and I can see how much progress he's made." She extended her hand.

Hastings took it in both of his and held on to it a few seconds too long. "Your son has a great deal of natural talent." He took in every detail of Becka's appearance in his intense fashion, and then swept his gaze around the room. "I've enjoyed working with him," he added.

Jack was anxious to get Hastings out of the house as quickly as possible. "I came back to pick up some stuff for practice," he explained, though no one seemed to be listening. He took the stairs two at a time. He could hear Hastings's voice behind him.

"I can see that your son takes after you," he was saying.

Jack removed the sword and scabbard from its box and managed to get it into the duffle bag from his closet. He added several towels from the linen closet for padding, and zipped it closed. When he came downstairs, Becka was leaning against the door frame, laughing at something Hastings had said, twisting a tendril of hair around her finger. The wizard was smiling, but Jack couldn't help but think there was something *predatory* in his posture.

"All set," Jack said, rather loudly.

"How late will you be?" Becka looked from one to the other.

"Is eight-thirty all right?" Hastings asked. "We're getting a bit of a late start."

"That's fine," Becka said. "Jack and I are flexible." And then they were finally out the door.

Jack put the duffle bag in the backseat and climbed into the front. "Where are we going?" he asked as the car pulled away from the curb.

Hastings didn't respond. He appeared to be lost in thought. Jack repeated his question.

"I thought we'd practice outside this time." As usual, Hastings didn't provide a complete answer. Jack soon realized they were headed for Perry Park. He had been there hundreds of times through his childhood. It was the largest and least developed of Trinity's municipal parks, heavily wooded and remote, with few hiking trails. It was an inland park, and the parks along the lakeshore always received the heaviest use, especially in the spring and summer.

Hastings seemed to know where he was going. After traveling several miles along the road, he pulled into a parking lot at one of the trailheads. There were no other cars in the lot. Hastings slung a small backpack over his shoulder. "Let's go. Bring the sword."

They hiked for perhaps a mile and half into the woods. Hastings maintained a rapid pace, offering little but directions. When a stream intersected the trail, Hastings walked up along the streambed for a few hundred yards, then struck off to the right through the woods again until they came to a small clearing. It appeared as if the trees had been felled some years ago. Small shrubs were beginning to fill in here and there, but it was mostly tall grasses and some brambles, as Jack quickly discovered. The late-day sunlight streamed down into the meadow. This, then, was their destination.

Jack set the duffle bag on the ground and unzipped it. He delivered his sword from its nest of towels, strapped the scabbard around his waist, and cinched it tight. He drew his weapon. It felt good to have it in his hand again. He turned it this way and that so it caught the light, then moved gracefully through his stances, adjusting to the larger blade. As before, it felt light in his hand, weightless. Hastings watched this for some time, occasionally making a suggestion.

"We're going to have to handle your training differently now that you're using the Shadowslayer," he said finally. "I cannot serve as your opponent. We'll do the best we can with the tools we have." There was a brief flash of a smile. He opened his backpack and pulled out some metal stakes and a hammer. He walked the perimeter of the clearing, pounding in nine stakes in all. Then he stood at the center of the meadow and spoke some words in the now-familiar language of wizardry. Jack tried his best to commit the words to memory. An eerie silence descended. Jack realized that he could no longer hear the sounds from the surrounding forest. The area outside the boundaries marked by the stakes became smudged and surreal.

Nick had said that Hastings was a powerful wizard, but his teacher had never displayed his abilities until now.

Hastings walked back to Jack. "That will keep anyone from interfering with us," he explained. "I will be sending some warriors against you. Your job is to defend yourself against them, and kill them if you can."

Jack was bewildered. "Warriors? What are you talking

about?" He looked wildly around the empty clearing.

"Don't worry. Think of it as a kind of video game, but on a rather . . . larger scale." The wizard stepped to the side of the clearing, leaving Jack alone in the center. Moments later, a massive man in a tunic and leggings punched through the smudged boundary at the far end of the meadow. His fair hair was plaited into braids that hung to his broad shoulders, and he sported a robust red beard. He carried a large axe in one hand and a sword in the other. He wore neither armor nor helmet. He looked a bit disoriented at first, but then his eyes lit on Jack.

"What is this? They send a mere child against me? Go back to your mother, boy, until you've grown!" he shouted. Jack glanced helplessly over at Hastings, who stood calmly, feet apart, arms folded, at the edge of the trees.

Receiving no answer from Jack, the man strode toward him, swinging his axe as he came. It seemed light in his hands, like a toy. The insults grew louder and more colorful. "Go back to she that whelped you, before I send you to hell!" the man shouted.

"Is he real?" Jack shouted to Hastings. Hastings said nothing.

The man was now close enough that Jack could see the beads that decorated the plaits in his hair and the broad metal bands that enclosed his massive arms. His stench was overpowering, a reek of sweat and steel and raw physical power.

"Is he real?" Jack shouted again desperately. There was no answer.

And then the man was upon him. In a sudden panic,

Jack raised his sword to block the blow, but it was too late. The man had his axe up, it was descending. Jack felt a cold pain at his shoulder, and there was a darkness before his eyes. When his vision cleared, he was flat on his face in the grass. He'd landed in a patch of brambles, and thorns pierced his palms and forearms. When he lifted his head, he saw that the man was gone.

"Well now, Jack," Hastings said from the sidelines. "I'm afraid you've been beheaded. Not a good start." He sounded amused.

Jack scrambled to his feet, picking briars out of his skin, his clothes. "It would have been nice to know the rules of the game before we started!" he fumed.

"But you know the rules of the game," Hastings replied. "We've been studying them all along. The Rules of Engagement. Now you just have to apply them."

"He cut off my head, but I'm still alive," Jack pointed out.

Hastings shrugged. "Those are the rules of this particular game, under the charm I used to call him up. We can't afford to lose you in practice. Let's try again."

He nodded to the end of the clearing again. This time a man on horseback entered the clearing, wearing chain mail and carrying a lance.

"Give way!" the man roared. "Or die today!"

Somehow, Jack knew that he was not expected to give way. He searched for his sword in the tall grass and retrieved it. "Dismount!" he shouted back. "As you can see, I'm on foot!" He hoped the other man would see that there was no honor in trampling him.

The knight clambered down from his warhorse. He wore a helm and hauberk, but his face was uncovered. He appeared to be in his twenties or thirties, clean shaven and quite handsome. The man approached with his blade drawn, a mace swinging from his other hand. Jack raised his sword and flowed into a fighting stance. Shadowslayer flamed up, eager for blood, and Jack was astounded to see that his opponent looked a little frightened.

His words were bold, however. "Give way, boy. I think ye must be squire to some brave knight who comes behind you."

"There's just me," Jack replied, wishing devoutly that he did have a backup.

"Well then, prepare to defend yourself!" The man charged forward, sword extended, but Jack was ready this time, and parried the blow. There was a tremendous strength behind it, and the blow shook Jack's arm to the shoulder. He ducked, and the mace sang as it cleaved the air where his head had been. He spun flames from his own sword, and the man blocked them with his blade. Jack thrust him backward with a concussion of air.

Jack felt more confident now. Although the man was definitely stronger, Jack was quick on his feet, and the routine was familiar from the bouts at the fitness center. After several minutes of well-matched swordplay, Jack put a bolt through his blade that sent the knight's sword flying and knocked him to the ground. The man sat up, looking dazed, his sword arm hanging useless. No one was more surprised than Jack, who glanced over at Hastings for further instructions.

"Finish him," his teacher said.

"No," said Jack, lowering his sword and backing away.

It was the knight's turn to be surprised. After a few seconds, the knight dissolved and was gone. His horse, too.

Hastings strode onto the field, eyes glittering. "You did an excellent job in that last bout," he said. "An excellent job. Now, why couldn't you follow through?"

"I don't want to kill anybody," Jack explained, shrugging his shoulders. He'd never expected to be apologizing for it.

"That is your gift, Warrior," Hastings snapped. "Killing people. Get used to it."

"Well, maybe I don't want this gift," Jack said. "I never asked for it." He angrily stuck his blade into the ground and folded his arms.

The wizard's voice softened a little. "I told you to think of it as a video game."

Jack shivered, looking around the meadow, then stuck out his chin stubbornly. "This is no video game," he replied.

"Well, it's nothing like a real battle," Hastings said. Jack was struck by the bitterness in his voice. Once again, Jack wished he knew something more about his teacher, where he'd come from, and what drove him. There was a brief, uncomfortable pause.

"Who are they?" Jack asked, meaning his opponents.

"They are warriors," Hastings replied. "Champions from the past, long dead. Under the rules, they are trapped in the next world. Thus, they are available to us for training when I call them." He rubbed his jaw. "As you know, there are not many live warriors left to joust with. Perhaps the modern word is scrimmage."

So that was what the passage in the rules had meant. That means you can't ever get away, Jack thought. Not even after you're dead. "Who wrote these rules, anyway?"

"They are part of the covenant, signed by representatives of the five guilds at the founding."

Jack recalled the story in his Weirbook of the dragon and the five cousins.

Hastings put his hand on Jack's shoulder, and Jack could feel his power like electricity into the bone. "What will you do, Jack, when someone really tries to kill you?" he asked.

"Then I suppose I will kill them back," Jack replied.

"You can't kill them back," Hastings said. "Because by then you'll be dead."

Jack got the point. "So I suppose I'll have to kill them first." And Hastings seemed satisfied with that answer.

By the time they'd left the meadow, Jack had fought ten opponents, and his record was six and four.

From then on, Jack and Hastings practiced at the meadow at least twice a week. Sometimes they went on a Saturday, so they could spend more time. Jack was always bruised and exhausted after these bouts, and as the weather grew warmer, he discovered that fighting was hot and thirsty work.

Hastings never pressured him again to finish off someone he'd disabled, but Jack gave and received some serious blows in the heat of the fight, some of which were "mortal" on both sides. The cuts he survived were painful when he received them, so he assumed his opponents felt the same. Once the bout was over, however, nothing remained but the aches and pains. Part of the rules of the summoning, Hastings explained. The wizard carried a bottle of fiery liquid he gave Jack to drink once or twice after a particularly difficult bout. It killed the pain remarkably well, though Jack suspected it didn't comply with Trinity High School's zero tolerance drug and alcohol policy.

His record was continually improving, although Hastings always seemed to have new challenges to throw at him. Sometimes he fought two or three warriors at a time. Sometimes, his opponents were women. That took some getting used to, but he found those bouts were as tough as any of his other fights. Once, he fought a teenager only a little older than he was. He was in a more modern style of dress, perhaps from the nineteenth century. Jack disarmed him fairly quickly.

"He was pretty young," he commented to Hastings. "And poorly trained."

"Yes, he was," Hastings replied.

"Are warriors often as young as me?" Jack asked.

"And younger," said Hastings grimly. And he would not say more about it. Jack had quit asking questions about a lot of things. He still didn't understand how learning to fight with a sword would protect him from his wizard enemies. It wasn't as if he could walk around Trinity with a sword on his hip. He felt that he was being prepared for some kind of challenge, but had no idea what. More and more it seemed like his life was under the control of others, particularly Hastings. Aunt Linda had abandoned him. He felt like a schizophrenic, with a foot in each of two worlds: the exquisite normalcy of school and the risk and mystery of the Weirworld. Dull acquiescence seemed to alternate with a bright anger that was more and more difficult to control.

His love life was out of control, too, and at the same time totally unsatisfactory. Although Leesha was officially going out with Lobeck, it seemed Jack was back on her A-list. She never missed an opportunity to come on to him, no matter who was around. As a result, Jack was on Lobeck's list, too. A different list.

Ellen seemed as stressed and preoccupied and touchy as Jack. She'd stepped up her skills clinics with the team as the season progressed, drilling them with an increasing intensity. She and Hastings functioned like competing assistant coaches.

And then several things happened in rapid succession right at the end of the school year that put the new cadence of his life in disarray.

THE STREET FIGHT

Soccer season ran into June, and the Trinity varsity team made the playoffs. Jack was a starter, playing midfielder and forward. Will played defense, and Fitch played goalie and midfield. The district championship game against Benjamin Harrison High School was scheduled the same night as Leesha's birthday party. Jack contributed the winning goal from midfield, but twisted his ankle. The final score was three to two.

The locker room emptied out quickly, since most of the team was going to Leesha's party. Jack took his time, because he wasn't particularly eager to get there. By the time the trainer finished wrapping Jack's ankle and he had showered and dressed, he was alone. The party was a few blocks west, at the Lakeside Club. Jack limped to the parking lot, wishing he'd thought to catch a ride, and not looking forward to the walk to Leesha's.

Someone stepped out of the shadows in the entryway of the building. Jack flinched and brought up his hands up in defense.

"Jack! It's me." It was Ellen. She stood with her back to the lamppost, her face in shadow.

"What are you still doing here? Everyone's gone."

"I wanted to . . . to say good game, Jack. You were awesome."

"Oh. Well, thanks." He felt inordinately pleased. "I wasn't sure if you'd come."

She rolled her eyes, as if to say, *Duh!* "How's your ankle?"

"It'll do. Be a little stiff, I guess." He rotated his foot to demonstrate.

"That's good." She straightened then, and said briskly, "Well, good night." She turned to go.

"Wait," Jack called. Ellen swung back around. "When can we get together?"

She glanced around, as if she thought he might be talking to someone else. "Get together?"

"Yeah, you know. Hang out. Now that soccer season's over, we'll both have more time."

She shrugged. "What are you doing now?"

"I . . . ah . . . was going to Leesha's party."

"Happy birthday, Leesha." She turned away again.

Jack caught her arm. "Let's do something else."

She stuffed her hands in her jeans pockets, rocking back on her heels, looking down her long nose at him. "Are you serious? Isn't she expecting you?"

"Look, give me a break, Ellen. Leesha and I are not together. She totally creeps me out."

Ellen looked down at her feet and pushed a rock around with the toe of her sneaker. Then she looked up and smiled crookedly. "All right. What do you want to do?"

Jack cast about for ideas. "I could walk you home."

She raised an eyebrow. "You're injured."

"I'll lean on you."

If Jack leaned on Ellen more than was strictly necessary, she didn't object.

The air was soft and muggy as they exited into the parking lot, promising summer ahead. Ellen and Jack walked down Bank Street and headed for the square. Jack realized he didn't even know where Ellen lived.

"I live close to the lake," she explained when he asked. "On Walnut. In one of those apartment buildings."

They walked on in silence for half a block, moving slow, though Jack's ankle was loosening up.

"What do you want to do when you graduate?" Ellen asked. "If you could do anything you wanted."

"Me?" Jack thought a moment. "Well, I used to think I'd sail around the world."

"Are you a sailor?"

Jack nodded. "My dad and I used to sail all the time. He lives in Boston now. He has a sailboat there, and we're talking about building another."

"You must be close to your dad."

"Not really. I haven't seen him for nearly a year." Ellen didn't question him further, which was one of the things he liked about her. "Have you ever been sailing?"

She shook her head.

"I'll take you sometime this summer, if you want. I mean, I guess I'm going to be in England for most of the summer, but—"

"England!" She stared at him. "Are you going with Mr. Hastings?"

"No, my mother is teaching a course there. Something about British influences on Appalachian culture. What about Hastings?"

"He's taking the Chaucerian Society on a tour. Will and Fitch are going. I thought you knew."

Jack shook his head. He really was losing touch. "What about you? Aren't you going?"

She shook her head. "No, I can't go. I'm going to be away all summer. At camp." She released a long breath and looked up at him, as if debating whether to go on. "I might not be back in the fall."

Jack felt like his insides were collapsing. "What? Why not?"

"My dad's on temporary assignment with Ohio Power." Ohio Power had a plant just outside Trinity. "The time is about up. So we'll most likely be going."

He stopped walking and turned to her. "Ellen. I'm sorry. That sucks."

"I wanted to tell you before. I've known for a while." She shrugged. "We've moved around a lot. I'm used to it."

Jack had always thought that living all his life in a place where everyone knew his history was a disadvantage. Now he wasn't so sure. "You'd think he could stay in one place until you graduate, at least."

"Yes, well." She shook her head. "I wonder if we'll ever see each other again."

Jack's own future looked a bit cloudy at the moment. "We have till I leave for England, at least. We'll try and make the most of it."

By now they had crossed the square and turned on to Lake Avenue.

"Do you know how to dance?" she asked as they reached the public beach parking lot. He looked up, startled by the question. She rushed ahead. "I mean, I don't know how to dance, and I thought if you knew how, maybe you could teach me. Or if you don't know how, maybe we . . ."

She stopped in midsentence. Jack looked up to see someone in the parking lot. Three someones. It was Garrett Lobeck and his two friends, Harkness and Leonard. They were leaning against a pickup truck with an open case of beer in the bed.

"Well, if it isn't the hero of the game," Lobeck sneered. "We looked for you at the party. Wanted to make a toast." He finished what appeared to be the latest of many beers, crumpled the can in his fist, and tossed it on the ground. He fished another out of the case and Jack heard the *"poosh"* as he opened it. "Leesha was looking for you, too. She was really pissed."

"Oh. Well. See you tomorrow," Jack said. He nodded to Harkness and Leonard, who were on the varsity team. "Good game."

He took Ellen's arm and started to make a circle around the trio, but Lobeck moved into Jack's path. "Who do you think you are? Your cheap shot kept me off the varsity team."

"Go away, Lobeck," Jack said wearily. "Forget about it, will you?"

"I'll forget about it when I've had a shot of my own," Lobeck lunged forward, swinging at Jack; but the combination of the beer and Jack's quick sidestep sent his fist sailing past Jack's right ear. Like a large truck, it took a while for Lobeck to get turned around again. "Stand still and fight!" he bellowed.

"I don't want to fight you, Garrett," Jack replied. He shot a sideways glance at Leonard and Harkness, to see if they were going to join in. They were blocking his path, but just watching for now. He jerked his head at Ellen. "Ellen. Go. Please."

Ellen clenched her fists. "Don't be idiots. Jack's your teammate. What's the matter with you?" She looked ready to throw a punch herself.

You're not helping, Jack thought. If there was going to be a fight, he didn't particularly want Ellen there to see it.

"Oh, so now his girlfriend is going to protect him." Leonard laughed, a harsh, wheezing sound. Sensing blood in the water, they were beginning to circle, like sharks in a feeding frenzy. It wasn't looking good.

Lobeck charged him again. Jack managed to avoid the blow a second time, but then someone grabbed him from behind and pinned his arms. It must have been Harkness. "Hit him once, and then let's go." The voice came over his shoulder, along with a noxious whiff of beer.

Lobeck was on his way, a murderous look on his face,

and Jack had a feeling he wouldn't miss this time. He remembered a confusion charm, something from his lessons with Nick. He spoke the words quickly, under his breath, and Lobeck's mad-dog expression turned to one of bewilderment. He looked from Jack to Harkness and back again. "Now, what was I doing?" he asked, completely clueless. He started stumbling aimlessly down the sidewalk.

"Hey!" Harkness called after him. "Are you gonna hit him or what?"

Lobeck swiveled back around. "What?" His bleary eyes took in the scene. "Oh, yeah." He headed back in Jack's direction.

Great. Jack wrenched free of Harkness and turned in time to see Ellen slam both feet into Harkness's right kneecap. Soccer training paid off, apparently.

Harkness yelped and fell back, clutching at his leg; but by then Lobeck was incoming. His right fist smashed into Jack's cheek and right eye with stunning force, and then his left, and right again plowed into Jack's middle. Jack saw stars and felt blood flow, warm and wet, into his nose. It was as if the bones in his face had been driven into his eyes. He stumbled forward a step, desperately sucking in air to replace what had been driven out of him. And then rage and instinct took over.

He swept his arm forward, fingers extended, and a concussion of air pounded into Lobeck's midsection, sending him flying to land, hard, on the blacktop.

Anger still flared in Jack, and power, white and hot. He snatched up a large tree branch, holding it across his body like a quarterstaff, and advanced on Lobeck, who lay on his back, momentarily stunned. As awareness returned, disbelief crowded onto his face, and then fright. He pushed up on his elbows, scuffling with his feet, trying to scramble backward out of danger. He came up against the low stone wall that ran along the perimeter of the parking lot. Not a tall barrier, but tall enough to trap him. Jack stood over Lobeck, feet braced apart. A shimmering flame ran along his weapon as he raised it above his head, turning it vertical for the killing blow.

"Jack! No!" Ellen's voice cut into his blood rage. He shook his head fiercely, focused on the task at hand. Lobeck's eyes were wide and his mouth was moving, pleading or praying, he couldn't tell.

"Jack! Oh, God! Jack!" Ellen gripped his elbow and wrenched his arm back with amazing strength.

Self-awareness flooded in. Dismayed, he flung the burning branch away from him. It flew end over end in a high arc, clear across the parking lot, a flaming pinwheel that extinguished itself in the lake. He drew in a painful breath and turned back to the others.

Harkness sat on the blacktop, doubled over, holding his leg, swearing softly. Leonard gaped, openmouthed at Jack and Lobeck. He showed no eagerness to mix in. Ellen stood as if rooted to the ground, hands raised, face pale and horrified. Lobeck propped up on his elbows, looking like the end of a very bad day. For a long moment, nobody moved.

Jack's eye was already swelling, so he could scarcely force it open, and blood poured from his nose and welled up inside his mouth. He wiped the back of his hand across his face, and it came away bloody. "Let's go," he muttered to Ellen, using the other hand to take her by the arm. She gasped and recoiled from his touch, and he quickly released her. "I'm . . . I'm okay now. Promise. Let's get out of here."

None of the three boys made any move to stop them.

The walk to Ellen's house was miserable. His face was on fire and every breath hurt. He'd failed at his most important task: keeping his magical powers under cover and under control. Ellen was probably scared to death, and no wonder. He had come within a heartbeat of killing a drunken Garrett Lobeck in a street fight. What was he turning into?

Perhaps his use of power had already exposed him. His luck couldn't hold out forever. It was a beautiful night under a full moon, the party at Lakeside just letting out. Anyone could have been walking along the lakeshore and seen what had happened. He looked about warily. Nothing moved on the quiet street but him and Ellen. Their long shadows extended out ahead of them, collected under the streetlights, and then stretched out again.

There were at least four witnesses. The human mind had a remarkable ability both to discount what it sees and make reality conform to expectation. And Lobeck and his friends had been well wasted on beer. But this was the second time he'd lost control with Lobeck. Hard to imagine he'd get away with it again.

Ellen was another story. She was perfectly sober and nobody's fool.

She didn't ask him any questions. In fact, she said nothing at all on the way down Walnut Street. Just walked ahead fiercely, head down, hands in her pockets.

"Ellen, listen, I—"

"Shut up, Jack."

So Jack occupied himself by thinking about what he was going to tell his mother.

By the time they arrived on Ellen's front porch, Jack had pretty much decided against attempting a kiss good night under the circumstances, with Ellen feeling the way she did, and with his face in the condition it was in. He'd been planning on it before the fight broke out.

Ellen glanced uneasily over her shoulder into the dark interior of the apartment. She seemed painfully eager for him to leave. Jack figured this wasn't a good time for an introduction.

"Good night, Ellen," he said, the words muffled in his damaged mouth. "I'm sorry about what happened. I had a great time up till then."

To his surprise, Ellen leaned in and brushed her lips over his undamaged cheek. "Good night, Jack," she said. "I'm sorry, too." Then she disappeared into the building.

When he arrived back on Jefferson Street, he had little hope his mother would have gone to bed. She'd been at the game, and he expected she would wait up for him for a little celebration and a rehash of the match. He was right. The Downey house was ablaze with lights. A big sign posted on the front door said, "Welcome home, hero!" He didn't feel much like a hero just at that moment. He reached for the knob, but the door opened before he could touch it. And the person in the doorway was Linda Downey.

"Jack!" she said, sounding delighted, and then "Jack!" again, horrified, when she caught a clear look at his face under the porch light. Then Becka was there, and the welcome home party turned into a first-aid and interrogation session.

"So you mean to tell me you were *fighting*? You know I've always told you to walk away from a fight." Becka had always had strong ties to the peace movement. Jack wondered what she would say if she could see what he had been doing in the meadow.

"Believe me, I tried to walk away. I don't usually pick fights with people twice my size."

"Oh, I don't know, Jack," Aunt Linda said. "You look like you might be able to hold your own against almost anybody." She had been staring fixedly at him, and at first he had assumed it was because of his swollen eye.

"That's not helping, Linda," Becka snapped.

"There were three of them," Jack explained to his aunt.

"Was it someone from Harrison?" Becka asked, referring to the other soccer team. "Or Harrison fans?"

"It was Garrett Lobeck and his friends. They're on my team."

"Then why would they want to beat you up?" Becka looked mystified. "Especially after that play you made?"

"It's hard to explain," Jack muttered. "It's kind of complicated."

Becka rose to her feet. "Well, I'm calling Bill Lobeck right now. I'm tired of those sons of his terrorizing this town." She reached for the phone.

"I wouldn't do that, Mom," Jack said hastily. "I mean, I'm not sure how Garrett's doing right now." Both women swiveled to look at him. "I kind of knocked him down. Then we left."

"Who is we?" Linda asked.

"Remember Ellen Stephenson, Mom? I was walking her home."

Becka was ready to call somebody. "Maybe we should call Ellen's parents, just to make sure she's all right," she suggested. "She must have been pretty frightened."

"Oh, I wouldn't say she was frightened, exactly," Jack said. Except of me, he thought. He almost smiled at the memory of Ellen going after Harkness, but it made his face hurt. "Listen. I don't think he'll bother me again. I'd really like to forget about the whole thing. I'm sure Garrett feels the same way."

"That sounds like a good idea," Aunt Linda said quickly. "Besides, we're having a party." She pointed to a large platter of shrimp on the table and bottles of wine and sparkling grape juice in ice buckets. A huge cake on the sideboard was inscribed with "We Are the Champions!" and a soccer ball.

"This is awesome," Jack said, grateful for the change in subject. "When did you do all this?"

"I was hoping to get here for the game, but my plane was delayed," Linda explained. "So we thought this would be a nice surprise."

"It's a great surprise," Jack said. "How long will you be staying?"

"I'm not sure," Aunt Linda replied.

Becka was pouring wine and grape juice into wine glasses. "It's good you came when you did. Much later and you might have missed us. Jack and I are leaving for England right after school is out."

"England!" Linda recovered quickly, accepting a glass of red wine. "You're going to England?"

Becka nodded. "Remember, we talked about it at your last visit. I'd hoped you could get us a lead on a house, but I haven't been able to reach you. But Thomas has a friend who has a cottage in Oxford. She'll be in the States all summer, so we're subletting. If you'll be home, we can visit you, but you don't have to feel obligated."

"That sounds . . . wonderful." Linda attempted a smile, but Jack had the sense that something was bothering her.

❦ CHAPTER ELEVEN ❧
UNDER SIEGE

The next morning was a Saturday, and Jack's class had scheduled an end-of-school excursion to Cedar Point, an amusement park on the lake. When he looked in the mirror in the bathroom, the right side of his face was an angry purple, and he could still hardly open his eye. *Great. I'll have to answer a thousand questions about this today.* He wished he could just stay home. But Will was supposed to pick him up in half an hour, and after their talk at Corcoran's, Jack was reluctant to cancel.

Aunt Linda was on the sunporch, drinking a cup of tea.

"Sorry I have to go out today," Jack apologized. "I wouldn't have planned it if I'd known you were coming."

"We can talk tonight, Jack. Have fun today." She looked subdued, almost as if she had been crying. "Did I tell you that you look different?" He nodded. "I probably notice it more than most people, because I've been away. You must be working out a lot."

"Three or four times a week."

"With Leander Hastings?"

"Yeah." He cleared his throat. "Where have you been all this time? I . . . I didn't know what to think. I was afraid Wylie had caught up with you, or something."

"I'm sorry. I laid a rather long false trail for him to follow. And then I had some . . . business to take care of, back home."

"You sound like you do this kind of thing all the time." Jack couldn't keep the bitterness from his voice.

"I have had considerable practice hiding from wizards, if that's what you mean." She started to say something else, but then there was a loud banging at the kitchen door.

"Come in!" Jack called. "We're on the porch."

"Jack! Where were you last night? We . . ." Will stopped in his tracks when he saw Linda. "Oh, hi, Ms. Downey," he said. Then he caught a full view of Jack's face. "Jeez! What happened to you?"

"I ran into Lobeck and friends after the game last night." That was going to be the short story, and Jack planned to stick with it.

"What? You win the game for us, and he clobbers you?"

"Just forget it. I think he'd had a few too many beers. Like a dozen. Which reminded him that he didn't make varsity."

"Is that why you didn't come to Leesha's party? She thought you were coming. Me and Fitch were looking for you."

Jack shook his head. "No. Actually, I was with Ellen. We . . . uh . . . decided to ditch the party," he said.

"Oh. All right, then." Will nodded. From his expression, he approved Jack's choice. "You didn't miss much. There were a lot of people drinking, a lot of people pretty messed up." Will raked his hand over his dark stubble of hair. "Maybe it's time someone taught Lobeck a lesson. Maybe I'll volunteer."

Jack blinked at him. Will's dark eyes were fierce and intent. Will had a certain *trajectory* about him. Like a great sailing ship, he was slow to turn, but once he got underway, look out.

"It's okay, Will. Really. I'm guessing he won't bother me again." Jack slung a small day pack over his shoulder. "I'm ready."

Will studied him a moment, shaking his head. "If you say so."

Fitch was waiting in the car, and Jack had to go through his story again. It was going to be a long day.

Ellen had promised to meet them around noon at one of the roller coasters. It was a beautiful day, hot and sunny, and Jack expected that practically the entire sophomore and junior classes and most of the teachers would be there.

Once they arrived at the park, Jack began to feel more cheerful. After some initial comments, no one asked too many questions about his face or the fight with Lobeck. The playoff victory made Jack something of a celebrity. He kept his eye out for Leesha, but didn't see her.

They rode on several of the bigger coasters right away,

assuming the park would be more crowded later on. Jack had always loved roller coasters, and he was beginning to realize that virtual danger had a lot more appeal than the real thing. By the time they sat in on a couple of the corny midway shows, it was almost noon, and time to meet Ellen.

She was waiting by the Blue Streak, wearing a white T-shirt, shorts, and flip-flops. When Will and Fitch tried to quiz her about the fight, she totally blew them off. Jack tried to catch her eye, to thank her, but she wouldn't look at him.

They rode the Blue Streak and tried some of the arcade games, and then it was time for lunch. They bought cherry slushies for dessert. It was getting hot, and the water rides beckoned.

"Let's go on Thunder Canyon," Will suggested. "It's time to get wet." He peeled off his T-shirt.

"I'm not done with my slushie." Jack lifted the paper cup.

"Let's leave them here," Ellen suggested, pointing to a broad railing by the lagoon. "The line isn't very long right now."

They all got soaked on Thunder Canyon. Since the line still wasn't very long, they rode twice more. They emerged, shaking like dogs, flinging water everywhere.

"You're not nearly wet enough, Jack!" Ellen grabbed his drink and threatened to empty it over his head. He threw up a hand, smacking her arm, and most of the contents cascaded into the fish pond below.

"Now look what you did!" Jack said, glad Ellen had

regained her sense of humor. It was practically the first time she'd spoken to him all day. He turned to see if the carp in the lagoon would go after the ice. Will was leaning over the railing, too, laughing, but then he looked puzzled. Jack followed his gaze. Dead fish were surfacing in a growing circle around the melting slush, their pale bellies shining against the murky amusement-park water. Hundreds of them.

For a moment, Jack froze, processing what he was seeing. Then his gaze met Will's, and the spell was broken. In one quick motion, Jack grabbed the cup with what was left of his drink and dropped it into the plastic bag he'd brought along for his wet clothes. He stuffed the bag into his day pack. Then he swept his arm across the railing, knocking the rest of the slushies into the lagoon. Ellen and Fitch wailed in protest when they saw their drinks fly from the rail.

"Sorry," Jack said. "My fault. I'll buy another round. Let's get lemonade this time." And he firmly ushered the still-protesting Fitch and Ellen away from the water. Will followed behind, shaking his head and frowning.

"This is interesting," Nick Snowbeard said, looking up from his microscope. He had set up a virtual chemical lab in his tiny kitchen. Jack and Aunt Linda were sitting at the kitchen table. Jack had put up a magical barrier so no one else would wander in. Nick was allowing his pupil to show off some of his accomplishments.

"It's an ancient Anglo-Saxon nerve poison. Fat soluble. Very quick and effective. Hard to trace. It takes very little." He stroked his beard. "I don't expect there's a carp left alive at Cedar Point."

"Who would have this kind of poison?" Jack asked. "Where would they get it?"

"It is plant-derived. It wouldn't be hard to make if you had the right ingredients. It's just not very well known. It must be someone in the family."

"If by family, you mean the Roses, then I think you're right on!" Jack exploded. "Who else would want to kill me?" He slumped in his chair.

"Who was at the park today?" Linda asked.

"Everybody I know," Jack said. "And a lot of people I don't." Leesha Middleton probably wanted to poison him just about now.

His aunt sighed, pulling her knees up under her chin. "Obviously, your secret is out to someone."

Nick was thoughtful. "Poison can so easily go astray. As it did in this case. Its a rather . . . inefficient way to kill someone."

Jack slammed his hand against the table. "They may have poisoned the entire western basin, but I don't think they'll lose any sleep over it. Don't you get it? *They know who I am! They know where I live.* What's to stop them from coming after me? Or Shadowslayer." He straightened in his chair. "One of the Seven Great Blades and it's hidden under my bed with my box of baseball cards. How long will it take to figure that one out?" He had a sudden urge to go back to the house, to make sure it was still there.

"I've set wards around the house," Nick said gently. "It

won't be easy to come after you here. And I'd be very surprised if they killed you outright."

"I feel so much better," Jack muttered.

"This might be some kind of warning. Or an attempt to panic you into running."

"Well, it's working."

Linda looked up. "Nicodemus. How is he doing with wizardry?"

"Jack has a surprising aptitude for wizardry, despite his warrior stone."

"Are we talking about parlor tricks and whimsy, or something he can really use?"

"He is much further along than that," Nick assured her. "He's done very well. He is not what I would call a powerful wizard, but he's more powerful than some who carry the stone. I've never seen anyone outside of the Wizard Guild who can do what he does."

"Tell me about your training, Jack," Aunt Linda said abruptly. Jack briefly reviewed the program, starting with the sessions at the fitness center and progressing to the bouts at the meadow. She frowned. "That's pretty much classical training," she said. "Didn't he cover anything else?"

Jack thought about it. "We spent some time working with a sling. There was some weaponless stuff, like wrestling and tai chi. I've been weight training on my own. But we've spent most of our time with the foils and with Shadowslayer at the meadow."

Linda hesitated before she asked the next question. "How is Leander Hastings as a teacher?"

"He knows what he's doing. He's been willing to

spend a lot of time with me, but he can be pretty demanding." Jack thought for a moment. "He has to be in total control. He answers only the questions he chooses to answer."

Linda nodded as if not surprised. "That sounds like Leander."

Jack couldn't help but think that it sounded like Linda as well. He was getting irritated at the interrogation. He had questions of his own he wanted to ask. Linda rose and began pacing back and forth in the small space between the table and the counter

"I don't think this trip to England is such a good idea," she said, not looking at Jack.

"What are you talking about?" Jack asked, surprised.

Linda spoke fast and persuasively. "If you go, Dr. Longbranch is going to want to see you. And I don't think that's such a good idea . . . as you are now."

Jack stood, feet slightly apart, arms folded. "Aunt Linda, I think it's time you were straight with me. People are trying to kill me. I think I deserve to know who and why."

"All right." Linda said, resting her hands on the back of her chair. "Do you remember I told you that the Weir has a history of fighting, mainly with each other?"

Jack nodded and sat down, suspecting that this was going to be a long and unpleasant story.

"There are actually two main branches of the family that have been battling for hundreds of years. It started with a pair of brothers. Do you remember the War of the Roses?"

"A civil war between two factions of British royalty. Lancaster and York, wasn't it?" Jack struggled to remember his British history. "Didn't that end with the Battle of Bosworth Field?" He and Nick had spent quite a bit of time on that. Understandably, the old wizard was an expert.

"Not for us. One branch of our family carried the red rose, and the other the white. For years after Bosworth, the fighting continued, with neither side really gaining the upper hand," Linda said. "By the sixteenth century, even the most bloodthirsty wizards of both houses realized things couldn't continue as they were. It was about that time that several hundred Weir immigrated to America to escape the ongoing warfare and the domination by wizards. They included representatives of all the guilds. We descend from that group of democrats, called the Bear clan. For those who stayed, a new system was developed, a system of tournaments."

Jack looked her in the eyes. "Nick told me about the Game."

Linda flinched, and her cheeks colored slightly. "The Game," she repeated. "So wizards were no longer involved in the actual fighting. The emphasis changed to recruiting warriors, training them . . . *breeding* them for certain powers and characteristics that would prove advantageous." She looked at Jack, then looked away. "Only, those efforts backfired. There was so much emphasis on the gift of power that they neglected the flesh and blood that carried it. Because of inbreeding, the line grew sickly, began to die out. That and the fact that warriors were dying in droves in the tournaments. Even the successful ones often didn't live long enough to have children."

"So why didn't they just stop fighting?"

"Lots of reasons. Tradition. Revenge. Control of a treasury of magical artifacts, the last of their kind. That's right," she said, noting Jack's reaction. "The winner of the tournaments takes control of the Wizard Council, which governs the guilds. Those who have come to power through the system are unlikely to change it. Our family is an aristocracy: privileged and idle, with little to do but spin intrigue.

"So, back in the 1700s, when they were running out of warriors in the Old World, someone in the European guilds must have remembered those who had left for America two centuries before. They have extensive records. They're really big on genealogy.

"The branch in America had severed its ties with the Roses, using the Silver Bear as our emblem. We have also intermarried extensively with Anaweir, people without the gift. As a result, not everyone inherits. Maybe that's why you were born without a stone. But many people in this branch of the family carry the gifts and are physically healthy. And they're vulnerable because they either don't know about their gifts or haven't been trained to use them. They are unaffiliated, which means they lack protection.

"So the Roses began tracking us down. They would find those who carried the crystals, particularly the warrior trait. And those people would disappear. They are particularly fond of stealing children and raising them for the Game. It was a long time before we understood what was happening. But there were some of us in the family who studied the old ways, who knew the traditions, who understood the significance of the Weirbooks."

"Where's the rest of the family?" Jack asked.

"All over," Linda replied. "There are still several big strongholds in Britain, but they are all over the world. These are really rich and powerful people, Jack. These are people who can see the future and control others. They have no trouble making a living."

Jack thought about his aunt, who always had plenty of money and no visible means of support. "Are you telling me these tournaments are going on all the time, and nobody knows about it?"

"Not so many anymore, because of the shortage of warriors. But they do go on." Linda shrugged. "The tournament system has worked well, from a wizard point of view. It saves lives and property. You see, wizards aren't allowed to attack each other under the Rules of Engagement, which haven't been changed since they were written in the sixteenth century. The other guilds, of course, are fair game."

Jack remembered the book of fighting rules Hastings had given him. "The rules. Oh, right. I have those." His day pack was lying on the table. He reached into the side pocket and retrieved the slim volume.

Linda reacted as if Jack had pulled a snake from his pack. "Where did you get that?" she demanded.

"Mr. Hastings gave it to me. I've been studying it."

"Well, you won't be needing it, because you won't be fighting anyone," his aunt said flatly.

"Then why do I have to go through all this training?" Jack stuffed the book back into his pack, more confused than ever.

Linda gripped his arm, blinking back tears. "Jack, I'm just doing my best, every day, to keep you alive. When you were born, I had to involve Jessamine Longbranch, or you would have died. She is the premier wizard of the White Rose. She gave you a warrior stone with the assumption that you will eventually fight for them. I managed to convince her that she should leave you where you are, that you could be trained later, that it would be difficult for the Red Rose to find you in Trinity." Aunt Linda smiled wanly. "You know I can be very persuasive. And up until recently, you've remained hidden.

"The premier wizard of the Red Rose is a man named Geoffrey Wylie. He was the man you met at the graveyard. Since the White Rose has known you were here all along, I can only assume Wylie's group is behind the poison. But it doesn't really make sense. If they know who you are, they'd only kill you as a last resort."

Nick nodded. "If a wizard wanted to kill you, he wouldn't poison you. He would act more directly. But Wylie wouldn't kill you. He would capture you and call a tournament. If the White Rose can't field a player, he would win by default." He rubbed his beard thoughtfully. "I haven't seen any sign of wizards in Trinity since the day of the soccer tryouts. If they're still in town, they're in hiding, maybe because of Hastings. I don't think we should panic just yet."

Linda frowned. "If Dr. Longbranch realizes the Red

Rose is on to you, she'll take you right away." She noticed Jack's lack of comprehension, and rushed on. "She'll take you for training. I know something of what they do to warriors to prepare them for the Game." Her voice trailed off, as if she suddenly realized to whom she was speaking.

"You're nearly grown, Jack. Dr. Longbranch won't wait much longer to take you in any event. So I contacted Hastings. He was the one who suggested we retrieve the sword and train you in secret. He thought Shadowslayer might make the difference, might level the playing field."

"Who exactly is Hastings?" Jack asked.

"I've known him for a long time. He descends from the Bear line, as we do. He is a powerful wizard, and he's always had a strong interest in warriors and warrior training. He has long been a defender of the lesser guilds, what are called the Anawizard Weir, or nonwizard Weir. I knew he would be an excellent teacher."

Jack was beginning to understand just how bleak the situation was. Trinity didn't seem safe at all anymore. It seemed too small a hole to hide in. Maybe it was time to leave town.

"Look, Aunt Linda, I have to go to England. My mother already bought the tickets. She's been talking for months about all we're going to do."

"Can you avoid seeing Dr. Longbranch?"

"I think Mom's already called her to tell her we're coming."

Linda looked resigned. "Then you're going to have to start taking Weirsbane again."

"No!" Jack stood, backing away from them. "I'm done

with that stuff. You promised."

"But, Jack, she's going to suspect something. The change in you has been, well, remarkable."

"I'm a teenager. Teenagers change." Jack shook his head. "I won't take it. I mean it. I'd rather die." Even as he said it, he was a little amazed at himself. He couldn't remember ever saying no to Linda.

Linda looked surprised, also, but kept any comment on it to herself. "All right, Jack. If that's how you feel."

The week after the Cedar Point trip was exam week, the last week of school. When Will arrived at Jack's house that Monday morning, he found the kitchen door locked. Looking through the screen, he could see Jack with his head down, asleep at the table, his cereal uneaten. Will had to bang on the door several times before Jack awakened, wild-eyed. When Jack saw who it was, he got up and let Will in, relocking the door behind him.

"So you're locking your doors now," Will observed. He motioned for Jack to finish his cereal and poured himself half a bowl. Jack looked terrible. His black eye was now turning green and yellow. There were dark circles under the other eye. He might be a physical masterpiece, but he looked like an emotional train wreck. "Were you up late studying social studies last night?"

"Social studies? Uh, yeah." Jack mechanically shoveled soggy cereal into his mouth.

"Fitch says he can get together with us tonight to study math. Ellen can't make it. I guess she has some relatives visiting all week."

Jack shrugged as if he didn't care one way or the other. "Okay."

"Listen, Jack." Will hesitated. "I was wondering if your problem is something the police could help with?"

It seemed to take a moment for Will's words to register. Jack stared at him. "What do you mean?"

"Well, I'm wondering if you and your aunt are in some kind of trouble. It seems like every time she visits, things happen." Jack didn't say anything, so Will hurried on. "My Uncle Ross is a sergeant on the Trinity police force. Maybe we could go talk to him. Just informally, you know. He might be able to give you some advice."

Jack shook his head. There was an air of resignation about him that bothered Will. "No, it's okay. Everything's going okay," he repeated unconvincingly. "We're leaving for England in another week or two."

Will nodded. "Well, you're not the only one who's traveling this summer. Did you know that me and Fitch are going to England, too?"

That roused Jack from his lethargy. "Right. Ellen told me. But I don't know much about it."

"Mr. Hastings set it up. The Chaucerian Society is spending a month in England. We'll overlap with you, because you'll be there most of the summer, right?"

Jack nodded. "I guess. But how can Fitch afford to go to England?"

"There was some private foundation. Mr. Hastings had us all writing essays. Fitch's was really impressive. We're all getting some support, but he's getting a full scholarship."

Just then Will heard someone descending the back staircase to the kitchen. It was Linda Downey. Will regarded her with a peculiar mixture of hostility and fascination. Will was convinced that Jack's beautiful aunt was somehow responsible for Jack's troubles.

"Hi, Jack. Hi, Will." Linda greeted them warmly, but her smile faded when she saw Will's expression. Jack was oblivious. "I'll drive you two boys to school."

Will was disappointed. He had been hoping for private time to talk to Jack, to try to get to the bottom of the events at Cedar Point, to try to persuade him to talk to Uncle Ross. He couldn't think of any other way to help.

Jack nodded. "Sure, okay," he said, as if it were all the same to him. "I'll get my book bag."

Aunt Linda had rented a small silver sports car this trip. Ordinarily, Will would have begged for a chance to drive it, but this time they rode the short distance to Trinity High School in silence. Linda pulled up in front of the high school. As Jack climbed out, Linda leaned back over the gearshift toward Will, speaking so only he could hear. "Please keep an eye on him, Will."

Will looked up in surprise. She was close, very close; she had those impossibly blue eyes fixed on him, and she looked absolutely serious, almost pleading.

Oh, God, he said to himself, feeling the blood rush to his face.

She extended a slip of paper. "Here's my cell phone number. Call me if anything unusual happens."

"Sure. Okay." Their fingers touched as he accepted it. Reluctantly, he slid away, across the seat, and unfolded himself onto the sidewalk. He stood uncertainly, clutching the paper in his hand, watching as Linda drove away.

After that, Will found it difficult to concentrate on his exam, and was almost grateful when time was called. He and Jack turned in their social studies books and walked back to their lockers to collect materials to study for math. Jack's locker was next to Will's, and it was standing open. It looked as if it had been ransacked. "I must have left my locker unlocked," Jack said to Will, shaking his head. "I'm really losing it."

And then suddenly Penworthy was there. "Mr. Swift, I need you to come to the office immediately." Penworthy looked so nervous he was literally twitching.

Jack blinked at him. "Is it about my locker?"

"You might say so." The principal's mouth twisted up into a knot of distaste whenever he stopped speaking.

"It's all right," Jack reassured him. "I don't think anything's missing."

"I told you to come with me," the principal repeated. "You can leave your things here." Something in his tone made Will swing around to watch. Penworthy was practically pushing Jack down the hallway, and Jack was looking back over his shoulder at Will. Mystified, Will trailed along at a discreet distance. The principal hurried Jack to the front of the building and into the administrative office. Will walked into the outer office just in time to see Penworthy's inner office door close. The secretary looked up inquiringly.

"Uh, I'm waiting for someone to pick me up," Will said. He sat down in a chair by the door. "They'll be here any minute." Linda's words came back to him. *Keep an eye on him, Will.* She was counting on him. He didn't plan on leaving until he found out what was going on.

When Jack entered the principal's office, he saw two men seated at a small table. They were dressed casually in sweatshirts and jeans. Both looked to be in their thirties, rather rough looking. One was dark with a stubble of beard, and the other was blond and clean shaven with a prominent scar that ran down his jawline. Both looked like they worked out. They rose in unison with matching puzzled expressions when Jack came into the room. "You're sure this is him?" one of them asked Penworthy, nodding at Jack.

"This is Jackson Swift," Penworthy said deferentially. He sat down behind his desk and motioned Jack to an empty chair across the table from the two men. Jack took the seat, watching the two men warily. The men studied him as if they were seeing something unexpected.

Each of the strangers produced a leatherette folder that flipped open to reveal a badge. The dark man spoke. "Jack, I'm Brad Hansford, this is Mike Sowicky. We're with Narcotics, Trinity Police Department. We'd like you to answer a few questions."

Jack was baffled. He knew several of the police officers on the Trinity force, including Will's uncle Ross, but he'd never seen either of these two before. He looked from one to the other of the men, and then over at Penworthy. The principal's hands were leaving damp spots on the desk blotter. "What's this all about?"

Sowicky spoke up this time. "Jack, we searched your

locker this morning and we found this." He tossed two plastic bags onto the table. One contained a green leafy material, the other a handful of pills and capsules.

"Wait a minute!" Jack protested. "I never saw that stuff before in my life."

"That's why we want to talk to you, Jack. We'd like to clear this up." It was Hansford, the dark detective again. His voice was soothing.

Jack's mind was slow to process, empty of useful thought. "Why were you searching my locker?" he asked finally, buying time.

"We received a tip that you might be involved in drug trafficking," Sowicky said. "So we contacted Mr. Penworthy, here. He's been a great help." He smiled at the principal, who looked distressed and important at the same time.

"Look, you have the wrong person. I don't sell drugs!" Dreaming. I must be dreaming again, Jack told himself. Only, how to wake himself up?

"Where'd you get the black eye, Jack?" Sowicky asked. "Are you in some kind of trouble?"

Jack started to say something, but thought better of it. He knew he was in serious trouble, and he couldn't understand why. Who would want to plant drugs in his locker? Sure, there were some people who wanted him dead and others who wanted to take him captive, but why would anyone want him to go to jail? He struggled to think clearly, but his brain seemed unusually sluggish.

These would be undercover cops, given the way they were dressed. But weren't they supposed to offer him a lawyer before they started asking questions? He tried to puzzle it out, but his mind wouldn't respond.

Hansford was speaking again. "Why don't we go down to the station house, ask you a few questions. We've already called your parents. They said they'd meet us down there."

"But I have an exam in two hours!" Jack said, then felt stupid that he'd said it.

Hansford smiled. He was definitely the friendlier of the two. "With any luck, we'll clear this up, and you'll be back here in time to take it."

Jack closed his eyes. Something fluttered in the back of his mind, like tiny wings. No, not wings. Words. A soothing litany. *Go to the station house. Talk about it. Everything will be fine.* He stiffened. They said they'd talked to his parents. But his dad was in Boston. Not a chance they'd spoken with him. And his mother would insist on driving him herself.

And then it came to him. He opened his eyes. Hansford was looking steadily at Jack, concentrating, and Jack could feel the power that was being brought to bear. *Go to the station house, everything will be all right,* the insistent voice said.

The men were wizards.

Jack took a deep breath, fighting back panic. Above all, he knew he must not reveal what he knew about the deadly game being played. His only advantage was the fact that they thought he was just an untrained high school boy.

It must be the Red Rose. His gaze slid to Penworthy. A

whole school full of Penworthys wouldn't be enough to stop them. He needed help.

Jack stood up. "I think I'm going to be sick," he announced, clutching at his midsection. And it wasn't far from the truth. "I need to go. I'll be back in a minute."

The wizards stirred unhappily. "Why don't we just get going, Jack?" Hansford suggested. "You'll feel better as soon as you're out in the fresh air."

"I'm serious," Jack replied, his voice rising. "I'm going to barf."

Penworthy leaped to his feet. His office was carpeted in pale peach. "The restroom is just two doors down. You two can go with him if you like."

Reluctantly, Hansford and Sowicky followed Jack into the outer office. Will was sitting in a chair by the door and looked up when Jack emerged from Penworthy's office accompanied by the two "detectives." Will was about to say something, but at that moment Jack caught his foot around the leg of a chair and fell practically into Will's lap. With his mouth next to Will's ear, Jack whispered, "Will, I'm in trouble. Find Hastings, quick. Tell him." Hansford and Sowicky each grabbed an arm and lifted Jack to his feet and out the door.

Will sat for a moment, dumfounded. Hastings? What did he have to do with anything? But he got to his feet quickly, recalling the desperation in Jack's face. "Where's Mr. Hastings?" he demanded of Miss Prentiss, the secretary, who was staring avidly after Jack and his escort.

"Well, I'm sure I don't know," she replied. "I know he's

in the building, but it's exam week, so everyone's schedule is a little—"

Will put up a hand to stop the flow of words. "Look, it's important. I've got to find him right away."

Penworthy appeared in the doorway of his office, nervously straightening his tie. "Mr. Childers, I don't like the tone you're taking. When we see Mr. Hastings, we'll let him know you're looking for him."

Will turned and glared at the principal, reached out and put a hand on Penworthy's shoulder. Given the difference in their sizes, the gesture was eminently threatening. "I'm not playing around, Mr. Penworthy. If you know where he is, you need to tell me, or . . . or everyone's going to be sorry." Both the secretary and the principal stared at Will, who never raised his voice to anyone.

Penworthy took a step back, swallowed, and seemed to shrink even further. "I don't know where he is. He might be helping with some of the exams. The intercom's still broken, so you'll have to look for him."

"Who were those men and where were they going with Jack?" Will demanded.

"They're police officers. They're taking him to the restroom. He's not feeling well."

"If you see Mr. Hastings, tell him Jack Swift needs his help." Will spun on his heel and charged out of the office.

It seemed like a hopeless task. The building was huge, and Hastings could be in any of a hundred classrooms. Because the classroom doors lacked windows, that meant opening a hundred doors. He went down the hallway at a trot, throwing open doors, startling proctors and test takers, asking everyone he saw if they knew Hastings's whereabouts. Finally, he rounded a corner and practically ran into Fitch.

"Whoa, watch it, Will. If you run over someone, there could be casualties." Fitch stopped laughing when he saw Will's face.

Will explained the situation in a rush. Time was passing, and he was getting nowhere.

"Look," he said to Fitch. "You keep looking for Hastings. I'm going to call Linda. She gave me her cell phone number."

He sprinted to the bank of phones outside the cafeteria and dialed. She answered almost immediately. From the background noise, it sounded like she was in her car.

"Ms. Downey, this is Will. Jack's in some kind of trouble. He sent me to look for Mr. Hastings, but I can't find him."

There was a moment of silence. Then Linda's voice snapped over the phone. "Where's Jack now?"

"The last I saw, he was leaving the principal's office with two men."

"Will, listen to me. We'll be there as soon as we can. Find Hastings." And she clicked off.

Jack's two captors kept a tight grip on him. Their hands burned his skin through his shirt. He thought they might try to force him outside right then and there, but the hallway was crowded with students, and Jack doubled over, complaining loudly about feeling sick. Somebody—Jack didn't know who—called after him. Jack didn't look back.

The two wizards headed for the restroom, apparently taking Jack at his word.

Hansford was still playing his mind games. *You feel fine, Jack,* the voice inside his head said. *Just cooperate, and everything will be all right.* Once in the restroom, Jack locked himself in a stall and made a great noise of retching. He had no idea what Will would do with his message. What if he couldn't find Hastings? Jack had made up his mind he wasn't going anywhere with Hansford and Sowicky. It just didn't seem that there was any future in it.

The wizards were growing impatient. "Come on," Sowicky said, pounding on the cubicle door. "Let's not prolong this."

"Give me a minute," Jack said through the door. "I don't want to puke in your car."

"We don't care, Jack," Hansford said. "It's time to go. Your parents will be wondering where you are."

"Listen," Jack said weakly. "Maybe I could come down with my parents a little later. After my exam. They'll want to call their lawyer anyway."

"You won't need a lawyer," Sowicky said bluntly, then added hastily, "because this is very informal. Now come out now, or we're coming in after you."

Jack considered his options. A restroom stall door wouldn't keep the two wizards at bay for long. He debated trying one of the attack charms Nick had taught him. Only, he knew he wasn't terribly powerful in wizardry, and he had no idea what he was up against. He decided it might be better to continue to play dumb until they got outside, then try to take them by surprise where there was less risk to other people and a better chance of escape.

He flushed and unlocked the door. But as soon as he stepped through the doorway, Sowicky slammed a hand against his throat, pinning him against the frame of the stall, cutting off his air supply and effectively silencing him. He heard Hansford speak a charm, and it was as if hot metal had been flushed through his veins. All his limbs were suddenly too heavy to lift. An immobilization charm, if he read it right. Too late.

And then Sowicky jerked him away from the wall and slammed him facedown on the floor; somebody's knee was in his back, and one arm was being twisted back painfully behind him until he thought his shoulder would give way. Then the other arm, and something was being clamped over his wrists, binding them tightly together.

Time moved slowly now, and all of his senses were on full alert. The familiar school restroom stench was in his nose, the ceramic cold against his bruised face. There was dirt in the grout between the gray and burgundy tiles on the floor, Trinity High School colors. He had a split second to wonder if that would be the last thing he would ever see, if they would kill him then and there. Then he realized that they probably wouldn't bind his hands if they meant to kill him.

"Playtime's over, Jack," someone hissed. It was Hansford. The nice one. They rolled him over so he was lying uncomfortably on his bound arms, looking up into their faces, one on either side. Sowicky slid Jack's T-shirt and vest up to expose his chest.

Hansford fished a silver cone from the neckline of his sweatshirt, similar to the one Dr. Longbranch used, only smaller. He placed it against Jack's skin, held it there a moment, nodded briskly to his partner, and then replaced it under his shirt. Jack tried desperately to roll away, but didn't even manage a twitch.

"Listen close," Sowicky said. "We're taking you out of here alive, since you're worth a fortune as you are, and nothing to us dead. Come with us quietly, and no one gets hurt. But we'll kill anyone who gets in our way. I want you to think about that before you make a scene on our way out."

Just then Jack heard the restroom door open. He looked up to see Leesha Middleton framed in the doorway.

He wanted to cry out, to warn her to get away.

Then he wondered what she was doing in the men's room.

But she shut the door behind her and came toward them, knelt next to him on the tile floor. She smiled and ruffled his hair in a proprietary manner. "So you got him," she said.

Jack opened and closed his mouth like a landed bass.

"I thought you said he was untrained," Hansford said. "We couldn't detect any leaking magic at all. We had to take your word for it."

"Which should be good enough for you." Leesha slid her fingertips under Jack's shirt, peeling it away from the vest. "What have we here?" She fingered the vest. "Untold secrets? You think you know a person."

Jack was thinking pretty much the same thing.

Leesha sat down on the floor next to him and cradled his head in her lap, gently stroking his cheek. "You're not as pretty as when I last saw you. Looks like my boyfriend beat you up. Serves you right for ditching my party." She sighed theatrically. "Oh, Jack, what a fool I've been."

Me, too. "Who are you?" Jack whispered. He wished he could squirm, even a little, to relieve the stress on his arms. "Who do you work for?" Each question was worth a little more time.

"Me? I'm a wizard. Dr. Longbranch hired me to keep an eye on you last fall. I couldn't understand why Longbranch considered you worth watching, so I decided to find out. I worked so hard on you, Jack. I ferreted out all your boring secrets, but my timing was all wrong. At the time, you were totally ignorant, and you had nothing to tell me. And Longbranch had you doped up on Weirsbane, so your body didn't leak magic, either."

Jack could remember little about his dates with Leesha. A rather pleasant blur, nothing more.

"Now I work for myself," Leesha went on. "And I've earned whatever I get, this time, believe me—stuck in this podunk town, making nice with hicks and idiots. Though I must say, it wasn't all unpleasant." She leaned over and kissed him.

"Which reminds me." She rummaged one-handed in her purse and produced a small bottle. She uncorked it with her teeth. Gripping his jaw, she forced his mouth open and dumped the contents in, stroking his throat so he swallowed most of it. It seemed to be something she'd had practice at.

The taste was familiar, and Leesha confirmed it. "Weirsbane. To prevent any nasty warrior surprises. A few minutes to let that take effect, and we'll be on our way."

"How did you . . . how did you find out?"

"Well, I must say, the change in your physical attributes sparked an interest. And then Leander Hastings shows up in Trinity, which told me something was up."

"You know Hastings?"

Leesha actually shivered. "That bleeding-heart traitor? We all know him. After he arrived, it seemed like you were always together. So I figured I'd slip you something at the party, take you into a back room, and see what I could find out. When you didn't show, I went out looking for you. And wasn't I surprised to see you blow poor Garrett clear across the parking lot." She tapped herself on the forehead. "I mean, duh!"

Hansford cleared his throat. "Speaking of Hastings, maybe we should get going."

"What are you going to do with me?" Jack asked quickly. Leesha was having a good time proving how stupid he'd been. Perhaps he could delay the inevitable a little longer.

"That depends. Both Houses are eager—make that *desperate* to get their hands on you. That should drive the price up."

"You're traders," Jack said, finally understanding. "You mean to . . . to sell me." His stomach contracted, and he thought he really would be sick. Only, flat on his back as he was, unable to move, he would probably drown in it. He forced the thought away.

"That's right, Jack. One deal like this and we're set for life," Sowicky said. "You're what we call a one-of-a-kind item. No more hours spent in dusty libraries and small-town courthouses, no more digging two-bit sooth-sayers and sorcerers out of their hidey holes to sell for a pittance."

"I think he's ready." Leesha stood and dusted off the back of her skirt. "Gotta go, Jack. Alicia Middleton wants nothing to do with a suspected drug dealer. But I'll see you later. Promise." She looked in the mirror, corrected her lipstick, pushed through the doorway, and was gone.

Hansford and Sowicky each gripped an arm and hauled Jack upright, so he dangled between them, helpless.

"Now, we're going to walk out of here, quickly and quietly," Sowicky said. He spoke a charm, and strength flooded back into Jack. He gave it about a second, then put his head down and plowed into Sowicky's midsection. The wizard fell hard, banging his head against the wall with a satisfying thump. Jack twisted and jumped high, slamming his right foot into Hansford's groin. Only, with his hands tied, Jack couldn't break his fall, and slammed painfully into the edge of the sink. The Weirsbane was working, dulling his reflexes, throwing his physical instincts into disarray.

Someone, Sowicky, he supposed it was, gripped him by the hair, forcing his head back into the bowl. The wizard turned the water on full blast, and Jack was drown-ing, spluttering and gasping, taking in water instead of air. Sowicky drove his fingers into Jack's midsection, sending power and pain ripping through him. When he tried to scream, he only sucked in more water. He twisted and turned, but could not avoid the wizard's touch.

After what seemed like an eternity, they lifted his head out of the sink and shoved him down to his knees on the floor. Sowicky gave him a sharp blow to the back, and Jack spewed water onto the tiles from his nose and mouth. But the wizards' hands under his arms kept him from falling forward onto his face.

"Amazing, isn't it, how much you can hurt a person without doing any real damage," Hansford said softly. "That's just a crude demonstration, Jack. We know how to make you real sorry in ways you've never thought of. Don't mess with us."

They lifted Jack to his feet again. Keeping a hold on each arm, they practically carried him out of the restroom. Jack noticed with some small satisfaction that Hansford was limping badly.

Jack scanned the corridor as best he could, his eyes streaming from the assault of the water, unable to wipe his face. There were still quite a few students around. The buzz of conversation stopped gradually, as those loitering in the hallway noticed the trio making their way to the door, the two men dragging their prisoner between them, Jack with his hair plastered down and dripping, his hands tied behind his back. The crowd in the hallway parted before them, the students backing up against the lockers on either side as if they wished they could crawl inside. Someone said, "Jack?" in a small and frightened voice. He didn't see who it was.

Then he saw Will and Penworthy standing by the door of the office. Jack wondered what Will was doing there, if he'd managed to find Hastings, but he didn't want to ask in front of the traders. Penworthy's mouth was hanging open. The two wizards spotted the principal, and Hansford seemed to be debating whether to offer an explanation or not. Finally, he said, loud enough for everyone to hear, "Sorry. He kind of went crazy in there. Must've been the drugs. It's okay now."

Will took a step toward them. "Jack, what's going on?" His voice was quiet, but he had his fists clenched, and looked ready to jump at a word.

"No, Will." Jack shook his head, acutely conscious of the wizards' promise in the restroom. "It's okay. I'll be all right. I need to go with them."

Will took another step forward, as if to block their path. The outside door opened, and in strode his mother with Aunt Linda close behind. Jack swore softly. What were they doing here? Becka looked from Penworthy to the scene of Jack being dragged out by the two wizards. The expression on her face was dangerous. But it was Linda who spoke.

"Stop right there!" she commanded the traders. They came to a halt, staring, as if they were too surprised to do anything but obey.

Becka turned to the principal. "Leotis, I think you have some explaining to do."

Leotis Penworthy looked more nervous than ever. He motioned to the two men in turn. "Becka, this is Mr. Hansford and Mr. Sowicky from the police department. They need to ask Jack some questions. I thought you were going to meet them down at the police station."

"I knew nothing about this until Will Childers called us fifteen minutes ago." Jack recognized her lawyer voice. "I want to know what's going on here."

Jack's heart sank. His mother would not be intimidated by the police. She would never allow them to walk out with him unchallenged. Becka might be an adversary to be reckoned with in a courtroom, but she was no match for wizards. And Linda was standing beside her sister, the full knowledge of the danger in her face, trying to decide what move to make. *Please, God*, Jack prayed. *Not this.* It was up to him to stop it.

He focused on his mother. "Mom. Listen to me. These men are not the police."

She looked at Jack, then shifted her gaze to the two wizards. Sowicky tightened his grip on Jack's arm, a warning. Becka would brush aside any concerns about her own safety, so he used the argument that he knew would convince her. "They'll kill me if you interfere. They can do it in a heartbeat. The only way I have a chance is if you let me go with them. I'm serious."

She gasped. "Jack," she whispered, her voice breaking over the single syllable. "Please. This has to be some kind of mistake. You have the wrong person. Don't hurt him." Jack was aware of movement behind him, the slight shifting of bodies that told him there were still students in the hallway.

"Please, Mom. Aunt Linda. Let us go. Do this for me." His eyes slid to Linda, willing her to stay in place as well.

She was studying the two wizards, sizing them up.

"Take me instead," Linda suggested. "I ought to be worth something to the Trade." The voice alone was enough to melt hearts, and now she glowed, as if illuminated from within. Jack felt a sudden push of power directed at the two wizards. The traders practically staggered under it.

Hansford thrust his free hand at Linda, and she flew backward and hit the wall, hard. She must have lost focus with the impact, because the effect of the spell was blunted momentarily. She lay there, dazed, for a moment.

"Let's take her with us," Sowicky pleaded with Hansford, who seemed to be in charge. "We'll trade the boy and keep the enchanter for ourselves. No one else needs to know."

Becka looked at Sowicky, then at Linda, frowning.

Hansford shook his head. "No. I don't deal in enchanters anymore. Before you know it, she'll have us cutting each other's throats. We'll have our hands full as it is. Let's get out of here before she starts in again."

Both men were looking edgy, as if they might lose control at any moment. "Let's go," Jack said urgently, hoping to get them out of there before they changed their minds about Linda.

"I'm glad you've decided to be reasonable," Hansford muttered, shoving him toward the front doors.

At least until I get into the parking lot, Jack thought. The idea of being auctioned off to the Roses made him shudder. *I'll make them kill me first*, he swore silently.

When they came through the doors to the outside, the

heat and light of the summer day hit Jack like a physical blow, disorienting him for a moment. Someone shouted, "Down, Jack!"

With a kind of war cry, he wrenched himself away from the wizards and flung himself backward onto the pavement, landing painfully on his bound arms, scraping his hands along the rough concrete. In the same instant, something shrieked through the air, just above his head, something that carried the scent of fireworks and ozone. Someone screamed. Hansford or Sowicky. Both, he hoped. He lifted his head.

Hansford lay facedown on the concrete in front of the door. He was ripped nearly in half, his body contorted in a way that was inconsistent with life. Blood was spreading in a pool around him. Sowicky stood next to him, legs braced apart, looking wildly about for the source of the attack. The trader flung out his arm in a flat arc, launching flames in all directions, muttering charms desperately. He bent slightly, reaching for Jack where he lay on the ground, clutching the front of his shirt, preparing to haul him to his feet, to use him as a shield.

Then there was a hard concussion, like a sonic boom, that set Jack's ears ringing. Sowicky went flying, spread-eagled, taking the front of Jack's shirt with him. He collided with a car halfway across the parking lot with a sickening crunch. Sowicky lay unmoving, draped across the hood of the car.

Leander Hastings stepped past Jack and nudged Hansford with his foot. Jack had no doubt that Hansford was dead, and it was hard to believe Sowicky could have survived his landing, either. Then Hastings knelt beside Jack. "Are you all right?" His face was grim, fierce.

"I'm okay," Jack said hoarsely. He rolled onto his side. Now he was facing the dead wizard, blood and tissue on the ground.

"Good. We don't have much time." Hastings took a quick look about the parking lot, then extended his hands over the wizard at his feet. He murmured a few words, and power leaped from his fingers. The body shimmered, then seemed to *disassemble* before Jack's eyes, dissolving and seeping into the pavement. Jack shut his eyes, shivering. After a moment, he heard Hastings walking away from him to see to the other trader.

Jack felt like staying where he was, but he used his skinned and battered hands to push himself into a sitting position. There was no sign of Hansford, no blood staining the concrete. It was as if he'd dreamed it. He struggled to his feet. The borders of the parking lot had the smudged appearance that denoted a wizard's wall. The world beyond was indistinct. Hastings was walking back toward him, having disposed of the other body.

"What . . . what did you do with them?" Jack stammered.

"They're fifty feet down. That should be deep enough." He was hard, cold, implacable, frightening; but when he turned to Jack, his expression softened.

Hastings took his elbow gently and turned him, then closed his hands over the cuffs on his wrists. Jack felt the tingle of power against his forearms, and his hands were free. He rotated his shoulders, gasping with pain as he did so. Hastings placed his hands on them, power trickled in, and the pain eased. He heard the wizard's voice behind him, unexpectedly kind. "It's all right, Jack. You're safe for now." For some reason, this gesture brought tears to his eyes, and he found himself trembling. The hands remained, soothing him.

"Leesha Middleton's still in there, I think. She's working for Dr. Longbranch. But she's a trader. She knows who you are." Jack knew he was babbling, but he couldn't seem to help it.

"It's all right. She's likely gone by now. She's going to have more than me to worry about when Jessamine finds out what she's been up to."

Jack realized he was hearing a repetitive thud, like something hitting the school's double doors from the inside. Jack twisted and looked back at Hastings, and saw a smile ghost across the wizard's face.

"I thought you would never come out of there. I didn't want to start anything inside, with all those people." He gestured at the doors. "I put up a barrier, to keep them from mixing in. I suppose I should let them out before the police arrive. Are you ready to deal with them?" When Jack nodded, Hastings said, "Just pretend you're in shock and let me do the talking. People will expect you to be incoherent anyway." From somewhere, not far away, Jack could hear the sound of sirens.

Hastings swept away the wizard wall, and suddenly the sirens were much louder. He gestured toward the school building, spoke a charm. The double doors burst open, and Will Childers came flying through them, obviously surprised when they suddenly gave way to his shoulder. He just managed to avoid landing flat on his face. Becka and Linda were right behind him.

Becka let out a cry when she saw Jack; then led him over to the steps and made him sit down. She and Linda sat on either side of him, each cradling one of his bloody hands, smearing their clothes, but they didn't seem to notice.

Hastings stood on the sidewalk, staring at Linda. Her gaze kept sliding to the wizard, then away when he caught her at it, a kind of thrust and parry between them. Jack remembered what Nick had said. *They haven't seen each other for years.*

Fitch had appeared out of nowhere. He and Will stood slightly to one side, saying nothing, still watchful, waiting for someone to explain.

Three police cars skidded screaming into the lot. Uniformed officers poured from the cars, guns drawn.

"They ran that way," Hastings said, pointing to the athletic fields at the rear of the school. "Two men wearing jeans and sweatshirts. One blond, the other dark haired. They may be armed."

More police cars arrived, and officers poured past them, swarming across the athletic field and into the neighborhood beyond. A crowd of the curious was growing, students and teachers who had left the school, as well as new arrivals for the afternoon exams. Two policemen herded them into the teacher's parking lot, behind a yellow tape barrier. Every officer in Trinity must be out here, Jack thought. The police force just wasn't that large.

He allowed Becka and Linda to fuss over him, trying not to make eye contact with anyone.

"Are you all right, Jack?"

Jack looked up to see a bulky, sandy-haired man with a mustache. It was Will's uncle, Ross Childers.

"Just bruised. And skinned, I guess."

"I'd like to ask you some questions that might help us catch them, and then we'll have you looked after." He glanced at Becka. She rested her hand on Jack's shoulder, as if for protection. "Did you know those men, Jack?"

He shook his head. "I never saw them before today." *Truth*.

"Any reason anyone would be out to get you? Are you in any kind of trouble?"

He shook his head again. *Lie*.

"Becka? You come into an inheritance or something? Make any new enemies down at the courthouse?"

She considered before she answered, "No inheritance. Can't think of anyone in particular."

"Exactly how'd you get away, son?" he asked.

Someone spoke over his shoulder, answering the question for him. It was Hastings. "Will Childers told me there was some kind of standoff in the office. I came up the hallway and saw what was happening. So I went out the side door and circled around front, hoping to surprise them, which I did. Jack managed to get away in the confusion, and they ran." All of which was true, except for that last part.

"That right, Will?" Ross fixed his gray eyes on his nephew. Will nodded, glancing at Hastings.

Becka stood and embraced Hastings. "Mr. Hastings, I can't tell you how grateful I am," she said. "If it hadn't been for you, I don't know what would have happened."

Linda smiled tentatively at Hastings, and extended her hand to the wizard. "Thank you, Lee." He took it, looking down at her. It was like watching a small-scale electrical storm between two people.

In the days that followed, a story of sorts emerged. The kidnappers had abandoned their getaway van in the school parking lot. It had been stolen that afternoon from a mall in Cleveland. There were a series of heated meetings involving Becka, the police, and Penworthy. Why hadn't the principal asked for better identification from the bogus policemen? Why hadn't he called Becka when the subject of searching Jack's locker had come up in the first place? Penworthy could explain none of it. Jack actually felt sorry for the little man. Whatever his faults, the principal had no defense against wizardry.

Leesha Middleton never returned to school. There was some concern that she might have run afoul of the kidnappers, but then they heard that her parents transferred her to a private school in Boston, where she would be safer.

The police continued to question Jack. Once Jack had the story line, he stuck with it, but he could tell things weren't quite adding up as far as Will's uncle was concerned. Becka the lawyer would sit in on these question-and-answer sessions, and every now and then would put her arm around Jack and murmur, "He's the victim, Ross, remember?"

For his part, Jack wished he shared Hastings's ability to deflect questions.

His aunt was hard to pin down as well. Each witness remembered Linda's offer to swap herself for Jack a little differently. Someone even remembered her speaking of *the Trade*, and the kidnappers saying something about "enchanters," but she just looked bewildered when Ross brought it up.

"Ross, how should I know what they were talking about? I have no idea what I said. I was just trying to persuade them to let Jack go."

The story created quite a splash in the local media, and was even picked up by some national outlets. Camera crews from the Cleveland stations camped out in front of their house for a few days, but for some reason none of the video they shot ever turned out. Linda persuaded Becka and Jack to make themselves strictly unavailable to reporters, in hopes that the story would die down quickly. It would be a disaster if news of the attack reached Jessamine Longbranch.

Somehow, Jack made it through the rest of exam week. Each day Hastings or Nick drove him to and from school and camped in the hallway outside his exams. Will and Fitch and Ellen came to Jack's house nearly every night to study. There was always a wizard within shouting distance.

Jack felt as though he were in prison. He'd always traveled freely all over town on his bike and on foot; more recently he'd been driving. Now he couldn't make a move without an escort. All the while knowing that if the Red

Rose couldn't get to him, they would go after the people he cared about.

Will and Fitch and Ellen were the only friends Jack wanted to see, the only ones who didn't ask him a hundred questions, who didn't have any hidden agendas. But he knew that by spending time with them, he was putting them in danger.

It was impossible to get a moment alone with Ellen. This was the only time they would likely have, and it was running out.

Jack's lessons with Hastings were suspended; so Jack could now spend hours sharpening his wizardry skills with Nick. He had been shaken by the traders' ability to immobilize him so easily. Now he focused on defenses against spell-casting.

"The key to defense against wizardry is to stay alert," Nick advised him. "The spoken charm is like any other weapon. Take a dagger, for instance. If your enemy catches you unawares, he can slip it between your ribs before you have time to react. If a wizard casts a charm, you must speak the counter-charm before his takes effect. Failing that, you must interrupt the incantation. Otherwise, you may not ever get the chance. Fortunately, it is much easier to stop a spell than to cast one." That was good news to Jack, whose powers of wizardry were limited. He spent hours reviewing charms and counter-charms.

On the evening of the last day of exams, Jack was sprawled on his bed reading science fiction, seeking escape, glad to be done with studying for a while. There was a light knock on his door. It was Becka. "Can I talk to you a minute?" When he nodded, she came in and sat down on the bed beside him.

"Jack, I was just wondering"—she twisted her hands in her lap, turned the opal ring that had belonged to her grandmother—"is there anything you'd like to talk about?"

Jack put his finger in the book he was reading to mark his place and sat up straighter. "What do you mean?"

"What I mean to say is, you seem different, somehow. Like you're stressed. You've always been . . . temperamental, but lately you fly off the handle at things that didn't used to bother you. All of a sudden, you're working out all the time." She reached out a hand and gently touched his bicep. "Not that there's anything wrong with that, but you've never been interested in bodybuilding before. . . ." Her voice trailed off. "And . . . now this episode at school."

She swallowed. "I know your father and I have always been busy with a thousand things, but you've always been so *low maintenance*. You've seemed to thrive, despite the divorce. But now . . ."

"Come on, Mom," Jack said uncomfortably. "It's not like you've neglected me."

"I know I have a rather . . . strong personality." Becka slid a look at him. "But I want you to know you can tell me anything at all."

"Okay," Jack said cautiously. "Anything at all. I'll remember that."

"So, is there anything you'd like to tell me now?" Becka looked up from studying her hands.

Jack sighed, because he had both arms around a great

big lie that he couldn't let go of. Could never let go of. He started with a truth. "I love you, Mom," he said. And ended with a lie. "I'm sure everything's fine now."

Some instinct was pricking at her, and she was unconvinced. She gave him a look that said so. "You know, Jack, I'm afraid. I almost lost you when you were a baby. That would have broken my heart, because I would have always imagined what might have been, the boy you would have grown to be. But—if I lost you now, it would be much worse. Because now I know how very special you are." And she smiled sadly, kissed him, and left the room.

Linda was beginning to agree with Jack: England couldn't be much riskier than staying in Trinity. Although it was common knowledge they were going, Linda didn't want anyone to know exactly when or how. The kidnapping attempt was a blessing in disguise, because it enabled her to convince Becka to go along with her plans. They finally decided they would leave a week earlier than scheduled, and fly from Pittsburgh rather than Cleveland.

The Chaucerian Society was preparing for its trip abroad as well. Ten members were going, with Will's parents as chaperones. Fitch was busy checking books out of the library and searching online, studying every aspect of British history and culture. His enthusiasm was infectious. Even Jack was becoming more excited about his own summer plans.

Hastings and Linda encountered each other often during this period, when Jack's teacher was picking him up or dropping him off, or stopped by for a visit. They were always polite and courteous to each other, but Jack sensed a frisson of energy in the air when they were together, like heat lightning on a stifling day. Hastings seemed uncharacteristically unsure of himself. Jack sometimes noticed him standing, watching her intently, one hand wrapped around the other forearm, as if working a problem.

When the time came for Jack to pack for his trip, he couldn't bring himself to leave Shadowslayer behind. He put the blade in its case and then in a large carry-on duffle bag, placing a simple charm on it so no one would open it up. Jack was beginning to see how his gifts could smooth the way for him, particularly when it came to dealing with Anaweir.

He sorted through his other magical weapons. Jack hadn't looked at Blaise's mirror since the night Nick had returned it to him. Now he unwound it from its leather wrapping and turned it over and over in his hands. Finally, he peered into the cloudy glass.

It cleared to reveal the nave of a medieval church. Candles guttered in the corners, making little headway against the dark. A body lay on a rude pallet on the floor, covered by a rough blanket. It was surrounded by a solemn guard of warriors. Two women knelt next to the body, heads bowed, praying, their soft voices the only sound in the stillness. Demons lurked in the shadows, circling the bier, advancing and receding, the women's prayers keeping them at bay.

Jack squinted, trying to make out who the players were. Surely this scene was from the past. Yet, the women seemed to be wearing modern clothes. The image faded, replaced by the reflection of his own face.

Obscure, as always, Jack thought. Totally useless. Still, he slid Blaise's mirror into his carry-on. He could use all the help he could get.

Nick would maintain the fiction that the house was occupied for two weeks after they left, then join them in Oxford. He seemed unenthusiastic about visiting Britain. "It's too noisy over there," the old wizard explained to Jack. "You'll see what I mean when you get there. Besides, the food is bad. The British have never mastered the dessert course."

"I wish you were coming with us," Jack admitted. "I feel like I need a *caretaker* more than ever."

"Just remember who you are, Jack," the old man said. "The world will try to change you into someone else. Don't let them. That's the best advice anyone can give you."

Jack didn't share the change in schedule with anyone, not even Will and Fitch and Ellen. But he invited them over for dinner the night before their real departure. All the suitcases were packed and hidden away, everything ready for the morning. They ate out on the side porch. Aunt Linda kept everybody laughing with her cutting imitations of various Trinity personalities. Usually Becka tried to rein in her irreverent sister, but tonight she laughed along with everyone else. Nicodemus Snowbeard told a very old, very romantic story about kings and queens, misapprehensions, and unrequited love. The hero Leander Hastings was a special guest, and he and Becka got into such a heated discussion about medieval art that the others had to beg them to call a truce.

"Fine," Becka said, tilting up her chin and lifting her glass. "I will desist, though I will not give. I would like to propose a toast to Will Childers, Harmon Fitch, and Leander Hastings, brave men all, who helped to save my son's life."

Hastings raised his glass, smiled at Becka, and some awareness fluttered at the edges of Jack's consciousness. "Perhaps we'll meet in England, then," the wizard said.

As dusk fell, Snowbeard lit the lanterns on the porch railing, and the fireflies flared in the shadows under the trees.

There seemed to be a little magic in everyone that night. The air was thick with it. Jack sat back in a wicker chair against the house, quietly alert to it all. Linda and Hastings shared the glider, a little space between them, talking. Will and Fitch tossed a ball back and forth in the yard, the white sphere barely visible in the dimming light. Jack had the melancholy feeling that something important was changing or passing away, that they might never be together again, in just this way.

Ellen sat down in the chair opposite him. She wore a long flowing skirt and a sleeveless white sweater. Jack could not remember seeing her in anything but pants before. Since the weather had warmed, her skin had taken on a rich golden color from working in the garden. Gardening seemed to agree with her, because she was looking very . . . fit, Jack thought.

"I like your mom," Ellen said wistfully.

Jack glanced over to where Becka was now deep in a conversation with Hastings and Linda. "She can be kind of intense at times," he said.

"Yes," Ellen said. She never required lengthy explanations. She swung her feet, her bare toes peeking out from under the skirt. "This is a nice town." She looked out at Jefferson Street, where the gas lamps were beginning to glow. The sound of children playing carried in the soft air. "I wish you weren't going to England."

"Yes, well." Jack stared out at the street. Ellen was leaving for Wisconsin the next day, and probably wouldn't be back in the fall. "You're going away also, and I don't even know if you'll be back."

"I know," she said.

And then Becka was there. "Would you like something else to drink, Ellen?"

"No." Ellen rose to her feet. "I've got to get going. I've still got some packing to do. Thanks for having me over, Ms. Downey. Dinner was great. I hope you have a wonderful summer."

Jack walked her down the steps and into the shadows at the side of the porch.

Ellen took his hands in hers. "Good-bye, Jack. Be careful."

She released him, but Jack grabbed her wrist and pulled her back toward him. Drawing her in close, he tilted her face up and kissed her. Their first real kiss, and he didn't want it to be their last, so he kissed her again, taking his time, wondering why he'd waited so long.

When finally he broke away, Ellen stayed in place, eyes closed, face turned up. As if she wanted to prolong it, too.

Resting his forehead against hers, he said, "Bye, Ellen. I'll e-mail you when I get there."

She swallowed hard, then turned away. Jack watched as she moved across the lawn, her white sweater pale against the darkness until she turned the corner.

❧ CHAPTER TWELVE ❧
A VISIT WITH DR. LONGBRANCH

Linda had booked rooms for herself, Jack, and Becka in a small, elegant hotel on Thurloe Place, near the Victoria and Albert Museum and Kensington Gardens. Jack's room was bright and airy, and opened out onto a garden. He threw open the garden doors and breathed deeply. Roses. He slid the bag with the sword in it under his bed, laid wards along the perimeter of the room, and collapsed, exhausted, on the bed.

From the time the plane had landed, he had been overwhelmed with a feeling of homecoming, although he'd never been to England before. From the street signs to the buses to the greenery to the architecture, everything was uncannily familiar. What was more disconcerting was the constant murmuring, a cacophony of voices of the Weirlind long dead. They were everywhere, calling from church graveyards and gardens and old buildings. "Welcome the warrior," they whispered. He had begun to understand what Nick meant by noise. He hardly felt he'd slipped into town unnoticed.

Once they were unpacked, he and Becka had lunch in the hotel dining room. Linda had other business to take care of, she'd said. Although they had traveled all night, Becka was full of plans. "Harrods is just up the street, so we'll have to go there. We can walk over to Kensington Palace, and you can see the gardens and the Serpentine, and walk along Rotten Row." She waved her fork in the air. "Then, tomorrow we'll go over to Buckingham Palace in the morning, and maybe see the Tower in the afternoon." She grinned wickedly. "I think you'll like that."

"Sounds great, Mom." After all that had happened, Jack was genuinely looking forward to being a tourist.

He and Becka toured Kensington and Knightsbridge that afternoon, and all three spent the next day seeing tourist London: Buckingham Palace and Big Ben, Trafalgar Square and the Tower.

Jack found Westminster Abbey exhausting, and not because of jet lag. They began their tour in the shrine of Edward the Confessor. A sour-looking cleric delivered a rather long, boring speech about the history of the church, while ghost warriors drifted above his head and shoulders, gesturing urgently to Jack. Their voices echoed against stone like a tuneless choir. They trailed him through the Lady Chapel, where were buried the three great female adversaries of Tudor times: Elizabeth I, Mary Tudor, and Mary, Queen of Scots. PARTNERS BOTH IN

THRONE AND GRAVE, HERE REST WE TWO SISTERS, ELIZA-
BETH AND MARY, IN THE HOPE OF THE RESURRECTION.

Jack paused at the tombs of Henry the VII and
Elizabeth of York. Their marriage had ended the War of
the Roses. Officially, at least. Here the Weirlind became
almost frantic. A gaunt ghost soldier seized Jack by the
arm. His gray flesh was nearly translucent. A great gash
beneath his chin stretched from ear to ear.

"Beware, Warrior!" he intoned, reminiscent of Caesar's
ghost. "Beware the Ghyll!"

Jack allowed Becka and Linda to get a little ahead of
him, then spun around and hissed, "Will you leave me in
peace?"

"Beware, Warrior!" the ghost repeated. "They'll pin a
rose on your breast, the White of York or the Red of
Lancaster, and send ye out to the butcher's field!"

"Look, I have no intention of fighting anybody," Jack
retorted, then clamped his mouth shut. An overweight
couple in matching Bermuda shorts and tank tops was
staring at him. One of them raised a digital camera and
snapped his picture.

"Jack, will you come on?" Becka stood framed in
the entrance of the Lady Chapel, tapping her foot impatiently. "You've been totally distracted today!"

"Sorry." Jack followed her toward the front of the
sanctuary. "After lunch, do you think we could go some-
place where there aren't so many ghosts?"

"Beware!" the ghost called after him. If he'd had a
chain, he would have rattled it.

For the next several days, they immersed themselves in

London. They went to the theater, ate in pubs and Indian restaurants, and took the train to Kew Gardens. There was a full-day tour to Bath and Salisbury Cathedral and Stonehenge. Stonehenge turned out to be another spot that spoke to Jack.

Jack shopped for a gift for Ellen, a British football club jersey. Manchester United or Chelsea? He bought both. He labored over a postcard for an hour. Wrote "Hope you're having fun!" and scratched it out. Finally sketched out a brief list of sights they'd seen and ended with, "Miss you. Wish you were here." He posted it to her Trinity address, hoping her parents would forward it. He e-mailed her from an Internet cafe, but got no response.

Becka had scheduled an appointment for Jack with Jessamine Longbranch on their last day in London. Both Linda and Jack were trying not to think about it, but it came quickly nonetheless. The night before the appointment, they had dinner at a Thai restaurant in Knightsbridge. Lost in worry, Linda and Jack had little to say. Finally, over dessert, Linda convinced Becka to take a tour to the William Morris Gallery while Linda took Jack to his appointment. It was sorcery, plain and simple. But they both felt better with Becka out of danger.

The next morning Jack and Linda took the underground to St. James Park. Longbranch's offices were in Westminster, near Parliament Square. All the way there, Linda second-guessed their decision to keep the appointment, even after they'd exited the train and left the stale air of the underground station behind. Linda was sure Dr. Longbranch would contact Becka to reschedule if they didn't show. The next time it might be Becka and Jack alone.

The building was ancient, and the elevator was only a little less so, but Dr. Longbranch's offices were elegantly appointed, with expensive fabrics and antique furniture. The receptionist offered them tea, which they declined. They were the only ones in the waiting room. Soon, a nurse led them to an exam room. It was really more of an office, without the cold medical feel Jack was used to in American clinics. The nurse weighed him in his sock feet, then directed Jack to take off his shirt and sit up on the exam table. Jack removed both shirt and vest and set them next to him on the table.

He glanced down at himself. The star-shaped surgical scar gleamed faintly over his breastbone. He realized he must look pretty pale. His chest had not seen the sun all summer. Linda seemed even more unsettled, seeing the changes in him, the muscles that stood out along his arms and across his chest. She paced nervously.

Finally, Jessamine Longbranch swept into the room. She was dressed in silk trousers and an elegant sweater, a pristine white lab coat over top, that unusual stethoscope draped around her neck. She was carrying a folder, his file, he assumed. It struck Jack that she didn't look any older, but then he remembered that wizards don't show their age like other people.

She stopped just in front of Jack and looked him up and down, holding the folder close to her chest. "Well, Jackson," she said, drawing out his name. "I do believe you've grown." Something in the way she said it made him feel even more self-conscious than before. She glanced at Linda. "Becka couldn't come? That's too bad."

She kept talking as she examined him, her fingers full of power, sending off tiny electrical shocks as they touched his skin. He flinched and gritted his teeth. "Now, don't tense up, Jack. That's better. I understand this is your first trip to London? I hope your mother and aunt have been showing you around?"

Jack nodded, then gasped as she ran her hot hands over the muscles in his back. "Ah . . . we've seen a lot in a short time," he managed to say. "I'm really enjoying it." He didn't remember his previous sessions with Longbranch as being quite so *physical*.

"As you should," said the doctor. "Land of your ancestors, I believe? Have you been to the Tower? Thrilling, really. All those stories of torture and murder." Dr. Longbranch kept up a constant stream of conversation, asking questions about their stay in London as she checked Jack's blood pressure and pressed her strange stethoscope against his chest. She had him jump down from the table and walk across the room and back, watching him, arms folded, as he did so. The exam took longer than usual, but he told himself that perhaps it was because he had come such a long way to see the her. She'd never shown nearly so much interest in him before. Finally, the doctor stepped back and looked him up and down approvingly. "You're in great shape, Jack. Tell me, when did you stop taking your medicine?"

She snapped out the question, and it took Jack by surprise, like a quick blade under the ribs, as Nick would say.

It took him a moment to respond. "I don't know what you're talking about," he stammered.

Linda spoke up. "Jack and Becka have always been very good about following instructions, Jessamine." Her face had lost its color.

"Is that so, Linda? I was thinking Jack here looks like someone who likes to break the rules. Have you ever heard of the White Rose?" Another quick blade, but this time Jack was better prepared for it. He considered a moment, then said, "Wasn't that a battle emblem in the War of the Roses? York carried the white rose, Lancaster the red."

"Very good!" She moved to the side of the examination table and ran her fingertips lightly across his shoulder. He tensed as the current went through him. She didn't seem to be making any attempt to blunt its effects. "You've been studying your history. There's a great deal of history in this part of the world. Much more than most people realize. And your family has been in the thick of it, did you know that?" Now she was stroking him, petting him like a dog. "I think it's time you became better acquainted with it. I know some people who can teach you." The change in her voice warned him, and he was prepared for the charm when it came. She spoke it quickly, tightening her fingers on the back of his neck, a simple immobilization charm. He spoke the counter charm under his breath before she could complete it. Then he stilled himself, looking as immobile as he could. He didn't have to pretend to be frightened.

"Jessamine, what the hell are you doing?" Linda's voice was sharp.

"I must tell you, this is a wonderful surprise," Jessamine said. "I thought it would take months to get him into fighting condition, and now I find you've done it for me."

"Listen to me," Linda said urgently, persuasively. "I don't know what you're thinking, but he's just a boy. The only reason he's alive today is because he's been hidden. As soon as the Red Rose finds out about him, he'll be a target."

Jessamine laughed. "He doesn't look like a boy to me. He has gained six inches in height and forty-five pounds since my last exam, and it's all muscle. He's breathtaking." Her voice hardened. "You do remember our bargain, don't you? It's time to give him up, Linda. We need to begin his training. We really haven't any choice. I would have come after him in Trinity had you not arranged to bring him to me here. The Red Rose has called a tournament for Midsummer's Day." She paused. "It appears they will put forward a champion."

"That's impossible!" Linda exclaimed. "How could they have managed that? You would have known about it before now."

"We are working on locating and eliminating their player," Dr. Longbranch said coldly. "But we cannot exclude the possibility that we will fail. If we cannot answer the challenge, we will forfeit. And that will not happen." She smiled. "If we succeed in taking their player, the Red Rose will forfeit. And even if the tournament goes forward, perhaps Jack will win. I must admit, I'm optimistic now that I've seen him in the flesh."

"He can't possibly be prepared for a tournament by Midsummer's Day," Linda persisted. "He doesn't know anything about fighting."

The doctor tapped her long nails against his shoulder. "He was born to this, Linda. He'll figure it out. My trainers can bring out the killer in anyone. I just hope they don't damage this beautiful body too much." She must have seen some reaction to that in Jack's face, because she cupped her hand under his chin and turned his face to look at her. "Don't be frightened, my mongrel. I know you'll catch on fast." She eyed him speculatively. "They say a mixed breed is often stronger than its parents. I wonder if he'll pass down the warrior stone to his offspring. An interesting question."

She went on, as if thinking aloud, "Perhaps if he survives the tournament, we'll breed him. Would you like that, Jack?" she asked, as if she were offering him a treat for rolling over. Jack was mortified. He felt the blood rush to his face, and then she said, "Look, he's blushing." As if he were a cute puppy.

Jack looked at his aunt, sending her a desperate message. *Let's get out of here.*

"That's enough, Jessamine," Linda warned. She nodded slightly to Jack, and he slid his hips to the edge of the table.

Dr. Longbranch was speaking rapidly now, all business, focusing on Linda. "Here is the story. Unfortunately, Jack either slipped or jumped into the Thames from Westminster Bridge shortly after his appointment with me. You saw him fall. There will be several other witnesses. I recollect that he seemed preoccupied, depressed when I examined him. The body will never be found. You will convince your sister of this. Do you understand me?"

It was clear that Jessamine had little interest in whether the story stuck or not. "Actually, I had rather hoped Becka might come to the appointment with Jack. We've found that the presence of family members can be very motivating during training. Well, no matter. I have some people here who will take him north and work with him intensively until the tournament. Then there's the matter of locating a suitable blade."

Linda nodded at Jack over Dr. Longbranch's shoulder, an almost imperceptible movement. Jack pressed his fingers against the surgeon's collarbone and released power into her, knocking her to the floor.

Jack shoved his feet into his shoes and yanked his vest on over his head. He jumped from the table, and the two of them raced back down the hallway toward the reception area. They burst into the elegant waiting room to find the receptionist gone and two bulky-looking men leafing through magazines. Jack's escorts, apparently. Wizards, certainly. The two men looked up as if surprised, and Jack said, "I left my sword outside," and he and Linda walked swiftly past them and out the door into the corridor. Jack hoped the wizards would go back to see what had happened to the doctor, which might buy them some time.

But when they opened the accordion doors to the elevator, the car wasn't there. They could hear it toiling somewhere far below. He knew his simple charm wouldn't keep Dr. Longbranch down for long.

"The stairs!" Jack exclaimed. Jessamine's office was on the ninth floor. They took the stairs, two at a time, careening across the narrow landings, flinging themselves around corners. Jack was acutely conscious of the sound of the elevator laboring in the shaft next to the stairwell.

They reached the ground floor just in time to see Dr. Longbranch and the wizards of the White Rose exiting the elevator. Jack and Linda charged for the front door, which burst into flames in front of them. Throwing their arms over their faces, they plunged into the flames and through them, and out into the fresh air.

They were on Victoria Street, just off Parliament Square. "Head for the river!" Linda hissed. The sidewalk was packed with tourists and government workers out for their lunch hour. When Jack looked back, the doorway was still in flames, but none of the Anaweir seemed to notice. Some looked curiously at Jack, who was pulling his sweatshirt on over his vest. They melted into the crowds taking photographs of Big Ben and the Westminster Bridge. Westminster Bridge! The site of the accident Dr. Longbranch had planned for him.

They kept moving with the crowds toward the water. Should they cross the river? Hide in a building? Only, Jack didn't know the area and was afraid of being trapped. He was leaning in to ask Linda what she thought when something hit him hard in the chest, sending him flying to the pavement. He sat up in time to see the two wizards from the waiting room running toward them. They had aimed at Linda, and Jack had stepped into the way at the last minute. Once again, his vest had turned the blow.

Linda helped Jack to his feet and they ran a zigzag across the square, keeping close together. The wizards fired only when they thought they had a clear shot at Linda. It seemed they meant to take Jack alive. The two groups caused a kind of ripple as they moved through the crowd. There were no weapons in evidence, so there was no panic, but people had to scramble to get out of the way of the pursued and pursuers. Someone shouted at them as they passed, "Watch where you're going, you bloody idiots!"

They were on Broad Sanctuary Street. This gave Jack an idea. "Does Westminster Abbey count as a church?" The Abbey was still some distance away.

"What are you talking about?"

"Does it count as a church?"

"Good idea," Linda said.

"Never mind. Let's go in here." A smaller church stood in front of the abbey itself. An elaborate maypole dance was in progress in the churchyard. Young girls and ladies in medieval gowns were weaving broad ribbons into an intricate pattern around the pole. Jack and Linda ducked under the ribbons and sprinted for the door of the church. Just as they reached the threshold, something struck Jack on the shoulder where his vest didn't protect him, almost spinning him around. It stung badly, but he managed to stumble into the sanctuary.

It was cool and quiet inside. Tourists clustered around the stained-glass windows and the marble memorials in the side aisles. Jack and Linda dropped into the nearest pew, glancing behind to see if anyone had followed them in. No one had.

Jack's shoulder was beginning to throb, but when he pulled his sweatshirt away, he could see neither a bruise nor a mark where the skin had been wounded.

A woman in a sensible skirt and sweater approached them. "Welcome to St. Margaret's. There will be a tour beginning in ten minutes up by the east window." She gestured at an elaborate stained glass window at one end of the nave.

"Can we just sit here for a few minutes?" Aunt Linda asked. "We're in need of a little prayer."

The woman smiled and moved away. And Jack did say a few prayers once he'd caught his breath. Linda sat bolt upright, hands braced against the seat of the pew, eyes closed. Jack wasn't sure if she was praying or not.

He wondered how many wizards were waiting outside. Enough to cover all the exits? *Maybe I'll just stay here.* Didn't fugitives in medieval times take sanctuary in churches in order to avoid the law? There was something familiar about the vaulted ceilings, the worn stone floor, the quality of the light. As if he'd been here before.

As they sat, his shoulder stiffened, became more and more painful, and drew his attention like the bite of a poisonous insect. When it was too much to ignore, he nudged Aunt Linda. "I think something hit me, outside the church. Maybe you should take a look."

She lifted his shirt away and touched his arm with the tips of her fingers. The area was bright red now; swollen, and hot to the touch.

"Damn!" Linda released a long breath. "It must have

been a wizard's graffe," she said. "It's a kind of magical dagger."

"But it didn't break the skin," Jack pointed out.

"It doesn't have to. It's really an enchantment. Very clever on their part, actually. Only a skilled wizard can treat it. They know we can't stay in here."

"I thought . . . I thought magic wouldn't work in a church."

"The damage is already done. Your body's just responding to it."

"What happens if it isn't treated?" This was another one of those questions that Jack had to ask, although he was sure he wouldn't like the answer.

"You'll die." They sat in silence for a few minutes. Linda bowed her head, dropping her clasped hands between her knees. Her shoulders shook, and he realized she was crying.

"Don't worry," he said, awkwardly patting her arm. "It's okay. I'll think of something."

At this, Linda straightened, swiping away tears with the heel of her hand. "No, Jack," she replied. "I will." She pulled out her cell phone and slid to the far end of the pew and started punching in numbers.

Jack's shoulder reverberated with pain, a cold flame that spread into his neck. He couldn't seem to get comfortable. He tried speaking a few healing and soothing charms, but nothing seemed to make any difference. He'd read somewhere that wizards are unable to heal themselves. Let alone mongrels, as Dr. Longbranch put it.

The shadows at the front of the nave organized

themselves into a half dozen medieval ghost warriors who solemnly processed down the aisle to Jack's pew, their helmets under their arms. They knelt in the aisle next to him, a semicircle of men who appeared to have come straight from battle. They ranged in age from about thirteen to middle age.

Their leader was a red-bearded man in a bloodstained tunic, embroidered over with red roses. The hilt of his sword protruded over his shoulder. "Did we not tell ye to stay away, lad? Did we not warn you?"

Jack licked his lips and looked about. No one else seemed to notice the invasion of Weirlind. "I had to come."

The warrior looked back at his companions. "He had to come," he repeated, lifting his hands in exasperation.

"*He had to come,*" the Weirlind whispered, their voices like the wind through icy branches.

Turning back to Jack, the warrior said, "And where is Shadowslayer?"

"I . . . I left it back in my room," Jack admitted, feeling besieged.

The red-bearded man raised an eyebrow. "So ye went abroad among wizards with naught but your hands?" He turned to the guard and added, "Leaving his blade behind."

"*Leaving his blade behind*" came the echo, like a kind of Greek chorus.

"Ah, well," the warrior said. "Now ye've taken a mortal wound." He rested a gloved hand on Jack's knee. "Don't worry, lad. We'll keep vigil with the lady until the end. Vigil for the Warrior Heir!" he said to the others.

"*Vigil for the Heir!*"

"Jack!"

The warriors drew back, but did not disperse. Jack turned to see Linda beside him.

She took his hand between hers. "Don't worry. I reached Hastings. He's coming from Canterbury. It's about sixty miles away."

"How long does it take?"

Whether Jack meant the graffe or the trip from Canterbury, the answer was the same.

"I don't know," his aunt said.

Groups of tourists came and went. Jack felt worse and worse. He propped himself in the corner of the pew to keep from falling over. He was alternately chilled and overheated. Even worse, he was beginning to see things, dark shadowy things like demons crouched in the corners of the church. The walls writhed and quaked, advanced and receded. The Weirlind huddled disconsolately in the aisle, whispering among themselves.

Linda found a drinking fountain in the entrance to the sanctuary and brought him some water in a paper cup, which he drank greedily. She brought him two more cups.

Then someone slipped into the pew in front of him. It was Jessamine Longbranch. She looked shimmery and monstrous to Jack, who was having trouble focusing his eyes. He raised both hands, feebly, to keep her away. The Weirlind stirred and muttered.

"Jack, you don't look well. Not nearly as well as you looked in my office this morning."

"Get out of this church, Jessamine, before God finds out you're in here," Linda whispered fiercely.

"Do you know what's wrong with you, Jack?" The doctor's voice was probably meant to be soothing, but without its usual overlay of wizardry, it only sounded thick and sinister.

"Wizard's graffe," Jack tried to reply, but it was difficult to say with his tongue so thick in his mouth.

"Come outside, Jack, and we'll take care of you. Otherwise, you'll be dead before the day is over." She turned to Linda. "You at least should know better than to try this kind of a stunt."

"Get out of here, Jessamine," Linda repeated.

Dr. Longbranch shrugged. "We'll be outside. Let us know when you're ready to give him up." She raked back her dark fall of hair. "I can see already that Jack is very talented. I would hate to see him go to waste." She reached out her hand to him, and he shrank back into the pew like a cornered animal. She tucked a strand of damp hair behind his ear. Then she stood and walked out of the church, the heels of her shoes clicking on the stone floor.

Did the end of the day mean sundown or midnight? Could be important, he thought, but then he couldn't remember why. He knew there was something he desperately needed to say. "Aunt Linda." It came out as a scratchy whisper. She slid close to him and cradled his head in her arms, being careful of his shoulder, leaning in so she could hear him. "Aunt Linda, please don't let her take me. Please. I don't care . . . what happens. Promise."

Linda promised, tears dripping down her face.

The woman who had greeted them when they entered the church had returned. She looked concerned. "Is your son ill?" she asked Linda.

"Nephew," Linda corrected her automatically. "He is ill, but it's a spiritual kind of sickness," she explained.

"Is it?" The woman raised her eyebrows. Jack was stretched out full length on the hard pew, his head in Linda's lap. He was shivering, delirious, muttering to himself. "Are you sure we shouldn't take him to hospital?"

"Please. He needs to stay in here," Linda said desperately. "Or he'll be lost."

The woman hesitated. "Perhaps we can make him more comfortable." She disappeared for a few moments and reappeared with a thin bedroll and blankets. "I suppose I should introduce myself. My name is Sarah Barham. I am one of the church docents, but I also run a ministry for the homeless," she explained. "We accept donations here at the church. So we have some bedding here."

"My name is Linda Downey," Linda replied. "And this is Jack. We really appreciate your help."

When Leander Hastings arrived half an hour later, Jack lay on a mattress in a corner of the church. Linda and Sarah Barham knelt next to him, praying. They were ringed by kneeling ghost warriors, in vigil. Jack looked near death, his freckles standing out against the pallor of his skin, his breathing a shallow and ineffective rasp. The warriors faded back as Hastings approached, muttering unhappily.

Linda leaped to her feet when she saw him. "Hurry, Leander. I'd almost given him up." When the wizard hesitated, she said, "Come on! There couldn't possibly be any problem with healing a person in a church!"

Hastings knelt next to Jack and rested his hand on the injured shoulder. It was red and shiny and swollen, with long red streaks that extended all the way from his arm to his chest. Jack moaned and tried to twist away.

"Hold him down."

Linda and Sarah each pinned one of Jack's wrists to the floor. Hastings placed his hands over the wound, speaking a charm slowly and distinctly. The skin immediately blistered up, turning a nasty green and yellow, as if the poison had risen and collected just under the skin.

Sarah Barham cleared her throat. "What is he, a priest?" she asked Linda.

"Not exactly," Linda replied.

Hastings waited a minute, keeping his hands in place, then spoke a different charm. Minutes passed, and there was no change. Then, slowly, Jack's complexion lost its waxy appearance. His breathing grew less ragged and his whole body relaxed. Hastings smiled up at the two women. He was pale and perspiring, his green eyes muddy with exhaustion. He removed his hands; the blistering had subsided.

The church docent looked from Jack to Hastings. "Well. I thought he was going to die," she admitted.

"Me, too," Hastings said shortly. He stood and wiped his hands on his trousers. "Is there any other way out of this church?" he asked softly. "Besides the obvious?"

"There is another door," Sarah said. "At the south-east end. But it's usually not open to the public," she added.

"Could we use it?" Hastings smiled at the woman. "Please? The boy's in danger."

"Well." She looked at Jack, and back at Hastings. "I suppose so. I'll show you where it is."

Hastings turned to Linda. "I need you to stall those wizards outside as long as possible. Don't let them know that he's gone. Better yet, see if you can convince them he's dead." He reached out and brushed her cheek with the back of his knuckles. "Be careful. I think we can assume they'll be angry."

"Wizards!" Sarah took a step back, her hand flying to her mouth as if she had suddenly realized that the tall stranger did have a certain supernatural look about him.

"So to speak," said Hastings, smiling in a disarming fashion. "The boy's involved himself with a cult." He bent and lifted Jack again. Jack frowned and muttered something. "One more thing: Linda, can you get to Canterbury and take over my Chaucerian Society? They're at Dovecote Hostelry in the old city. We're visiting all the scenes of the great murders. Tomorrow they want to see where Becket was killed. They're a bloodthirsty lot, it seems."

Linda nodded, without speaking.

Hastings followed the bewildered Sarah Barham to the rear of the church and disappeared. Linda arranged the bedclothes to look like a recumbent form. Then she stationed herself next to the pallet to wait.

Sarah Barham allowed Linda to stay beyond the official church closing time of four-thirty. The enchanter kept her vigil, seated on the floor, her back against the wall. Daylight faded behind the stained-glass windows as the interior lights kindled. It was after nine P.M. when Jessamine Longbranch reentered the church to find Linda dozing at her post. The wizard stood, hands on hips, gazing down at Linda.

"I suppose the boy's dead?" She motioned at Linda's arrangement of bedclothes on the floor.

"Yes," Linda replied.

"You little fool!" The words were full of venom. "I can't believe you would sacrifice your nephew like this. Why not let him fight, and at least give him a chance?"

"You cast the graffe, Jessamine, I didn't. You can explain it to the rest of your House. Jack said he'd rather die than end up in your hands. I honored his choice."

"I'm most displeased. I think I'll pay your sister Becka a visit. She's staying on Thurloe Place, isn't she?" Dr. Longbranch stalked from the church.

Linda rang Becka repeatedly, but there was no answer. She lounged at the church until about midnight, then slipped out the back door.

The Chaucerian Society was a flexible group. When Linda introduced herself as an expert in medieval myth and magic who would be replacing Leander Hastings for a few days, there was hardly a ripple of concern. The boys in particular were pleased with the change. The notable exceptions were Will and Fitch, who knew that Linda Downey surfacing unexpectedly meant that trouble would follow.

Linda was a good choice for the assignment. She was an ardent Anglophile, and shared her family's interest in English literature and medieval studies. She had lived much of her life in England, and was able to add detail and color to the information provided by the official cathedral guide. They were all suitably impressed with the sheer nastiness of a murder in church. We weren't far from that last night, Linda thought. She wondered where Jack and Hastings had gotten to. She'd heard he had a house in Cumbria, perhaps they'd gone there.

She tried to call Becka several times during the day, but there was no answer in the hotel room in London. Becka surely wouldn't leave for Oxford without Jack. She left a message at Devon House for Becka to call her in Canterbury. The story she had devised was that they had spotted the kidnappers in London, and although Hastings had taken Jack to a safe place, they were all in danger.

There were no messages when Linda returned to Hastings's room. There was sparse evidence of his presence: a book on the table, a leather shaving kit in the washroom, a sweater draped across the foot of the bed. Impulsively, she pressed the wool to her face, breathing in his scent. Embarrassed, she dropped it on the bed.

By now, Becka might be frantic. What if she called Dr. Longbranch? Surely now that the wizard thought Jack was dead, she would leave Becka alone, despite her threat in the church. Unless Longbranch decided to use Becka to take revenge on Linda for the double cross.

And where were Jack and Hastings? Hastings owned property somewhere in Cumbria. Perhaps they had gone up there. Maybe Hastings had called Becka and told her some story on his own. Anything was possible.

There was a knock at the door. When she pulled it open, Will and Fitch stood in the hallway, Fitch with a folder under his arm. They looked to be on a mission.

"Hello, Ms. Downey. We need to talk to you. If . . . are you busy?" Will shifted from foot to foot.

"Not at all. Please, come in! Would you like some tea or something?" Linda looked from one to the other.

Fitch shook his head. "We came because we want to know why you're here and what it has to do with Jack," he said bluntly.

"I see. Well, won't you sit down?" She gestured toward a little table next to a window that overlooked the narrow street below.

They arranged themselves as best they could, seeming overlarge for the delicate table, all elbows and knees and long legs and wary determination.

Fitch dropped his folder on the table and said, "So where's Jack? And why are you filling in for Mr. Hastings?"

Linda steepled her hands and rested her chin on her fingertips, studying them. They had earned the right to information. Without them, Jack would no doubt be dead or worse. "Jack's had trouble again since coming to London. He had to leave with Mr. Hastings. That's why I'm here."

"Listen, we're tired of being clueless." Will placed his

palms flat against the table. "Jack won't tell us anything. He just says not to worry, there's nothing we can do. Crap like that. We think you can tell us what's going on."

"I can do that. It's up to you to decide what you want to believe." Linda could make them believe Jack had been kidnapped by aliens if she wanted to. But, this time, she preferred to convince them by non-magical means. She took a deep breath.

"Jack should have been a wizard, but he was implanted with a warrior stone when he was a baby."

Fitch squinted at her doubtfully, as if trying to decide if she were joking. "Implanted with a . . . what?"

"A Weirstone. Those who carry a warrior stone have certain magical attributes that manifest when they come of age—"

"Right." Fitch rolled his eyes. "Jack Swift is . . . is some kind of gladiator with superpowers. Is that what you're saying?"

Linda nodded. "There are other stones and other guilds, of which wizards are the most powerful. Wizards play warriors in tournaments called the Game. Only there aren't many warriors left. So Jack is what you might call a rare find. Because of that, wizards are after him, trying to capture or kill him."

"Hold on," Will said, scowling. "Wizards? Like in a fairy tale?"

"Well, more like a nightmare, I suppose. They are crafters of magic, using spells and charms. Unlike warriors, wizards have no specific physical manifestation, but rather a powerful presence."

Will slammed his hands down on the table. "Fine. If you're not going to tell us the truth, just say so and quit wasting our time."

"Will." Fitch put a hand on Will's shoulder. "Remember the dude in the graveyard, and the flaming sword and all that?"

"That was a wizard. In fact…" Linda hesitated, then went on. "In fact, there are a number of wizards who live right in Trinity."

"Like who?" Fitch demanded, searching her face for clues. Then his eyes widened behind his glasses. "Mr. Hastings, I'll bet."

Reluctantly, Linda nodded.

"Who else?" Fitch thrust his chin forward, clearly in interrogation mode.

"Well, there's Nick Snowbeard. And Leesha Middleton."

"Nick? And Leesha-frigging-Middleton? The princess?"

"Well, yes," Linda said. "She was working with those men who tried to kidnap Jack from the high school."

"No way!" Fitch shuddered.

"Don't tell me Lobeck was involved, too?" Will said.

Linda shook her head. "A bully and a jerk, maybe, but not a wizard."

"Not unless they come in stupid," Fitch added. "Are we going to be able to see Jack while we're here?"

Linda hesitated. "I don't know. I'm not even sure where he is right now."

Fitch tapped his folder with his fingertips. "What does this have to do with his grandmother and the graveyard?"

"Susannah had the same gift, the same stone as Jack. She was a warrior like he is. That was her sword you dug up. We were hoping he could use it to protect himself."

"Can a Weirstone be stolen?"

"Not without killing the bearer."

"But could it be stolen? Like, if you cut somebody open? Would someone have any reason for doing that, maybe to implant it in someone else? Like Jack?"

Linda thought a moment. "Weirstones have some magical power in themselves. Wizards sometimes buy them off traders and use them as talismans. Jack's the only person I've heard of who had a stone implanted. That was because he was missing his."

"I was thinking about Jack's grandmother, Susannah Downey, and how she died. Whenever I see that star-shaped scar on Jack's chest, I think of it."

"What are you talking about?" Linda looked from one boy to the other. "She died in an accident. Didn't you say she fell from a horse?"

Fitch nodded. He opened the folder. "But the cause of death was a hole in her chest. It said in the paper that maybe she fell onto a fence post or something. Look." He pulled a microfilm printout from his folder. "I ended up with this when we went to the library. It sounded kind of far-fetched to me. I don't imagine forensics were very sophisticated in those days." He passed the paper to Linda. It was Susannah's obituary.

Linda scanned it quickly, then read it again more slowly. "'Lee Hastens, a visitor in the township, found her lying in the woods back of the family farm in the late evening. Although known to be a capable horsewoman, Mrs. Downey took a fall onto a fence post. She had a severe gash to the chest, which was the cause of death.'" A tiny flame of an idea kindled in the back of Linda's mind. It burned with greater and greater intensity, no matter how hard she tried to put it out.

Fitch broke into her thoughts. "Maybe it's because we've been talking about all these murders in the past few days. And now the Weirstones. Could Susannah have been murdered, and her stone stolen?" Fitch stopped, peering at Linda. "What's the matter?"

"It's Jack," Linda whispered. "I'm afraid I've made a terrible mistake."

⊛ CHAPTER THIRTEEN ೲ
CUMBRIA

Jack remembered little about his last hours in the church. He lay mortally wounded, the Weirlind keeping vigil around him. A vast darkness threatened to overtake him, but somehow was kept at bay by the music of women's voices praying. He clung to the sound as to a lifeline, and then finally there was a new voice and a new prayer, and the darkness receded and the throbbing in his shoulder eased. Someone lifted him up, and there was fresh air and rain on his face. He was carried some distance through the rain, and then bundled into the backseat of a car. He remembered the scent and feel of leather against his face. Someone lifted his head and poured a burning liquid down his throat, and then he slept. He awoke once to darkness and the slamming of car doors and what might have been his mother's voice. He tried to call to her, but it was impossible to stay awake.

When he finally awoke again, it was to a soft daylight that intruded into sleep. He rolled over and buried his face in the pillow to force the light away. He was in a large bed that was made up with rather coarse linens with a light coverlet over the top. He was dressed in unfamiliar clothing: shorts and a T-shirt. Memory began to overtake him, and he sat up quickly, too quickly, became dizzy, and lay back against his pillows.

The chamber was virtually bare, as if carved from rock, with stone walls and a stone floor, a fireplace, and a single, unadorned window. There was an arched wooden door at the far end of the room. Apart from the bed, the only furnishings were a stand with a basin and pitcher on it, a small bedside table with sorcerer's bottles lined up on it, two plain wooden chairs, and a rocker drawn up next to the bed. A jeweled case stood propped against the hearth. It was Shadowslayer, his sword, and next to it, on the hearthstone, lay Blaise's mirror in its leather wrapping. How did those get here? He'd left them at the hotel, under charms of protection.

He desperately tried to remember what had happened at the end of the long afternoon in the church. There was no twinge or tenderness in his shoulder, no remnant of the wizard's graffe. Had Hastings arrived in time, or was he in the hands of the White Rose? That thought made him get up and swing his legs over the side of the bed. He meant to retrieve his sword. If they were foolish enough to leave him a weapon, he intended to take advantage of it.

Just then, the door opened, and his mother came in. Becka was wearing jeans and a bulky sweater, barefoot despite the chill of the stone floor. She carried a tray with a pot of tea and a generous breakfast.

"Mom!" Jack was amazed and overjoyed to see her. Becka carefully set the tray down on the bedside table and then pulled him into her arms. They sat there on the edge of the bed for a long minute.

Finally Becka sat down and looked at him. "You seem much better, Jack. I was so worried when Leander came to get me. You looked terrible."

There was toast and marmalade, bacon and eggs, and some kind of smoked fish. Jack spread the marmalade onto his toast, stalling for time while he conjured up a question. Jack wasn't sure how his condition would have been explained.

"Did Mr. Hastings tell you what happened?"

She frowned, as if she were trying hard to remember. "He said you had caught a . . . a virus, and what you needed was some rest and peace and quiet. So we came up here." She stroked the hair away from his forehead. "Would you like me to get you something to read? There's a wonderful library downstairs."

Jack stopped chewing and stared at his mother. This was not at all the response he had anticipated. He expected a thousand questions he couldn't answer. He wondered how Hastings had handled her, why she had not insisted on his going to a hospital. Though, perhaps he already knew the answer to that question.

"Where are we?" he asked, looking about the room. "And how long have I been . . . sick?"

"This is Leander's house. We've been here three days."

Jack glanced around the room again. It was as spare as the man himself. The only color was from the sorcerer's bottles on the table. Hastings had never mentioned any connection to England, let alone that he had a house here. But it made sense, if Hastings knew Aunt Linda. "Are we still in London?" Something about the quality of the light and the stillness outside told him they were not.

"This is Cumbria. In the north of England. We're in the mountains, actually, not far from Scotland."

Jack wondered how recent events would affect the rest of their time in England, wondered if wizards would soon be chasing him all over Britain. "What about Oxford? Aren't they expecting you?"

"I have all summer to get to Oxford." She spoke languidly, as if there were no longer any urgency about getting there. She sat down in the rocker. "Jack, eat your breakfast before it gets cold. You haven't eaten for three days, and you need to get your strength back."

Why had Hastings brought his mother up here? Perhaps to help care for him, but it certainly made matters awkward. He didn't see how they could hope to keep his problems secret much longer anyway. He felt like his whole life was unraveling, and threatening to shred his family in the bargain.

He pushed his breakfast aside for the moment and slid out of bed. It was unexpectedly high, and his feet hit the stone floor with a smack. The shutters over the window stood open, and the morning air was chilly. His clothes were nowhere in sight.

The view through the window caught his eye. They

were perhaps three stories up, looking out to a beautiful landscape of mountains and green hillsides, the foothills shrouded in mist.

And then the door opened and Leander Hastings walked in. He too was dressed in a heavy sweater against the cool morning. He seemed surprised to see Jack up and walking around. "Becka!" he said, smiling. "It looks like your son is definitely on the mend." He came and stood behind her, resting his hands on her shoulders. There was an ownership about the gesture that set Jack's teeth on edge.

"He looks much better," Becka agreed, half turning to look up into the wizard's face. "But I can't get him to eat much breakfast."

Hastings crossed to the window and looked over Jack's shoulder. "Beautiful, isn't it? I feel renewed each time I come here."

Jack turned away rudely. "Mom, I think I'd like to do some reading after breakfast after all. Do you think you could go down and find me a couple of books?"

Becka actually looked at Hastings for an answer. The wizard nodded. "That's a good idea," he said. "Jack and I need to talk anyway. I'll come get you in a little while."

Becka rose from the rocker and kissed Jack on his forehead. "Try and eat a little more," she said, and left the room. Hastings gazed after her until the door shut behind her.

Jack broadened his stance, resting his fists on his hips. "What's wrong with her?"

Hastings sat down in the rocker next to the bed. "There's nothing wrong with your mother. She's fine." He might have smiled, but didn't when he saw the expression on Jack's face.

"You've put a spell on her," Jack persisted. "She's not acting like herself."

"I haven't used any charms on her unnecessarily," Hastings replied, shrugging like an innocent man. "Though I may have to . . . direct her a bit more now that you're up and about."

"You should never have brought her up here."

"I see." Hastings toyed with an unusual ring on his left ring finger. It was a beautifully faceted stone set in an ornate gold setting, and it spun out light in a thousand colors. "I've kept your mother safe," he said. "By now, the Roses are certainly looking for her. I don't know what more you want from me."

Jack didn't know what else to say to the man who had once again saved his life. So he said nothing.

"Sit down, Jack." Hastings motioned to the other chair, looking like a man with an unpleasant job to do. Reluctantly, Jack sat. Hastings waved a hand at the breakfast tray. "Better eat." Jack surveyed the tray, then grudgingly picked up a piece of toast. "How are you feeling?" the wizard asked.

"I'm feeling good," Jack admitted. "It's like I had a bad dream."

"A very bad dream," Hastings agreed. "Your shoulder should be fine, with no stiffness at all. As long as the charm is destroyed in time, all is mended."

"I don't really remember what happened." He finished the slice of toast and started in on his eggs.

"After the charm was broken, I carried you to my car. Linda stayed behind to distract Dr. Longbranch and the others. I thought it best to stop and retrieve your mother. I knew she would be worried about you when you and Linda didn't return, and I was afraid she might go to see Dr. Longbranch. So I brought her up here."

"I didn't know you had a house here."

"This house is the ancestral home of my family, though I acquired it only a few years ago. This is the Lake District, the land of the poets, one of the magical places in Britain." Jack looked up to see Hastings still watching him, as if sizing him up. It made him uneasy.

"Why don't you tell me what's going on?" Jack sat back a bit from his breakfast. "What do you want from me?"

"Had you heard that there is a tournament scheduled for Midsummer's Day?" Hastings's face was expressionless.

"Dr. Longbranch told us about it." Jack thought hard. A lot had happened since his visit to Longbranch's office. "She said the Red Rose had issued a challenge, that they had a champion. She wants me to fight."

Hastings nodded. "She does. And so do I." The words hung heavily in the air between them.

Understanding came slowly, like the change in light that comes with the onset of bad weather. Their eyes locked briefly, and Jack's breath was stolen from him. So many puzzles, so many inconsistencies, and now it all made sense. And then he was angry, at Hastings and at his own stupidity.

"That was your plan all along, wasn't it?" His voice

trembled, despite his efforts to keep it steady. He shoved his breakfast tray away and leaned forward. "That's what you were preparing me for, all the formal training, the bouts in the meadow, everything!"

Hastings nodded. "Yes." He didn't look up, still focused on the ring.

"This trip to England: was that your idea also?" His mother had decided this on her own, hadn't she? He tried to remember.

The wizard spread his fingers in a gesture of confession. "I would have arranged for you to come to England this summer one way or another. I thought perhaps with the Chaucerian Society, but as it happened, you traveled with Becka."

"So you lied to Aunt Linda," Jack continued. "Making her think she could keep me out of this."

"Yes. I lied." Hastings was unapologetic. "Your aunt handed me the rather challenging task of keeping you alive. We simply disagree on strategy."

"Well, you've chosen the wrong person. You can't make me fight for you. If it comes to that, I'll throw the match."

"There is no 'throwing' of the tournament. It's a fight to the death."

"Then you'll have to find someone else to sacrifice."

"Make no mistake. Either way, you will be sacrificed."

Jack looked up, thinking he heard a threat. But Hastings's expression was a mixture of sympathy and impatience.

The wizard leaned back and closed his eyes. "Face the

facts, Jack. As far as you are concerned, this all started maybe three or four months ago, with the trip to the graveyard, right? In the past three weeks, you have been attacked three times. That's just a taste of things to come."

Hastings opened his eyes, fixed Jack with his green-eyed gaze. "Remember, the White Rose has left you entirely alone up until now. As soon as they realize you're alive, they'll come after you again, too. Perhaps the Red Rose tried to poison you. If not, they certainly know who you are now, since the incident at school. And then there are the traders to consider. You're worth a bloody fortune. And the world is full of adventurers who will try to claim it."

Jack could stay in his seat no longer. He rose and walked back to the window. The mists were burning off in the low places, disintegrating into ragged streamers in the still air. Some sheep had wandered into view on one of the far hills. He wished he could just fly away from this place, from who he was, from his past and his future.

Hastings was relentless. "Assuming you make it home from here, what do you think you'll go back to? Trinity will become a battleground for wizards. Your friends, each person in your family will be a point of vulnerability, particularly Anaweir." He paused. "You've seen your mother. I brought her here as an example to you. All I have to do is speak a charm, and she'll do anything I tell her to do. I can demonstrate if you'd like."

"Go to hell," Jack muttered into the crystalline air.

"Which means she will be at the mercy of any wizard from either house who tracks her down. Your father,

Will, and Fitch: no one will be safe. How many of *them* are you willing to sacrifice?" Hastings joined Jack at the window. His voice grew softer. "Trust me, I know. Even if you sleep with one eye open, I give you six months to a year. And even if you survive, you'll end up alone. You see, there are no rules out there."

Jack rested his face against the cool stone surrounding the window. He thought of Trinity, of its quiet tree-lined avenues, the stone buildings of the university, the gaudy gingerbread of Jefferson Street. And then he imagined a barren ruin in its place. "Why do they do it? These tournaments, I mean?"

Hastings spoke patiently, as if delivering a history lesson. "These are ruthless, powerful people with time on their hands and the means to destroy each other. This system meets a lot of needs. It allows the settling of disputes with minimal bloodshed. Wizards claim to be heir to the legacy of the Dragon of Dungeon Ghyll. By contract, we own you. By that point of view, warriors are considered property. And are therefore . . . expendable."

Jack thought of Jessamine Longbranch and how she had treated him. Like he was some animal that could be used and then put out to stud. Jack's hand stole to where the star-shaped scar lay under his shirt. "They should have let me die, back then," he whispered. "I'd be better off."

"Well, they didn't. And now we have to deal with what is." He touched Jack's arm, and Jack flinched.

"What do you know about it? You're a . . . a . . ."

"I know all about it." Hastings voice was so soft, Jack might have missed it.

I could kill myself, Jack thought. He looked over the stone sill of the window, judged the drop to the courtyard below. It would probably be enough. Of course, he could end up paralyzed. Then they couldn't make him fight. He sighed and pressed his palms into his eyelids. Even his hands were callused from swordplay. He was sixteen years old. He didn't want to be dead or crippled. He wanted to graduate from high school and go to college and fall in love. None of which seemed very likely now.

"What happens if I fight?" Jack realized he had crossed a line.

"All warriors in the Game are associated with a sponsor. There is some protection in that, for you and your family, once you are declared. If you win: fame, fortune. And, based on the current shortage of warriors, probably a considerable respite before you have to fight again."

Hastings cleared his throat. "Until I heard that the Red Rose was fielding a champion, I had hoped no one would be able to meet your challenge. If the challenge isn't answered, the Game is forfeited. As good as a win, and not so bloody." Hastings almost smiled. "You don't have much experience, but your weapon may make the difference."

"Will I be able to go home again? Afterward?" If I win, he thought. After I kill somebody. Jack knew he could have killed Garrett Lobeck. But he wouldn't be facing Garrett Lobeck. Jack thrust the thought from his mind.

Hastings thought a moment. "I don't know, Jack. That's probably a question for you to answer. You are already quite different from the boy who went to Coal Grove." He ran his hand through his hair and leaned against the wall. "It is not fair, and these are not attractive choices. Look at it this way: even if you lose the tournament, your family and friends will be safe." He paused, a heartbeat. "But I don't intend for you to lose."

"What happens at the tournament?"

"It's a celebration over several days: ceremony, wagering, and posturing on both sides. Then the champions fight each other in one-to-one combat. Everything is regulated by the Rules of Engagement."

"Where is it held?"

"Here in Cumbria, traditionally; though it's a movable feast. The last one was held in Australia."

"What do you get out of it?"

"Perhaps a chance to change the system. Perhaps a chance to save your life. No guarantees, either way."

Did he really have a choice? Jack had no doubt Hastings could force him to participate, whether he wanted to or not. He was just like any other wizard when it came to pushing people around. Hastings acted like he had some kind of personal rule book he played by. If so, it was indecipherable to Jack.

It was all pretty hopeless. The best he could do was to try to limit the risk to his family. Perhaps this would be easier than throwing himself out a window.

The soft breath of the mountains cooled his flushed skin, whispered a warning. "I'll play," he said, without turning away from the window.

Hastings released a long breath. Jack wondered if it was a sigh of relief.

"I thought you would." Hastings said.

"What about Aunt Linda?" She would be furious with him, but there was nothing he could do about that. My choice. My life and my death.

"I'm hoping the tournament will be over before she knows you're playing." Hastings shook his head. "She is going to be very angry with me. Perhaps angry is not so bad as indifferent." He gazed out of the window.

Jack couldn't stop himself. "But how could you . . . weren't you . . ?" His voice trailed away under Hastings's clear-eyed scrutiny.

"Yes. We were together once." He half smiled. "You know, Jack, all of the women in your family are full of magic, whether they inherit the stone or not. They are among the casualties of this war." With some effort, Hastings shook off his melancholy. "I will make arrangements for us to attend the tournament, then." He turned to go.

But Jack still had a question. "So if the Red Rose already has a champion, I assume that I will be fighting for the White Rose?"

The wizard stopped and turned back, looking surprised and almost amused.

"No, Jack. I thought you understood. You will be playing for me."

ᚱ CHAPTER FOURTEEN ᚱ
WHEN LOVERS MEET

Jack went back into training the day following his conversation with Hastings. The routine of it was almost soothing. The idea of a deadline was also appealing compared to the cat-and-mouse game that had been going on for months. Every morning he ran for miles through the mists, up and down the treacherous hills surrounding the stone house. Hastings ran with him.

They would return to the house and have breakfast with Becka. The stone house was almost a castle, with sheer, fortresslike walls that dropped to a grassy plain surrounded by hills. Informal gardens stretched from the back door to the wooded area at the foot of the fells. The first floor of the house included a great hall, a library, and kitchen and dining areas. There were at least six bedrooms upstairs. Jack never saw any staff around, although there always seemed to be food and drink available whenever they were hungry. Perhaps it was all done through sorcery.

After breakfast, they worked with their foils in the meadow behind the house. Now the focus was no longer on defense but on offense, on penetrating his opponent's defenses, the delivery of a killing stroke. And every afternoon Hastings sent warriors against Jack. Some were new to him, while others were familiar from his previous bouts.

Now there was no need to put up a barrier when he fought, to keep away prying eyes. No one came anywhere near, except for the occasional sheep that wandered down the hillsides. Somehow, Hastings kept Becka away from the bouts, though whether through personal charm or wizardry, Jack didn't know.

Jack realized Hastings was concerned about his lack of experience. Despite relentless coaching and the quality of his weapon, it was hard to get around the fact that Jack had been in training for only a few months. The same could be true of his opponent, but he couldn't count on that.

Jack wished he knew more about the warriors he fought against in practice; about their previous lives, how they'd come to be warriors, how many tournaments they'd fought in, how they'd died. Well, maybe not that last part.

On his third afternoon of training, a young man exploded into the meadow, Jack's fifth opponent of the afternoon. The man's brown hair was drawn into a queue decorated with feathers, and he wore fringed buckskins. He carried a hatchet in one hand, a curved sword in the other, and a knife was belted at his waist. He appeared to be a New World frontiersman of the seventeenth or eighteenth century. He charged at Jack with a bloodcurdling howl.

Jack put up his hand. "Wait a minute!"

For a moment, Jack didn't think the man had heard him. He kept coming, full speed, like he meant to take Jack's head off without breaking stride. But finally, at the last minute, the man slowed and skidded to a stop just outside the reach of Jack's sword.

"What d'you mean, wait a minute?" The man scowled indignantly. "You called me to a bout, and I came as ordered. Now, go to." He spread his arms wide, a weapon in each hand, ready to receive Jack's charge.

"Well," Jack said uncertainly. "I thought perhaps we could talk a little first."

"Talk a little?" The warrior snorted, then spat on the ground. "What the devil for? We're fighting, not making love."

"I was just wondering where you were from, how you became a warrior, things like that." Out of the corner of his eye, Jack could see Hastings standing by, hands on hips, shaking his head. Probably rolling his eyes, too, but he was too far away to see.

"Why do you care about that?" the warrior demanded.

"I thought we probably have something in common," Jack persisted. "Being as we're both warriors, you know."

The warrior looked him up and down, at Jack's sweat-shirt and athletic shoes. "You don't look like any warrior *I've* ever seen. If you must know, I started out fighting against the French when I was fourteen. When I tired of that, I went and lived with the Shawnee. Then I was captured by wizards. They chained me up and put me on board a ship back to the Old Country. Put me into the hands of the Warriormasters. I would've cut my own mother's throat by the time they finished wi' me.

"I probably fought eight or ten bouts over here before I bought it. And I think what we have in common is that a bloody wizard has us by the privates." He jerked a thumb at Hastings. "Now, go to, before he does something neither one of us will like."

Reluctantly, Jack brought the tip of his blade up and assumed a ready stance.

"Wait a minute!" This time it was Hastings. The wizard was striding purposefully across the field.

"Now you've done it," the other warrior muttered to Jack, swearing softly. He swung around to face Hastings. "It's not my fault!" he shouted, when Hastings was still twenty feet away. "I wanted to fight 'im, but he'd ruther talk. But give me a chance, and I promise I'll give him a game." He wiped the sweat from his face with his grimy sleeve and shifted his feet nervously.

"What's your name?" Hastings asked the warrior.

"Brooks, m'lord," the warrior replied, licking his lips. "Jeremiah's my Christian name, m'lord."

"Did I hear you say you'd fought in a number of tournaments?" As Hastings drew close, the warrior backed away.

"I did say that, sir." Jeremiah Brooks spoke reluctantly, as if unsure whether to admit it or not.

Hastings nodded. "Good. I need you to help my student, here."

"That's just what I was about, m'lord," the warrior said, turning back to Jack and crouching as if to spring.

"No!" Hastings said quickly. "I had something else in mind. Something a bit more . . . direct."

Brooks began to backpedal. "Please, m'lord. I came to fight a bout, and I'm willing. Don't spell me."

"I won't hurt you," Hastings assured him.

Not reassured, Brooks turned to run, but Hastings extended his hands and the air shimmered around the frontiersman. He was bound tightly, his hands at his sides, his weapons useless. He tried to squirm free, unsuccessfully. His eyes were fixed on Hastings, wide with fear.

Now it was Jack's turn. "Don't hurt him," he protested.

"Don't you start," Hastings snapped. "I'm not going to hurt him. I'm just going to *borrow* what he knows on your behalf. Come here, Jack."

"What are you going to do?" Jack asked warily.

"If we're going to work together, you're going to have to trust me now and then," Hastings growled. "I *said* come here."

Angrily, Jack slammed Shadowslayer into his scabbard and crossed the distance between them, and stood next to Brooks. Hastings shoved them both to their knees and squatted, facing them. He placed his hands on their heads. Brooks was muttering softly to himself, swearing or praying. Swearing, Jack guessed, based on what he'd heard so far.

"I'm going to try to edit this, Jack, but it's an art and not a science, so bear with me," Hastings said, which made no sense at all. The wizard closed his eyes, concentrating, speaking a charm, and then the power begin to flow through his fingers. Jack felt as if his scalp were being stretched away from his skull, heat and light pouring into his mind, an invasion. He wanted to twist away from the wizard's hand, but found he couldn't move.

His breath came quick and shallow, in ineffective gasps. He thought he cried out, and then images began to slide across his consciousness, slowly at first, and then faster, like bright frames in a jumbled videotape. There were landscapes: dense green forests, never touched by an axe, the ground open under a canopy of trees, an Indian trail that twisted and turned, following a creek with a Shawnee name that sang over the rocks as it descended to the Ohio. A broad valley, shrouded in mist, surrounded by mountains, filled with bones, where warriors were brought to fight.

There were people: red-coated British regulars, scruffy colonials who could slide through the forest as well as any Shawnee, a girl in a tavern with hair the color of buttercups and a blouse that slid softly from her shoulders. Wizards, hard-faced and ruthless, with their black arts, with their metal collars and chains, who tortured him until he begged for the chance to kill somebody, who put fear into him for the first time in his life. The warriors who came to him, tall and short, some of them very young, but none of them very old. He read their faces, could see hope and then death in their eyes.

And sensations: the scent of rain racing across the lakes. The ring and spark of steel on steel. The stench of too many unwashed men, too long together. The quick and deadly dance of the Game. The yielding of flesh and bone to his blade, and the wet sucking sound as he freed it. And in the end, that soft slipping away of life as he lay flat on his back staring up at the sky, the blood pumping from his body, knowing that someone else would fight the next time.

When Hastings released him, Jack fell forward onto his face and lay there, trembling, for a long time. He didn't want to look at the other two, because he didn't want them to see him crying. He could hear Hastings speaking softly, to Brooks, he assumed. When he finally lifted his head, the warrior was gone.

From then on, Jack knew all about Brooks—too much. For all intents and purposes, he was the heir of the warrior's experiences, but whether that boded well or ill for him, he didn't know. He had a body memory of bloodshed, in the New World and the Old. He could tell which way a man would go in a fight by a shift in his weight, or the look in his eyes. He could throw a hatchet and hit a tree a hundred paces off. He didn't have to try it, he just knew he could. He feared wizards and their burning hands the way some men feared snakes and flying things: with an irrational and paralyzing terror.

There were other things. He knew the taste of pemmican, and venison, and squirrel. It wasn't until Becka commented on it that he realized he'd acquired a colorful new vocabulary. After that, he tried his best to keep his tongue in check.

Be careful what you wish for. Once again, he was angry with Hastings, who had given him a history he'd never asked for. At the same time he knew it for the gift it was.

He won the next ten bouts he fought.

The days went by, more than the few Becka had promised, and still she stayed. She was an almost ethereal presence, drifting through the corridors and gardens, reading in the courtyard, writing poetry. Because Jack and Hastings spent a lot of time in practice, she spent considerable time alone. But she never complained.

The three of them always had dinner together. In the evenings after supper, Becka and Hastings would go for long walks in the hills. It was during those times that Jack took advantage of the library. It was a wonderful collection of books, some rare and valuable: English literature, studies of the great philosophers, scientific works, volumes about Eastern mysticism. The contents of a glass case in one corner held a particular fascination for Jack. It was a collection of books on wizardry. Although it was protected by a locking charm, it was one that Jack could easily disable. So he spent hours reading through ancient texts, some in Latin, some in Middle English, some in French (which he had taken in school, but there wasn't much overlap in vocabulary). He wished Nick were there to translate. He could use some advice anyway.

Jack had been careful not to reveal anything about his

training in wizardry to Hastings. He figured that keeping it a secret might be an advantage in a game where he had few advantages to claim.

After fighting most of the day, Jack was always exhausted by early evening, and fell into bed early. Not even his reluctance to leave his mother alone with Leander Hastings could keep him awake.

Jack was ambivalent over Becka's continuing presence. He was well aware that his mother would never approve of his decision to fight in the tournament, but he welcomed the chance to spend what might be his last days with her before Midsummer's Day.

Sometimes he gazed into Blaise's mirror, hoping it would reveal something. But a mist lay over the silver surface like the fog that shrouded the mountains at sunset.

Then came an evening ten days into his stay in Cumbria and four days prior to Midsummer's Day. Becka and Hastings had gone out walking as usual. Jack was deep in a book on *convertere*, that is, the art of transforming one thing into another. He heard a sound as of a door closing elsewhere in the house. He thought perhaps that his mother and Hastings had returned early. Quickly he returned the book to its shelf, closed the cabinet, and reapplied the locking charm.

He heard no voices filtering down the hallway, no one calling his name. Curious, he crept to the door of the library and looked up and down the hall. Empty. Could it have been the wind? He thought it was unlikely any breeze could have moved the heavy wooden doors in that place. An intruder? Perhaps the wizards of the Red or

White Rose had tracked them there.

Shadowslayer was in the Great Hall, where he'd left it after practice. He slipped noiselessly down the hall to the huge, two-story entry and scanned the room beyond. It was dimly illuminated by the fading light that leaked through the gallery windows. There was no sign of anyone or anything moving on the main floor or on the gallery above. His sword still leaned against the corner of the hearth. He took a deep breath and sprinted across the flagstones that separated him from his weapon. He had reached the apron of the huge fireplace when he heard a noise behind him. He seized his sword and spun around in a half crouch and came face-to-face with Linda Downey.

"Jack!" She grabbed him and held him tight, careful to avoid the blade as she did so. "I knew you couldn't be too far from your sword." She patted his sword arm, then released him and looked him over carefully. "Are you all right? Is your shoulder healed?"

Jack nodded, completely undone by this turn of events. He carefully set his sword back on the hearth and retreated until his back was against the masonry. His mind was spinning madly. What now?

Linda didn't give him much time to think about it. She seemed to be in a considerable hurry. "Where's Hastings?" she demanded.

Jack found his voice. "He's out for a walk, I think."

"Good. We've got to get out of here before he gets back." She picked up the case and the sword, and handed them both back to Jack.

"H-how did you find us?" Jack stammered.

"I knew he owned property up here. It just took me a while to trace it. Come on, Jack," she said urgently. "You're in danger here."

"I can't just leave," Jack protested.

"We'll write him a note when we're far away," Linda replied grimly. "With no return address."

"Mom is here," Jack said finally.

"Becka?" Linda exclaimed. "I've been worried sick about her. Has she been here all this time? Thank God she's all right." And, then, after a pause, "But, what is she doing here?"

"Hastings thought it was best if she weren't searching the town for me, asking questions, perhaps going back to Dr. Longbranch." Jack shrugged unconvincingly.

"Is she in the house?" Linda asked quickly.

Jack shook his head. "She's out walking with him."

Linda stared at him for a moment, then appeared to come to a decision. "Never mind. I need to get you to safety, then I'll come back for Becka. Nick's waiting for us in Oxford. From there, we'll find a safer place." There was a mixture of enchantment and desperation in her voice. "Please, Jack. You've got to come with me now."

"Can't you at least stay for a cup of tea?" The voice came from the doorway. "Or a glass of wine for old times' sake?" It was Hastings, with an armload of kindling, Becka just behind him. "I was just about to light a fire." He turned to Becka. "Look, Becka, your sister has come to visit."

"Linda!" Becka embraced her sister. "How did you

find us? I wanted to call you, but there's no phone up here. You've seen Jack? He's much better."

Linda withdrew enough from Becka's embrace to glare at Hastings. "Lee, this is just like you."

Becka stared at them, looking from one to the other. "Do you two know each other?"

Hastings looked up from the hearth, resting his forearms on his knees. "Becka, forgive me. Would you mind fetching us some wine?"

Becka nodded, pursing her lips thoughtfully. "Let me see if I can find us something in the kitchen." She disappeared.

"So you've left the Chaucerian Society behind," Hastings said, standing up. He pointed at the kindling and it burst into flame. "I hope they're in good hands." He was studiously avoiding looking at the enchanter, which wouldn't have been easy for any man.

"They are safe enough," she replied. "Will's parents are with them. They're leaving for their tour to Scotland and Ireland. Which you should know, since you set it up."

Hastings nodded. "So perhaps . . . perhaps you can stay a few days?" He looked at her quickly, then away. To Jack's surprise, he sounded hopeful, almost eager.

Linda was having none of it. "Look, I appreciate all you've done, but I think it's time Jack and Becka went to Oxford," she said evenly. "My car is not far away, and I've come to drive them there."

Hastings folded his arms, making an exasperated sound. "D'you really think Jack can go down to Oxford? With every wizard in the United Kingdom hunting him?"

"Well, they can't stay up here!" Linda muttered, balling her hands into fists.

"Who are you worried about? Jack or Becka?" He raised a hand to prevent an onslaught of words. "Don't you see? Jessamine knows who he is. So does Geoffrey. It's over."

Jack could stand the game playing no longer. "I've decided to fight in the tournament, Aunt Linda," he said.

"Jack!" She turned on Hastings. "You were supposed to prevent this! What kind of charm have you laid on him?" she demanded.

Hastings sighed. "Had I wanted to force him into it, I could have taken him a long time ago and saved myself considerable trouble."

Becka returned with a bottle of wine and some glasses. She scanned the angry faces and poured a glass for Linda first. "Maybe you'll feel better after you've had some wine," Becka suggested calmly, handing it to her.

"There's more than one way to spellbind a person," Linda said darkly, then caught herself, sliding a glance at her sister. "Becka, I need to talk to Leander in private."

Becka handed a glass of wine to Hastings and laid a hand on his arm, a gesture of support. "Linda, I want to know why you're being so rude to him. He saved Jack's life back in Trinity. When Jack was taken ill in London, he invited us to come up here so he could recover. He's been nothing but kind to Jack and me. Then you show up here unannounced and treat him like a villain in his own house."

"Leander!" Linda vibrated with anger.

"Oh, all right!" Reluctantly, Hastings set his wine down on the table. He put an arm around Becka and muttered a few words under his breath. Becka froze where she stood, eyes open, lips parted, as if she were about to say something. Hastings lifted her and settled her gently on the couch. Then he picked up his glass again, holding it in front of him like a shield. "Speak your piece, if you feel you must."

Linda swung around to face Jack. "Jack, if you participate in this barbaric system, you will just perpetuate it."

Hastings drained his glass quickly and refilled it from the bottle on the table. "Linda, you will not be allowed to interfere with this," he said softly.

"So now you've taken to using sixteen-year-old boys to get your revenge, is that it?"

"If I could do it myself, don't you think I would? You know me better than that."

Jack was absolutely lost. "What are you two talking about?" he demanded. He dropped wearily into a chair.

Linda's voice was brittle and cold. "Didn't you tell me once that Mr. Hastings always chooses what he wants to talk about? I assume he didn't choose to tell you about his family."

Jack shook his head, already depressed. He knew he was about to hear another old story. He felt like his life had been entirely ruined by events that had occurred long before he was born.

"Leander's older sister, Carrie, was born a warrior. Lee's childhood was spent moving from place to place, as his family tried to avoid the Roses." Linda took a sip of wine. Hastings was staring into the fire. "It didn't help. Geoffrey Wylie found her when she was eighteen, and claimed her for the Red Rose." Her voice softened. "She never even made it to a tournament, because the White Rose got to her first. His father and brother were killed, and his mother was never the same. Leander was ten at the time."

"Wylie?" Jack repeated.

She glanced at Jack. "It's a story that has been played out a thousand times in our family. Only, Leander has been obsessed with fighting Wylie and the Roses ever since. So when I was looking for someone to help me protect you from the Roses, I thought of him. I never thought he would choose to embrace the system that killed his sister." She threw what remained of her wine in Hastings's face.

Hastings caught Linda's wrist with one hand and shook the wine glass from it. It shattered on the flagstones, scattering drops of wine like blood on the hearth. He wiped wine out of his eyes with the other hand. "Don't make me lose my temper, Linda." His voice was deceptively gentle.

Linda didn't back away, but leaned in to him, standing on tiptoe to get close to his face. "Why? Is that what happened to Susannah?"

The daylight had fled completely, and the room was illuminated only by magic and the flames on the hearth. For a moment the little scene was like an engraving, the tall wizard, the tiny enchanter, both spinning out fragments of light; Jack and his mother, everyone frozen.

Then Hastings released his grip on Linda's wrist and stepped back. The two stared at each other for a long moment. "Something like that," he said. He sat down in a chair by the fireplace and put his face in his hands.

Jack looked from his aunt to Hastings and back again. Linda leaned wearily against the fireplace. "Jack, meet the man who murdered your great-great grandmother."

"But that was a hundred years ago," Jack protested. "And she fell from a horse!" None of this was making sense.

"No, she didn't, Jack." Hastings straightened, but did not look at him. "Susannah was a warrior, but she was a pacifist. She wouldn't help me fight the Roses, nor would she allow me to train her son. When she learned what my purpose was, she wanted nothing more to do with me. I could not convince her that running and hiding always fail in the end."

"So you killed her, and you took her stone," Linda said quietly.

He flinched. "Not exactly. She killed herself because of me. There is a difference, if a small one. She offered her stone, and I took it." Hastings extended his left hand; the stone in his ring shone brilliantly. "I use it to remind myself of what I did, and what I lost. It . . . is a source of power, but if I could take it all back, I would, in a heartbeat."

Jack remembered the scene in Blaise's mirror, the young, red-haired woman he'd thought was his mother, the struggle at the top of the cliff. She'd buried the dagger in her own breast. That, at least, was the truth.

There was a brief silence, broken only by the snap of resin in the fire, and then Jack spoke. "How did you know?" he asked his aunt.

"It was in her obituary. Her body was found by Lee Hastens, Hastings to us. They weren't so fussy about spelling in those days. She had a chest wound, but I am sure it was not difficult for a wizard to plant a story about a fall from a horse. Will and Fitch had it partly figured out."

"But that was a hundred years ago," Jack repeated stubbornly.

There was a faint smile on Hastings's face. "I am much older than you think I am, Jack. We wizards are long-lived and have long memories. Why do you think this barbaric tournament system has gone on as long as it has?"

"What about Susannah's son?" Jack was slowly putting the story together. "What happened to him?"

"His name was Andrew," Hastings replied. "Your great-grandfather. I helped him escape with his father after Susannah's death. I kept track of him, kept the Roses away from him, but chose not to interfere with him after Susannah died." There was a century of pain in his voice.

The man in the mirror had wept, rocking the young woman in his arms. "You were in love with Susannah," Jack said. "And you're the one who tends her grave." The words came back to him. *Wizards have long memories.*

Hastings did not dispute it. He stretched his long legs out in front of him and stared moodily into the fire.

After a moment, Linda said in a voice that would cut diamonds, "So, Jack, it appears that Mr. Hastings is working his way down through the Downey women. First your great-great grandmother, then me. Perhaps your mother is next."

"Just stop it!" Jack said it loudly enough to shut them both up. He felt that he was getting way too much information, but still not enough to understand. He'd never seen his aunt in such a state, ever, and he hoped he never would again. There was a raw, primitive edge to her anger that was bewildering. Now they were both staring at him.

"Becka is my mother," Jack went on, more quietly. "She's a great lawyer and a civil libertarian, and she'll always back the underdog in a fight. She loves medieval literature, and she makes her students love it, too. She likes to garden and take in strays. And she has *nothing* at all to do with this."

"That's what wizards do, Jack," Linda said evenly. "They go after whatever they want, and run over other people in the process. And it looks like you're on course to be the next sacrifice in Mr. Hastings's quest for revenge."

Hastings spread his fingers. "I didn't ask for this job. You asked me to save him, and I'm doing the best I can." He smiled bitterly. "Don't you see? I've failed. More than a hundred years I've been fighting the Roses, trying to organize a rebellion against this system, training warriors to defend themselves, pulling off daring raids and rescues. And for what? The Warrior Guild has been wiped out, for all intents and purposes." His voice softened. "I'm not telling you anything you don't know. *You've* been fighting this war since you were Jack's age. From what I've heard, you're still fighting. Just not with me." He held her gaze for a long moment, and then looked away, toward the fire.

Linda looked stricken. "Lee, I—"

"Even that's not enough for them," Hastings growled. "Now Jessamine Longbranch is trying to figure out how to create new warriors. Next they'll be digging up the bodies of those they've murdered and cutting them apart." He touched the ring on his finger self-consciously.

"So it's time to change strategies. I've been cutting off the arms of the beast, and it's done no good. This time I'm going after the heart."

"You're going to try to gain control of the council," Linda whispered. "And the artifacts."

Hastings nodded. "If I play Jack, and win, I'll own the Wizard Council and all their cache of magical weapons under their damned rules, at least until the next tournament. And there won't be another, if I can prevent it." He looked at Jack. "As I told you, I had hoped neither House would be able to come up with a player. They would forfeit, and you wouldn't have to fight."

"Well, maybe you can find the Red Rose player and eliminate him," Linda said acidly, mimicking Dr. Longbranch. "That would be perfect."

Hastings slammed his fist against the table, rattling the crockery. "Do you have a better suggestion? I wouldn't have done this if I didn't think it was Jack's best chance. It's too late. What do you think his future is going to be like? Where are you planning to hide? They're going to butcher him sooner or later, just like the rest of the

Weirlind, and there's nothing you or I can do about it. And if they take him to play, you know what they'll do to him, don't you? At least if I sponsor him, that won't happen."

"Mr. Hastings told me that both the Red and the White Rose will be hunting for me now," Jack said with little emotion. "He said they would go after my family in order to get to me. Is that true?"

Linda sighed. "That has been the pattern," she admitted.

"No matter where I go, they'll track me down. I can never go home." Jack shook his head. "I'm already tired of this, and it's only been a few months. I can't do this for a lifetime. At least this is clean and simple."

There was a brief silence. "Where are they holding the tournament?" Linda asked.

Hastings shrugged. "At Raven's Ghyll, perhaps."

Linda drew in a quick breath. "What makes you think you would get out of there alive? The members of the council will draw lots to choose who has the honor of cutting your throat."

Hastings smiled. "As a sponsor, I will be protected."

"Until someone gets you alone. Wizard's rules are meant to be broken," Linda said. To Jack's surprise, there were tears in her eyes. "Leander, maybe you are determined to get yourself killed, but leave Jack out of it."

"I'm already in it, Aunt Linda," Jack said quietly. Maybe it was the effect of the merger with Brooks, but there was some part of him that was no longer a child.

Linda seemed to sense it, too. "You're different," she whispered. "First your body, and now . . ." The tears had escaped and were now sliding down her cheeks. "You're sixteen years old," she said softly. "You're too young for this fight."

"I never picked it," Jack said. He turned to Hastings, feeling unusually calm and resolute. "You need to let my mother go now. Aunt Linda can take her back. Whatever you two can cook up between you to keep her from worrying is fine. I'll be at your bout. But I don't want her involved with this or with you. I think I deserve that much."

"Jack, I'm sorry. I'll send your mother back with Linda," Hastings said. He knelt beside Becka and took her hands. He spoke quietly, and although Jack was listening intently, he couldn't make out most of the charm. Becka blinked and sat up, looking confused.

"Becka, Linda is here to drive you down to Oxford. Jack's going to stay on with me for a few days. We're going camping in Langdale Pikes. I'll drive him down to you next week." Jack was beginning to recognize the sound of wizardry.

Becka stared at him a moment, then nodded. "I suppose I knew we couldn't stay here forever," she said. "But thank you for your . . . hospitality. I know you'll have fun, sweetheart," she said to Jack, managing a smile. "It will just take a minute to get my things." She looked as if she wanted to say something else, but then lost the train of it. She stood, wrapping her arms about herself, then turned and fled up the stairs.

Hastings looked after her for a long moment, then turned to Linda. "She'll sleep all the way home, and when she wakes up, she won't remember much about her stay here. She'll not worry, though, because she'll know Jack is camping with me."

"I'm not leaving you here, Jack," Aunt Linda said stubbornly. "Don't you think your mother will catch on when you're dead?"

"There's nothing you can do," Jack replied. "I'll be fine," he said with more confidence than he felt. "Besides, I might win."

Becka returned with her bag. Linda gave Jack a fierce hug, her face wet with tears. Becka gave him a considerably drier one. And then they were out the door.

With the women gone, the manor had the feel of a dead place. The wizard and the warrior stood awkwardly for a moment, at a loss for words. At some level Jack had known it would come to this, from the first time he'd seen Hastings in Trinity. Even then, he'd seen the deadliness in him, and somehow sensed his tragic history as well. More and more, there were no revelations, but simply the uncovering of truths long known but dimly remembered. Everything had been written long ago. Their destinies were linked.

As for Hastings, the wizard seemed more vulnerable than before, flawed, somehow eminently human. A man who considered himself a failure at his life's work. Who was, perhaps, heading to his death in Raven's Ghyll, and bringing Jack along.

❦ CHAPTER FIFTEEN ❧
RAVEN'S GHYLL

Fells. It was a fit name for these mountains, Jack decided. They were full of old magic, lost souls, and melancholy. And on this day they were full of rain and mist as well. He and Hastings had left their car in a parking lot some distance outside of Keswick. As they climbed higher and higher, the weather grew more brutal. Summer in the Lake District felt like November in Ohio. Jack wore a heavy jacket he had borrowed from Hastings, climbing pants, a thick sweater, and sturdy hiking boots. He carried his other clothes in a backpack, and his sword was slung across his back to leave his hands free for scrambling over the unforgiving terrain.

Hastings set an unrelenting pace, always upward, following a path that Jack could barely pick out on the treacherous rock.

The peak loomed up before them. Ravenshead,

Hastings called it. But its stark melancholy suited Jack in his present mood.

They climbed farther into the ravine, keeping the peak on their left-hand side. Their route coincided with a stream that leaped and tumbled among the broken stones. The rocks along the streambed were wet and slippery underfoot. They climbed almost vertically the last hundred yards until they came to a place where the water seemed to explode from a cliff face.

"This is the water gate to Raven's Ghyll." Hastings had to shout over the roar of the falls. This left Jack as clueless as before. But he knew that Raven's Ghyll was their destination, the traditional site of the tournament. Hastings had suggested they enter the back way, for safety reasons.

"The Rules of Engagement are not in force until you are officially registered for the tournament," Hastings had said. "I don't want to risk an ambush along the way." Jack remembered what Linda had said about the members of the council wanting to cut Hastings's throat, and assumed that the wizard might have personal reasons for slipping in unnoticed. As if the terrain and weather were not bad enough, the idea of an ambush had infused their journey with just that extra element of suspense. Jack found himself reacting to every little noise and flicker of movement.

Hastings boosted himself easily onto a small platform of rock next to the falls and extended a hand to Jack so he could climb up after him. All of the stones and handholds were slippery with spray. Hastings pointed into the falls. "We're going in there."

There was a scant eight inches of ledge along the side of the gorge. By flattening themselves against the cliff and hugging the cold rock face, they were able to slide past the falls and into a rock chamber that lay beyond. It was cold and shrouded in vapor from the thundering falls. Jack could look out past the cascading water and see how far they had climbed.

At the back of the vault a narrow path snaked up between two massive blocks of stone. That was their road. They were hardly hiking anymore, but climbing. Any steeper and they would have needed ropes, Jack thought, tightening his fingers around stones above his head and hauling himself upward, trying not to think about what would happen if he slipped.

His thoughts wandered to his opponent, putting flesh on the bones of speculation. Hastings had guessed that Jack's opponent must be young, or the Red Rose would have called a tournament before now. The White Rose had held the cup for years, a situation that rankled the other House. Since most warriors were taken as young children, he'd probably been in training for years. Perhaps he looked forward to this fight with anticipation instead of dread.

Another half hour of hard climbing, and they were over the rim and looking down on Raven's Ghyll.

They couldn't see much. The valley was shrouded by a shimmering cloud that might have been mist, but which even Jack's uneducated eyes recognized as a wizard's barrier.

"How did you know how to get through here?" Jack

asked, struggling to catch his breath and hoping to delay the wizard long enough to do so.

"I've had to get in and out of Raven's Ghyll unseen in the past," Hastings replied. The wizard wasn't even breathing hard. Hastings unslung his backpack and produced two lightweight cloaks. He pulled one on over his clothes and handed the other to Jack. "Put this on," he directed. Jack put his cloak on and pulled up the hood.

"Have you ever been in a tournament before?" Jack asked.

"I've never actually participated, but I've disrupted a few." Hastings reached into his pack and drew from it a small object, which he handed to Jack. It was a roughly-hewn gray stone, oval, about the size of the palm of his hand. It was covered with unfamiliar runes and symbols, and hung from a finely-wrought silver chain. It seemed to absorb light rather than reflect it.

Jack looked up at Hastings. "Put it on," the wizard said. "I'd like to surprise them, if I can." He didn't offer any further explanation.

Jack slipped the chain over his head and pushed the stone into the neckline of his sweatshirt. It lay against the skin of his chest, creating a slight tingling sensation. The wizard laid a hand on his arm, spoke a few words of Latin, and disappeared.

"Hastings!" Jack could still feel the burn of the wizard's hand.

"We're both invisible, Jack. The stone is called a *dyrne sefa*. Created by sorcerers. It allows us powers uncommon even to wizards. Now, stay close so I don't lose you." And he pressed ahead, more slowly now, descending the inner side of the hills that enclosed the Ghyll. The footing was tricky, and Jack had to concentrate to keep from stumbling and to stay within reach of Hastings.

As they approached the barrier, the wizard spoke a charm, and a ragged rent appeared in the mist before them. They stepped through, and it closed behind them. Now they could see clearly.

Raven's Ghyll was a broad, shallow valley surrounded on all sides by sheer cliffs and frowning fells. Snow-fed streams tumbled from the flanks of Ravenshead and meandered across the valley floor, cutting it into meadows and parks quilted with trees, and finally escaping through the ravine they'd just climbed. At the far end of the basin, halfway up the slope, a large castle was built into the hill. It had been constructed of the native rock, and resembled an outcropping, part of the landscape. It was surrounded on three sides by terraced gardens that sloped down to the floor of the Ghyll.

Far above their heads, halfway up the slope of Ravenshead, something caught the light, reflecting it into Jack's eyes. He squinted, shading his eyes. A crystalline boulder protruded from the granite, as if trying to escape its drab prison. It must be huge, tons of stone, he thought, to appear so prominent from this distance. It had several shining faces, and was bluntly pointed at the end. The brilliance he was seeing was not reflected sunlight, but rather came from the heart of the stone itself.

"What's that?" he asked Hastings, pointing, then

remembering that Hastings couldn't see him. "That shiny rock up there?"

He could hear amusement in Hastings's voice. "Hardly a rock, Jack. That's Ravenshead, soul of the mountain, otherwise called the Weirstone, the Dragon's Tooth. It is said that the crystals we carry originated from that stone, freed and shaped by a magic more powerful than any known today." He paused. "It is the stone that keeps us imprisoned," he added softly.

Jack didn't understand. "What do you mean?"

"The Rules of Engagement are part of the covenant that keeps the dragon sleeping in the mountain. If the rules are broken, the dragon will awake."

"Is that true?" Jack shivered, gazing up at the stone that shimmered like a beacon on the hillside, while the top of the mountain was still shrouded in mist.

Hastings shrugged—Jack was sure he did, though he couldn't see it. "That's what they say," he repeated.

The weather was better in the valley than it had been on the fells, though everything dripped with moisture from the recent rain. The wall of stone around them diverted the relentless wind, which made it noticeably warmer. The grasses of the meadow were lush, deep greens and yellows where the buttercups bloomed. It was almost sunny, although the light had an odd, incandescent quality from the wizard's mist.

Between them and the castle, the Ghyll boiled with activity. Buildings and tents and trailers were scattered along both sides of the vale, as if tossed there randomly by a giant hand. People swarmed across the meadows, all seemingly in a hurry. Bright pennants flew from many of the temporary structures. Some bore a white rose, and others red. The smell of food came faintly to them. It reminded Jack of a Renaissance fair he had attended years ago. Or how he imagined a gypsy encampment might look.

A large space had been left free of buildings on the valley floor just before the castle walls. Teams of workers were constructing reviewing stands on either side. He assumed that was to be the site of the tournament. The thought left him numb.

"Who organizes all this?" he asked Hastings.

"His name is Claude D'Orsay," Hastings said shortly. "He is a wizard, and the lineal Master of Games of the Weir. The Ghyll is the seat of the Wizard Guild, the legendary source of their power. For centuries, his family has had the job of keeping peace among the heirs. Under the rules, the Master is a chancellor who works with the head of the Wizard Council, the Holder of the Tournament Cup."

He paused. "The Master of Games is supposed to be neutral in these affairs, but D'Orsay has always been a political player, more powerful than he should be. He administers the rules—for example—the one that says that wizards are not allowed to attack each other except through the warriors. Only, he overlooks a lot when it suits him," he said dryly.

Jack had wondered why Linda seemed to think Hastings was in danger, despite the protection of the rules. "Where did all this come from?" He waved a hand, then remembered again he was invisible. "All these buildings. How did they get here?"

Hastings laughed. "We *are* wizards, after all. What with servants and so on, we can set up rather quickly. It will all be gone the day after the bout."

The two picked their way down a stony path to the valley floor. Soon they were fighting their way through crowds of people who seemed startled at their touch.

Jack's head was spinning, filled with a cacophony of voices, living wizards and dead warriors, an overwhelming din that grew as he approached the keep. The dead voices were warning him. *Away the warrior*, they pleaded. *For this is where they spill your blood.* The floor of the valley was a killing ground, watered with blood, salted with bones, the resting place of hundreds of warriors. It was brutally familiar, courtesy of Jeremiah Brooks. He tried to lick his lips, but his mouth was dry. He remembered coming there a captive, in full knowledge of what lay ahead.

Hastings disabled the invisibility charm as they approached the festival grounds. They were assigned quarters in a permanent structure, a cottage in the manor garden. It was small and comfortable, with two bedrooms and a large room that served as living room, kitchen, and parlor, centered around a large stone fireplace. Jack was cold and tired and grimy after his trip up the mountain. Fortunately, the place had a shower. He spent considerable time under the hot spray, and emerged to find new clothes piled on his bed: heavy canvas pants; a white shirt with full sleeves; and a long tunic, navy blue with a device embroidered on the back and down the sleeves. It was a silver dragon rampant, if Jack recalled his heraldic terminology correctly. He and Nick had spent time studying heraldry a year or two ago. He never thought it would have any practical application. His old clothes, including Mercedes's vest, were gone.

Whatever. He was beyond having an opinion about fashion. The clothes fit perfectly, and were lightweight and comfortable. He caught a glimpse of himself in the mirror. He looked like a young knight or squire dressed for a feast day. His mind flashed back to the golden-haired warrior from his dream.

When he returned to the front room, Hastings was just hanging up the telephone. The wizard nodded approvingly when he saw Jack. "You look fit to play a part," he said. Hastings was dressed in his usual dark colors, but he wore a short cloak in the same midnight blue color as Jack's tunic, fastened at one shoulder with a silver clasp in the shape of a dragon.

"Well, the Game is going forward," Hastings said. "The Red Rose must have managed to get their champion here in one piece, because they are declaring the tournament as we speak, down at the lists. All interested parties are expected to be present. Are you ready?"

Jack nodded, hoping it was true. "What will happen today?"

"The bans, or announcement of the tournament, is made by the sponsor putting forward a champion. Any challengers declare themselves. Then the contestants are qualified. Lots of pageantry." Hastings tossed Jack his cloak, which was still damp, and pulled on his own. "Let's maintain our anonymity for as long as possible, shall we?" Jack pulled the cloak on over his clothes and tugged the hood up over his damp hair. Hastings carried a large, leather-bound book under his arm. Jack realized with a start that it was his Weirbook.

Events were moving forward briskly, giving him little time to think. Maybe that's how they convince young men to go to war, Jack thought. You're just swept along until you find yourself looking death in the face, and you wonder how it ever happened.

One of the galleries had been completed alongside the playing field, and a large crowd was already seated there. Many sported devices carrying the white or red rose. Some were in contemporary clothes, but most had dressed in medieval style for the occasion. There were more men than women, and appeared to be mostly young to middle age, but then you could never tell with wizards. He saw no children, and he was glad of that. He was sure it was entirely wizards in the crowd. He could feel the hard push of power from the stands.

And still, the voices clamored inside his head. *Away the warrior.* He forced himself to ignore them. *You're going to kill somebody here, or be killed.* It was as simple as that.

Front and center in the stands, there was a small area of box seats roped off for dignitaries. Several finely dressed wizards were seated there. Jessamine Longbranch sat above the judges' box, surrounded by a crowd in White Rose livery. She was dressed in a green velvet riding dress, cut very low in front, with embroidered white roses and thorns emphasizing the neckline. Her shining black hair was pulled away from her face with a green velvet band. She held something that looked like a baton or a riding crop in her right hand, slapping it absently across her other palm. She didn't look happy. Jack was glad of the cover of the cloak, given his last encounter with the wizard. He pulled the hood forward to further cover his face. He had to admit, the woman intimidated him.

Hastings pointed to a man with aristocratic features and dark, close-cropped hair who was leaning back in his seat, gesturing with fine-boned hands, talking to the man next to him. "Claude D'Orsay," Hastings said. "The others are members of the Wizard Council, who are judges of the field. Dr. Longbranch is representing the White Rose. She is current Holder of the Tournament Cup."

Hastings and Jack joined the crowd milling at the edge of the gallery. Several wizards in livery of the Red Rose were clustered together on the field. Jack recognized the gray-bearded wizard from the graveyard, the one with the burned face.

"Geoffrey Wylie," Hastings murmured. "Premier wizard of the Red Rose." There was an intensity about Hastings that hadn't been there before, like that of a wolf who has caught the scent of blood. Jack recalled what Linda had said, that Wylie had killed Hastings's sister. "Pity," Hastings added. "Looks like he's had some sort of magical accident." Wylie was reading from a thick, leather-bound book.

"What are they doing?" Jack whispered to Hastings.

"They are reading their contestant's ancestry, proving that he is a legitimate warrior heir to the Weir. That is a first step to qualifying for the tournament." Hastings broadened his stance and folded his arms under the cloak. "This could take a while."

Jack looked around to see if he could spot the other warrior, but couldn't pick anyone out. Obviously, the Red Rose sponsors were maintaining their own sense of mystery.

Wylie was fairly far along in the family tree, and it took only ten or fifteen minutes to wrap things up somewhere in the tenth century. He took a few more minutes to outline plans for the tournament, should a challenger appear. It was to be held on Midsummer's Day, two days hence, two P.M., Raven's Ghyll Field, under the Rules of Engagement.

D'Orsay, who was obviously bored with the proceedings, returned his attention to the field when the announcements were finished. The five wizards seated in the boxes held a brief discussion, and then D'Orsay said, "Contingent on documentation of the same, the genealogy is accepted. The Red Rose shall submit said documentation. Contingent on verification of the stone, the warrior appears to qualify."

A cheer went up from the crowd, at least from those wearing the livery of the Red Rose. It had been three years since the last tournament.

D'Orsay was speaking again. "The tournament is declared by the Red Rose. Are there any challengers?"

There was a long pause. The crowd was silent, everyone looking around for someone to step forward.

"From the White Rose?" D'Orsay prompted, looking at Longbranch.

"The White Rose can put forward no champion at this time," Dr. Longbranch said reluctantly.

A murmur of disappointment ran through the crowd. It appeared there would be no tournament after all.

"What happened to their last champion?" Jack whispered to Hastings.

"Killed himself," he whispered back. He rested a hand on Jack's shoulder a moment, tightening his grip. "Now we're for it. Remember what we talked about."

He moved away from Jack, closer to the judges' box. "We will challenge the Red Rose," he announced in a clear voice.

D'Orsay scanned the crowd, trying to determine who had spoken. "Is it the White Rose after all?" he asked.

Hastings stepped onto the field, into the sunlight. "I am the player's sponsor," he said. "Neither the White Rose nor the Red." And he ripped back his hood.

There was a moment of stunned silence. Then, "Hastings!" D'Orsay exclaimed in disbelief, the name spoken as an epithet. The other judges of the field stood to get a better look. "What are you doing here?" the Master demanded angrily.

A ripple ran through the crowd, seated spectators standing to see better, turning to one another. Some seemed to know the identity of the tall stranger, and were being kept busy explaining.

Hastings shrugged as if it were obvious. "I'm here to play," he said, smiling.

Geoffrey Wylie was smiling also, but his grin was nasty. "We're so glad you've come, Leander. This is most con-

venient. The Red Rose has unfinished business with you."
He turned to his colleagues on the field. "Take him!" Four
red-clad wizards advanced on Hastings, hands out-
stretched, wizard fire leaping from their fingers like
Roman candles.

It happened so fast that Jack stood frozen, unsure
whether to try to intervene. Hastings had told him to stay
put. But the wizard didn't seem to need his help. He threw
out his right arm, and the air between him and the Red
Rose shimmered, solidified, a barrier that turned the wizard attack for the moment, sending the flames careening
out over the cowering crowd. With his left hand, he pulled
a small book from under his cloak.

"What about the rules, Claude?" Hastings thrust the
book into the air. "As a wizard and potential sponsor, I am
protected. Call them off."

"This man has incited the servant guilds," Wylie
argued. "He's a traitor who has spilled wizard blood in
defiance of the rules. He doesn't deserve their protection."

"Prove it." Hastings swiveled, still holding the rules
aloft so everyone in the crowd could see. "Of course, I've
always believed that blood is blood: wizard or warrior,
enchanter or sorcerer or seer."

"That's not what the rules say," Wylie snapped.
"Why don't you read them for a change?"

"Give over!" D'Orsay said reluctantly, shaking his head
at Wylie. "Desist, or you'll be disqualified."

Wylie gestured, and the wizard posse stopped. "I
should have cut your throat when I had the chance." He

turned to D'Orsay. "This is preposterous. He cannot be a sponsor. This can't be allowed! The tournament holds between the Roses."

"Where is it written?" Hastings asked coolly. He extended the rules toward Wylie. "Show me."

But Wylie persisted. He had just seen an obvious forfeit turn into a possible contest. "This game is based on centuries of tradition! No one else has ever been allowed to play."

"Has anyone else ever tried to field a candidate?" Hastings looked from one to the other. Wylie and D'Orsay were speechless for a moment.

"What house do you represent?" D'Orsay asked warily.

"The Silver Dragon." Hastings shed his plain cloak completely and folded it over his arm, revealing the blue cloak with the dragon device beneath. A rumble went through the crowd again. The Silver Dragon? Whoever had heard of the Silver Dragon?

Jack glanced into the gallery, at Jessamine Longbranch. She was watching the proceedings, frowning, tapping her chin with her bloodred nails. Apparently she hadn't yet made up her mind what this turn of events meant to the White Rose.

"You must field a warrior, Hastings," D'Orsay said, then condescendingly, confident this condition could not be met, "or you can't play."

"I have a player who qualifies," Hastings replied. He was still alert, like an arrow drawn back and ready to fly, keeping his back to the open field, his face to the Red and White Roses in the gallery.

The crowd reacted to this with loud approval. Suddenly, it looked as if the tournament might actually go forward.

Wylie turned to D'Orsay for help. "We need a ruling," he said plaintively. "This is ridiculous."

D'Orsay sighed. "There's nothing in the rules to exclude the Silver Dragon. I don't know why he can't present his player. Perhaps he doesn't even qualify." He nodded to Hastings. "Proceed." Wylie stood fuming at the edge of the field.

Hastings opened Jack's book, found his place. "Jackson Thomas Swift, son of Rebecca Downey and Thomas Swift—"

Now Jessamine Longbranch surged to her feet. "That is impossible!" she shouted. "Jack Swift is dead!" She leaned forward out of the box, and almost out of her dress, to the delight of the crowd in the stands.

Hastings frowned at her. "Dr. Longbranch, isn't it? Despite all your best efforts . . . and yours, too," he said, nodding at Wylie, "Jack Swift is very much alive."

Longbranch scanned the gallery, fists clenched, spinning off white-hot sparks into the crowd around her. Jack shrank further back into his cloak, acutely conscious of his missing vest.

"May I continue?" Hastings asked D'Orsay mildly. The Master nodded, speechless. Hastings continued to read through generations of Downeys, Hales, and other names less familiar. The genealogy was liberally sprinkled with Heirs, warriors and wizards mostly. It was twenty minutes before they found themselves back in the twelfth century, and came to a stopping place.

The judges conversed for a longer time, this time, and there was some loud arguing and dramatic gesturing involved. Finally, D'Orsay nodded and turned back to the field. He didn't look happy. "The genealogy is in order. There is nothing in the Rules of Engagement that precludes his participation. The warrior appears to qualify, pending documentation of the same, and assuming he passes the physical test."

The crowd exploded in cheers. They had come for a spectacle, and now they would have one. Longbranch and Wylie mounted a vigorous protest. Wylie wanted to set aside the genealogy altogether, while Longbranch was willing to accept the genealogy, but was protesting Hastings's sponsorship. D'Orsay was becoming more and more annoyed, although Jack suspected it was rooted in his inability to find a reason to disqualify Hastings or his player. Any excuse would have to be convincing, given the mood of the crowd. Finally, he held up a hand.

"Dr. Longbranch, you can file a grievance after the fact, if you would like. Mr. Wylie, we have already ruled on the genealogy. Please be quiet or there will be a forfeit."

That possibility appealed to Jack, but Wylie shut up immediately.

D'Orsay sighed. There was one more chance to keep Hastings out of the tournament. "The physical test. Produce your warrior."

Jack looked quickly at Hastings, who nodded almost imperceptibly. Jack strode out onto the field, shedding his cloak as he came. The crowd leaped up to get a first look at the challenger. Jack could feel the wizard heat behind him. It was almost enough to blow him off his feet.

. One of the field judges climbed down out of the box, carrying a stethoscope similar to the one Dr. Longbranch used. He lifted Jack's tunic and pressed the silver cone against the skin of his chest. After a moment, he removed it and stepped away, surveying Jack with interest. He turned to D'Orsay and announced, "There is a warrior stone. He qualifies."

There was pandemonium. It was several minutes before order could be restored.

Jessamine Longbranch stood again. Jack looked up into those black eyes, remembered the last "examination" in her office, and shuddered. "I own this boy, Claude. He was stolen from me by trickery. Now that he's turned up alive, you must return my property to me."

D'Orsay shook his head. "Jess, we can't decide that right now. As I said, file your grievance, and we'll see. Mr. Wylie, your candidate?"

Wylie looked across the field. The warrior of the Red Rose was already approaching them. Jack squinted, shading his eyes. He appeared young, not more than Jack's age and perhaps not as tall. He wore a white tunic with red trim and a red rose emblazoned on the front, knee-length leather boots, and a close-fitting hood covering his hair and most of his face. Jack was transfixed. There was something familiar about the stranger, in the graceful way he moved and carried himself. The warrior faced the judges, and the stethoscope was applied. The judge wielding it stepped back, startled, for a moment. Then he turned to D'Orsay. "There is a warrior stone. She qualifies," he said.

The warrior turned to Jack and pulled off the hood. Brown shoulder-length hair tumbled down. The face was unmistakable. It was Ellen Stephenson.

"Hullo, Jack," she said.

❦ CHAPTER SIXTEEN ❧
A SUMMONS TO COURT

Jack lay on his back in his bed, staring at the ceiling. It was still early evening, but the drapes had been drawn to keep people from peering in the windows. He could hear the noise of the crowd outside, waxing and waning. More and more spectators were arriving all the time as news spread that the tournament would actually go forward. It seemed certain that the Ghyll would be full to capacity before long, if it weren't already. It was a feast, a festival, a celebration of the ancient sacrament of violence and death.

Every so often there would be a pounding at the door. Groups of newcomers were anxious to meet the Silver Dragon's player. Hastings quickly sent them on their way. He had already spent considerable time laying traps and putting up barriers along the perimeter of the cottage, not trusting that his many enemies would play by the rules. Now it had the embattled feeling of a fortress.

The sounds of music and gaeity came faintly to Jack's ears. Tavern tents had sprung up everywhere, selling high-potency wizard's brews of various kinds. There seemed to be a great deal of serious drinking going on.

Ellen Stephenson. Waves of self-doubt rolled over him. Stupid. He was stupid. He was so tired of being stupid. How could he have missed it?

Little clues came back to him. The fact that he never seemed to have to explain anything to Ellen. Her mysterious past and home life. He'd never met her parents, nor had anyone else that he could recall. How had she managed that in the small town of Trinity? Another stupid question. With a little wizardry, anything was possible.

She was always going to lessons. Piano lessons, he'd been told. Or she had relatives visiting. He'd admired her sleek, muscular body, her athletic moves. From working in the garden, she'd said. No wonder she hadn't been afraid of Garrett Lobeck or his friends. She could have turned them into hamburger.

Jack glanced over at Shadowslayer propped against the wall. He'd heard of people in tight places killing themselves by falling on their swords. The idea was appealing, but he didn't think he could manage it.

Hastings appeared in the doorway. "Come and have some supper," he said.

"No, thanks," Jack said listlessly.

The wizard stared at him for a moment, then snapped, "Get up and get in here." He stalked back into the main room.

Jack lay there for a moment, then sighed and swung his legs over the side of the bed.

Hastings had put out a supper of cold roast beef, cheese, hard rolls, horseradish sauce, potato salad, fruit, and cake. Jack was actually hungry, despite his black mood. He hadn't had anything substantial to eat since they'd hiked up the mountain. That seemed like a long time ago. Jack sat down at the table and filled his plate. Hastings set a glass of cider in front of him.

Hastings sat across the table from Jack, picking at his food, the look on his face unreadable. He was drinking a tall glass of dark English beer, quite rapidly. The two said little until Jack was finishing his second piece of cake. Then Hastings set his empty glass on the table, leaned back a bit, and said, "You knew going into this that it would come to a fight, and that one of you would end up dead."

Jack put his fork down. "I didn't know it would be her." He paused. "Did you?"

Hastings shook his head. "No. Something about her caught my attention at the high school, but I never pursued it. She must be very disciplined."

"I can't kill Ellen Stephenson," Jack muttered.

"You don't even know Ellen Stephenson." Hastings tilted his head back and surveyed Jack from under his heavy brows. "The girl you thought you knew does not exist. She is not the person you'll be fighting. From what I understand, she's been in training for years. She's a killer, Jack. She'll cut your heart out."

"Well, maybe *you* wouldn't understand. I'm just not

into killing women," Jack snapped. As soon as the words were out of his mouth, he knew he had made a mistake. But by then he was flat on the floor and the wizard was towering over him. After a moment, Hastings extended his hand and helped him to his feet.

"I'm sorry," Hastings said stiffly. "Like you, it appears I have a control problem." The two sat down again. After a pause, he said, "I once asked you what you would do if someone tried to kill you."

"I said I would kill them first," Jack said, remembering.

"She'll kill you if she can," the wizard said. "I didn't bring you here to have you slaughtered."

What he didn't say was that maybe Jack wouldn't have a chance against her, even if he made his best effort. *Not the thing to say to your player before a bout.*

There came another pounding at the door. Hastings answered. Jack could hear voices, but it didn't sound like the fan club this time. When the wizard returned, he dropped an envelope on the table. "It seems there have been some grievances filed concerning your participation in the tournament," he said. He ripped open the envelope and scanned the paper quickly, then tossed it onto the table. "There's a suit by one Linda Downey claiming that you are not a warrior born at all, but a wizard. That a warrior's stone was fraudulently implanted in you by one Jessamine Longbranch. Creative," he said. "I wonder if they'll buy it. The other is a suit by Jessamine Longbranch claiming that you are her property fraudulently stolen from her by one Leander Hastings. The remedy suggested is that you play in the tournament as the champion of the White Rose."

"I'll never do that," Jack said with conviction. "I don't know what I'm going to do, but I'll never do that."

"Well." Hastings drummed his fingers on the table. "You may find that she can be very persuasive. And considering who is making the ruling, it might not go our way."

And Jack couldn't help but wonder what outcome Hastings hoped for. If Aunt Linda won her suit, he would be out a warrior.

Fitch peered up at the frowning façade of the Carlisle Citadel Railway station, blinking against the falling raindrops, then he returned to at his guidebook.

The station dates to 1847. It was designed by Sir William Tite, who also designed The Bank of England and the Royal Exchange in London. Tite used a Tudor Gothic style to harmonise with the crenellated towers of the nearby Citadel. Carlisle Castle was once the prison of Mary, Queen of Scots. It was captured by Bonnie Prince Charlie in 1745.

If the railway stations look like castles, what must the castles be like?

"Fitch! Will you come on? We only have an hour. If we don't find something for lunch, we're going to starve all the way to Edinburgh!" From the expression on Will's face, this would be a completely preventable tragedy.

"There'll probably be a food car on the Edinburgh train," Fitch suggested.

"Cadbury Dairy won't do it. And I don't want to miss the train."

"Chill, Will. In a minute." Fitch pulled out a digital camera and snapped several photographs, including one of Will looking annoyed. The camera was borrowed from the media center at school. Officially, Fitch was covering the tour for the school Web site. He zipped it back into the pocket of his rain jacket. "I wish we had time to tour the castle."

"Right." Will squinted out at the dismal scene. "Aren't you castled out?"

Fitch scanned the map in his guidebook and made a quick calculation. "Look, the Citadel and cathedral are just over there. I can be up and back in an hour. Buy me something for lunch, a meat pie, maybe. I'll pay you back."

"My parents will be pissed if you miss the train," Will warned.

"I won't." Fitch hunched his shoulders against the weather and Will's disapproval, and crossed the court between the train station and the Citadel, skirting the sodden flower gardens. He had time for a quick look around, at least.

After circling and photographing the Citadel towers, Fitch turned on to English Street, heading for the cathedral, whose spires poked above the surrounding buildings. He jostled through crowds of tourists driven from the lakes into town by the weather. Ahead of him, a girl in a bright red slicker stepped from a doorway, catching a fistful of her dark curls to keep them from flying in the wind. As she turned, Fitch caught a full view of her face.

It was Leesha Middleton, recent high-school student. And wizard.

He ducked his head and thrust himself backward into an entryway, colliding with a woman overburdened with packages.

"You appalling young hooligan! D'you know what these ornaments cost?" She shook a bejeweled finger under his nose.

He'd blundered into one of those year-round Christmas shops. Automatically muttering apologies, he peered out into the street again. Leesha looked both ways, then turned north, toward the cathedral.

What was she doing here? *Hunting Jack* was the obvious answer. Could he be somewhere nearby? Leaving the tongue-lashing behind, Fitch stepped out onto the street, following Leesha. Somehow, he had to find Jack and warn him. It didn't matter if he missed the train.

Leesha walked briskly, seeming confident of the way. They passed a small church at the edge of the cathedral close, then the cathedral itself, turning left onto Castle Street. I may see the castle after all, Fitch thought. But Leesha skirted the fortifications, making for a park near the river. She disappeared into the woods, and Fitch put on speed, looking for the spot of red to guide him.

It was gloomy under the trees. When the wind blew, water showered down from the leaves overhead. The riverside was nearly deserted, the more sensible tourists having taken refuge in the pubs and cafes in the city center. Where had she gone? He pivoted, swiping rain from his face.

His only warning was a slight sound behind him. Then a hot grip on his shoulder and the words, driving him down, down into the soggy leaves. He lay flat on his face in the wet muck, but couldn't turn his head to clear his mouth and nose. In a moment of panic, he thought he might suffocate, but hot hands shoved him over onto his back. He lay there, helpless, blinking against the raindrops that spiraled down on him from the canopy above.

Leesha knelt next to him. She pressed her bare knee against his windpipe until spots swam before his eyes. Finally, she released the pressure, and he sucked in great lungfuls of air. She sat down on the wet ground next to him with a sigh.

"I never liked you very much, *Harmon*," she said. She pulled a lipstick from her pink purse and reapplied it. Then drew her knees up until her skirt nearly disappeared. "Always telling Jack he should break up with me."

She came up on her knees again, leaning over him. She gripped the heavy chain around his neck and yanked him half upright. The metal heated, burned into his flesh. "What the hell do you think you are, with your grungy Salvation Army clothes, living in that dump over on Madison like a bunch of cockroaches? Nothing, that's what." She spat in his face, then released him. He fell backward like a rag doll, bouncing a little.

"We're going to go see Jack. Would you like that?" She smoothed the wet hair away from his forehead, noticed the hoop in his right ear, and tugged at it experimentally. Tugged again, harder, until blood trickled into his ear. Fitch took a deep breath and closed his eyes. "Oh, *Harmon*," she whispered. "You should see your face! You scare so easily."

She stood, brushing wet leaves off her skirt. "You sit tight. I'm going to go get Will."

The hearing on the suits was to be held the next morning at ten A.M. in the great hall of the castle. Only "interested" parties were permitted to attend. That didn't include the thousands of spectators who collected outside. Rumors were flying in the Ghyll. The oddsmakers in the colorful blue-and-white striped betting tents along the midway were in a quandary. A huge crowd of people was gathered outside of the cottage when Jack and Hastings left for the hall. "Jack! Jack!" they chanted.

As they pressed through the crowd, Jack felt a hot wizard hand fasten around his arm, and not gently. He turned to face an athletic-looking man with stick-straight black hair, dressed in the livery of the Red Rose. He had a thin, cruel mouth and a shadow of beard along his jaw.

"Hello, Jack. I'm Simon Paige, Ellen's trainer. I've been working with her for years. I just wanted you to know that I can't wait to see your blood spilled tomorrow." His lips drew back from his teeth in a parody of a smile. "Don't worry. I told her to take her time. We want to make sure we give these people their money's worth."

Angrily, Jack shook off the wizard's hand. Simon Paige was laughing as he turned away.

The guild had set up a makeshift court in one end of the great hall. D'Orsay and the other judges were sitting on a raised dais and rows of chairs were drawn up around the platform.

Hastings's hand on Jack's shoulder kept him moving to

the front of the hall. "Most of these people are members of the Council of Wizards, the guild's governing body," the wizard explained. Jack and Hastings were directed to chairs just in front of the dais, where the judges could look down on them.

Jack spotted Linda sitting at one end of the front row, surrounded by several of the Jefferson Street neighbors. What were they doing here? Jack caught Linda's eye, and she nodded to him, managing a smile. Iris and Blaise lifted their hands in greeting.

Hastings frowned at Linda. "She should have sent a proxy. This is no place for an enchanter." Jack wondered what he meant.

Jessamine Longbranch and several wizards of the White Rose were also seated together at the front. The surgeon smiled at Jack as if he were chocolate.

Geoffrey Wylie swept up the center aisle, into a swarm of red wizards. Before he sat down, he surveyed the crowd. When his gaze lit on Linda, he flinched as if startled. Lifting his hand to his scarred cheek, he scowled at some unpleasant memory. He continued to watch her after he sat down, running his tongue over his damaged lips. Jack looked for Ellen, but didn't see her.

D'Orsay called the court to order. "This is an informal hearing called to rule on two suits that have been filed relative to the participation of the warrior representing the Silver Dragon in the tournament scheduled for tomorrow." He spread several papers out in front of him. "It appears these two claims are closely related. We will take testimony relative to them both, and then rule in the order that makes the most sense to the court. First, we must rule whether Jackson Swift is indeed a warrior, despite the fact that he seems to meet the usual criteria. I would like to ask the plaintiff in the matter to explain herself."

Linda Downey rose to her feet. She was dressed for court in a loose black tunic and trousers, and her hair was uncharacteristically subdued. Her skin was pale, almost translucent, her lips a bruised purple-red. She moved with an unconscious grace, like the progress of light across the stage.

Her presence was having an effect on the judges. They leaned forward to get a better look at the enchanter.

"Thank you, Master D'Orsay. I will be brief. The details of the matter are in my deposition. I am the aunt of the player in question, and am also his godmother. His mother is my sister, and Anaweir. His father is also Anaweir. Jack was born a wizard, Weirflesh without a stone." She paused, and a murmur ran through the gallery.

"I asked Dr. Longbranch if she could replace his Weirstone. She took that opportunity to implant a warrior's stone into my nephew instead of the wizard stone he needed. Apparently by so doing she hoped to create a warrior from a wizard."

Linda motioned to Jack. "If you examine him, you will find the surgical scar from the implantation. There is no provision for created warriors under the rules. It was a nasty and inappropriate experiment on another wizard. What we have here is a boy who, under the Rules of Engagement, should never have qualified for a tournament, although it is easy to see why he seemed to meet the criteria."

Jack was surprised to see that Linda seemed comfortable in this role, despite the audience of wizards. *Perhaps my mother is not the only lawyer in the family.*

"What proof do you have that the boy was a wizard?" D'Orsay asked. "Rather than a warrior born without a stone?"

"Jack's Weirbook identifies him as a wizard, and includes the usual chapter on charms and incantations. It's the same Weirbook that Leander Hastings used to present him on the field."

"Is this true?" D'Orsay looked at Hastings. Jack's Weirbook lay on the table in front of him.

"It is true. The Weirbook identifies Jack as a wizard." Hastings handed the book to D'Orsay and looked over at Linda. She avoided his gaze.

Once again, a murmur ran through the crowd. Did Hastings mean to disqualify his own player?

The judges looked thoughtful. Jack closed his eyes. It was a bold move. He wondered if it could work. He felt like someone with a terminal illness who had been given news of a possible cure.

"I have several of Jack's neighbors here to testify as well, if need be. They know the history of his case, what was done to Jack." Linda crossed in front of the crowd again, ending in front of the judges. "In rendering a decision, it's important to consider the long-term consequences. Dr. Longbranch has transformed a wizard into a warrior. Acceptance of this procedure could put other wizards at risk in the future and subvert the intent of the Rules of Engagement. After all, the rules were meant to prevent direct combat between wizards."

D'Orsay turned to Hastings. "Mr. Hastings, you are the boy's sponsor. Do you have any response to this?"

Hastings shrugged. "Jack carries a warrior stone, and I have trained him as such. However, I'll not contest the judge's ruling. I have no desire to play a wizard in a tournament, if the ruling goes that way." He put his hot hand on Jack's shoulder, but it felt somehow reassuring.

He's going to save me from this if he can, Jack thought with surprise. No matter what it does to his own plans. Jack looked up at his aunt, who was staring at Hastings with an unreadable expression.

D'Orsay turned to Jessamine Longbranch. "Dr. Longbranch?"

The doctor rose to her feet. She faced the judges, turning her back on Linda. "First of all, you should all be aware that you are being charmed by an enchanter and beguiled by a renegade. They've conspired to prevent the tournament from going forward. We should have all stopped our ears before they began speaking." The judges smiled.

"The enchanter called me in the first place because her nephew was Weirflesh born without a stone, and so was dying. She was desperate. Because I am a cardiothoracic surgeon, I thought I could save the boy. As it happened, a warrior stone . . . ah . . . became available when a warrior I was training suffered an accident. I implanted the crystal with Ms. Downey's full knowledge and consent. The stone restored him. I did it with the intent of raising the child to fight for the White Rose. That was our bargain from the beginning."

"I asked you to place a wizard stone," Linda replied. "I never agreed to this. I didn't know what you'd done until afterward. The fact is, he's still a wizard, and always has been. He doesn't belong here."

"A verdict in my favor in this case has few implications for wizards," Dr. Longbranch went on, as if Linda hadn't spoken. "It's not as if I removed a wizard's stone and replaced it with another. The boy was for all intents and purposes *Anaweir*, a nothing, and I made him into something by placing a stone. He should be grateful for it."

She was about to continue, but then looked off to the right, where there was something of a commotion. "I believe I have a witness to present. Ms. Middleton?"

Leesha Middleton came into the room, pushing someone ahead of her. Two someones. Will Childers and Harmon Fitch.

His friends were walking under their own power, looking back over their shoulders at Leesha as if eager to keep a certain distance between them and her. Jack swore under his breath. Hastings was right. No one was safe. The wizards of the Roses were never going to leave his family and friends alone. Not unless he managed to get himself killed or disqualified.

He was surprised to see that Leesha was still working for Longbranch after the double cross with the traders. But then, Longbranch would have had no way of knowing any of that. The traders were dead and gone, thanks to Hastings.

Jessamine Longbranch frowned at Leesha. "I told you to bring the boy's mother," she hissed. "Who is this?"

Leesha shrugged. "I couldn't get to her. The old man has her hidden away." Jack looked at Aunt Linda, and she mouthed the word, "Snowbeard."

"This is Will Childers and Harmon Fitch." She gave each of them a little push in turn. Will looked like he wanted to push back, but thought better of it. "They are Jack's childhood friends. They'll do." Leesha and Longbranch exchanged a look, and Jack sat up straighter, wondering what this was about.

"Well, they'll have to do, now, won't they?" Dr. Longbranch snapped. She paused, composed herself, and turned to the boys, who stood bewildered in front of the judges. "Which one of you is Will? Ah. Let's start with you, Will. We were having a discussion about Jack's surgery years ago, and we were hoping you could help." Longbranch's voice was soothing. "What has Jack told you about it?"

Will looked at Jack. "I . . . I don't know much about it. Why don't you ask Jack?" he added, nodding to his friend.

"We're asking you," Dr. Longbranch said, a dangerous edge to her voice.

Will swallowed audibly. "All right, then. When Jack was born, he had a heart problem. This Dr. Longbranch—I guess that's you—fixed it. That's what I know." The words came out in a rush.

"So I saved his life, based on what you know?" Longbranch asked.

Will nodded.

"No one is disputing that," Linda said.

"You've known Jack all his life, is that right?" Longbranch went on.

Will nodded. "Pretty much. As long as I can remember."

"Have you ever known Jack as a young boy to demonstrate any signs of special powers. Something you might call wizardry?"

Will frowned. "Uh, no, not really."

She turned to Fitch. "Have you ever seen any signs of wizardry in Jackson Swift?"

Fitch cleared his throat. "I don't know what you mean by wizardry," he replied, hunching his shoulders as if for protection.

"No? Let me demonstrate." Longbranch put a hand on Fitch's shoulder. He stiffened, cried out, tried to twist away, then sank to his knees, his face going gray with pain and shock. Will took three long steps and launched himself at the wizard. She extended her other hand, palm outward, and Will dropped as if axed.

Jack tried to push up out of his chair, but Hastings shoved him back. "It won't help. Believe me."

"She's abusing her own witnesses!" Linda appealed to D'Orsay, spreading her hands in frustration. The Master shrugged, as if to say that Longbranch could do whatever she wanted. They were her witnesses, after all, and Anaweir at that.

"Now then, Harmon," Dr. Longbranch murmured, finally releasing him. "Don't waste our time."

"I never noticed anything until recently," Fitch gasped,

ducking away from the doctor's hand. "In March. When he blew Garrett Lobeck across a soccer field. And then there was the fight in the graveyard, with . . . with flames and all. But maybe that was because of the magical sword," he added lamely.

"Thank you," the doctor said. "We all know wizardry manifests at a very young age. One would expect the wizard Jack to have shown some signs of it, something even Anaweir would notice." She waved her hand at Will and Fitch. Will was struggling to sit up, and Fitch was helping. "On the other hand, the warrior trait comes on after puberty, which was when Jack began to display his . . . talents."

"He was suppressed, and you know it," Linda said tightly. "He was taking Weirsbane. He didn't manifest until he stopped taking it."

"The woman is a liar." Dr. Longbranch spread her fingers. "The medication was a placebo. I prescribed it in order to keep track of him, so his parents would have to come back to me for more. That was Linda Downey's suggestion also, that I leave him with his parents instead of taking him when he was a baby. She promised to give him up when he was ready for training."

Now, for the first time, Longbranch faced Linda. "This enchanter has never understood her appropriate role. She has been rude and uncooperative from the very beginning. She should not be up here telling wizards what to do. In my opinion, someone on the council should volunteer to take charge of her. The girl needs a guarantor who can provide some *discipline*."

Hastings swore softly. When Jack looked around the

room, he could see several male council members leaning forward eagerly. It seemed there would be no shortage of volunteers willing to take on the problem of Linda Downey. Geoffrey Wylie stood, and his hand opened, revealing something metallic that caught the light, a hinged silver piece, like a collar.

"I'll accept responsibility for the enchanter," he said hoarsely.

Now Hastings half rose out of his chair, but Iris Bolingame was already standing.

"She already has a guarantor, Master D'Orsay," Iris said, "I am her friend, and I stand for the enchanter." She glared around at the other wizards, as if daring them to dispute her. Linda stood, cheeks flaming, eyes downcast, and saying nothing. Now it was clear to Jack why Linda had brought the neighbors along. He remembered the Rules of Engagement, and the description of the enchanter role he had assumed was archaic. No matter how articulate, an enchanter needed a sponsor in a gathering of wizards.

Wylie shrugged as if he didn't really care, and sat down again. The collar disappeared.

Longbranch seemed a little taken aback by Iris, but recovered quickly. "Perhaps you should teach her some manners, then," she snapped. She walked back along the front of the dais, stopping just in front of Jack.

"The fact is, it is the Weirstone, and nothing else, that determines the nature of an Heir. It doesn't matter what Jack Swift was to begin with. He is a warrior now, and so qualified to play in the tournament. He would be dead if not for me. In that sense, I created him, so I own him." She reached out and slid her hand to the back of his neck, pulling his face in close to hers. His flesh burned under her touch. "And you'd better play well, my mongrel, or your two friends will pay the price," she breathed, just loud enough for him to hear. Jack stared at her, horrified, then pushed her hand away. Her nails left long scratches on his skin.

And then he understood: Longbranch already knew what the outcome of the suit would be, was confident he would be back under her control in time for the Game. That was why his friends had been brought to the Ghyll. Longbranch had been given no opportunity to bring out the killer in him, as she'd promised back in London, so she planned to use Will and Fitch to force him to play. To "motivate" him, as she put it. He looked from Jessamine Longbranch to Claude D'Orsay, and knew the fix was in. Will and Fitch sat huddled together on the steps, as if for mutual protection. As if that would make any difference. Jack shivered.

"Jack Swift would be dead if not for me," Leander Hastings announced.

Longbranch's head snapped up. "Leander Hastings has been a thorn in our sides for years. He has done everything in his power to sabotage the Game. Why would he try to field a player if he didn't have an ulterior motive?"

Hastings stood. "Dr. Longbranch has told you it was her intent to play Jack in the Game. How do we know what was intended, or agreed upon seventeen years ago? There was no contract. The stone was placed under false pretenses. The White Rose has had minimal contact with

Jack ever since. Whatever training he has received, I have provided. Two weeks ago, Dr. Longbranch tried to murder him with a graffe, and almost succeeded. It is through my efforts that he is still alive. If only for that reason, I say the boy is mine.

"I brought Jack to the Game as his sponsor. I presented his genealogy and secured his approval as a player. Now your petitioner proposes to strip him from me. In matters of the Game, possession has always been the law. Who will bring a warrior to play in future knowing he might well be stolen? If Jack is deemed fit to play, he should play for me." Hastings remained standing.

He must know he can't win this, Jack thought. He's nobody's fool.

D'Orsay conversed briefly with the other judges, then turned to face the court. "Here is my ruling," he said. "On the first issue, whether Jack Swift is warrior or wizard, I rule against the petitioner. It is the stone that determines what he is, and nothing else."

Jack released his breath and looked over at Aunt Linda. She had her eyes closed, chin resting on her clasped hands as if praying. The hope of a reprieve was over.

Hastings was still standing, and now he spoke quickly, before D'Orsay could continue. "If Jack remains under my sponsorship, I'm willing to sweeten the deal."

D'Orsay and the other judges looked up with interest. Longbranch looked wary. Hastings stood calmly, one hand grasping the other forearm. "If Jack wins, I'll expect the usual award. I will be Holder of the Cup and Master of Council. If Jack loses, I will submit to whatever *justice* the council deems appropriate for past crimes. After the Game and outside of the rules."

There was a shocked silence. Again, Jack tried to rise, but now Hastings's hand was on his shoulder, full of power, keeping him in his seat.

"What makes you think you can trust him?" Jessamine Longbranch demanded, her voice going shrill.

"What's trust got to do with it?" Hastings asked, smiling. "You can do as you like. I am here, outnumbered, in the Ghyll. You have plenty of witnesses to the agreement. If you would like me to sign something . . ." He shrugged.

D'Orsay regarded Hastings thoughtfully, his lower lip caught behind his upper teeth. Then he studied Jack, no doubt evaluating his chances against the player for the Red Rose. He turned to the other judges, and there was another brief conference. When he turned back to the petitioners, he was smiling.

"On this issue of sponsorship, we will leave matters as they are. It appears the Silver Dragon has more invested in this boy than the White Rose, despite their early involvement. And we accept Mr. Hastings's proposal. We will prepare the appropriate documents for his signature." He rubbed his hands together, once, twice, like a man at table anticipating a feast. He nodded to the assembly. "You may go."

Thus, the judges had managed to issue a ruling that made nobody happy. The crowd cleared quickly, except for Jack's small group of supporters. Longbranch and Leesha left Will and Fitch sitting alone on the steps, discarded.

As soon as Hastings released him, Jack turned on him angrily. "Why'd you have to do that? You don't think there's enough pressure on me already? Now if I lose, you put your head in a noose."

"Most likely not a noose, Jack," Hastings replied. "I'm sure they'll think of something more . . . creative." At Jack's stricken expression, he sobered. "Look, did you want to play for the White Rose tomorrow? I had to give them a reason to rule my way. Claude D'Orsay would never have left you under my control otherwise. He has too many reasons not to. Don't ever expect fair play from wizards."

And suddenly, Linda Downey stood in front of them, chin thrust forward. "Damn you, Leander." She was pale, her blue eyes bright with heat.

Hastings looked at her, startled. "What did I do?" He seemed genuinely puzzled.

"You really don't care, do you? You're just as reckless as always. You are bound and determined to end up dead before this is over. Damn you," she repeated with feeling.

Hastings glanced at Jack, then back at her. "And I suppose you weren't taking a chance, coming in here? He shook his head, smiled a little. "Cheer up. Jack will think you have no confidence in him."

"I believe in Jack. It's *you* I wonder about, Leander." She turned back to Jack. "We'll be here for you, Jack," she said, nodding at the neighbors. "We'll think of something," she promised.

Will and Fitch still sat on the steps, afraid to move, like parishioners in an unforgiving church. "Hey, Will. Hey,

Fitch," Jack said, crossing to where they sat. "I can't say I'm glad to see you. Are you all right?"

Will's eye socket was going purple from when his face had hit the stone floor, but otherwise he seemed none the worse for wear.

"Hey, Jack," Fitch said morosely. "I'm sorry I didn't do better with answering those questions. But when she . . . It was like I couldn't help myself."

"It was like I was drugged or something," Will added.

"You did fine," Jack said, raising his hands to stop the apologies. "If anyone's to blame, it's me. How'd you get here, anyway?"

"It was Leesha," Will said, opening and closing his hands as if throttling her. "She set a trap for us in Carlisle and we walked right in."

"God, I'm sorry," Jack began.

Fitch twitched impatiently. "Right, let's all agree straight off we're all sorry to be here. Now what?"

Jack was at a loss for what to do with his friends now that they were here. This was not a safe place for Anaweir.

"Why don't you come back to the cottage with us until we decide what to do?" Hastings suggested. "I think it's best if we keep you out of traffic."

As it turned out, someone was happy with the verdict. Word had leaked to the crowd outside, and a great cheer erupted when Jack appeared. Once again, there were long lines at the betting parlors. The spectators tossed tiny gold and silver balls that exploded into flowers and miniature fireworks that rained down on their heads. Jack had seen them for sale in several of the booths that lined the Ghyll.

Despite Hastings's efforts to keep them at bay, women crowded forward, trying to embrace Jack, thrusting favors into his hands. Will and Fitch were jostled and pushed this way and that by the mob trying to get to Jack. All in all, he was glad to reach the refuge of the cottage and shake the flower petals from his hair.

"They act like you're a rock star or something," Fitch said in amazement.

"More like a gladiator, I guess." Jack shrugged, still distracted by the events in the courtroom.

While Hastings went out in search of lunch, Jack brought his friends up to date on all that had happened. The one piece Will found hard to accept was Ellen Stephenson.

"It can't be true," he said, shaking his head. "She wouldn't. She's our friend. Plus, you're all she ever talked about. Well, you and soccer," he amended.

"That was before she knew who I am. Or *what* I am, rather." Jack spread a chamois over the table and laid out his weapons, oil, and honing tools. All except Shadowslayer, who never lost her edge.

"Well, she had a hundred chances to kill you in Trinity," Will persisted. "Why didn't she?"

Jack shook his head. "I have no idea." Methodically, he tried the edges, used the polishing stone, applied a thin coating of oil.

"Is she any good?" Will asked, looking over his shoulder.

"How should I know? I've never even seen her play a video game." He took a deep breath, released it. "I hear she's been training for years."

"Maybe it's magic," Fitch suggested. "Maybe it just looks like Ellen Stephenson. Maybe they figured it would be hard for you to . . ." He didn't finish the sentence.

Jack rather liked that idea. "I guess anything is possible," he said slowly.

"I can't believe Mr. Hastings is making you do this," Will said angrily. "Fight in this tournament, I mean."

"Well," said Jack, "We don't have much choice." He thought of what Jessamine Longbranch had said about Will and Fitch. At least Hastings had saved them from their intended role as hostages. Small blessings. That was what he had to focus on. "They would've caught up to me sooner or later. At least this way, it's on our terms."

Will was not impressed. "Right. Our terms. And either you or Ellen end up dead. Why can't the four of us just slip out of here?" He gestured at Shadowslayer. "We'll be like the Four Musketeers. With two swords."

Jack didn't know what to say. He was beginning to realize how terribly expendable they were, warriors and Anaweir alike. All Will and Fitch had to do was get between a wizard and something he wanted, and they would be history.

Hastings returned with two roasted chickens, bread and salad, and bottles of cider and soda.

"I have been trying to find an escort for you two," Hastings said after a while, passing Will another quarter chicken. "But Linda and the neighbors won't leave before the tournament. They're hoping to prevent it," he said. "You'll need help to get through the wizard's mist, and a guide to get back to Keswick."

"I'm not going anywhere without Jack," Will said stubbornly. "Forget it."

"Me neither." Fitch delicately separated chicken from the bone.

Hastings sighed. "You're both in danger here."

"And Jack isn't?" Will said meanly. He licked his fingers and took a swig of soda.

"I don't want you at the tournament tomorrow, either of you," Jack said suddenly. "Promise me you won't come."

"I won't promise anything," Will said. He looked up at Hastings. "Only, my parents are probably going out of their minds."

"All right," Hastings said, putting up a hand. "You have to stay anyway until I can devise a safe way to get you out of here. I'll get some kind of message to your parents. God knows what."

Jack and Hastings spent much of the rest of that day surveying the field and talking strategy. He had a strong sense of déjà vu as he walked up and down between the galleries, reliving Brooks's memories of slaughter. Ellen and her trainer walked the field on the other side. There might as well have been an ocean between them.

A banquet was held that evening in the hall of the castle for players and sponsors and invited guests. The dais had been removed, and a table set up in a large U shape extending halfway down the length of the hall. The White Rose was well represented, despite the fact that they were not fielding a player. Jessamine Longbranch was, after all, still Master of the Council, at least until after the tournament. Leesha Middleton was resplendent, dressed all in black, like the spider she was, her hair entwined with white roses.

The Silver Dragon delegation occupied only a small part of one arm of the table. Linda, Iris, Mercedes, and Blaise were there, in addition to Jack and Hastings. Will and Fitch came also, since they were safer in company. There was always the chance that Ellen's handlers would decide to take hostages of their own. Besides, Hastings suggested they might as well see as much of the spectacle as they could.

Intimidation seemed to be the order of the evening. Jack was dressed in a new tunic in the Silver Dragon colors, even more elaborate than the one he'd worn earlier in the day. Shadowslayer was belted at his waist. Jack quickly discovered that it was highly inconvenient to sit at a table wearing a sword. Hastings wore black and silver. Although he claimed he had never fielded a player, he seemed at home amidst the pageantry associated with the Game.

D'Orsay, Longbranch, and other high officials were seated at a table that connected the two arms of the U-shaped table. Red Rose representatives occupied almost the entire other arm of the table. Ellen entered between Geoffrey Wylie and Simon Paige. She wore a ceremonial white battle tunic with sprigs of red roses and a pure gold-mail bishop's mantle over her shoulders. A short dagger was sheathed at her waist. Much more practical for dining than a sword. Her hair was done up in a thick braid that circled her head. She looked beautiful. And dangerous.

They seated Ellen as far away from Jack as she could be, and still be at the same table. He supposed that was to prevent any early skirmishes. Not that he planned on starting anything, but he wanted desperately to talk to her. He spun mental messages out to that effect, but she was very careful never to meet his eyes.

The food was elaborate and beautifully displayed, including thirty-five courses, many of which Jack didn't recognize, along with potent wines and liqueurs. Even tasting some of them was enough to set his head to spinning. Several times Hastings had to intercept Will or Fitch before they tried something particularly exotic. "That will most likely kill you," he explained. After that, they became considerably less adventurous.

After dinner, thousands of bubbles were released into the hall. They burst open, releasing tiny birds, or butterflies, or showers of precious stones. This seemed to be routine entertainment to most of the people in attendance.

Geoffrey Wylie was invited to propose a toast on behalf of the tournament sponsor, so to speak. He launched into a long and bloodthirsty history of the Red Rose, finishing with a prediction of what he expected to happen to Jack on the field the next day.

"Thousands of warriors have been sacrificed to hallow this ground. Tomorrow we will continue that tradition. The warrior of the Red Rose will rip out the still-beating heart of the Silver Dragon and water the Ghyll with his blood."

Will put his hands over his ears, which some of the wizards seemed to find amusing. Fitch sat, pale and silent, folding and refolding his napkin. Ellen stared straight ahead, chin up, looking capable of most anything. Jack sat impassively. He was learning to just skip over the next day and land softly in the nothingness beyond. When the toast was concluded, there was enthusiastic clapping and cheering from the Red Rose contingent, except for Ellen. Bad form, Jack guessed.

Afterward, Hastings got up and proposed his own toast, which was considerably briefer. "I would like to propose a toast in memory of all who have given their lives over the centuries to make this bloody tradition possible." At this, the Silver Dragon representatives raised their goblets, but many of the guests said later that the toast was in poor taste.

After dinner, Jack tried to get close to Ellen, but her handlers hustled her off quickly. He kept close enough to see them head into the west wing, rather than out the front door. So he knew she was staying in the castle itself.

Hastings remained after, for a briefing on plans for the Game the next day. Linda and Iris stayed with him. Jack and his friends walked back to their cottage, running the gauntlet of fans once again, some reaching out to touch him, others asking for autographs. When they were back inside, Will flopped miserably on Jack's bed. "I ate that big dinner, and then I wanted to throw up during the toast," he said.

"Ellen looked really different," Fitch said. "Sort of cold and fierce and unfamiliar." He studied Jack. "What are you going to do tomorrow? Do you have a plan?"

"Don't worry about it," Jack said shortly. "Won't do

any good anyway." He removed his sword and tunic and replaced them with a sweatshirt. The *dyrne sefa* was still lying on the wardrobe where he'd left it when he'd showered that first day. Was it just a day ago that he had arrived in the Ghyll? He hung the stone around his neck, found Blaise's mirror in his duffle bag, and tucked it into his waistband. Then he unlatched the window.

"What are you doing?" Will demanded.

"I'm going out for a while. See if you can keep Hastings from finding out I'm gone." Jack lifted himself to the stone sill, swung his legs over, and dropped to the ground. He leaned back through the window. "Better close up after me. I'll tap when I'm ready to come in. Don't sleep so sound you don't hear me."

Will reached through the open window and grabbed a fistful of Jack's sweatshirt. "You're going to go out walking through that mob? You'll probably come home with a knife in your back."

"They'll have to find me first." Jack spoke the invisibility charm he'd made sure to memorize when Hastings used it. Will let go quickly, swearing, when Jack disappeared.

He was the champion of the Silver Dragon, the talk of the ghyll, the one whose name was on everyone's lips and tournament garb. Customers spilled from the tavern tents, danced in the pavilions under the trees, laid down their coin in the betting parlors. Private parties were just getting under way. But no one noticed as he made his way in the shadows between the cottage and the keep.

The young maid didn't see him slip inside the castle as

she stood, smoking, outside the kitchen door. He moved quickly along the corridors in the service part of the building, working his way to the west wing, always turning left when he had the chance. At first he could smell the cooking from the feast, then that faded, and he passed through laundry and storage areas. He encountered a number of servants, mostly Anaweir. Eventually he found himself in what looked like the family quarters. Now wizards passed him in the corridors. He said nothing, and fortunately they didn't seem to mark his presence.

He had no particular plan for finding out where Ellen was housed, and was beginning to realize just how impossible it might be to find her in the warren of corridors. Especially if she was already in her room. Then he heard a familiar voice coming from around a corner. Instinctively, he flattened himself against the cold stone of the wall behind him as Paige and Wylie came into view. Apparently they were at a parting of the ways, because they paused a moment at the intersection, a foot away from Jack. He struggled to control his breathing, knowing he would be history if those two wizards were to spot him in a deserted corridor.

Wylie handed a book to Paige. It was the Rules of Engagement. "Have her look it over one more time," the wizard said. "I don't want any missteps tomorrow."

"She has it memorized," Paige replied. "It's like breathing for her. There won't be any problem." He was full of confidence.

"Let's hope you're right," Wylie said with a trace of a smile. "Better get some sleep. I have some meetings yet tonight."

Wylie continued on down the corridor, and Paige turned past Jack, passing close enough to touch. Jack followed him at a cautious distance. Paige took a few more turns, and then they were in a short corridor that dead-ended into two doors at the end. He knocked sharply on one of the doors. There was a long pause, and then Ellen opened it. She was wearing a short silk nightshirt and had taken her hair down. Jack approached as close as he dared. She had only opened the door a little, but Jack was in luck, because Paige shoved it open the rest of the way and plowed into the room. Jack managed to slip in after him.

"You feeling all right?" Paige glared around the room. "You didn't eat much at the banquet. We don't want to take any chances so close to the event."

"I'm fine," Ellen replied, putting her hand out for the book. "I didn't want to break training with all that rich food."

Paige handed her the book. "Are you clear on strategy?"

"I'm clear," Ellen replied, not meeting the wizard's eyes. She was obviously ill at ease, eager for her trainer to leave, and trying hard to hide it.

Paige persisted. "The boy is stronger, so that's what you have to watch out for. Plus his reach is longer. Don't let him get inside, not even once. If you can't get at the body, go after his sword arm. He won't expect that. He's green, inexperienced. Don't go for the throat immediately. Try for a gut wound. Once you have him incapacitated, bleed him."

"Bleed him," Ellen repeated dutifully.

"You know, take your time. Cut him up slowly. The crowd will love it. Only, as I said, don't take any chances. Cut out his heart to finish him off."

Jack was finding he liked Simon Paige less every time he opened his mouth.

"Is that all?" Ellen looked at the floor.

The trainer reached out, caught Ellen's chin, lifted it so she was looking at him. "You won't disappoint me." It was not a question.

"No," she whispered, pale as ashes, gray eyes clouded by some memory of pain.

"I'll be next door." The wizard backed out of the room and Ellen shut the door behind him. She slipped the dead bolt into place and rested her face against the heavy wood of the door. The dagger she'd worn at dinner lay on a table next to the bed. Her sword leaned against the wall. Jack sat down at the table between Ellen and her weaponry, arranging himself carefully in the chair. First he dissolved the noticeability charm. Then he spoke a charm to secure the door.

At his first words, Ellen spun around, grabbing for a weapon that wasn't there. "Jack!" she whispered. "How did you . . . ?" She turned and released the dead bolt and yanked at the door, but it wouldn't budge.

"It won't open," said Jack. "Don't get Paige involved. I want to talk to you."

Ellen flattened herself against the door, still searching the room. "Are you looking for this?" Jack held up the dagger by the point, and then laid it back on the table. "Please, sit down for a minute. I won't take much time."

Ellen finally sat down in an armchair across the room from Jack. She perched on the edge, palms braced against the seat as if she expected him to spring at any moment. "What are you doing here?" she demanded. "How'd you get in here?"

"I need to ask you a few questions," Jack said.

Ellen was regaining some of her confidence. She looked him over carefully. "You're either crazy or stupid. Paige is right next door."

"Call him in if you want." Jack sat back in his chair, affecting indifference. He really had no idea what Ellen would do, but he'd seen her interaction with her trainer, and he took a chance.

After a moment, she said, "What did you want to ask me?"

"Why did you come to Trinity?" Jack asked bluntly.

She stared at him for a moment, then rolled her eyes as if he were an idiot. "I came to kill you, Jack." She flexed her hands in front of her. "Or capture you, rather. Only, I didn't know it was you, at the time. Wylie found out the White Rose had a young warrior hidden in Trinity. So I came to the high school to find you.

She paused. "There was a huge flare-up of power the day of the soccer tryouts. Paige and Wylie came after you, but I guess practice had already broken up. So we knew for sure that it must be someone on the team. But after that there was nothing, not a hint."

"I . . . ah . . . met Wylie in Coal Grove," Jack admitted. "He tried to take my sword away from me."

"That was you?" Ellen studied him speculatively.

"Paige told me about that. Wylie had been reading the history of the Seven. He hoped to find me one of the blades. Wylie was sure you were Anaweir since he could detect no stone. He credited the sword with all the fireworks. Are you the one who did that to him? Burned up his face, I mean?"

Jack shook his head. "It was burned when I first saw him. Looked fresh."

Ellen studied him, as if not sure whether to believe him. "Wylie left town after that. Paige said he was hunting an enchanter, some agent of the White Rose who had stolen the blade. I guess that was your aunt. Wylie never connected you to Trinity. Then Hastings arrived and Paige went into hiding. I was the outside man. The spotter. And all that time you and the sword were under our noses. It's kind of funny when you think about it." But she didn't smile.

"I didn't spot you, either," Jack pointed out.

"After all these years, I'm good at keeping my power under control. How else do you think I've stayed alive? I guess you never think your enemy is as clever as you are," she added.

She dropped her hands into her lap. "Eventually, I convinced myself it wasn't you. Maybe I didn't want to believe it was you. And I was really getting into the whole small-town scene, the soccer team and everything. I'd never lived anywhere like Trinity. Hell, I don't think I've ever lived nine months in one place."

"So you knew about Hastings?" Jack persisted.

Ellen nodded. "We assumed he must be trying to get

to you first. We thought that was why he was focusing on the soccer team. But he was working with a number of players, and then there was the Chaucerian Society. That threw us off, because you weren't involved with that." She shrugged. "I thought for sure it was Will. He's built, you know, and it took a while for you . . . for you to . . ." She seemed to lose her train of thought. She was looking at Jack's chest and shoulders.

"Was that why you hung out with Will?"

"At first, yes. But I finally realized he was Anaweir, and he became a friend. Fitch, too." She looked up at Jack. "I was surprised to see them at the banquet."

"They were brought here as hostages, to make sure I perform."

Ellen frowned. "Hastings?"

Jack shook his head. "Longbranch. She's pissed I'm playing for Hastings." The conversation died for a moment. "Where are you from?" Jack asked.

Ellen shrugged. "I don't know." She got up and started pacing back and forth. "They've never told me. I must've been kidnapped as a baby. As far back as I can remember, Paige has been my coach." She shuddered and wrapped her arms around herself.

Jack thought about what Hastings had said. *You know what they do to warriors to get them ready for the Game.* She was obviously scared to death of Simon Paige. He wanted to do something, to put his arms around her, or at least to take her hands, tell her how sorry he was, but he sat stupidly, knowing she might not react well to such a gesture.

"All the time you were tucked away in Trinity in your

wonderful old house with your wonderful quirky mother, I've been on the run. I've seen the world. I can speak seven languages. I belong nowhere, and I have no one. I always leave in the middle of the night. No good-byes for me. Meanwhile, you've had the same friends all your life."

"It's not my fault," Jack whispered. He was finally realizing what Aunt Linda's intervention had meant. She had saved him from that life so he could stay in Trinity, with Becka, and grow up as he had. Things could have been very different. He thought of Jessamine Longbranch, and shivered.

Ellen was still pacing, still angry. "And all this time I've been training, week in, week out, since I was three years old. You have no idea what they've done to me." She paused, swallowed, then went on. "Not only was I born for this, I was raised for it, too. Tomorrow is the payoff," she said, dropping back into her chair.

Jack felt the need to change the subject. "So it was the fight with Lobeck that tipped you off?"

Ellen nodded. "I still can't believe you took that shot to the face before you let him have it. I was trying to help you out without giving myself away. You have a lot more control than I do."

It was time for the jackpot question. He pulled the mirror from his waistband and toyed with it, then turned it so he could see Ellen's face. "So you told Paige, and then he tried to poison me at Cedar Point."

She was shaking her head before he finished speaking. "Swift, you are so stupid sometimes."

"What do you mean?"

"Wylie wanted to make sure of you before he called a tournament, so he could win the cup by default. Why risk his warrior unnecessarily? But they wouldn't have killed you unless they had to. They planned to capture you. With the two of us, he and Paige could start a . . ." Here, the words seemed to catch in her throat. "They wanted to start a breeding program, all right? Raise warriors for the Game." She stopped again, her cheeks flaming with embarrassment. She poked a glittering strand of hair behind her ear. "God only knows why I'm telling you all this."

Jack didn't know what to say. This was the girl who sat in front of him in homeroom. Someone whose biggest problem should be whether she'd make the soccer team, or how she would pay for college. He took a deep breath, then cleared his throat. "If Paige and Wylie didn't try to poison me, then who did?"

"That was me."

"*You* tried to kill me?" Jack stared at her, speechless. *She would rather see me dead, than . . .*

"Idiot." She blew out her breath in disgust. "If I'd wanted to kill you, you'd be dead. And I wouldn't poison you. That's not my style."

"What is your style, then?" Jack demanded. "Forgive me if I'm a little lost, here."

She pointed at the dagger on the table. "That's more like it, I guess." She tilted her head, studying him. "I knew it was only a matter of time before you were discovered. Trinity just isn't that big. I poisoned your drink and then dumped it into the lagoon. That was supposed to scare you away, make you leave town. I thought I'd give you a taste of what I've been through. But you didn't leave."

"I wanted to run," Jack admitted. "But I had nowhere to go."

"You don't run *toward* anything, Jack, you just run away. That's how it's done. Anyway, the next thing we know, fireworks are going off at the high school and you and Hastings are hip-deep in it. We couldn't figure that out. The kidnappers, I mean. We thought we had everyone accounted for."

"Traders," Jack said bluntly. "Leesha Middleton was working with them."

"I should have known!" Ellen scowled. "So Paige is finally clued in, but now you and your family are completely inaccessible. Wizards and wards everywhere. When you disappeared, the story was, you'd gone to England. The Red Rose assumed you'd gone to fight, so they called a tournament so they could set the date and location."

"You could have avoided this," Jack pointed out. "*You* always had access, even after the kidnapping failed. "It would have been easy enough, a blade in the throat, a quick getaway. Why am I still alive?" He looked down into the mirror and waited for her answer. For the truth.

"I don't know! Paige was always pestering me about it. He made things . . . very unpleasant. I kept telling him there was never an opportunity, that Snowbeard or Hastings were always around. I just kept thinking of your . . . your mother finding you, all that mess. I guess I'd rather have a fair fight, one with rules. And now we're going to have one."

She picked up the *Rules of Engagement* and began leafing through it. "It's time to get going, Jack. Considering I have a ten-year head start, I'd suggest you study hard," she said mockingly. "Don't think Shadowslayer will save you. I'll have your blade when this is all over. And get that thing away from me!" She pointed to the mirror.

Jack shrugged and returned it to his place under his sweatshirt. He considered what he had seen. "I don't want to fight you, Ellen," he said.

"Don't you think it's a little late for that?" Her voice was cruel. "Lots of people will be disappointed. They're looking forward to seeing someone killed."

"I don't want to kill you," Jack said.

"I hardly think that will be a problem," she said coldly. She gestured at the weapon on the table. "Maybe you'd better take your advantage while you can."

Jack stood up. "Good night, Ellen." He moved to the door, dissolved the locking charm, slipped silently through, and was gone.

⊛ CHAPTER SEVENTEEN ⊛
THE GAME

Jack slept fitfully the first part of the night, but in the early morning hours he fell into a deep and healing sleep. He awoke to a commotion outside and then the sound of Will swearing at the window. Partisans of the Red Rose were pre-enacting the tournament outside the cottage. As might be expected, Jack was getting the worst of it.

"Don't encourage them, Will," Jack said, without moving. He felt strangely at peace. He lay back on the pillows and said a prayer for the day ahead. He'd finally left behind the dreadful whiplash of possible outcomes for the tournament. He knew what he was and wasn't capable of. And now he had a rudimentary plan. It was not a great plan, nor one that was likely to get him out alive. But it was a kind of template, nevertheless.

Jack slid out of bed and got into the shower. He made the water as hot as he could endure, and stood under it for a long time. Then he pulled on his T-shirt and shorts, towel-dried his hair, and measured out his medicine and swallowed it. Everything had the divinity, the significance of a ritual being carried out for the last time.

He pulled out Blaise's mirror and turned it so it reflected back the light. He was afraid to look into it, unable not to.

When Jack looked into the glass, he saw a young man standing in a clearing. His hair was a red-gold color and hung to his shoulders. It gleamed in the shafts of sunlight that poured through a rooftop of trees. He was arrayed for battle, in gleaming chain mail and carrying a sword. The Shadowslayer. He carried a helmet under one arm.

But then perhaps the battle had already occurred, because the warrior was surrounded by bodies. Hundreds of men lay about him, some of them cut to pieces, men who had died fighting. There was something uncannily familiar about the features of the man. Jack lifted his hand, ran it over his own face.

The bodies on the field. Were they friends or enemies? Jack didn't know.

Hastings had already gone. Will paced from room to room like a caged animal looking for a way out. Fitch was morose, his face a study in dread. It didn't look like they'd slept much. When Jack came back from Ellen's, Will and Fitch had asked him about the visit. Jack said only, "It's Ellen, all right."

After breakfast, Jack sat down at the little desk in the front room and found some paper and envelopes in the drawer. He began writing letters—to his parents, to Aunt

Linda, Will, Fitch, Nick Snowbeard—and Ellen. He sealed them up and addressed them neatly. He tried to leave them with Will and Fitch in turn, but they backed away, looking panicked.

"You're crazy, Jack," Will said. "Stop thinking like that."

Jack shrugged and left them on the desk. He wondered how his death would be explained if he died at Raven's Ghyll. Fortunately, that was not his problem.

Hastings returned, stamping wet grass from his boots in the entryway. He had been down at the lists, surveying the field conditions. "Bloody wet, but it's still in the shade. The weather's fair, so it should dry off by afternoon." Jack and Hastings had been over the field a number of times the day before. It was relatively flat, considering the terrain surrounding it, but made treacherous by small gullies and streambeds that tunneled through it. Stands of tall grass and small bushes made them difficult to see. Jack estimated the entire field of play was about the size of a soccer field. It seemed overgenerous for two people.

Hastings was uncharacteristically edgy. Maybe he's regretting the bargain he made, Jack thought. Given all of Ellen's years of training, Jack didn't exactly look like the horse to back. Unless you were betting on a legendary sword.

The wizard fussed over Jack's weaponry. He'd laid out Shadowslayer along with a short dagger, a small shield, a mace, and a sling. There was also a razor-sharp axe, similar to the one Jeremiah Brooks had carried. The weight and use of it was familiar to Jack, courtesy of the frontiersman.

The cottage hummed with tension. Will was so angry with Hastings that he could hardly look at him. Jack spent a half hour reviewing the Rules of Engagement, but he found himself reading and rereading the same paragraph. Fitch tried unsuccessfully to concentrate on the Weirbook. It was almost a relief when it was time to get ready.

Jack methodically pulled on the heavy canvas breeches, tunic, boots, and a bishop's mantle made of chain mail. The Rules of Engagement permitted little in the way of armor. He slid his arms into leather gauntlets, laced them up using his teeth. He belted his sword around his waist and picked up the small shield. "This is all I'll need," he said, and left the rest where it was.

Hastings frowned. As Jack pushed past him, the wizard put out a hand to stop him. "This plan only works if you win," he said quietly.

"Who does it work for?" Jack asked, swinging around to face him. They looked at each other for a long moment, and then Jack nodded to his friends. "Could you guys find my gloves? I think I left them in the bedroom."

The boys were eager to do something, anything. They disappeared into the other room. "I don't see them," Fitch was saying, when Jack pulled the door shut and locked it.

"Hey!" Will pounded on the door. "Jack! Let us out of here!"

Jack spoke through the door. "You're better off in here. Trust me. I'll see you in a little while."

There was a rising storm of protest from behind the door. Someone threw himself against the other side of it, and the door shivered with the impact. It was a good, sturdy door, however, and Jack thought it would hold. He turned to Hastings. "Let's go."

Jack had estimated the galleries would hold several thousand people. He understood there was a great deal of money riding on the match, though he deliberately hadn't asked about the odds.

Apparently the parties had gone on all night. Servants with trolleys were hauling away empty bottles and other debris from private pavilions. The day was growing pleasantly warm. Pleasant in the stands, Jack knew, but it would be deadly hot on the field.

There were still open seats in the reserved section and box seats, but they were filling fast. The galleries were splashed with bright patches of red and white, shot with occasional silver. Pennants bearing the red and white rose snapped in the breeze. Here and there a spectator had even raised a hastily-assembled pennant for the Silver Dragon. Influential council members had erected tents along the sidelines. Jack glanced into one of them and saw an elaborate buffet laid out inside. Beer and wine were already flowing freely. The cries of vendors rang out over the hubbub of the crowd. By now, the sky was a white-washed blue. It was a beautiful day.

A lusty cheer rose from the crowd when they spotted Jack walking along the sidelines. Jack was popular even among those who had bet on his opponent. It was common knowledge that he had been in training for only a few months. Some of those present had watched him working out with Hastings the day before. Everyone agreed that the Warrior of the Silver Dragon had considerable talent. Given a little more experience, he would be outstanding. Too bad he wouldn't be back, said some.

Linda, Mercedes, Blaise, and Iris were all waiting at the side of the field. Linda's face was haggard, and her eyes red-rimmed from crying. She wore jeans and a baggy sweatshirt, intentionally nondescript. She embraced Jack for a long moment, then held him out at arm's length. "You haven't changed your mind?"

Jack wasn't sure that changing his mind was still an option, but he shook his head. "No, I'm in." When he saw how stricken she looked, he said, "Look, it will all work out. Why don't you go up and stay with Will and Fitch at the cottage until it's over? Not that they'll be very good company."

Her body stiffened, and her chin came up stubbornly. "If you're in, I'm staying."

And someone else was there as well. Jack saw a figure crossing the field, tall and gaunt, shoving a staff out into the grass ahead of him, showing his age but moving fast. It was Nicodemus Snowbeard, the Silver Bear.

"Nick!" Jack embraced the wizard. "I heard you were here. You're right, you know. It is too noisy in England."

"And the food is still bad," Snowbeard added. "Whoever put steak and kidneys together in a pie made a serious error in judgement." He looked Jack over carefully. "You're looking rather deadly, my boy."

"More deadly than I feel," Jack admitted.

The wizard smiled a little sadly. "Do you remember what I told you when you left Trinity?"

Jack inclined his head. "You told me to remember who I am."

Snowbeard nodded. "Hastings has made you a Dragon, but you'll always be a member of the Silver Bear clan. Don't let them turn you into something you're not. Your strength comes from that consistency."

Jack nodded. "I won't forget."

Snowbeard and Linda and the neighbors formed a circle around Jack. He felt the power in it, the love flowing to him from all around. He was surrounded by faces, all familiar from his childhood. Mercedes said, "Remember Jack's party, and the giving of gifts sixteen years ago today." She circled his neck with a chain, fastening the clasp. From it hung an amulet, a silver bear. She put a hand on his head, speaking a benediction. "Keep him safe today." Keep him safe today, they all repeated, solemnly. Feeling somehow more confident, Jack slid the bear inside his neckline so it rested against his skin. He still wasn't sure what outcome to hope for.

There was an excited stirring, and then another cheer went up. Ellen Stephenson had arrived at the lists amid an escort of wizards. She wore a red tunic overlaid with rosebuds in a deeper color, tan leggings and tall boots. Her sword was belted around her waist, and a sling hung over her shoulder. Her braided hair glittered in the afternoon sun like a crown.

Jack released a long breath at the sight of her. Though surrounded by wizards, she was absolutely alone. He said his own prayer on her behalf, one voice among the thousands, not caring whether it made sense or not.

Keep her safe today.

By now the galleries were packed, and D'Orsay and the judges were making their way to their seats. A table in front of the viewing stand held a large gold chalice. That must be Cup, the trophy of the day. Next to the chalice was an elaborate leather-bound volume. *The Rules of Engagement,* Jack thought, in case someone had to refer to them on a point of order.

At the stroke of two, three elaborately clad trumpeters advanced to the edge of the field and blew a fanfare. The warriors and their sponsors approached the judges' box, Jack with Hastings, and Ellen with Geoffrey Wylie. Jack glanced over at Ellen. She looked straight ahead to the judges, her face pale and haggard, dark circles under her eyes. Maybe she'd been up all night studying the rules. Except she already knew them by heart. *Like breathing,* Paige had said.

Claude D'Orsay was turned out in a dove-gray tunic, a ceremonial sword belted about his waist. A red-and-white stole draped over his shoulders identified him as Master of the Game. He looked down at the players and their sponsors. "This tournament has been called by the Red Rose for Midsummer's Day, two P.M., at Raven's Ghyll," he proclaimed in a voice that carried to the far end of the galleries. "The Bans were said on the nineteenth of June. The challenge has been accepted by the Silver Dragon. The defending champion, the White Rose, has brought forward no champion, thus is in forfeit. The tournament chalice and associated real and monetary property will be awarded to the sponsor of the winner of the match. By the rules, the winner's sponsor ascends as Master of the Council of Wizards until a new tournament is called. The tournament is fought *à outrance*, to the death, under the Rules of Engagement as published by the guild, A.D. 1532." He rested his hand on the volume on the table. "All disputes are to be decided by the judges of the field based on the rules." He looked at Jack and Ellen. "Do you understand?"

They both nodded.

"You will adhere to the rules or forfeit the match. Any warrior in forfeit will be put to death by the sword, and his heart delivered to the judges." He turned to Wylie and Hastings. "There is to be no interference from the galleries, and no wizardry on the part of the sponsors, wagerers, or spectators." He paused. "There will be a five-minute interlude after each half hour of play. The judges may stop play at any time for a point of order.

"The wagering windows should now be closed for this match and sponsors shall leave the field."

Hastings put a hand on Jack's shoulder. "You can win this if you have the heart to do it," he said. "And if you do win, it will be the end of this bloody Game if I can help it." He gazed across the field at Ellen, then turned and walked to the sidelines.

Ellen and Jack were left alone at midfield, facing each other, perhaps ten feet apart. She stood, lightly balanced, her face expressionless. The sun was just past being directly overhead, and the shadows around their feet had diminished to nothing. The light caught Ellen's hair as she tilted her head, and then reflected off the shield slung over her left arm. She looked down at Shadowslayer, and back up at Jack. A breeze snapped the pennants above the gallery, but the crowd was quiet.

"Go to," said D'Orsay.

The tournament was almost over before it started. Ellen fished a dagger from a sheath at her belt and threw it, end over end, at Jack. He just managed to get his shield up to chest level, and the blade glanced off and landed somewhere in the grass. The crowd gasped. Ellen shrugged the sling off her shoulder in one fluid motion. Jack drew his sword just in time to deflect a swarm of flaming stars with his shield and the flat of his blade. They splintered into shards of blue sparks that showered over him, momentarily blinding him.

Ellen drew her own sword and thrust it forward, spinning long tongues of flame off the tip. Jack brought up his sword to defend against it. It was like blocking a goal kick in soccer from midfield: at that distance there was always plenty of time to intercept. He wondered if Ellen might be wary of confronting Shadowslayer at short distance.

But when the aerial assault proved ineffective, Ellen moved in closer with her sword. The merits of his weapon aside, swordplay had always been one of Jack's strengths, and now he was also benefiting from Brooks's experience. He found he could hold his own very well. Ellen was quick and accurate, but Jack was stronger, and his weapon made him more powerful still. When he slammed his blade against hers, she almost lost her hold on it. Sometimes she had to grip the hilt with both hands, which closed her reach even more, leaving her vulnerable to a quick thrust from the side. But Jack never seized the opening. His play was strictly defensive, although at times he stepped into the space between them and forced her backward.

Ellen flowed gracefully from stance to stance, and Jack moved to meet her. Her play was instinctive, breathtaking, a dance learned from birth. Her blade hissed and sang, a bright blur in the sunlight. Although he often felt clumsy in opposition, he found he could anticipate her moves fairly well. Another gift from Brooks. It was a deadly pas de deux in which the dancers never embraced, yet each was exquisitely attuned to his partner's every move. Ellen frowned and swiped sweat from her eyes. Perhaps she was surprised they were so well matched.

The noise from the crowd had receded to a buzzing in Jack's ears, but he could feel the intimidating presence of thousands of wizards as an almost physical pressure. He tried to narrow his focus to the small space between them, the reach of Ellen's sword. He was relieved when the half hour was finally called. His life was measured in thirty-minute segments now.

Sweat poured from Jack's face, despite the coolness of the day. Hastings handed him a large bottle of water, which he drained. The wizard watched him critically, hands on hips. "You're going to regret those missed opportunities, Jack. Sooner or later, you'll get careless or she'll get lucky. You'll never match her move for move. Use your power against her. Go to her left side. She has trouble with her back hand."

He doesn't miss a thing, Jack thought, but didn't reply. He toweled off his face and sent up a prayer for another half hour. Time was called again, and they returned to the field. Ellen was more aggressive than before. Her sword was everywhere, and once it slashed through the fabric of his tunic but missed him. With the increased intensity, however, she grew a little careless, and when Jack delivered a heavy blow to her blade near the hilt, it went flying from her hand.

Ellen froze for a moment, then leaped after her weapon. She landed rolling, and scooped it up, bringing it into a defensive position while she was still flat on her back. Jack dropped the point of his sword and stood waiting until she was back on her feet. This drew a mixed reaction from the crowd: silent disbelief and a few scattered boos.

Ellen had a peculiar look on her face, which was soon replaced by irritation. She stepped in close to Jack. "What's the matter, Jack? Do you think you have to give me a break because I'm a girl?" she demanded.

Jack shrugged. "I told you, Ellen, I don't want to kill you."

"Well, that makes my job easier!" she retorted. With a thrust of her sword she penetrated Jack's defenses and sliced into his right arm above the leather.

His shield smashed against her blade with a clang and a spray of sparks, shoving it aside, and he backpedaled out of range. Suddenly, he could hear the thunder of the crowd again, reacting to the blow. It was amazing how much it hurt, and it was all Jack could do to keep from dropping his sword. His pretty coat was torn from wrist to elbow, and quickly soaked with blood. *Go after his sword arm*, Paige had said, and it seemed she was taking her trainer's advice. Ellen came back after him grimly, leading with her sword, pursuing her advantage. She slashed at him, one, two, three times; and Jack found he was having trouble stopping her blade.

In desperation, he threw out a charm. Ellen all but bounced off the shimmering barrier that suddenly sprang up between them. She remained on her feet, but only just, and launched herself at Jack again, with the same result. Then she stood, sword at her side, breathing hard, cheeks flushed, staring as if dumbfounded.

There was pandemonium. The crowd came to its feet. Geoffrey Wylie furiously jabbed his finger at Leander Hastings. "Point of order!" he shouted. "The Silver Dragon is interfering with the match!"

Hastings looked baffled. He scanned the crowd, focusing on the Jefferson Street neighbors, as if thinking that perhaps Iris or Snowbeard had intervened. Iris was turned around, gesturing, speaking to Snowbeard, who shrugged his shoulders innocently. Hastings's gaze drifted to Linda Downey, who did not look innocent at all. He pursed his lips and turned to D'Orsay.

"I had nothing to do with this," he said. "I don't know whose charm it is."

Meanwhile, Jack examined the gash in his arm as best he could. Fortunately, it seemed to be a flesh wound only. He opened and closed his hand. Everything seemed to be in working order. His muscles and tendons were intact. It was bleeding, not heavily, but it was definitely distracting. Ellen stared at him through the shimmer wall, head tilted, feet apart.

D'Orsay addressed the crowd at large. "To repeat: there is to be no wizardry or other interference from the sponsors or galleries under the Rules of Engagement. This is your last warning."

Wylie was still protesting. "It was Hastings. It must have been. Who else?"

D'Orsay silenced him with a look and pointed at the barrier. It dissolved away, dwindling until it sparkled like a dew upon the grass. The match resumed.

This time, both players were a bit off balance. Jack's arm was still bleeding, leaving smears of blood along the right side of his tunic. It was also throbbing, which made it hard to concentrate. Ellen seemed skittish, no doubt waiting for the next charm to fall. She seemed relieved when the half hour was called. It already seemed like they had been fighting forever. Jack wondered how long the average match lasted. Something else he'd failed to find out. Ellen probably knew to the minute.

Hastings was not allowed to use wizardry to heal up Jack's arm, so he applied a salve and bandaged it tightly. Jack drank another bottle of water while Hastings lectured him about his lack of offense. "You're stronger than she is," he pointed out. "But it will do you no good if you never land a blow."

"I know what I'm doing," Jack said shortly.

"If you lose fairly, that's one thing. But I won't see you sacrifice yourself, if that's what you have in mind." He laid a hot hand on Jack's shoulder. "I can make you fight, you know."

"Then make me," Jack retorted. "Only, now that I'm

on the field, you'd better do it without wizardry." He nodded at the judges. Hastings's eyes glittered, but he was stuck, and knew it.

When the fight resumed, Ellen seemed to have adopted a new strategy. She launched a constant stream of taunts and challenges. She seemed to be trying to make him angry. "Come on, Jack, are you afraid to fight me?" she called to him. "Don't make me chase you around the field. Are you just a little man with a big sword? Do you always run from women?" and so on.

Jack tried to ignore it. He had less strength in his thrust now, which had been his primary advantage. Sometimes he needed both hands to counter one of Ellen's blows. He continued with his basic defensive posture, parrying Ellen's attacks as best he could. She became bolder as she realized he was mounting no offense. Finally, she feinted left and then lunged forward, leading with her sword, and got inside his blade again. Jack desperately threw up a hand, and suddenly Ellen was waving a large spray of gladiolas in place of her sword. She stared at the flowers in her hand and then at Jack, finally understanding. "It's you," she whispered.

Ellen wasn't the only one who had caught on. Now Wylie had a new target. "It is the boy!" he cried, clearly amazed. "It is obvious he has been trained in wizardry!" He glared accusingly at Hastings.

"If the boy has been trained in wizardry, it was not by me," Hastings replied, his eyes on Linda Downey. She looked boldly back at him. He turned to D'Orsay. "And if he were truly a warrior, it wouldn't matter. He'd never be able to put it to use."

"This is unacceptable," Wylie fumed. "The warrior of the Silver Dragon should forfeit the match, and his sponsor should be sanctioned."

"Where is it written?" Hastings asked abruptly. He turned to Claude D'Orsay, hands on hips.

Wylie was sputtering. "Everyone knows it. It doesn't have to be written. The High Magic is not tricks and trifles to be practiced by the Anawizard Weir. Who knows what harm might come of this?"

Jack found it interesting that all communication took place through the sponsors, as if he and Ellen were incapable of answering a question.

"Where is it written?" Hastings persisted.

D'Orsay sighed. "It says in the Rules of Engagement that there is to be no wizardry or other interference from the gallery or sponsors."

"That is just my point." Hastings waved a hand at the assembly. "There is no wizardry from the gallery. This is wizardry on the field. The rules do not speak to that."

D'Orsay was at a loss for a moment. "Warriors are not supposed to be trained as wizards," he said finally.

"That is not written either," Hastings replied. He pulled a small volume of the rules from his tunic. The page was already marked. He read from the book. "'The Game may also be played as personal combat between two warriors. Only hand weapons are to be used, including blades, slings, cudgels, mace and morningstar. The outcome of the match will depend on the weapons chosen, along with whatever personal talent, skill, and training the warrior brings to the match.' There is nothing here to exclude wizardry. *You* have already ruled him a warrior. If he is, then Jack's use of wizardry is perfectly legal."

D'Orsay was still paging through the ancient volume on the table, as if he might have overlooked a passage that would save him. He finally stopped, stared at Jack, and then looked back at Hastings. His face was a study. It was clear that he believed himself the victim of a clever conspiracy. Jack was a wizard wolf in warrior's clothing. The Master of the Games had been had, and now he knew very well what the outcome of the match would be. The Silver Dragon would prevail, and Leander Hastings would be Master of the Council at the end of it all.

Claude D'Orsay did not like being made a fool.

He smoothed his elegant coat, straightened his stole of office, freed the lace from his sleeves, taking his time. "Well then," he said deliberately. "It appears we shall have to change the rules."

There was a moment of silence, and then a great clamor broke out in the crowd, for and against.

Now it was Hastings's turn to protest. "You cannot amend the rules in the middle of a match," he said angrily.

"Where is it written?" Wylie asked mockingly.

"You must not," Hastings repeated. "The warriors must fight under the rules as proclaimed."

D'Orsay turned and consulted with the other judges. The crowd was on its feet, roaring opinions. Ellen stood holding her strange bouquet, saying nothing. Jack felt a little dizzy, and wished he could sit down for just a little while.

D'Orsay turned back to the sponsors. "By order of the Judges of the Field, in consideration of the current situation, we will amend the Rules of Engagement. There is to be no wizardry or use of High Magic by the players in the Game. Let it be so written." Someone produced a pen. He opened the leather-bound book, found the last page, and scrawled something into it.

The light changed, as if a shadow passed across the landscape. A cold breeze sprang up, lifting the damp hair from Jack's forehead and drying the sweat from his exposed flesh. He scanned the sky. A bank of clouds had appeared, rolling over the fells, a dark line on the horizon. They were a strange, gray-green color, the leading edge boiling like vapors from a nasty brew. A change in the weather was on its way.

Some of the judges cast their eyes skyward, but D'Orsay was unaware, or pretended to be. He pointed at Ellen, restoring her sword.

"If my player is using wizardry, then he must be a wizard," Hastings persisted. "And if so, you must reverse yesterday's ruling and disqualify him from the game."

D'Orsay smiled. "There is nothing that I *must* do, Hastings. There will be a five-minute interlude. Control your warrior, or he will forfeit."

Hastings shook his head, and the muscle was working in his jaw again. Jack dropped wearily into a chair on the sidelines. Hastings handed him another bottle of water, which he gulped greedily.

"So you've been studying out of school," the wizard murmured.

Jack was too tired to respond, but stared straight ahead. After almost an hour and a half of play, he had little fight left in him.

"This is wrong," Hastings said with conviction. "I know it is."

"The whole thing is wrong," Jack retorted. He threw his head back and watched the clouds foaming overhead.

"If you use the High Magic again, you will forfeit," Hastings said quietly. "They will cut out your heart."

"Maybe that's best," Jack replied. He was beyond caring. He thought of Brooks, lying on his back, that gentle letting go of life. All of it, out of his hands.

"Warriors to the field," D'Orsay was calling.

Somehow, Jack pushed himself up and out of his chair. The point of his sword drew a line in the grass as he stumbled back out on the field. Ellen looked weary as well, and when D'Orsay said, "Go to," there was little response for a moment. Then Ellen raised her sword and grimly moved forward, and Jack retreated. Ellen wasn't talking anymore, but was businesslike and mechanical, doggedly pressing him farther downfield than before. Shadowslayer blazed as he parried Ellen's sturdy blows. The sword was a part of him, but all his parts were heavy now, his arms and legs like lead, his breathing labored. At least the pain in his arm seemed distant now, like it was someone else's.

It was more and more difficult to stay focused. The wind blew harder, and he smelled rain in the air. He found himself thinking about sailing, about the time he was caught in a gale, racing for shore with a storm behind him, spray breaking over the bow of the boat as he plunged through the swells. He had to force himself back to the business at hand. Ellen. Ellen was beautiful, graceful, determined. Ellen was doing her best to kill him. He blocked another killing blow and stepped back again.

He stepped into space. Jack hadn't noticed that he had reached the banks of one of the small streambeds. He flailed a moment, seeking his balance, and then toppled backward. As he fell, his foot caught in the roots of a small shrub that grew on the bank of the creek. There was a nasty crack as the bone in his ankle gave way. He landed with his hips in the creek and his shoulders partway up the opposite bank.

Jack broke into a cold sweat. The pain in his ankle overcame everything else. He managed to free his foot, crying out as he did so, but it hung at an impossible angle. Shadowslayer had landed a few yards away, but it might have as well have been a mile. He had no other weapon. Perhaps he should have gone with the dagger, too, back at the start. Not that it would change anything.

Well, it's over, he thought. Although he had anticipated this, the idea of *ending* frightened him. He desperately pushed himself partway up the slope on his elbows, so he was half sitting up. He saw Ellen appear at the top of the opposite bank. She stared at him a moment, and then jumped down, her boots landing in the soft mud next to him. She looked very tall from his angle of sight, lying on his back in the small ravine. Though he couldn't see the crowd, he could hear them well enough. He supposed he could use wizardry to hold her off, and let the judges eviscerate him, to spare her the job. But maybe they would ask Ellen to do it for them. Maybe she would prefer to do it herself.

Now she was between him and the sky, filling his field of vision, and she let the point of her sword drop until it rested lightly at the base of his throat. Jack closed his eyes, trying not to swallow.

After a long moment, the blade was lifted, and Ellen said something. He didn't understand her at first, and she repeated it impatiently. "Get up, Jack." He opened his eyes to see her leaning over him, the expression on her face unreadable.

She was taunting him again. "Go ahead," he said wearily. "Take your match. This is the payoff, as you said." Then he remembered what Paige had said. Perhaps Ellen would "bleed" him now that he was helpless. Slowly cut him into little pieces. Well, he wasn't going to bring it up.

"Get up, Jack," she said again, more urgently, and she extended him a hand.

He stared at her. "I can't," he whispered. "My leg is broken. I'm done."

"You have to get up," she said stubbornly. She knelt beside him, pushed up his pants leg, drew her belt knife, and efficiently cut away his boot and sock. She ran her fingers lightly over his ankle. It was swelling rapidly, and had turned an odd purple color. When she looked back at him, her face was streaked with tears.

"I can't do it, Jack," she said fiercely. "I don't know why, but I can't kill you." She reached beneath her tunic and pulled out a small wizard's bottle. She pulled the cork with her teeth, grabbed a fistful of his hair, lifted his head, and poured it into his mouth. Poisoning wasn't her style, she'd said. Poison or no, Jack swallowed it down. The liquid was warm from being next to her body.

It was the same potion Hastings had used at the meadow, and it took most of the pain away. Probably highly illegal under the rules, he thought. Jack watched helplessly as Ellen unstrapped a long knife in its sheath from her back. She laid it alongside his foot and ankle and secured it with her sling. He gasped when she straightened his foot, but the drug was in him, and it wasn't too bad.

She worked rapidly, muttering to herself the whole time. "If you would just give me a reason to kill you, maybe I could do it; but no, you won't take the bait, not even when I cut you, not even when I provoke you. You just dance, so pretty with your blue eyes and your fine-looking . . ." She looked up and saw Jack staring at her. "So Hastings never taught you how to splint a broken bone? That's what you get for taking the short course."

The crowd and judges must have seen Jack fall into the streambed, and Ellen jump down after him; but because of the fall of the land and the distance, they couldn't quite tell what was going on. Now Jack could hear D'Orsay's voice over the din. "Warriors, is there a winner?"

"Come on, Jack," Ellen said, tying off her work. "You've got to get up or you'll forfeit." She was trembling, and there were spots of high color on her cheeks.

"Ellen, I can't fight you on a broken leg," Jack protested. He just wanted to lay back on the grassy slope and let the stream rush over him.

But she was not to be deterred. "Don't worry about that," she said grimly. She picked up his sword and placed it in his left hand. Then she moved to his right side, seized his wrist and pulled him to his feet, draping his right arm over her shoulders and throwing her arm around his waist so she carried most of his weight. His nose was full of the scent of her next to him, an intoxicating mixture of flowers and sweat. Not like any soldier Brooks had ever encountered. She was amazingly strong. She half pushed, half lifted him up the slope.

The two warriors emerged from the ravine, clinging to each other. Jack of the Silver Dragon was limping badly, one boot gone, carrying his sword in the wrong hand.

The Warrior of the Red Rose gasped, "There is no winner."

D'Orsay was speechless for a moment. And then he snapped, "Approach the judges, warriors."

Jack gathered all his strength and tried to help Ellen maneuver them forward. Hastings and Wylie were standing below the judges' box. Hastings looked amazed, his eyes traveling from Jack to Ellen, while Wylie looked furious, as usual.

"Explain this," D'Orsay demanded, for once addressing the warriors directly.

Ellen looked the Master of Games in the eye. "The match is over. There is no winner. It is a draw." An unhappy rumble rolled through the crowd.

"There can be no draw," D'Orsay replied. "Under the

rules it is a fight to the death."

"Not this time," Ellen said boldly. "The fight is over, and nobody is dead. I think you've had your money's worth. You can all go home now!" she shouted to the crowd.

D'Orsay's voice was cold. "Sponsors, control your warriors."

Hastings gave an almost imperceptible shrug. His warrior was upright only through the grace of his opponent. Wylie, on the other hand, was in Ellen's face immediately.

"What's the matter with you?" he hissed. "Finish him off, and let's be done with this." He made as if to grab her sword arm, as if he intended to settle the matter himself, but she threw him off hard. He landed in the grass. "You're a killer, Ellen!" he shouted. "You've trained for this for a lifetime. Now do what comes naturally!"

Ellen pointed her sword at Wylie and flame ran along the blade. "Be careful what you wish for," she said coldly. A shudder ran through the crowd. Warriors threatening wizards. It was against the laws of nature. As if to commemorate it, there was a blaze of lightning, a crash of thunder, and the first fat drops of rain splattered down.

D'Orsay came to his feet, his calm disinterest shattered. He pointed at Jack and Ellen. "For violations of the Rules of Engagement, your lives are hereby forfeit!" The other judges stood as well, and the death sentence was mirrored in their eyes.

"No!" Hastings stepped between the judges and the two warriors. "This tournament has been flawed from the start. Do you really mean to sacrifice the last remaining warriors for a set of rules you can't even adhere to yourself? What rules have they violated? The loser in the tournament dies, but there is no loser here. The rules do not speak to this."

The two wizards glared at each other. "For someone who has never played by the rules, you've become quite an expert, haven't you? If the rules don't speak to this," D'Orsay said softly, "we'll just change the rules again." He pointed at Hastings. "We have made our decision. Get out of the way."

"No," Hastings said again. He flung out his arm, and light exploded from his fingertips. A shimmering enclosure descended around Ellen and Jack, like a house spun of glass. Suddenly, the sound of the crowd was blunted, and the rain no longer touched them.

All five judges pointed at the barrier, speaking a dissolving charm. The wall fell away, but Hastings threw up another in time to turn a blizzard of blue wizard flame that ricocheted and exploded over the field like fireworks.

The crowd shifted uneasily, some of the spectators throwing up their arms to shield their faces against the rain and the flames arcing over them. The sun had disappeared entirely, and the Ghyll was shrouded in a dim twilight, although it was just after four in the afternoon. There was a low rumble that might have been thunder, but it was more persistent, as if the hills were speaking with a thousand voices. The din surrounded them, growing louder and louder. The fells glowed eerily in the darkness, as if lit from an unseen source. High up on the slope of Ravenshead, the Weirstone stood out against the black shoulder of the mountain like a blue flame.

The beleaguered trio on the lists hardly noticed. It was only a matter of time before the five wizards in the gallery overcame the one on the field. Jack desperately tried to follow the charms that were flying back and forth. He wanted to help, but it was beyond his skill. Hastings constantly shifted position, staying between the judges and the warriors. The judges were aiming for the players, but would hardly have hesitated to blow Hastings away to get to them. The five judges descended out of the stands, clearly meaning to surround the warriors and launch an attack from all directions, which would be more difficult to defend against. Wylie screamed something, but whether he was pleading for his warrior or encouraging her would-be executioners, Jack couldn't tell.

Mercedes and Blaise, Snowbeard, Iris, and Linda joined Hastings on the field and formed a tight circle around Jack and Ellen. Snowbeard and Iris sent their own flames into the air, throwing up barriers as fast as the council could tear them down. The rain came down hard and flames flickered on the undersides of the clouds, white lightning and blue wizard fire. Now the roar of the battle competed with the howl of the storm. Many in the audience were fleeing their seats, fear of dying having overcome their love of spectacle.

Suddenly the earth itself shuddered. Jack could feel it shimmying beneath his feet, like logs rolling down a hillside. Ellen lost her hold on him, and he was pitched to the ground. Flat on his back, the cold rain in his face, and the pain renewed in his shattered leg, Jack couldn't help but think about Brooks dying on this very field. But he could still feel a vibration, an earthquake, he thought at first. Cautiously, he propped himself on his elbows. His view of the field was blocked by the rest of his party, most of whom were on their hands and knees, attempting to get back on their feet. When he looked up at the surrounding hills, he could see a vast shadow flowing down their flanks, pooling at the bottom and spreading outward across the Ghyll. A huge fissure had opened in Raven's Ghyll Field, and an army was pouring from it.

Up in the cottage, Will had grown increasingly agitated as the afternoon waned. He had tried the door and window a hundred times, had even tried to force his massive shoulders through the chimney. Fitch lay on Jack's bed as if in a trance. In fact, he was listening. Trapped in the back bedroom, he hadn't been able to see any of the tournament, but he could hear the roar of the crowd, so he knew it wasn't over. But now the sound he was hearing was more like screaming, full of panic and dismay. He'd felt the weather change and the wind come up. Now the light had gone and the building shuddered under the assault of the gale. Rain and hail crashed against the windows, and the wild, electric scent of the storm came through the walls.

It's the end of the world, Fitch thought. And we're going to die in here. Just then, the ground heaved and the floor buckled, setting the flagstones up at a crazy angle. Slate and plaster fell around them, dust filling their lungs and stinging their eyes. Part of the wall next to the fireplace shifted and split away from the masonry. There was no daylight to speak of, but now the wind and rain howled through a large gap in the wall.

"Come on!" Will shouted to Fitch over the growing din. "Let's get out of here before this place collapses!" Fitch scraped and skinned his shoulders and knees and elbows, leaving blood on some of the stones, but he managed to slide through the gap. Will squeezed through behind him.

As soon as Fitch stepped outside, the rain slammed against his face so hard he could barely see. He found himself in the castle garden, looking down on Raven's Ghyll Field.

At first it looked as if the ground itself were on the march, in ghostly gray waves across the valley. Then he could see it was an army of sorts, a motley army whose soldiers seemed drawn from many lands and many times. There were men and women, and some were mere children. Some were armored, others lightly clad, and they carried a variety of weapons. Here and there were splashes of red-gold: warriors with hair the color of Jack's.

Fitch could hear drums and the wild scream of bagpipes. The warriors had overrun the midway, tents, and trailers at the other end of the valley. The structures were burning, the smoke from the flames adding to the gloom.

"No way," Fitch breathed. The cottage no longer seemed like a sanctuary, with its walls falling down around them.

Spectators from the galleries fled past them. Others appeared frozen in their seats. Fitch scanned the chaotic scene, looking for Jack. Finally he spotted what looked like a private war going on before the galleries. Hastings, Linda, and some of the neighbors from Jefferson Street were in a tight circle, under siege by a group of wizards who were attacking relentlessly in what looked like a spectacular light show. He could see Jack and Ellen at the center of the circle, sitting on the ground, holding each other tightly. Fitch shook his head. None of this was making sense.

The long arms of the shadow army reached out to enclose the battle on the field. The warriors swung axes and broadswords, slaughtering any wizards who got in their way. Few of the wizards had time to respond, and those that did were impossibly outnumbered. Hastings and the Silver Dragon group, facing outward, stopped and stared in disbelief, but the tournament judges did not see their peril until a muscular Celtic warrior with bright red–gold hair seized one of them and ran him through with his sword. He tossed the dead man to the ground, the blood running from his blade in the rain. The battle came to a swift halt after that. D'Orsay and the four remaining judges formed a tight circle of their own.

There was a breathless pause as warriors and wizards faced one another, though small groups of warriors continued their work at the fringes of the crowd. The ranks of the army parted, and two women walked toward them. One was quite young, not much older than Jack, and she had a head of dark curls. She was dressed in a white linen shirt and trousers from another century, and moved with an elegant, athletic grace. The other was somewhat older, taller than the other woman, with bright, strawberry-blond hair. She wore a long dress that seemed to float over the grass. They stopped in front of the Silver Dragon partisans, and the older one spoke. "The Game is over," she announced. "Where are the warriors?"

Her voice was eerily familiar. Jack had heard it once before, one night in a graveyard. In another age, it seemed. Ellen helped him to his feet, and they moved awkwardly to the front of the circle, he limping, she supporting him. As he approached the woman who had called for him, he was startled again by her resemblance to his mother. He had seen her before only in pictures.

"Hello, Jack," she said, smiling. "I see you've taken good care of my sword." She gestured at Shadowslayer. "I think you've had more use of it than I ever did."

"Susannah," Jack whispered. He was aware of tightly controlled energy, the presence of Hastings just behind him. He turned. The wizard stared at the two women as if he had seen a ghost, which in truth he had.

The younger woman spoke. "Lee, what a man you have become." She ran forward and threw her arms around Hastings, and he held her tightly, the joy on his face overlaid with wonder.

"Carrie," he whispered, his voice hoarse with emotion. "I can't believe it. You look the same."

Carrie smiled at him, and Jack could see the resemblance between the two: strong noses, high cheekbones, dark curls plastered to their heads. "I've been dead for more than a hundred years, and you've been living. Living marks a person. That is the difference." She released him and stepped back.

It was all Jack could do to stay upright, even with Ellen's support. The earthquake might be over, but his head was spinning. Every part of his body competed for attention.

Susannah noticed. "Can someone get the boy a chair?" she asked. "I think he has been through enough today. Get two chairs," she added, looking at Ellen.

Two warriors pulled down chairs from the judges' box and set them in the grass. Jack was startled to see that both warriors looked familiar. One of them was Jeremiah Brooks, and the other was the young knight he had fought at the meadow, in the first bout he'd won.

Brooks helped Jack to his seat, being careful of his ripped arm and injured leg, Ellen assisting on his other side. "Looks like you took a beating today, my friend," he observed laconically. He nodded at Ellen. "Being as we're almost brothers and all, I'd suggest you say yes the next time the lady asks for a tumble." He rubbed his nose and grinned at Jack, who stared at him, too tired to be embarrassed.

The knight brought a bottle of water, turning it over curiously in his hands before handing it to Jack. "I always appreciated that you would not kill me," he explained. "There comes a time for all of us to die, but you can't imagine what it is like to go through that over and over." He jerked a thumb at Ellen. "She always killed everybody."

Ellen looked chastened. She perched uneasily on the edge of her chair, as if unsure whether she might need to fight her way out of there. Jack shared his bottle of water with her, then sat back and half closed his eyes. His leg was throbbing, and he felt nauseous. After a minute, Ellen got up and set her chair in front of him, then propped his leg up on it. "You should elevate it to keep the swelling down," she suggested. She sat on the grass next to his seat and leaned her head against his hip, seeming oblivious to the water that ran in rivulets across the ground. The rain had slowed almost to a stop.

"Susannah," Hastings began awkwardly. She turned to him, acknowledging him for the first time.

"Hello, Lee."

"Susannah, I'm sorry," he said simply.

She ran her fingers through her streaming hair. "I did not see my son grow up. That is difficult to forgive."

"I'm not asking you to forgive me." The wizard's hand was extended, something shining in his palm. It was the ring with Susannah's stone. "I think I should return this to you."

She studied him a moment. "A hundred years is a long time to hold a grudge," she said, "for both of us. Carrie and I are asking you to let go of yours, and I will part with mine." She paused. "I have no use for the stone, now or ever. Keep it, and remember me by it. I believe you've learned something since I last saw you."

Hastings looked as if he would say more, but D'Orsay shoved forward. "Why have you brought this army to the Ghyll?" he demanded. "You have destroyed our property and disrupted our tournament."

Susannah turned to him. "Your tournament was already in a shambles before we arrived." She lifted her skirts and climbed into the judges' box.

"It is unlawful for this gang of warriors to come into the Ghyll uninvited. The Warrior Dead are not to cross unless called, according to the rules. You've already murdered a judge," D'Orsay continued. "I hope you understand you will be held to account for this."

Susannah was no longer smiling. "You never minded it when we were murdering each other." She reached for the leather-bound volume of the *Rules of Engagement*. "Are you ready to write some more rules, Master D'Orsay?"

"What are you doing?" he snapped. "Leave that alone."

"We have some amendments of our own to suggest," she said calmly. "Now that you've waked the dragon."

The look on D'Orsay's face was a mixture of incredulity and fear.

"You see, the Rules of Engagement have held us in bondage since 1532. The covenant was written, bound in the bones of the earth—the Ravenshead stone—never to be changed. The rules of the tournament, the relationship between wizards and warriors. Our place in limbo, always waiting to be called to slaughter. But you've opened the book. First you violated the rules by playing a wizard, and then you dared change them. You are the lineal Master of the Games, and you did it here in the shadow of the stone, the lair of the dragon. They must be reconsecrated. That's why we're here." She waved a hand at the assembled army.

"We are the dragon."

"It was not our intent to open the rules to amendment. We'll put them back the way they were," D'Orsay said quickly.

"We've decided we don't like the way they were." Susannah slid the book across the table toward D'Orsay.

"This is wizard business," the Gamemaster protested. "The rules cannot be changed without a vote of the council."

Susannah surveyed the wizards present. "I think we have adequate representation here. We'll take a voice vote. However, I must point out that some among us will be very touchy about the outcome." She nodded at the sea of warriors. D'Orsay looked at them, then back at her. His face had lost its color. Susannah smiled. "You must understand that there is a risk associated with maintaining an army, even an army of the dead. There is always the risk of mutiny. Now, Master D'Orsay, the rules?"

Reluctantly, D'Orsay climbed into the judges' box and sat down in front of the table. He slid the book over, flipped to the first blank page, and picked up his pen.

Susannah dictated, "Amendment number one. The tournament system as it has existed since 1532 is abolished."

D'Orsay put down his pen. "That's impossible," he said. "You would destroy our most important tradition. This is the system that has kept us at peace."

"Second," Susannah continued, ignoring him. "All guilds of the Weir are equal under the rules. There are no codified superior/subordinate relationships among wizards, warriors, enchanters, sorcerers, or any other class."

D'Orsay was still shaking his head, but he had picked up his pen and was writing.

Susannah looked out over the crowd, as if thinking. Linda Downey advanced to the edge of the judges' box, leaned forward, and spoke urgently to her.

"Third," Susannah said, "the town of Trinity, Ohio is established as a sanctuary. The Weir are to carry out no killings, kidnappings, mind magic, spellbindings, or other black arts within its boundaries."

D'Orsay kept scribbling, struggling to keep up.

Susannah looked over at Carrie and then at the rest of the assembly, then turned back to D'Orsay. "Fourth. Wizards may no longer call forth the Warrior Dead at will. However, the Warrior Dead will return in force if these amendments are violated."

D'Orsay finished writing. "Is that it?" he asked sourly.

"One more thing. Henceforth, the rules cannot be changed except by majority vote of a council in which all guilds of the Weir are equally represented, each with a single vote."

When D'Orsay was finished, he angrily pushed the book toward Susannah. She read what was written and nodded. "Now for the vote. All in favor say aye."

D'Orsay and the four judges looked at one another, then out at the army, and hesitated. But only for a moment. "Aye," they mumbled.

"Opposed? No? It's unanimous then," Susannah said with satisfaction. She closed the book with a thud. "We like the rules better this way." She turned and extended her hands to the Weirstone. "We are all heirs of the Weirstone, and submit these mended rules which would govern all of the magical guilds."

The stone flared up, casting a cold blue light over the Ghyll and everyone in it. And deep beneath the star-shaped scar, Jack the wizard heir felt the warrior stone in his breast respond.

Susannah stood for a moment, her arms wrapped around herself, eyes closed. Then she sighed and opened them. "Now it is time for us to cross." She turned and saw Nicodemus Snowbeard standing there, leaning on his staff, the wind whipping the clothes around his gaunt frame.

"That was good work, Susannah," the wizard said, smiling. "I'm proud of you." He embraced her carefully, as if she might break.

"It's good to see you, too, Old Bear," she said, throwing her arms about him in turn. They stood like that for some minutes. Hastings stood nearby, watching, his head tilted, as if trying to work a puzzle that was missing pieces.

Jack drifted into semiconsciousness, but roused himself when a small group of warriors approached him and Ellen. Brooks seemed to be in charge, but he also seemed unaccustomed to making speeches. "Look," he said finally, scratching himself under the collar of his leather shirt, pulling at his ear. "We really appreciate what you two did here, forcing them to change the rules and all," he said. "And if you'd ever like to call us up and have a go, we'd be up for it." He looked at Ellen and smiled a little arrogantly. "I think I could teach your woman here a thing or two. Just for fun, you know, and perhaps a pint or two of ale, to make it interesting," he added quickly, seeing Ellen bristle.

And Jack *remembered* how good a pint or two of ale could taste when a man was thirsty. Part of his varied education in the past six months. "Thank you," Jack said, "I'd like that. But maybe not for a while."

Carrie embraced Hastings once again. Her voice was quiet, her words for him alone. "I can't tell you what this has meant, to see you again. It's time for you to leave behind this obsession with revenge. You must find your own life." She looked at Linda, then back at Hastings. "Remember me, but you'll never find happiness if you live in the past."

Hastings held on to her hands. "I'll do as you say when this business is entirely finished." He nodded at the wreckage around them.

"A thin promise for your sister who loves you." She smiled, but there was already something tenuous about her, as if she were fading. "And now I have to go."

Hastings made as if to capture her with his arms. "Will you come back? Or perhaps I could come see you . . . where you are."

She shrugged. "Perhaps we shall travel more freely now, both ways. Only, it's hard for me to be very long in the world," she said wistfully.

He looked over her shoulder at Susannah, who still stood next to Snowbeard. "Good-bye, Susannah."

Susannah smiled. "Maybe we'll see each other again. You never know."

The two women stepped back with their comrades. The warrior army shimmered, grew insubstantial. For a moment, it lay like a mist in the Ghyll, and then dissipated in the wind. And with them went the galleries and all the trappings of the tournaments, the crowds and banners, the buildings that had been raised for the occasion. All that remained were the castle and the cottage in the castle garden, the permanent structures of the Ghyll. Even the chairs were gone, and Jack found himself suddenly sitting on the ground.

Jack and Ellen, Hastings and Linda, Mercedes, Blaise, Snowbeard, and Iris seemed to be the only living things in the valley, save a few sheep who grazed on the hillsides. Even the weather seemed to be clearing, and the wizard's mist no longer shrouded the sun, which blazed as it set behind Ravenshead.

"Will and Fitch!" Jack said suddenly. "I left them in the cottage." He tried to scramble to his feet, which he found was impossible. Ellen planted a hand firmly on his chest and pushed him back down.

"I'll go find them," Linda said quickly. She turned to the cottage.

"They're locked in," Jack added.

Linda looked at him curiously. "Well, they must have found a way out."

Two figures detached themselves from the side of the cottage and walked toward them. It was Will and Fitch. They were looking about in bewilderment. When they were close enough to be heard, Will shouted, "Where did everybody go?"

"Back home," Linda shouted back. "The tournament's over."

Will spotted Jack and Ellen sitting side by side on the grass. "I don't get it," he said slowly. "One of you is supposed to be dead." He glared at Ellen, daring her to defend herself. She made no such attempt. She lifted her shoulders, dropped them again, and looked away.

"Ellen could have killed me," Jack said quietly, "but she didn't. She saved my life."

"How come?" Fitch demanded. "After all this?"

Ellen turned scarlet and stared at the ground. "Maybe none of my opponents ever gave me flowers before," she mumbled.

Hastings knelt next to Jack. "Would you like me to look at your leg?" he asked, "or would you rather I took you into Keswick?"

"If you can treat it, go ahead," Jack said. "The arm, too, while you're at it." He lay back on the ground, closing his eyes to stop his head from spinning.

Hastings put his hand over the break and spoke his charm. It felt as though cold water were flowing over Jack's leg, carrying the pain and swelling away. A few more minutes, and the wizard went to work on his arm. Soon all pain was gone, and he was floating, comfortable, but unbelievably weary.

Hastings turned to Ellen. "Are you all right?" he asked.

Ellen didn't answer immediately. She untied the sling from around Jack's leg, using her teeth to free the knots. She draped it over her shoulder and restored the knife to the sheath on her back. Then she stood and jammed her sword back into its scabbard. "I'm fine," she said. "I'm sorry about all the trouble." She hesitated, then leaned down again and kissed Jack on the mouth, pressing him into the ground. "Good-bye, Jack. I need to get a few things from the castle, and then I've got to be on my way."

"What do you mean? Where are you going?" Jack demanded, struggling to sit up. Linda was on one side of him now, helping to support him.

Ellen shrugged. "I have no idea. At least I'm on my own now. Hey, don't worry," she added hastily when she saw Jack's face. "This is a way of life for me. Don't know where I came from, don't know where I'm going. I've always wanted to go back to Scotland. Maybe I'll go there." She glanced up at Hastings and the others warily, as if they might attempt to stop her.

"Come back to Trinity with us," Jack urged. "You said you liked it there."

Ellen laughed. "I'm sixteen years old, Jack. I have no family and no way to make a living. I can't exactly rent an apartment. And the thing I know best how to do is kill people. I think I'm sort of a high-risk individual, if you know what I mean." She was matter-of-fact, not asking for sympathy.

Surprisingly, it was shy Will who came to her defense. "You'll be fine," he said. "You have friends. We'll help you find a place to stay. I'll bet you could even learn not to kill people." He grinned. "And you're a cinch to make the girls' soccer team in the fall."

"Maybe Trinity would be the safest place for you," Linda said. "Now that it's a sanctuary. Who knows how the

Wizard Guild will react to what happened today? You might be a target. Besides, you have no money and no camping gear. And you can't exactly hike through Britain carrying a sword."

Ellen hesitated. "I don't usually stay in any one place for very long."

Hastings had been staring down the Ghyll, the expression on his face unreadable. Now he put his hand on Ellen's shoulder, and she flinched under his touch. "Why don't you finish the tour with the Chaucerian Society?" he suggested. "I can spend a little time debriefing you. We'll determine just how high risk you are. Then we can make a plan."

As always, there was no resisting Hastings. And so it was agreed.

More and more, there were no revelations, but simply the uncovering of truths long known but dimly remembered. Everything had been written long ago. There was nothing truly new in the world, but only the slow, circular march of time that revealed the old things once again.

"Way to skunk Jen DeBrock. She didn't even know you were there until you blew past her with the ball." Will grinned happily and signaled for the waitress. "But if it's anything like last season, you'll be seeing Garfield again in the playoffs. You only get one free one."

Jack counted some money out onto the table. "Too bad Slansky can't clone you, Ellen," he said. "That way he wouldn't have to choose. You could play goalie and forward at the same time."

Nothing got through Ellen when she was in front of

the goal. Trinity girls' fall soccer season had been a long series of shutouts for the opposing teams. It was the talk of the conference.

Soccer was a good outlet for Ellen's natural aggression. Which was a good thing, since she had little use for the social intrigues of a small-town high school.

Ellen grinned savagely. "I'd rather play forward. You know I like the attack, Jack." She held his eye for a long moment, then stood, slinging her team bag over her shoulder. "I'm heading back, Will. I told your mom I'd do the front yard. There's already a ton of leaves out there again."

"I said I'd do it!" he protested weakly. They both watched as she slammed through the front door of Corcoran's. Will was finding there were definite advantages to having Ellen as a houseguest.

Linda Downey had set it up. During the last part of the tour with the Chaucerian Society, she had told Will's parents some story that no one could remember about Ellen's parents moving away and Ellen wanting to finish high school in Trinity. Since Will's older sister had left for college they had an extra room, and they immediately offered it to Ellen. Maybe there was sorcery involved, but Will was happy with the arrangement and Hastings felt that Ellen posed little danger to anyone who didn't draw a blade on her.

She seemed eager to earn her keep. She was constantly chopping firewood or raking leaves or shoveling compost. She explained to her hosts that she came from a military family and was used to a very disciplined lifestyle. Besides, she liked to stay in shape.

Ellen had also joined the drama club, since she said she was used to playing various roles, and she signed up for girls' basketball. She had not yet made any close friends outside of their small group, but it was more for lack of common ground than anything else. She'd had a nontraditional childhood, to say the least—nightmarish, in fact. Jack worried about her, but she resolutely resisted any attempts to be drawn out.

The events of the spring and summer had left their mark. Jack's dreams were filled with bloodthirsty wizards, spells, ambushes, and deception. Sometimes he couldn't sleep, and when he did, he woke up screaming. He managed to persuade Becka that therapy wasn't likely to help in his case.

By fall, Trinity had had an entire summer to forget about the events at the end of the school year, since most of the players had spent the summer abroad. Some speculation resurfaced upon their return, but the town gradually fell into its usual autumn cadence, with the startup of classes at both the university and the high school, and with the departure of the summer residents. Some people noticed that Jack and Ellen seemed different after their trip to England, but then travel abroad can change a person.

"You want to hit some balls before it gets dark?" Will seemed inclined to allow Ellen to handle the leaves after all.

Jack shook his head. "Mr. Hastings is back in town. Mom asked him to dinner."

At first, they had seen a lot of Hastings. He spent long

hours with Ellen, questioning her about her training and the tactics of the Red Rose. It could have been awkward, given the history between them, but Ellen seemed to find it therapeutic.

After about a month, his appearances became more sporadic, sometimes coinciding with Linda's. She had been in and out of town more often than usual. To Becka's surprise, she had stayed the last part of the summer in Oxford with them, and had visited several times since their return to Trinity. It was as if she were unusually hungry for their company.

Linda and Hastings seemed to have overcome their differences about Jack's participation in the tournament, given the way things had turned out. Jack wasn't sure where their relationship was, otherwise. They spent considerable time together, discussing politics. But his aunt seemed determined to keep their relationship on a professional plane, which couldn't have been easy.

Trinity High School had a new assistant principal, though everyone agreed that Hastings would be missed. Discipline had never been a problem during his tenure, despite the fact that he'd rarely issued a detention. There was just something about him that made discipline unnecessary.

Becka often invited Hastings to dinner when she learned he was in town. She always said she wanted to thank him for what he had done that day at the high school, and for his hospitality while they were in England. But sometimes Jack caught her studying Hastings's face, as if eager to remember something lost. The wizard was a charming guest, but Jack had the sense that he was always under tight control, keeping her at arm's length.

Keeping a promise to Jack.

His feelings about the wizard were complex. Hastings had pledged his life to keep Jack out of Jessamine Longbranch's hands. The possibility still sent shudders through him. Considering the likely outcome had he chosen not to fight, the decision to play seemed like a good one in retrospect. But he knew that matters could have turned out very differently. Under the wizard's influence, he'd come close to doing murder.

On one of his visits, Hastings gave Jack three books on wizardry from his collection. Jack remembered them from the library in Cumbria. "If you keep up with your studies, you might find these useful." Then Hastings handed Jack a tiny, leather-bound book of attack charms. Jack examined it, surprised. He'd never seen it before. "I don't keep this one on the shelf," Hastings added with a faint smile. Jack stared at him, wondering how much the wizard knew, and how long he'd known it.

The Wizard Council had not yet responded to the events of Midsummer's Day. It was hard to imagine they would quietly accept the dismantling of the system they'd maintained for centuries. Perhaps even now they were plotting a countermove. Jack tried to put it out of his mind. There was nothing he could do about it, after all.

Nick Snowbeard slipped easily back into his role as caretaker when he returned to Trinity. He finished wallpapering the second floor of the house, and completed the renovation of the bathroom. Jack suspected there was more than a little sorcery involved. He still devoted time each day to tutoring Jack. Sometimes they focused on wizardry, sometimes other topics. There was less intensity to these sessions now, more like the old days.

Jack had never thought of Nick as anything but relaxed, but now it seemed that some kind of burden had slipped from the old wizard's shoulders. Perhaps it was the presence of the sanctuary. Nick often frequented the coffee houses and taverns down by the university, spending hours in philosophical dialogues with his friends. He also enjoyed walking along the lakeshore, often long after night had fallen, gazing out at the stars and the tumbling gray water. Sometimes Jack walked with him, old wizard and young warrior, as the cold northwest wind drove the scent of burning leaves inland.

"So I suppose you don't have to keep an eye on me anymore," Jack remarked. He hesitated to bring the subject up, but he wondered if the old man might have business elsewhere, and a sense of duty was keeping him in Trinity.

Snowbeard smiled at him, and put an arm about his shoulders. "Jack, this war has been going on for centuries. I've found it is wise to enjoy any time of truce, while recognizing it for what it is. A truce."

That wasn't exactly reassuring. Still, Jack couldn't help but feel optimistic. Freed from the effects of the Weirsbane, he'd been reborn to the race of the Weirlind. Despite their fractious interactions, he saw promise in his relationship with Ellen. And he felt safer than he had at any time since the day he took his sword out of the ground in Coal Grove.

And sometimes Jack or Ellen developed a restlessness, a need that couldn't be denied. Ellen might call Jack, or the other way around, and they would agree to meet at the meadow. Jack would throw up his wizard's barrier, and they would have at each other with their foils; or call up Brooks or some other old friends from the warrior army for a bout. Brooks taught Ellen a few moves, as promised, and she taught him not to underestimate women warriors.

They fought because they loved the dance, and the weight of a sword in their hands. The clash and spark of metal and hiss of flame was like music written just for them. They fought for glory, but not for blood. They were Weirlind, heirs of the warrior's stone. And they always slept better with blades beneath their beds.

MEET SEPH MCCAULEY: a good-looking sixteen-year-old who's used to getting his own way—with the help of a little magical persuasion. Seph will soon learn that in the world of the Weir, it takes more than mind games to get what you want: even if all you want is to survive.

Turn the page to read an excerpt from Seph's story, the companion novel to *The Warrior Heir*.

THE
WIZARD
HEIR

coming soon

Following a long stretch of unbroken trees, they reached a turnoff marked with a tasteful brick-and-stone sign that said THE HAVENS and PRIVATE PROPERTY. A high stone wall extended in both directions, as far as Seph could see. To keep the trees from wandering, no doubt. He blinked and rubbed his eyes. The wall had a smudged and fuzzy quality, as if shrouded in tendrils of mist.

Along the lane, the trees stood so close that Seph could have reached out and touched them. Their leafy tops arched and met overhead, sieving the light into frail streamers that scarcely colored the ground. The air hung thick with the scent of green things long dead and half decayed. They drove through dense woodland until finally the trees thinned and the light grew, and glimpses of the water and a freshening of the air said they'd reached their destination.

Each school he'd attended had been captured by a single image in his mind: the cavernous great hall at Dunham's Field School in Scotland; the view from the bell tower at St. Andrew's in Switzerland; Montreal illuminated at dusk in midwinter, where the sun seemed to set in midafternoon.

His dorm room was at one end of the building, isolated off a short corridor. Seph wasn't surprised to find he had a room to himself. Students at expensive schools were used to their own space, and plenty of it.

It was his custom to get introductions over with quickly. He walked down the hall, knocking on doors, but there was no answer until he reached the room at the far end of the hall, on the other side of the staircase. A solid, athletic-looking black student answered, clad only in swimming trunks. A silver amulet hung from a chain around his neck: a stylized hand. Protection against the evil eye.

Seph smiled and stuck out his hand. "I'm Seph McCauley. I just moved in at the other end of the hall." *Good social skills*, it always said in his evaluations, along with *Excels academically*.

"I'm Trevor Hill," the boy replied, grasping Seph's hand, then flinching and letting go quickly. "Whoa. You shocked me."

Seph shrugged, accepting no credit or blame. How often had he heard that one?

"I heard someone new was coming this week." Trevor's voice was like a slow-moving river: warm and rich with Southern silt. "Would y'all like to come in?"

Trevor stepped aside so Seph could enter. The room

was a mirror image of Seph's, but seemed smaller because it was crowded with extra furniture: a small refrigerator, a television, posters of sports figures. Seph's room was Spartan in comparison.

"This is cool!" Seph said. "Did you do all this in the last three weeks?"

"Nah, I've had the same room for three years." Trevor glanced nervously at his watch. "I guess we have a little time. You can clear the stuff off that chair and sit."

Seph sat in the desk chair. "Are you a senior?" he asked, trying to put the other boy at ease.

"Junior," Trevor replied. "I'm from Atlanta. Buckhead area. Got no business being so far north. I about freeze to death every fall." He snatched up a heavy sweatshirt from the bed and pulled it over his head.

"I'm a junior, too," Seph volunteered.

Trevor asked the inevitable question. "Where're you from?"

"I spent the summer in Toronto, and last year I went to school in Switzerland. So I'm used to the cold."

"Switzerland, huh?" Trevor quit looking nervous and started looking impressed. "Why'd you leave there?"

"It didn't work out." Seph rolled his eyes.

Trevor nodded, as if this answer weren't unexpected. "The Havens your parents' idea?" He gestured vaguely at their surroundings.

"My parents are dead. I have a guardian. A lawyer. He set it up," Seph replied, thinking that he should buy a T-shirt that said ORPHAN FROM TORONTO. It would save time in these situations.

"So what's the deal here? How do you get along with the staff?" Seph continued. Not that Trevor's advice was likely to be helpful in his case.

Trevor leaned forward, putting his hands on his knees. "Oh, I was in trouble a lot before I came here, too. You just need to follow the rules. Do that, and you'll be okay. They specialize in boys who've had problems other places."

"Really?" Great, Seph thought. I've landed in some kind of upperclass reform school. Trevor seemed normal enough, though, and he'd been here three years. "Do they kick you out if you break the rules?"

"No one gets expelled from the Havens," Trevor said. "You'll see. Their program is very—what they call—effective."

Something in the way he said *effective* sounded almost sinister. It made Seph want to change the subject. Trevor's laptop caught his eye. "I have my computer set up, but I don't see any jacks in my room. Is the cabling included, or do I have to pay for wiring?"

"We don't have our own Internet access," Trevor said.

Seph stared at him. "Why not? It's so easy. They could use a campus-wide wireless network if they didn't want to lay cable."

Trevor shook his head. "No, I mean, we're not allowed. They have computers in the library. You can do searches in there if you want, but they screen the sites."

"That's crazy. They can't do that. I have friends online." Seph didn't remember *that* being mentioned in the glossy brochure.

Trevor shrugged and looked at his watch again. "Well, it's about time for swimming. Y'all had better get changed if you don't want to be late."

Seph rubbed his aching temples. "I'm going to pass. It's been a long day already."

Trevor flinched, eyes widening in surprise. "Dr. Leicester excused you?"

"Not exactly."

Trevor stood up. "Then you'd better get ready."

It seemed like the visit was over, so Seph stood also. "Oka-ay, guess I'll get ready, then," he said.

"If you hurry up, I'll wait for you."

But Seph didn't hurry fast enough, because a few minutes later he heard Trevor at his door. "I'm going ahead. I'll see you down there."

Seph changed into his trunks and pulled his sweat-shirt and jeans on over them. Descending the stairs two at a time, he left the building and followed a wood-chip path back through the woods toward the waterfront. He didn't see any students around, so he figured they must've already gone down to the cove. A sign at the dock pointed him to his right, down the shoreline, to a well-worn path along the water.

The ocean foamed against rocks spattered with slime. Gulls burst into the air ahead of him, wheeling out over the water, screeching. Eventually, the path broke out of the trees at a place where the ocean cut back into the shoreline, creating a protected inlet, lined with stones, out of sight of the school buildings.

There must have been sixty boys in the water, their

heads sleek and dark against the gray surface. A few more were stripping off their sweatshirts on the shore. All of them looked miserably cold. Seph spotted Trevor already neck deep.

Dr. Leicester stood on the shoreline, dressed in a heavy sweatshirt, jeans, and windbreaker. When he saw Seph, he blew sharply on a whistle to get everyone's attention. "Boys, meet Joseph McCauley. This is his first day at the Havens, and he is late for swimming."

The reaction to this was remarkable. The other boys all looked away or looked down, as if they wanted to avoid any connection to Seph's transgression. Some of them peered back toward him when they thought Leicester wasn't looking.

Seph smiled, lifting his hands in apology. "Sorry. I got confused. I was waiting for you in the spa."

Laughter floated across the water, then was quickly stifled under Leicester's disapproving gaze. The headmaster didn't seem susceptible to Seph's legendary charm.

Seph left his clothes on a pile of rocks some distance from the water's edge and hobbled over the stony beach to the water. If he'd hoped that the water would be warmer than the air, he was disappointed. It was like stepping into snowmelt. His feet went numb immediately. He waded out to his knees, then to his waist, gasping.

The water was murky and unpleasant. The rocks along the bottom were slippery and invisible, so that, even in the cove, the waves threatened to knock him over. Something squirmed under his left foot, and he thrashed backward into unexpectedly deep water. His head went under, and he swallowed a mouthful. He came up like a sounding whale, spraying water everywhere.

He'd had enough. A few quick strokes took him back to the shallows. Shivering, teeth chattering, he hauled himself onto the shore. He'd almost made it back to his muddle of clothes when someone gripped his arm.

It was Trevor, covered in gooseflesh, lips pale with cold, water sliding off his dark body onto the rocks. "Just get in the water, Seph," he said, without meeting Seph's eyes. "Just do it. Come on." He put a cold hand on Seph's shoulder as if to urge him along.

Seph blinked at him. He looked over his shoulder at Dr. Leicester, who stood expressionless, watching. All right, he thought. If he was going to try to stay here two years, it was best not to get into a battle of wills on his first day. Gritting his teeth, he picked his way back across the beach and waded out into the water, not looking back to see if Trevor was following.

This time it seemed more tolerable. Maybe he was getting used to it. His extremities tingled as the feeling returned, and he was no longer shivering. He strode ahead more confidently, continuing until the water lapped at his collarbone. Though the sun was gone, intercepted by the surrounding trees, he felt almost warm.

He looked around. The other boys stood as if frozen, staring down at the water in disbelief. Another minute passed, and the surface of the water began to steam in the cold air. He might have been neck deep in the warm Caribbean.

No. This can't be happening. Seph looked over at

Leicester, who was deep in conversation with one of the boys on shore. He hadn't yet noticed that anything was amiss. Seph splashed toward a crowd of boys standing to one side, near the shoreline, positioning himself so that his head was just one of many pocking the gray surface. *Now, just relax,* he commanded himself, closing his eyes, breathing in and out slowly, trying to loosen his muscles, to empty his mind.

How long could he last? He was in trouble already, and it was just the first day.

He sorted through the littered memories of his school career. The homicidal ravens at St. Andrew's. The explosions and fires in Scotland. The wolves that had startled the nuns in Philadelphia.

By now, the water was close to spa temperature. All conversation in the cove had died. The swimmers looked down at the vapor collecting at the surface, rising up around them like morning mist on an upland lake. None of them said a word, to one another, or to Leicester.

Finally, the boy who had been speaking with the headmaster broke away and stepped into the water. He stumbled backward with a yelp of surprise and sat down, hard, on the rocks. Gregory Leicester swung around and stared at the boys in the water and the steam boiling up around them. He blinked once, twice, in surprise. Then he began searching the faces of the boys in the water until he found Seph.

Try as he might, Seph couldn't look away. The head-master stood, studying him as though he were a specimen on a slide. No questions, no disbelief, no challenge or confusion, only this intense and clinical scrutiny, as if he were looking into Seph's soul with full knowledge of what lay within. Then Leicester smiled as if it were Christmas.

Shuddering, Seph took a step backward.

The headmaster's gaze shifted to include the whole group. "Gentlemen, perhaps it is a bit brisk for swimming after all. You are dismissed to your own pursuits until dinner."

For a moment, no one moved. Then they began their exodus, silent as lemmings in reverse. Seph left the water on the far side of the cove, keeping as much distance between himself and Leicester as possible. He pulled his sweatshirt and jeans over his wet skin and picked up his shoes, unwilling to linger long enough to put them on. Slinging his towel about his shoulders, he followed the others toward the woods.

"Joseph."

Seph froze in midstride and stood waiting, without turning around. The headmaster's gaze pressed on the back of his neck.

"Come up to my office after dinner. I think it's time I explained a bit more about our program."

Seph nodded and walked on, into the indifferent forest.